NO TURNING BACK

Gorgon depressed the intercom's transmit button and ordered, "Target one and two for Norfolk."

From the missiles' launch vehicle, a woman's voice, barren of emotion, crackled back, "Positioning."

Carlucci returned to the window and stared, unblinking, at the twenty-three-foot missile pallet rising slowly on its hydraulic legs. When the platform reached an angle of sixty-seven degrees, the hydraulic pistons stopped, the warheads positioned.

"Arm one and two," Gorgon said.

"One and two arming," the woman's voice crackled. A pause, then, "Launch ready."

"Launch on my order."

Carlucci drew in a deep breath and held it. For an eternal moment the silence was deafening.

"Launch!"

CODE: ALPHA

JOSEPH MASSUCCI

LEISURE BOOKS ⎣ NEW YORK CITY

To Patricia

A LEISURE BOOK®

February 1997

Published by

Dorchester Publishing Co., Inc.
276 Fifth Avenue
New York, NY 10001

Printed in the United States of America.

CODE: ALPHA

Maximum Containment
Biohazard Level 4

Infectious Area
—Crash Door—
No Entrance

Prologue

U.S. Army BL-4 Biological Laboratory
Fort Detrick, Maryland
Monday, January 11

"We've got a breach!"

A horn blared in the lab's staging area, synchronized with a flashing red light. Both technicians were on their feet, checking the rows of screens on the tactical console.

"Do we have contamination?"

"Checking."

There came a high-pitched whine, followed by a metallic click.

"Autolock sequence complete."

"Jesus, he's sealed inside."

Burns, the center's chief engineer, pushed his wire-frame glasses up the bridge of his nose as he spun around to one of the computer monitors. "Talk to me, Ricky; what kind of situation do we have in there?"

Rick, the youngest technician to be assigned to Fort Detrick's maximum containment laboratory, jabbed one reset button after another, checking and rechecking the readouts. "I'm not getting anything."

Burns switched on the scanner. "Air particulates?"

"Zero. The air's clean. Whatever's happening in there is not in the air."

"He hit the manual alarm—must've torn his suit." Burns checked the video monitor and saw Dr. David French inside the BL-4 "hot suite" hunched over a lab bench like a near-sighted jeweler. He appeared to be cradling his arm, but Burns couldn't be sure because of the camera's angle. He punched the intercom. "Doctor, talk to me."

No answer.

"Jesus," Rick said, "he isn't moving."

"I want you to get the colonel down here *fast*."

There was genuine fear in Rick's eyes as he bolted from the lab's staging area, his footsteps echoing down the cinder-block corridor.

Burns pulled the receiver to his ear, nearly ripping the cord out of the wall. "Security, we have a Code Seventeen SIGMA alarm in BL-4. Repeat, a Code Seventeen SIGMA alarm in BL-4. Auto containment procedure completed."

Burns could hear a thin voice on the other end asking questions, but the siren masked the meaning of the words. He put a finger into his left ear and shouted, "I can't hear you. We have a Code Seventeen down here. Dr. French needs assistance, for chrissake. He may have breached his suit." Burns glanced up at the closed-circuit monitor. One of the cameras was still trained on the lab bench, but he could not see Dr. French. "Get Colonel Westbrook down here *now!*"

Julie Martinelli burst into the staging area, her white lab coat flowing behind her like a cape, her hard-soled shoes pounding the grated flooring. "What's happened?" she shouted over the siren. "Where's Dr. French?"

"Inside," Burns said. "He's locked inside."

Julie scanned the monitors and checked the readouts. "There's no air contamination. What the hell is he doing in there?"

"He hit the alarm," Burns shouted over the din.

"I can't hear a thing." Julie punched a console button and

silenced the siren; the red light, however, would keep flashing until the center's commander reset the security system.

"I don't see him." Julie panned the lab's two cameras first one way, then the other. "Where the hell is he?"

Burns shrugged. "He was at his lab bench a moment ago."

"David?" Julie said into the intercom. "Can you answer me please?"

Still no answer.

"I've got a bad feeling about this. I don't like the way he's been acting—that detached look of his, always in his own world like he's plotting something." Julie zoomed one of the camera's lenses in on Dr. French's lab bench and panned slowly. She could see the active gamma radiation unit . . . the beakers . . . the vials labeled GROUP A STREPTOCOCCAL VIRUS. . . .

"David, you stupid son of a bitch." Julie removed her lab coat and opened a suit locker with a bang.

Burns reeled away from the console. "May I ask what you're doing?"

She stepped into the one-piece, full-body polyurethane laboratory suit, a second skin she always called her prophylactic overcoat, and pulled it up to her waist. "I'm going inside."

"You're not going anywhere," Burns said. "Only the colonel can reset that door. Besides, security's on its way."

"I'm not waiting."

Burns stood defiantly in her way. "You don't have much—"

"Excuse me, please." Julie pushed past him and took a seat before one of the three computer workstations and brought up the lab's security interface.

ACCESS CONTROL CODE?

"Don't even think about it," Burns said. "The colonel gets a little testy when grad students start decompiling his security system's computer code."

She began typing, then entering, typing, entering.

LAB ACCESS DENIED

More typing.

MACRO COMPILED—PROCEED?

"Yes, please," she said to the screen, then jabbed the enter key.

PLEASE WAIT

"Julie, you're making me very nervous," Burns said, watching her.

MACRO COMPLETED

"Piece of cake," she said, then entered a final command.

AUTHORIZED

"Yes!"

"You're going to get my ass canned," Burns said.

Julie pulled the lab suit over her shoulders and thrust her arms into the sleeves, then fumbled to put each finger into the proper glove digit. Finished, she put on the hood and sealed it. She spun the releasing wheel on the vaultlike door until it pulled forward with a loud hiss. "If the colonel ever gets his ass down here, tell him I've got one huge problem for him to handle."

"Are you going to clue me in on what's—"

Julie closed the fourteen-inch-thick, two-ton, stainless-steel door behind her with a mechanical click. Burns shook his head and said to no one in particular, "You're a very dangerous young woman."

Inside the lab, Julie attached her suit to one of the spring-coiled air hoses hanging from the ceiling. The air supply hissed loudly in her ears, and the magnified view through her face shield distorted objects beyond arm's length.

The maximum containment laboratory was a claustrophobic compartment of centrifuges, incubators, freezers, benches and computing workstations. Cluttered, but very high-tech. Her eyes scanned the lab and saw no one. Above the even rhythm of her amplified breathing, she could hear Mozart's Piano Concerto no. 22 flowing from a dictating cassette recorder.

"David?"

No response. Julie stepped awkwardly to the lab bench. Her deep brown eyes scanned the bench's culture dishes, beakers . . . the active gamma radiation unit . . . the syringe . . . then across the rack of vials labeled GROUP A STREPTOCOCCAL

VIRUS and a second labeled TETRODOTOXIN. She began sweating inside the suit.

"God Almighty—"

"My . . . head hurts."

Julie whirled with a start. She recognized Dr. French's features inside his suit—his shaved head, his magnificent handlebar mustache. But something was wrong; she could see his contorted expression beneath his magnifying face shield, which made his eyes look like a pair of poached eggs.

Her anger swelled. "You son of a bitch. You did it, didn't you?"

She expected him to begin reciting one of his world-class philosophical lectures about stretching the limits of the scientific envelope. But he said nothing to her.

Julie began shouting at him, "David, you made me a promise. . . ."

She grew suddenly quiet. Her wide eyes stared at the drop of blood beading atop the fingertip of French's white polyurethane glove. A shot of adrenaline rushed through Julie's arteries, exploding in a tingling sensation at the roots of her hair. Was he even aware? she thought. "Your finger . . ."

He held out his finger to her as though it belonged to a helpless lab animal he had just infected. "Stupid . . . so stupid . . . a small distraction . . . I never felt the needle."

Julie touched his shoulder. "I'll take you into deconnnnnnn. . . ."

A ringing in Dr. French's ears made Julie's voice sound as though it came from the far end of a deep tunnel. His vision blurred and a wave of nausea swept through him. Sweat drenched the inside of his suit.

He forced a pathetic smile. "There's an army of red ants burrowing through my brain."

"Davvvviiiiidddddddddddd . . . ?"

Dr. French stared at her, his lower lip quivering. The sublime beauty of Mozart's concerto turned to discordant banging in his ears. "Julie, my head hurts—"

His chest tightened as though in a vise, and he coughed,

speckling his face shield with blood-laden mucus. He reached for a row of bottles on the table and realized to his horror that his hand no longer was his own. Julie stared transfixed at his trembling and twitching fingers. His arm began to undulate, wavy movements like those of an inept exotic dancer. He had lost all muscular control.

"Gancic . . . gancic . . . gancic . . ." He couldn't form the word.

Julie grabbed the doctor firmly by his shoulders and tried to ease him back onto a lab stool. The violent energy flooding his body caused him to lash out at her, catching her Plexiglas face shield at the chin. The blow drove her backward onto one of the lab's two scanning tunneling microscopes, rocking the seven-hundred-pound instrument. He could only watch, astonished, at what he had just done; he felt no exertion at all.

French collapsed in a heap, his face a grimacing mask of agony, his arms and legs flailing in a thrashing dance of death. He grabbed his suit at the neck and pulled it downward as though it were a bib, splitting the material.

"The heat . . . the awful heat!"

Julie, incredulous, watched as radical dehydration shrank the biochemist into a wizened caricature of his former self. Ruptured capillaries turned his skin black and blue. Patterns of bodily decay were exacerbated and accelerated, as in a time-lapse film, detailing the organism's utter devastation.

She stepped timidly back. "David . . . you stupid son of a bitch . . ."

Finally Dr. French grew still—it was over. He lay heaped in a twisted pile, the air flow from the ceiling-mounted hose giving his pulsating suit an illusion of life. Red and yellow sap oozed from the suit's tear, forming a loathsome puddle around him.

Julie knelt down and, breathing deeply, peered through the face shield at what was left of the doctor's face. His eyes flared open and gazed up at her through the magnified face shield. *Those eyes!* His face—a visage bubbling with secretions—had forfeited any claim to humanity. Dr. French had literally melted inside his suit.

His rubber hand grabbed her wrist with fingers that still possessed surprising strength. As she watched in horror, the ravaged flesh parted where the mouth should have been and tried to form words, failing miserably. The foul moan that erupted from his throat sounded like the last breath of a dying wolf.

Julie cried out. No sound at all penetrated the lab's fourteen-inch-thick metal walls.

PART ONE

The Winds of Death

"I thought we had banished forever what we all saw only a few months ago—a mother trying to protect her child, waving her arms against the invisible winds of death."

—President George Bush

Chapter One

Kumar, Iraq
Tuesday, January 12

Five miles outside the settlement, Tarra saw the first signs that something had gone terribly wrong: the fine bleached sand, swept up by a caravan of vehicles, veiled a procession of people and machines withdrawing from what could only be a battlefield. She drove past the surviving settlers—a few old men and motherless children, their heads swathed in *howhs*. Some of them wept bitterly; most simply walked in stunned disbelief. She drove past the soldiers dragging their rifles, retreating from an enemy their weapons could not touch. Finally her Jeep swept past the doctors and engineers, their solutions all proven impotent against the invader.

But this was not war.

Tarra drove on. She knew the desert well and navigated the Jeep with precision across its uneven roads. The desert was her home, and the price she had paid for growing up a rebellious desert child was the loss of her femininity to a tigerlike constitution. She negotiated the trail's curves too fast, chasing knots of dazed refugees up the dunes. She laughed at them all. Some men found her attractive—and so she was, with seductive features, short black hair and deep green eyes that could impale you. Tarra's attraction was not the allure gallant men dueled over; her beauty mirrored a feline in the wild, an animal that could not be tamed. Nor would any want to—her vicious contempt for men was legend in the region.

Tarra jerked the Jeep to a halt at the edge of the settlement, a collection of meager huts hastily cordoned off with thick spools of barbed wire and splashes of red paint denoting some cryptic Arabic warning. She dared go no farther.

Tarra turned to her lone passenger and smiled at him, her piercing eyes eager. For this lone man she harbored no contempt, only unyielding loyalty. He was a giant, intimidating to look at, dressed in a tailored silk suit and a civil red tie that set apart a dark face bloated by hatred. He responded to her mischievous smile with un-Arabic frigidity. His name was Banna, and his interest in the settlement was more than morbid curiosity.

He stood, peeled off his aviator-style sunglasses and raised a pair of high-powered binoculars to his dark, distant eyes. He could hear wailing in the distance, a far-off echo of mourning, but could not discern if the sound was human or animal. He scanned the settlement, searching for clues to the tragedy. To him this assessment was a game, a war exercise. At first he could see nothing unusual, just neglected wood-and-straw structures that had fought a generation-long war against the encroaching desert. Scores of huts, undamaged, stood empty. He saw no people, no activity of any kind, only sand; sand that lay in dunes and in rivulets; sand piled high against buildings. He zoomed in on the dirt road that cut the settlement in two. And then he saw them. Bodies. Dozens of them. Women huddled in doorways clutching their children, men draped across the road reaching futilely to help them. Carcasses of mules and dogs lay between them.

Kumar had become a settlement of corpses.

Banna removed the binoculars and let his war-trained mind consider how this could have happened. Poisoned water?

No—death had come too quickly, too completely. An air strike? There were no craters.

The railroad.

Banna focused the binoculars on a stretch of open track atop the far ridge three hundred yards upwind of the tiny settlement. Through the distant curtain of dust he could see the outline of a diesel locomotive pulled to a halt and several derailed cars lying in its wake. One was an overturned tank car for transporting hazardous liquids, its lethal contents long emptied. The people of Kumar had been unlucky. Their homes stood in the path of a wind that carried with it a death far more lethal than an advancing army. He grinned, finding amusement in this absurd tragedy; a man-made folly.

"Abdul Banna!" a voice called out to him.

Banna whirled to see who had shouted his name so openly. What he saw made him laugh loudly. There, walking toward him along the barbed-wire barricade, were several soldiers dressed in horrid-looking suits that allowed them to fight in a contaminated environment. Their suits were thick and bulky, with gloves and boots to match, each bearing the markings of Iraq's elite Republican Guard. But it was those gas masks with their extended snout and large glass eyes that would send children screaming for their mothers.

The lead soldier ordered the others to halt, while he alone approached the Jeep. The soldier removed his mask and let out a weary sigh. He was sweating terribly, the heavy suit consuming what little energy the day's events had not already taken from him. It had been a long day, worse than any he could remember in war. Banna knew this soldier. His name was Lt. Gen. Wafiq Sabri, Iraq's military chief of staff. Banna could see that the specter of another conflict with the West was killing him.

"I do not envy you, Sabri," Banna called down to him in Arabic. "But why do you summon me here? This is not my problem."

General Sabri climbed into the back of the Jeep and sat down heavily beside Banna, producing a cloud of dust from the leather seat. He ordered the woman behind the wheel to leave them, more curtly than he intended. Tarra looked questioningly at Banna.

"She will stay," Banna said.

The general, not comfortable in the presence of a woman, nodded wearily. He could not argue in the desert heat. "Tonight this settlement will be buried and with it all that has happened here today. By morning the train will finish its journey."

Banna shrugged. "Then what do you want from me?"

"Operation Harness. He wants it done just as you planned. Allah has given us a unique opportunity. You are to begin immediately."

Banna allowed a wry smirk. "I admire the president's conviction. He has conceded that his weapons and troops are useless to him."

"Your plan has given him new hope," Sabri said. "He will risk another holy war. Another air attack is imminent, yet we cannot fight the bandits in the sky and we have no navy. Our tanks are lost, our soldiers beaten. Now the murderers will strike again, this time to destroy our laboratories, which cannot yield enough uranium to power a clock. But you—"he thrust a finger at Banna—"you are his secret weapon. You can do what an army cannot. And may Allah save mankind from your wrath."

"I am only interested in his ability to pay."

General Sabri conceded with a nod. "The first eighty million pounds has been paid into the London branch of the Bank of Credit and Commerce International, just as you requested. You will report to me—"

"I will work with my own people. The plan is mine, as will be its execution. I shall divulge the details of Harness to no one, least of all to you. Once I leave here, you will not hear from me again. Like my weapon, I shall become invisible. There is no turning back, Sabri. Tell him he will have his victory."

The general and the mercenary stared at each other, two

soldiers with vastly different methods of warfare. Sabri knew there was no point debating the matter further with this man; there was nothing left to decide. A feeling of dread swelled within the general as he considered how the world would soon change because of the man seated next to him. He knew Banna was unstoppable, a warrior of great resources. He did not doubt for a moment that his terrible plan would succeed. "Then let it be done. May Allah be willing."

Banna scoffed at the general's prayer and wiped his forehead with a silk handkerchief. This was not Allah's affair. This was an economic decision—the Middle East nation could not defeat the alliance of force the superpowers had rallied against it. The inevitable strike must be done another way—Banna's way.

Sabri's eyes grew distant, as though blinded by the sun's reflection off the white sand. For a long moment he sat there, absorbing the heat, and said nothing.

Finally Banna said, "There is one more item that is not for negotiation: You are never to utter my name again."

Sabri understood; from this day Abdul Banna would cease to exist. "How will you be known?"

"I have a passion for Greek mythology." Banna replaced his aviator sunglasses and touched the chin of his charming Tarra. "Men dare not look her in the face, except by degrees: they mistake her for a Gorgon, instead of knowing her to be a Minerva."

She returned a devilish grin.

"I will be Gorgon."

Chapter Two

Anne Arundel County, Maryland
Thursday, January 14

Dr. Reinhard Sterling hailed the last cab outside Baltimore/
Washington International Airport, tossed his carry-on travel
bag and satchel into the backseat and climbed in after them.
He wanted to get far away from airports, a sentiment most
likely shared by his fellow travelers that night on Lufthansa
Flight 407 from Frankfurt. The flight had arrived three and a
half hours late, thanks to a bomb threat at the German airport.
Now he had to find his way to the U.S. capital at midnight
and, worse, function coherently at a 7:30 A.M. meeting with a
United States senator.

"Please take me to Washington," Dr. Sterling instructed
the driver in his German accent, still thick three decades after
becoming a United States citizen. "The Sutton House."

The driver, an affable old black man with a winning smile,
nodded and pulled his cab away from the terminal. He made
a quick mental tally of tonight's fares. *Jackpot!* More than
$400 for the day. His smile widened; this trip—$50 plus tip—
would net him his best night this week.

"Yes, sir," the cabby said to his fare. "Pretty late to be gettin' into town."

"Yes, very," Dr. Sterling said, his sixty-year-old face mirroring the strain of the last twenty-four hours. The biochemist was not in a conversational mood, something the cabby quickly picked up on. The cab pulled onto the Baltimore/Washington Expressway and headed southwest toward D.C., leaving behind the glow of the airport. The traffic this time of night was sparse, allowing them to make good time.

Dr. Sterling closed his eyes and relaxed for the first time since leaving Geneva. He even considered dozing during this final leg of his trip. Sleep had been elusive ever since he received the telex two nights before; in fact, the whole mood of his trip had changed following the hasty summons by Senator Baker. What originally began as a business visit and a brief address at a conference of fellow molecular biologists at Fort Detrick, now included an impossible schedule with a high-level meeting at the capitol. *All because of a lab researcher's stupid blunder.* Dr. Sterling first learned of the Fort Detrick accident in a news report along with the rest of the scientific community. But his colleagues didn't know what he knew. Senator Baker's telex confined his worst fears: the military had played God with terrible consequences. *Idiots!* He had known this day was inevitable.

Soon the late-night traffic thinned to a few specks of red taillights well ahead. The cabby tuned into an all-night talk station, one of the many devoting its programming tonight exclusively to news of the possibility of another war in the Persian Gulf.

"Do ya think Saddam has it?" the cabby offered over his shoulder. "The bomb, that is. Do you think he'll nuke the Jews?"

Dr. Sterling didn't answer. He had drifted into a fitful sleep, the gentle drone of the road serving as a sedative for his frayed nerves. The cabby shrugged and let his fare nap. He turned the radio low.

Dr. Sterling's nap proved to be a short one. When the cabdriver glanced up at his mirror, he saw another car approaching rapidly from behind. He swallowed hard when the car came so close to his bumper that its headlights disappeared below the cab's trunk.

"What the hell's he doin'?" He glanced in the mirror at his fare, who appeared to be sound asleep in the back.

A flashing blue light on the second car's dashboard blinked on.

"Shit."

The cabby glanced at his speedometer. Six miles over the speed limit—*a lousy six miles!* Exasperated, he pulled his cab onto the shoulder of the highway with a thump, gravel spraying against the undercarriage, and stopped. *So much for a jackpot night.*

The noise of the unscheduled stop startled Dr. Sterling awake. "What is it? Why are we stopping?"

"Cop," the cabby said, opening his door.

Disoriented, Dr. Sterling twisted his neck around and peered through the rear windshield. All he could see was the backlit silhouette of a hefty uniformed man wearing a Smokey-the-Bear hat.

"Please come back with me," the officer said. It was a command, not a polite request.

"Yes, sir." The cabby slid from the front seat and was gone.

Dr. Sterling heard the retreating gravel footsteps as the two headed back to the patrol car. He glanced at his watch, closed his eyes and scratched his closely cropped beard in frustration. Would he ever get to a bed tonight?

Suddenly the cab doors flew open and three people slid neatly inside. A powerful-looking woman with short black hair pushed Dr. Sterling roughly to the center of the backseat and jammed something metal into his ribs. He flinched in pain.

"What is this?" Dr. Sterling said. "Who are you people? What are you doing?" No one answered him. He appealed to the woman for an answer, but her amused look of contempt frightened him.

28

Code: Alpha

The man behind the wheel, a dark, grisly brute with a black beard and a squashed nose, put the cab in gear and pulled onto the expressway. The doctor's worst fears were realized when he saw the unmarked patrol car quickly pass them. He could see the uniformed officer with his round-brimmed hat, but no one else. What had happened to the cabdriver? And who were these people? *For God's sake, what is happening?*

Tarra passed Sterling's travel bag and satchel to a distinguished-looking gentleman in the front passenger seat. Dr. Carl Wynett, referred to by the others as "the Businessman," could have passed for Sterling's twin brother. Like Sterling, the man exuded an academic aura. He was of medium height, late fifties, a healthy head of silver hair, a large frame with an notable paunch and scientific eyes. He opened Sterling's well-traveled satchel, snapped on a pencil-thin flashlight and began a meticulous search of its contents.

Sterling watched him curiously. What did he want? What was he looking for? "Someone please tell me what this is about."

Tarra slipped an arm over Dr. Sterling's shoulders and applied pressure as a warning. "Do not ask questions." She spoke with a thick accent, possibly Arabic, but Sterling couldn't be sure. He smelled the strangest scent of perfume.

"Let him speak," ordered the Businessman. He, too, had an accent, which Dr. Sterling recognized as German, but the man's careful and deliberate phrasing suggested he was a student of languages.

Tarra poked Dr. Sterling cruelly in the ribs with her Walther. "Speak to him."

Dr. Sterling was too intimidated to speak.

Tarra poked him harder. "Speak!"

"Where . . . where are you taking me?"

Without looking up from his exploration of the doctor's satchel, the Businessman demanded, "Again."

Another vicious poke in the ribs.

"You can have my money . . . everything. I am carrying one thousand dollars."

Tarra laughed wickedly. "We do not need your money—"

"Be quiet!" the Businessman ordered her. He looked severely at Sterling. "Again!"

Sterling's breathing became more labored. He felt dizzy. "Please. I do not want trouble. I am a doctor—a biochemist. . . . I am to address a conference tomorrow in Maryland."

"I do not want trouble," said the Businessman, still rummaging through Sterling's satchel. The timbre and tone of his voice matched perfectly that of the doctor's. "I am a doctor—a biochemist." He even mimicked Sterling's facial expressions down to his nervous habit of scratching his beard. Hours of practiced skill were evident in the masquerade. "Tomorrow I will address my colleagues at a conference of the American Society of Microbiology convening at Fort Detrick."

The imitation was remarkable.

"You have him," the driver affirmed, grinning. Tarra agreed.

The Businessman closed the satchel and said, "I see the text of your speech and a working draft of a yet-untitled paper on enzymes. Still, there is something missing. Your secretary confirmed for me your seven-thirty appointment tomorrow morning at the capitol, yet I see no correspondence here related to that meeting. Surely you would bring it with you."

Dr. Sterling said nothing.

"Surely you brought it with you," the Businessman repeated tersely.

Tarra grabbed Dr. Sterling by the lapels and felt inside his suit. She retrieved a black leather billfold and passed it to the front. Sterling saw no point in resisting; these people would take what they wanted, with or without his cooperation. The Businessman rifled through airline tickets, a membership card for the National Academy of Science, a travel itinerary that included a hotel confirmation at the Sutton House, an employee ID for GenTech Laboratories—then he found a telex, which he read with particular interest.

"I have it," he said, directing his penlight's beam on the half-sheet of paper. "A personal invitation to meet with Senator Michael Baker tomorrow at seven-thirty A.M. to discuss a laboratory accident, it says. There are no details." He directed his light into Sterling's face. "Please elaborate for me, Doctor. Perhaps this meeting is about an unlawful gene-splicing experiment?"

It occurred to Dr. Sterling in one, wild instant. *These people are going to kill me.*

The Businessman signaled Tarra with an almost imperceptible nod of his head. She delivered two quick, hard blows with her elbow to Sterling's ribs, cracking two of them.

He shouted in agony—she possessed the strength of a solidly built man twice her size. Tarra poised her arm for another blow, but Dr. Sterling, winded and grimacing, waved her off. "I know only what was in the newspapers. No one has yet briefed me."

"You are lying."

"One mile," the driver warned, turning on the cab's inside dome light. They were out of time.

The Businessman stuffed Dr. Sterling's billfold inside his own suit coat, then studied the doctor's features like a plastic surgeon scrutinizing his work. "What have we missed?"

"His eyeglasses are different," Tarra noted.

"Give them to me."

Tarra removed his glasses and passed them to the front.

Dr. Sterling squinted helplessly as the inside of the car became a blur.

"His beard is thinner and has more white hairs," said the driver, scrutinizing the doctor in the rearview mirror.

"Yes, yes, I will take care of it. What else?"

"His rings and watch," Tarra said. These, too, she roughly removed and gave to the Businessman.

The cab pulled into a well-lit rest area and jerked to a stop beside a rented black Thunderbird Turbo Coupe. There were no other passenger vehicles parked here this time of night, just a couple of trucking rigs idling in the outer lot. The cab had barely stopped when the Businessman exited, taking Dr. Sterling's travel bag and satchel with him. He leaned back through

31

the opened window and said to his associates, "Are you absolutely clear on your instructions?"

Tarra nodded, her feline features exuding a cool look of confidence. "No one will find his remains."

Dr. Sterling, trembling, said in a remarkably calm voice, "I can get you money. As much as you want. My employer will give you whatever you want. Anything."

No one paid him the slightest notice. The condemned scientist looked hopefully at the faces of his abductors, searching for signs of compassion, a willingness to deal, but found only the hard, professional expressions of people who knew what they wanted and how to get it.

The Businessman vanished from the window and climbed behind the wheel of the Thunderbird. Less than a minute later, both cars were gone.

Chapter Three

Iraqi border
Friday, January 15
0200 hours

"Sir, we've got a problem," said naval pilot Capt. John Barron. One of the Marines' most experienced CH-53E Super Stallion helicopter pilots, Barron wouldn't voice a concern for the safety of his aircraft unless he was certain of danger.

Special Forces Maj. Joseph Marshall unbuckled himself from the forward observer seat and peered over the pilot's shoulder at the chopper's VDU display. The major's intense dark eyes remained fixed on the mischievous green dot that appeared and disappeared from the terrain features, moving away from the flight group in erratic patterns that could hardly be called regulation military flying. *The Russian gunship pilot is a fucking barnstormer,* Marshall thought. His hard facial lines grew tighter when the pilot switched his monitor to low-light level to show the rolling desert terrain four hundred feet below them. The major glanced out the windshield, then back to the monitor. The sandstorm had virtually blinded them. *We're too damned low for games.*

"What's our ETA?" he asked.

"Four minutes."

Marshall knew this joint assault mission with the Russians was a mistake. Too much politics. Not enough planning. No teamwork. The Russians never accepted the Western notion of antiterrorist special forces units. This mission was a political whitewash, a diplomatic agreement between allies to let the Russians nail the bastard who had downed one of their Aeroflot passenger airliners with a surface-to-air missile en route to Azerbaijan.

To hell with the Russians. Marshall wanted Gorgon for himself. U.S. intelligence said his training camp was out here. The Mossad's information reported likewise, as did the Russians'. *Don't grow impatient and careless—not with Gorgon so close!*

"The son of a bitch has broken formation," Barron said, watching the Russian chopper maneuver ahead of them. The strain was audible in his voice. "He's ahead of us now." Another wind gust buffeted the Super Stallion, knocking beads of sweat down the pilot's forehead. "He's dropped from our radar. And I can't see a thing through this shit. Jesus, what's that asshole doing?"

Marshall knew damn well what Ivan was doing. *They're going to level Gorgon's encampment with every missile on their gunships.* He glanced at the copilot seated to his left, Capt. David Johnson, who calmly handled the controls as though he were seated in a flight simulator instead of attacking the outpost of the world's most dangerous terrorist. Johnson gave the major a thumbs-up signal. Together the crew commanded the fastest and nimblest heavy chopper in the world, capable of high-speed, low-altitude penetration flights into hostile territory.

Marshall slapped Captain Barron's shoulder. "Let this weather cover us, not kill us. I'm not going to let Ivan force me to call a safety-of-flight abort."

"Yes, sir."

Marshall climbed back into the Super Stallion's troop compartment and scanned the twenty commandos under his command sitting shoulder to shoulder on drop seats, their gear strapped to the inside fuselage. Each wore identical dark camouflage suits; each carried the weapon of his choice—everything from Ingrams machine pistols to Franchi SPAS-12 semiautomatic military shotguns. No one spoke; no one moved about. His troops remained within themselves, anticipating the landing.

"Hang on, ladies," Marshall hollered, making his way aft. "ETA is three minutes."

"What's up, Joe?" It was Gunnery M.Sg. J. C. Williams, Marshall's right-hand man. The powerfully built black man had taught each of Marshall's troops how to put three consecutive rounds from a Remington 40XB sniper rifle through a one-inch washer at two hundred yards. Together Marshall and Williams had assembled and trained an elite squad that promised to handle any terrorist situation, in any environment, at any time. They were about to find out just how good that training was.

Marshall eased himself against the fuselage beside the sergeant. He looked pale, even under the compartment's dim red lights.

"Our Russian friends are singing from different sheet music," he said. "They're going in first to claim the prize—they'll flatten Gorgon's camp with their gunships. Ivan wants to make sure there isn't a single terrorist left alive for us when we storm off this transport."

Williams, his brow deeply furrowed, said in his resonant baritone voice, "Ivan wouldn't settle for no ground support duty. We're freaks to them. Air strikes, hard and bloody. That's what Afghanistan taught them. They'll let their machines do their talking—"

The missile warning signal screeched and the chopper gave a sudden yaw to starboard. "We've been acquired!" the pilot shouted over the intercom. "Dropping."

The pilot increased power and pitched the aircraft's nose down to the left to break the missile's radar lock. A gut-wrenching concussion to the aircraft's lower fuselage nearly tore the ship in two.

There was an outburst from the men. "Jesus Christ!" Williams yelled.

Marshall was on his feet in an instant, climbing into the cockpit. "Barron! Talk to me!"

There was a flash and detonation ahead of them. Marshall's hands instinctively shielded his face as the windshield exploded into a blizzard of Plexiglas. A terrible wind ripped through the cockpit, masking the sound of a dozen simultaneous instrument alarms. The chopper lurched violently, sputtering and spinning from the sky like a wounded bird. Captain Barron sat slumped, his head bouncing grotesquely. The copilot, his face a bloody river, groped for the control column, failing pathetically to control the chopper's descent.

Marshall clawed forward. In one wild motion he struck the pilot's buckle release and yanked Barron back out of the armored seat. Poor bastard would never file a rough-treatment charge. An instant later the major was wrestling with the cyclic, ignoring the blast of wind and sand pouring into his face through the shattered windscreen.

The cockpit lights were out. Only the glow of the warning indicators, lit up like Christmas, told the major what he already knew—the aircraft wouldn't be in the air much longer. They were out of the game. The second CH-53E *whump*ed overhead to take the lead and finish the mission.

Copilot Johnson groped for the controls. "I can get her down."

"Take your hands off!" Marshall barked.

The copilot sank back into his seat and rubbed a shaking hand over his oozing face. "Ground-launched missiles. Ivan's chopper flew right into our path when we took standard evasive action. Flew right into our fucking path! Couldn't maneuver. Two surface-to-air missiles detonated in our chaff. Get us down, Major. For God's sake, get us down!"

That was exactly what Marshall intended to do. But the current flowed heavily against him. The Super Stallion, swinging and sideslipping, spun an unpredictable path toward the ground. He allowed his eyes a quick scan of the instrument panel. The hydraulics were going; the VDU and TV monitor were gone. The cockpit display told Marshall he didn't stand a chance in hell of landing the transport in one piece. *Two hundred feet ... one hundred seventy ... one hundred forty ...* Even for an aircraft in perfect working condition, a sand-dune landing would be difficult. *Do something!*

Marshall's face, streaked with sweat, reflected a mixture of determination and desperation, the lives of twenty of Delta's finest depending on what he would do in the next seconds. He knew he could never bring the aircraft to a hover. *Try to autorotate it down—control the crash.*

"Impact positions," he shouted into the intercom.

One hundred ... fifty ...

As the altimeter approached zero, the chopper's airspeed was still much too high. He pulled up hard on the collective. The twin turbo engines screamed their final desperate cry and the vibration threatened to break his knuckles and tear apart the control column. The chopper dipped sharply as it hit the ground, an impact far less brutal than Marshall expected. The chopper skidded sideways like an out-of-control boxcar that had jumped the tracks, ten tons of momentum pushing it forward. There came a frightful concussion as the disintegrating rotors sheared off half the cockpit's roof. Miraculously the aircraft's cargo area remained intact. Marshall cut the ignition, killed the main electrics and activated the aircraft's fire-control system.

The aircraft came to a jarring halt on its side. For a few breathless seconds there was only stunned silence. The emergency fire lights silently warned him to hustle his ass.

Marshall heard the others in the troop compartment moving to evacuate. Williams called in to him, "We owe you a Coke, Joe!"

A shower of blood rained down on Marshall from the injured copilot now dangling above. "I got wounded in here," he shouted over his shoulder.

By the time Marshall unbuckled the copilot and pulled him into the troop compartment, his men had already evacuated through the partially opened rear ramp door. The night was cold. He dragged the injured airman through the shattered fuselage into a miserable desert storm, and several pairs of hands carried the copilot to safety.

"We got seven injuries, two serious," Williams reported, his words spitting out in short puffs of vapor. "What's left of Squad Six is on its way to Gorgon's camp on foot. They'll rendezvous with Haley Nine Zero in fourteen minutes."

Marshall didn't hear him. He watched the Russian gunship, an outdated Mi-4, continue its flight plan to the encampment. "My pilot's dead."

Williams didn't like the look of reprisal in the major's eyes. He touched Marshall's shoulder and shook his head. "Let it go, Joe. We came here to get Gorgon."

Chapter Four

Washington, D.C.
Friday, January 15
0738 hours

"Dr. Sterling, it's a pleasure to finally meet you," said Sen. Michael Baker, offering a sincere handshake to the man with Dr. Reinhard Sterling's appearance and identification papers. He led his guest to a plush couch in the center of a room that looked more like a university library than the office of a statesman. The room smelled of leather. The high ceiling allowed ample room for two walls of oak bookcases filled with impressively bound tomes. The senator loved books, not for the ideas they contained, but for the image they established for their owner.

Senator Baker, a jovial, rotund politician on the long end of his fifties, with pure white hair and flushed cheeks, tried his best to conceal a manila folder tucked under his left arm. He wasn't successful. The Businessman spotted it immediately and knew it was the reason Dr. Sterling had been summoned here. Shortly they both would be engrossed in its contents.

"I know you have a full day up at the institute, and my

day's a mess," the senator told his guest. "So I'll keep this short and sweet."

The two sat comfortably on the deep leather couch, like old friends. The senator could be quite affable when he wanted something, and today he wanted a lot from Dr. Sterling. He opened the manila folder and put on a pair of half-lens reading glasses that made him look like a flushed Ben Franklin.

"Dr. Sterling, I hope you will help me in what I pray won't become a national embarrassment."

"Certainly . . . if I can."

"When it comes to microbes and viruses, my experience is limited to an annual bout of the flu. But you, I understand, are one of the few people outside the military who are qualified to distinguish the natural from the man-made when it comes to microorganisms."

The Businessman gave Senator Baker a professional nod.

"Last week," the senator continued, his eyes on his folder, "the U.S. Army's chief biological engineer died in a freak accident at Fort Detrick. Perhaps you heard about it?"

The Businessman nodded. "Yes, I read the AP wire copy. It was Dr. David French. Very unfortunate. He and I met a year ago in Geneva."

"What hasn't been reported yet, and I implore you to keep this in strictest confidence, is that a Stanford doctoral candidate interning at Fort Detrick, a woman named Julie Martinelli, sent me a serious accusation related to that accident. In her letter, Miss Martinelli claims that Dr. French had synthesized a virus at the time of his death."

"May I know the nature of this virus?" the Businessman asked.

The senator dug deeper into the folder and produced another document. "Does this help you?"

The Businessman took the lab report and scanned it. "Most interesting. I was aware of Dr. French's pioneer work on a gamma radiation mutagenesis technique that would allow him to splice protein around the RNA strand of a virus. A remarkable achievement, if he was successful."

40

"If the virus he created was part of an offensive tactical weapon, it would be in gross violation of the 1972 Biological and Toxic Weapons Convention and the 1925 Geneva Protocol. Miss Martinelli was with Dr. French when he died, but has since been denied clearance to gather hard evidence to support her charges. So she has appealed to me to look into the matter. Now I am appealing to you."

The Businessman sank back into the overstuffed couch. "Interesting. How may I be of assistance?"

Senator Baker presented him with the woman's letter and a one-page biography of Julie Martinelli. "Miss Martinelli mentioned you by name. She knows you, or at least knows your work, and sent me this letter after learning that you would take part in the debate at the fort today. She says you can gain the clearance to access Detrick's maximum containment labs and that you would be able to determine the nature of Dr. French's work."

The Businessman scanned the letter and then read her biography. He suppressed a smile. *Beautiful.* Miss Martinelli was handing him a golden key to the city—a city of corpses. "Why doesn't she take her charge to the Defense Department? Or go to the press, if she feels this strongly?"

"Because of this." He passed the Businessman another sheet of paper, a research synopsis. "She attached that to her letter. French can't claim credit for the idea of his creation. That honor belongs to her, and she is not at all comfortable with becoming a mother of sorts."

"I am not following."

"Miss Martinelli believes her original thesis proposal could have spawned the incident that led to Dr. French's death. In that paper she proposes to genetically engineer a microorganism that may well prove useful as a biological weapon."

"Fascinating," the Businessman said, rapidly digesting the sheet's information. "She proposed to splice tetrodotoxin protein—the most potent neurotoxin known—around the RNA strand of a Group A streptococcal virus that causes rheumatic fever. Her goal was to create an airborne virus four hundred

41

times as lethal as conventional neurotoxins, with characteristics that would make it ideal for covert tactical biological warfare.''

Senator Baker raised a hand. "Because of the risks, she declined to go through with the experiment. She believes Dr. French's gene-splicing technique allowed him to create this new life-form, and the experiment caused his death. If her suspicions are correct, she fears she might be indirectly responsible for creating a terrible plague.''

"According to the autopsy report," he said, reading another page, "it appears as though he succeeded. Brilliantly so.''

Senator Baker peeled off his reading glasses, wearily rubbed his brow, then looked at the Businessman with genuine pleading in his eyes. "Dr. Sterling, I hope I am not being presumptuous by asking you to do me a very large favor. Before I can take Miss Martinelli's charges seriously and begin an investigation, I need to know the facts. Can I ask you to put one more item on your agenda today? I need a military outsider to ask the right people at Fort Detrick the right questions and, more important, to know when he hears the right answers. I will bow to your expertise to phrase those questions.''

A smile bloated the Businessman's silver beard, an unspoken agreement between friends. "Senator Baker, I would be only too happy to inquire on your behalf. And I promise to exercise the utmost discretion." *And thank you, Senator . . . and most of all you, Miss Martinelli . . . for making my trip here so immensely profitable.*

Chapter Five

A Bell Ranger jet helicopter *whump*ed over Fort Detrick's one-story barracks-style buildings and settled on a helipad just beyond the main gate. A gray sedan, its engine idling, sat waiting. The chopper's skids had hardly touched the tarmac when a uniformed young man with spit-polished shoes and a short haircut bolted from the car and crossed the pad to greet it. The helicopter's twin turbine engines sighed to an idle and a door opened behind the cockpit. The Businessman leaped to the ground, Dr. Sterling's well-traveled satchel tucked securely under his arm.

The uniformed soldier, a clean-cut American boy with a sincere grin, ducked under the blades and extended his hand to the visitor. "Dr. Sterling, I'm Lieutenant McPherson. I'll take you over to the conference."

The Businessman grabbed the offered hand, parted his neat silver beard with a forced grin and said with a heavy German accent, "I must ask you to make a detour. Please take me to see Colonel Westbrook immediately."

The lieutenant led the Businessman back to the car. "Sir,

43

your presentation was scheduled to begin ten minutes ago."

"Do as I ask, Lieutenant. And may we please hurry? I do not wish our chat to result in the death of more children."

Lieutenant McPherson delivered the Businessman to the compound's newest building, a three-story bunker made of sand-colored concrete. He stopped before the building's entrance, the home of the United States Army Medical Research Institute of Infectious Disease, or USAMRIID. A tangle of smokestacks and pipes lining the roof offered telltale clues to the institute's hazardous aerosol research. The Businessman smiled, beholding a monument to mankind's never-ending quest for new and exotic ways to kill off its own. Although there had been a notable attempt to make the building appear singularly uninteresting, he knew that in the event of a mishap, this concrete structure would attempt to safeguard the state against the biological equivalent of a nuclear meltdown.

The lieutenant escorted his guest through a set of double glass doors to the guard's station. There the Businessman forged an entry in the register and stood by impatiently while a security woman with serious blue eyes prepared a building ID tag.

"You need not announce me," he said to the woman, clipping the tag to his lapel. Then he turned to Lieutenant McPherson. "Thank you very much, Lieutenant. I will find my way from here."

The guard buzzed the Businessman through to the building's administration area, where he disappeared down the sterile hallway.

The polished captain rapped his knuckles hard three times on the door's metal frame leading into a large corner office.

"Enter," snapped Colonel Westbrook.

The slightly built, well-spoken young captain of thirty years marched into the colonel's office, jerked to attention before the huge desk, fixed his gaze on a point just above his superior's head and announced, "Dr. Reinhard Sterling to see you, sir. He has papers stating business on behalf of Senator Michael Baker.''

Dr. James Westbrook, a stocky colonel with closely cropped gray hair, glanced up from a *Baltimore Sun* article about the gory dismemberment of a Maryland cabdriver. "What the hell does he want?"

"Forgive my intrusion, Colonel," the Businessman said from the doorway, "but I must speak to you."

The colonel flashed his aide a frown. "Call Senator Baker's office and check this guy out."

The captain saluted, turned and was gone.

The Businessman took the captain's place before the colonel's gray metal desk, which reminded him of an aircraft carrier, and offered his hand. The center's commander stood and accepted the Businessman's firm grip, returning an expression as rigid as his uniform.

"I'm well aware of your work," Westbrook said in his Texas drawl. "Hell, everyone here is."

He waved the professor into one of three leather chairs facing his desk and stuck an ugly blue pipe into his mouth. Westbrook enjoyed pipes, a fact betrayed by his worn and discolored front teeth.

"I've read your work on biotechnology and genetic engineering. Impressive." Obligatory plaudits aside, the colonel slipped into a tone as serious as a bowl of boiled cauliflower. "I understand you're here today to help figure out what Hussein can do with his arsenal of chemical and biological weapons, if we give him a chance." He glanced at his watch with raised eyebrows. "You're late."

The Businessman took a seat and scanned the colonel's office trappings. The furniture, like the medals on the colonel's jacket, strove to impress visitors with his broad experience abroad—framed parchment from Egypt, bone carvings from China and countless wall masks from Africa. The Businessman merely saw Colonel Westbrook as an aging warrior who perhaps worried too much about making general. The Businessman pulled an envelope from his satchel and pushed it to the center of the colonel's desk.

"The conference will wait." He pointed to the envelope. "This must take priority."

The colonel gave his visitor a scowl. "What is this shit?"

"Senator Baker assured me you would cooperate. I have taken him at his word. I came here to investigate the death of Dr. David French. You could help matters immensely by keeping the tone of this meeting professional. Perhaps we can work together to dissuade the senator from conducting a full Senate hearing on this affair."

The colonel sat rigid—too rigid—and just stared at the man on the subservient side of his desk who reminded him of his college physics professor. *So that's what this is all about.* Westbrook wanted to cross his legs, to fidget just a bit, but he didn't dare move. He knew it was only a matter of time before Washington stuck its thick nose into this ugly business. *Your day of reckoning is here.*

"You're too late," the colonel said, choosing his words carefully. "Our investigation is over. Dr. French's death was an unfortunate accident. Poor bastard stuck himself with a contaminated needle. I'll get you a copy of the report."

"May I ask the nature of Dr. French's work?"

"Bolivian hemorrhagic fever."

"We must be honest with each other, Colonel Westbrook, if this meeting is to conclude on mutually beneficial terms. You will find among those papers an autopsy summary. The facts do not support death by hemorrhagic fever. An infection of that sort would not deplete a one-hundred-and-seventy-six-pound man of forty percent of his body fluids in thirty minutes. Nor am I aware of any virus that would."

Irritated, the colonel banged his pipe gavellike into a heavy glass ashtray. "Are you some sort of detective, Doctor? A fucking Sherlock Holmes wannabe?"

"I am a defense consultant—biogenetics. Senator Baker asked me to verify the facts of this case, a straightforward request, unless someone is hiding something. In which case I will simply turn the investigation over to the senator."

Colonel Westbrook slumped back into his padded chair, propped a foot up on his desk, removed the envelope's contents and unfolded the stack of papers. The top page was a letter to him from Senator Baker, chairman of the Defense Department Investigation Subcommittee, asking him as a personal favor to give Dr. Sterling his full cooperation. There was some mention buried in the text about a Senate hearing. Next was the autopsy report, the details of which he had personally censored. Very official. The more the colonel read, the more he realized how easily his cover-up attempt could backfire on him. He clearly saw himself as the scapegoat, if the real reason for Dr. French's death became public. In hindsight he realized there was still too much information in these documents, details from which a man with Dr. Sterling's credentials might glean volumes. *Who the hell sandbagged me into this?* He pulled a thin appointment book out of his shirt pocket, opened it to today's date and made a note to investigate everyone who had access to this information. He would have someone's head for this.

There came another three hard knocks on the door's frame. The colonel glanced up at his aide, who gave him a thumbs-up signal. "He checks out with Senator Baker."

The Businessman said, "I would now like to meet someone."

"Who?"

"Julie Martinelli."

Westbrook glanced up suddenly from his appointment book. So she was the one. He shook his head, scowling. "She's a nobody. A student working here thanks to the influence of her father, an army colonel. She can't tell you jack shit."

The Businessman withdrew a one-page biography the senator had given him and opened it on his lap. "Miss Martinelli is a Stanford graduate student six credits short of her Ph.D. in molecular biochemistry. She was a computer prodigy. At the age of five she could navigate through a mainframe system. At seven she could program in three machine languages. Along the way Miss Martinelli mastered algebra, geometry and calculus, all on her own. She entered Stanford at sixteen on the basis of a scientific visualization program to display cosmic string interaction, which she developed as a high-school science project. Then she turned her talents to biology—molecular bioengineering, to be specific. She developed seventeen revolutionary gene-mapping visualization programs, and is chairing a team to develop one of the most extensive genetic databases in the world. Her research paper proposing the use of chemical units of DNA as computing symbols has researchers in awe. She describes a memory bank constructed from a pound of DNA molecules suspended in a tank of fluid one meter square. The DNA molecules are synthesized with a chemical structure that represents numerical information. The vast amount of number-crunching that could be done in parallel as the reaction proceeds could potentially create the world's fastest supercomputer and store more information than all the memories of all the computers ever made. Everyone from computer scientists to physicists to molecular biologists is intrigued. I would very much like to meet your *nobody,* Colonel."

Westbrook's cheeks were flushed with anger. "You're on a wild-goose chase, for chrissake."

"Allow me to decide that, Colonel."

Colonel Westbrook, fighting to control his frustration-bred anger, let out a huff of cynical laughter and jabbed the mouthpiece end of his pipe at the Businessman. "Sterling, the work we do here at Detrick is vital to national security. We're looking at all sorts of crap brought back from the Persian Gulf that could potentially be loaded into a Scud warhead. I can't allow a goddamn schoolteacher to poke around in our business."

The Businessman shrugged innocently. "I am only asking to interview a graduate student—a nobody, you said. Please introduce me to Miss Martinelli. Or do I advise Senator Baker to begin his investigation?"

Chapter Six

The walk from Colonel Westbrook's office to the research area of USAMRIID impressed the Businessman. Electric eyes scanned the visitors and activated double doors that swung open, admitting them into a red-painted cinder block–and-concrete corridor, where white-coated technicians pushed carts of test tubes that clinked and echoed. Thick, bitter odors of nutrient broth and lab animals permeated the building's prisonlike atmosphere, smells the Businessman found invigorating.

Westbrook led the way through a second set of electric doors and down a long, battleship-gray corridor that ran the length of the USAMRIID building. On either side of the corridor, windows and doors offered glimpses inside labs where scientists and researchers were working. Above one door sealed from ceiling to floor with duct tape was a sign that read, INFECTIOUS AREA—CRASH DOOR—NO ENTRANCE. Access to any one of these labs might suit the Businessman's needs, but he vowed to be patient, vowed to play his masquerade for the highest payoff—he wanted access to a maximum-containment BL-4 lab.

The pair stopped before a partially open door devoid of identification and entered unannounced. The Businessman observed that the large, windowless room was a common academic office, barren of the test tubes and lab equipment that were the staples of Detrick. In their place, arranged neatly between file cabinets and book-laden metal desks, sat three computers: a Sun scientific workstation, an Apollo microcomputer, and a Macintosh PowerPC. A striking woman in her late twenties, with gorgeous black hair flowing over her shoulders and an attractive figure, was busy at the keyboard of the Mac, logged on to what the Businessman guessed was Stanford's mainframe. She was dressed for hunting, in a pair of khaki slacks and tan flannel shirt. The Businessman concluded that she was perhaps too preoccupied with her appearance to be an effective biochemist, and she radiated a self-confidence that he found conceited in one so young. Nevertheless, he could readily see that she also radiated a genuine intelligence. Gifted? He intended to find out.

"Miss Martinelli," Colonel Westbrook said, "this gentleman wants a word with you."

Startled, the woman spun around in her chair, her penetrating brown eyes taking in the visitor. There was a flicker of recognition.

"This is Dr. Reinhard Sterling," Westbrook said. "Says you and he have something to discuss."

There followed an awkward silence while Julie scrutinized the Businessman as though he were a homicide detective with an arrest warrant. He reminded her of the aging Captain Nemo from *Mysterious Island,* complete with a neat silver beard. She had been dreading this moment ever since sending Senator Baker that letter. There was no turning back.

Suddenly self-conscious at her hesitation, she stood, offered her hand and gave him a splendid smile. "A pleasure, Dr. Sterling. We've met before."

The Businessman accepted her proffered hand in both of his. "Have we now?"

"Yes, in Geneva, at last year's National Academy of Science conference. You were arguing against the regulations limiting the field of biotechnology. We spoke together briefly at a reception after your lecture.''

The Businessman let out a huff of relieved laughter and patted her hand affectionately. "Forgive me, Miss Martinelli, I meet so many students.''

She giggled infectiously. "No, forgive me. I hardly recognized you. Shame on you for putting on weight.''

"Yes, I must do something to reverse this,'' he said, touching his paunch. "Too many late dinners in hotel dining rooms.'' The two enjoyed an ice-breaking laugh.

"Are you on a social, Dr. Sterling,'' Westbrook interrupted, "or are you here to ask serious questions?''

The meeting's tone again turned somber. "Of course,'' the Businessman said. "My dear, you could humor an old professor by explaining what so lovely a biochemist is doing here at Fort Detrick.''

Julie smiled. "I'm a theoretical biochemist,'' she corrected him, then laughed pleasantly. She glanced warily at the colonel, then refreshed her smile, though it was conspicuously forced. "I can do better than explain. Please sit down.''

Julie massaged her cramped leg muscles before taking a seat in front of the Sun workstation. She had run that morning to help vent off tension that threatened another muscle spasm in her back, but only managed two miles instead of her usual five before the stiffness in her legs became too painful. She rolled a palm-sized optical mouse across a mirrorlike pad and double-clicked on an icon. The sparkle in her congenial eyes focused on an impressive color graphic she brought up on the high-resolution monitor. The Businessman wheeled a chair next to hers and watched a three-dimensional visualization of a protein molecule appear on the screen. The image reminded him of a bag of mixed-size colored pool balls suspended in a black void.

"The army allowed me use of one of its Crays to construct a theoretical model of the enzyme triosephosphate isomerase,'' she explained. "I used the center's Alliant FX-8 minisupercomputer to create this visualization. I'm in the process of animating it in realtime. I'm mapping its theoretical structure down to the genetic level.''

The Businessman, a frown pasted on his face, barely heard her chatter as he studied the computer-generated image. ''This is not right,'' he muttered. He wheeled around in his chair and glared at Westbrook with cold, dark eyes. ''You needn't stay, Colonel.'' He might as well have told Westbrook to fuck off.

Colonel Westbrook's jaw tightened. He scowled at Martinelli and said, ''I want to see you in my office when you're through here.'' He slammed the door on his way out.

''Young lady,'' the Businessman said, his kind, fatherly tone reduced to a cold monotone. ''This is not what Senator Baker nor I care to see. Please tell me about your plan to splice tetrodotoxin protein onto a Group A streptococcal virus.''

Julie glared at him. For days she had mentally prepared herself for this moment. Now, suddenly, she found herself facing a mental block. What would she tell him? Where would she begin? Her lovely features drew taut. She shook her head and said softly, ''This has become a nightmare, Doctor. I'm genuinely frightened about what's happened here.''

''Be assured that I will keep our conversation in strictest confidence.''

''I apologize for getting you into this. When I learned you were coming here, I knew you were one of the few people who could help me.''

The Businessman waved away her apology. ''You were correct to involve me. Please begin.''

She sighed, rolling her head and shoulders, loosening the stress-tightened muscles. ''For my original thesis,'' she began, ''I proposed a genetically reconstructed virus using neurotoxin protein. That's why Dr. French was so eager to sponsor my internship here. The army wanted to know if tetrodotoxin would be synthesized by the virus and, if so, could it live outside a test tube. The experiment had the potential to radically enhance the potency of the toxin and move the virus into the category of a T_4 supertoxin.''

The Businessman kept his features rigid, refusing to give

any clue to the excitement swelling inside him.

"But I never carried out the experiment," she said. "My thesis adviser—Dr. Nancy Shaw—convinced me there was a real possibility of a hazard if an anomaly of that sort somehow escaped this center." She gestured to the screen. "So I chose another project—something more useful."

"And you suspect that Dr. French went ahead with the experiment?"

She shrugged. "It all fits—his symptoms, the rapid rate of infestation. Everything. Of course he did it."

"I must see it. Take me to his lab."

Julie shook her head. "It's in maximum containment—a level-four hot suite. Only Colonel Westbrook can authorize entry."

The Businessman removed his glasses and wearily rubbed his eyes. "My dear Julie, we must have proof. Senator Baker suspects you are overreacting. If we do not do something, and without delay, the army will quickly and quietly bury this incident."

"Of course. Doctor, you must convince the senator that splitting the gene is far more hazardous than splitting an atom. Whatever French created must be destroyed. I don't want to become known as the person who helped create a virus that could wipe out the Eastern seaboard."

The Businessman sank back into the cheap fabric chair. "My dear Julie, it appears as though you already have."

Chapter Seven

USAMRIID
Maximum Containment BL-4 Laboratory

Colonel Westbrook escorted the Businessman down a concrete corridor beneath the USAMRIID building to a massive vault-like door. Theirs was the only foot traffic down the dead-end corridor. The colonel, his face a permanent scowl, did not like what he was about to do. He disliked visiting this lab, its entry authorized strictly on a need-to-know basis. Worse, he hated divulging its secrets to anyone, least of all to a civilian. And he hated to be near what was inside.

What choice did he have?

Thanks to Julie Martinelli, Dr. Sterling knew everything about French's blunder, and no doubt the world soon would know too. She had placed him in an unconscionable situation. Westbrook decided to discharge her this afternoon and end her career in military biochemistry. Fuck her lieutenant colonel father. He had no choice now but to show Sterling the virus and pray he had the brains to appreciate its strategic value to United States security. It was imperative that Senator Baker keep his mouth shut. The alternative was to endure a full-scale Senate investigation into this ugly affair, which could forever

change Detrick's charter to some docile avenue of cancer research. If that happened, he would lose his lab and with it his
shot of becoming a general.

"Ready?" Westbrook snapped.

The Businessman nodded, his inquisitive eyes eager.

Westbrook punched his personal ID code into a keypad next
to the door. A green pin light blinked on. There was a soft
buzz and a mechanical click. He pulled open the stainless-steel
door. "There's a step," he warned.

The Businessman stepped over the eight-inch sill and entered the lab's staging area, a cylindrical control center with
grated floors and walls lined with pipes. The door locked automatically behind them. They passed several panels of instrumentation that controlled the lab's environment down to
subtle shifts in air density. All automatic indicators glowed a
comforting green.

"This isn't the usual BL-4 configuration," the Businessman
remarked. "You've done an extensive retrofit. Keeping something secure inside, Colonel?"

"Just don't touch anything."

One wall was lined with lockers, like a fire-station dressing
room, containing full-bodied polyurethane suits. Without a
word of instruction Westbrook began undressing. The Businessman stripped naked, then selected one of the largest suits
on the rack and began dressing. Soon the Businessman stood
clad in full gear, his suit inflated; he knew the routine of entering a highly contagious pathogen research area. The colonel
moved awkwardly to don his polymer suit.

When he finished, the Businessman followed Westbrook to
a narrow door not unlike a bulkhead hatch on a freighter.
Westbrook spun the releasing wheel. The airtight door opened
with a loud hiss. A rush of air sucked past them into the lab;
negative pressure, the Businessman noted. His inquisitive eyes
scanned the laboratory outfitted with expensive centrifuges,
incubators, freezers and computing workstations. At the opposite end of the lab, sandwiched between two electron

microscopes, sat a DNA synthesizer. Most adequate, he concluded.

They were not alone. A figure, also dressed in a polyurethane suit, sat hunched over a lab bench that rose like a pedestal under a sophisticated exhaust hood that filtered away hazardous aerosols. The technician was carefully inserting a micropipette into a beaker, touching nothing, letting nothing touch him. He glanced up at the two, a frown conveying his annoyance at the intrusion. Clearly visitors were not welcome here. Visitors were a dangerous distraction in a lab where researchers routinely handled the most hazardous and least understood bacteria and viruses in the world.

Westbrook and his guest attached their air hoses to the central manifold and moved awkwardly into the lab, like deep-sea divers tethered to a surface ship. When the technician recognized the colonel behind the face shield, he put down the pipette and stood from the stool.

"You could have warned me," the technician said, his voice oddly amplified by a special cylinder mounted in his face shield over his mouth.

"Blame him," Westbrook said, gesturing over his shoulder at his guest. "This is Dr. Reinhard Sterling."

The technician's hand went out automatically, a civil offer the Businessman refused for sanitary reasons. The technician realized the mistake and withdrew his hand. "It's an honor, Dr. Sterling. My name is DeMarco. David DeMarco."

"The pleasure is mine."

"You and I are the only ones who know Sterling's down here," Westbrook informed the technician. "Let's keep it that way. Understand?"

"Yes, sir."

"Now kindly retrieve French's pathogen for us," Westbrook instructed as casually as asking a bartender for another beer.

The technician's grin faded beneath his face shield. "Sir?"

"Save it. Sterling's on official Defense Department business for Senator Baker. He knows all about French's fiasco.

Martinelli spilled her guts to him. I've agreed to show him the virus in return for his and the senator's word to keep French's work in strictest confidence. Now get me that specimen.''

"Yes, sir."

DeMarco opened a lab freezer, releasing a nitrogen-coolant mist that clung to the floor. Inside, arranged in neat rows on metal racks, sat two hundred tiny vials with plastic caps. Frozen within each glass container was a tiny sphere of plasma containing billions of viruses and bacteria, some exceedingly rare, named after the exotic, faraway places from which they had been found: Lassa, Ebola-Marburg, Junin, Machupo, Congo-Crimean Hemorrhagic Fever, West Nile encephalitis, among countless others. DeMarco brushed a gloved finger along the back row, then selected a vial from the collection of pathogens. He handed it to Westbrook, who, in turn, passed it to his guest.

"Here's what all the fuss is about," Westbrook said. "A sample of Dr. French's blood."

The Businessman held the unassuming vial close to his face shield. Scrawled across the label in barely legible handwriting was the name *Saint Vitus*.

The Businessman looked questioningly at Westbrook. "Why a saint?"

"It was my idea," DeMarco volunteered. "Thanks to French's infection, we know some of the symptoms include a sensation of burning in the extremities caused by contraction of the veins and arteries. As the disease progresses it causes convulsions, hallucinations and purging of bodily fluids wherever the tissues burst."

"I fail to see the connection."

"A fungal poison called ergot wiped out a third of Europe during the Dark Ages. Ingestion of tainted bread caused victims to collapse in the streets with convulsions. Others went insane. Some of those stricken fled to the shrine of Saint Vitus. This pilgrimage didn't do a thing for them, of course, but the trip at least took the victims away from the source of tainted grain, and some survived simply by changing their diet."

When the Businessman made no comment, DeMarco added, "We needed a code name. So I named it after the patron saint of epileptic convulsions."

"Indeed." The Businessman turned to the electron microscope. "Let me see it."

DeMarco reached into an incubator and carefully removed a glass slide from a slowly revolving tray. With prudent competence, the technician positioned the slide under the microscope's probe and fine-tuned the focus. Satisfied, he stepped aside.

The Businessman's face shield prevented him from getting his eyes close enough to the screen to take in a full view. Nevertheless, he could see the cytoplasm of French's blood cells deformed to alarming proportions. "How long have you incubated this tissue specimen?"

DeMarco glanced up at the lab's clock. "Seven minutes."

The Businessman stepped back from the screen, his incredulous features visible beneath the face shield. He had struck pay dirt. "Unbelievable. The cell's nucleus already is distorted beyond even the most formidable agents. Your pathogen is incredibly prolific. Dr. French has created a very interesting new life-form."

"It's routine business inside this lab," the colonel offered.

The Businessman shook his head. "None like this."

"You might find this interesting," DeMarco said. He retrieved a sealed plastic container from the workbench and presented it to his guest. "What do you see?"

The Businessman peered into it. At the bottom of the box lay a lab rat jerking with fatal convulsions.

"I see that soon you will be minus one lab rodent."

"This specimen is already dead," DeMarco said.

The Businessman looked at the lab technician, uncomprehending. "I do not understand."

"I killed this rat with chloroform more than an hour ago, then injected the virus directly into its brain. It's been convulsing ever since, though its movements are growing increasingly fainter."

"Are you claiming to have raised this animal from the dead?"

"Hardly." DeMarco raised the container closer to the Businessman's face shield. "The synthesized virus is feeding on the dopamine in its brain and is producing electrical charges as a by-product. We're observing the aftermath as muscle spasms. The result is an uncanny simulation of life. Extraordinary, isn't it?"

The Businessman waved it away. "It is the stuff of nightmares."

"Seen enough?" Westbrook asked.

"More than enough." The Businessman considered the Saint Vitus vial in his hand, proof that man had climbed yet another rung up the evolutionary ladder that separated him from his Creator. He couldn't believe his incredible good fortune. He had counted on obtaining one of the two known samples of the dreaded African Ebola virus. But the vial in his hand contained something extraordinarily different. Something that would allow him to double his fee to Gorgon.

"I assume you are aware, Colonel, that Dr. French's exploitation of molecular biology for military purposes is a criminal act."

"I beg your pardon?" Westbrook said.

"It was French's duty to preserve life. Instead he betrayed and perverted his oath to science and medicine by deliberately effecting the opposite." He held up the vial. "He created an agent of mass destruction that will guarantee his name a place on the list above the doctors at Auschwitz."

"Sterling, you're talking bullshit. That organism will never leave this lab."

"Colonel"—the Businessman stepped to the freezer and opened the stainless-steel door—"what else do you keep hidden in your house of horrors? A bug that does not kill, but simply puts its host into a lifelong coma? Or makes him violently ill after smelling a rose? Do you have something that can change the mental capacity of an entire city? Or suppresses a soldier's will to fight? I would wager you have all of that in here, and more.''

Westbrook's face flushed with anger. ''Mister, the purpose of this center is to defend the United States against a biological attack. Any crazy group with a kitchen and a couple of dollars' worth of specimens bought through a mail-order catalog can brew enough plague to assault any one of our cities. For chrissake, man, Iraq is recruiting experts from around the world to combine supertoxins for maximum killing effect, and maximum speed and action. We know they put botulinum toxins, enterotoxins and mycotoxins in their Scud warheads and fired them at our ground troops. We must have deterrents. We must find antidotes!''

The Businessman felt suddenly weary inside his suit. He wanted out of it, and quickly. He gestured DeMarco forward. ''Close up your circus from hell.''

DeMarco, stunned by the outburst, obediently swept past the Businessman to secure the freezer door. His gloved hand clasped the latch, but his muscles refused to cooperate. His vision blurred. Confused, he looked at the Businessman, who just watched him with clinical curiosity, making no effort to conceal a small needlelike object in his palm. All in one astonished moment, DeMarco realized the man who called himself Sterling had punctured his suit just below his right shoulder and injected him with something. Why? He tried to speak, to raise an accusation, but his tongue made only a lame sucking noise in the back of his throat. He clutched his shoulder to stem the leak; a futile gesture. And then the world turned black. DeMarco's eyes rolled up inside his head as he stumbled backward and collapsed with a crash between two lab benches.

''Jesus Christ!'' Westbrook jumped to the technician's side. ''Get security down here!''

The Businessman made no move to carry out Westbrook's order. Instead he reached into the freezer and withdrew a random vial labeled OROPOUCHE FEVER and dropped it onto the metal floor beside the colonel. The glass shattered with a sharp *tink*.

That got the colonel's attention. "What the f—"

The Businessman drove his huge rubber boot hard into Westbrook's face shield. It had all his weight behind it. The mask shattered, and the colonel fell backward. He was out cold.

The Businessman slipped the Saint Vitus vial in his suit's deep utility pocket, knelt down beside the colonel and thrust the needle into Westbrook's left shoulder. He returned to the freezer and withdrew several more vials from it. He began heaving them one at a time at the colonel. Some of the vials bounced off the colonel's plastic suit with a muted pop, while others shattered on the metal floor and cabinets, scattering their lethal contents over half the lab.

By the time the colonel recovered enough sensibility to open his eyes, his shattered face shield was covered with shards of contaminated ice crystals. His head spun, and he knew he could not stand. Dazed, he tried to brush away the mixture of ice and blood from his exposed face like a stunned skier after a bad spill, but his gloves could not reach beneath his shattered face shield. Another vial exploded on the floor by his feet. Then another. Westbrook looked at the Businessman, but his eyes would not focus. His brushing actions quickened as his senses cleared, then became frantic, bordering on panic.

"What in God's name are you doing?"

The Businessman, his eyes cold and calculating, offered no explanation as he hurled still more vials.

"You fuck!"

Colonel Westbrook struggled to rise, found that he couldn't and sank back wearily, his breath short and labored. The room began to spin. The melting ice had already started flooding the lab with billions of lethal viruses and bacteria.

"You fuck . . . you fuck . . ."

Finished, the Businessman disconnected his air hose from the manifold and walked to the lab's door as quickly as the suit would allow. He closed the hatch with a thud, spun the wheel and gave it a secure tug at the end of its threads. He entered a shower stall and doused his suit with phenolic disinfectant. Only when the timer had counted to zero did the automatic door admit him to the staging area. He went to work with practiced mastery. In fifteen seconds he had shut down the lab's communications, lights, electronics, ventilation and life-support systems. Rows of pin lights blinked from green to red. The computer displays, centrifuges, freezers, everything, systematically turned off. Only the overhead emergency lights inside the lab remained lit. He stepped to a console marked EMERGENCY and turned a final key. The console went dead, as did the lab's emergency lights. He stripped off the environment suit and put on his street clothes, carefully placing the Saint Vitus vial into a thermal canister inside his coat pocket.

The Businessman exited the lab and closed the outer door behind him with a solid click, sealing the colonel inside his tomb. The concrete hallway was empty; there was no indication that anybody knew or cared that one of the center's labs was now "hot." He rode the elevator to the main level and walked past the colonel's aide into Westbrook's office to retrieve his satchel. The thermal canister would keep its contents frozen for seven hours. He would need less than half that time to smuggle Saint Vitus out of the country.

"Did you see it?" said a voice behind him.

The Businessman whipped around. Julie Martinelli, her eyes anxious, looked questioningly at him from across the threshold.

"My dear Julie," he said slowly, "I did not expect—"

"Did French do it?"

The Businessman hugged the satchel close to his chest. Besides the thermal container, his satchel contained a Browning 9mm automatic. "You are a most persistent young woman."

"If you know, please tell me."

"Yes, your intuition was correct. I saw it. You needn't concern yourself any more. I will take this matter up with Senator Baker. Please forgive me, my dear Julie, but I have already kept the conference waiting too long."

"Where's Colonel Westbrook? He wanted to see me."

"He . . . was detained. Something to do with an indicator in the lab's staging area. I suspect he will return directly." He swept past her and walked briskly down the corridor. She looked curiously after him.

The Businessman's performance was over and now it was time for payment. He returned his ID tag to the reception guard, exited through the center's double glass doors and climbed into a waiting car—a black Thunderbird, a visitor's pass showing through the windshield. Tarra drove the car uneventfully across the parade grounds and through the Fort's main gate.

Colonel Westbrook grabbed the lab door's releasing wheel and pulled himself up to his knees, cursing the eternal darkness like a child. Not even the emergency lights remained lit. The disorientation caused by sudden and complete absence of light created in his mind images of indescribable horrors closing in an inescapable circle. Mustering all his strength he tried to move the wheel, but it would not budge. Fighting a concussion-induced unconsciousness, he felt for the emergency button and repeatedly punched it, but to no purpose. The lab was dead.

He sank wearily back to the floor, staring at eternal darkness. He listened to the slow, sinking whine of the lab's priceless equipment winding to a halt. Then silence. There was no one and nothing, only absolute, terrifying blackness. For the first time in the colonel's career, he was scared shitless.

For Colonel Westbrook, the unspeakable forces that surrounded him were not imagined. His face burned terribly and his extremities felt heavy and unresponsive. His lungs were congesting, and he could feel the onset of a peculiar headache. This was no illusion. His body temperature was rapidly melting the ice crystals. The room already was infested with billions of unseen organisms, with billions more released with each passing moment. Most of them had no known cure. He knew he was a dead man. The fight was finished. He had lost.

The air within the lab grew increasingly foul. *Good. Let me suffocate. Better to die that way than to face the alternative.*

"DeMarco!" he shouted, his voice phlegmy.

There was no sound of movement from the darkness. Perhaps the technician was already dead.

His thoughts returned to Sterling. A clever bastard. Very clever. He had guaranteed that no one would ever touch his corpse. Like a radioactive spill, it would take months of decontamination, perhaps years, before a team could enter the lab and determine what Sterling—or whatever his name was—had stolen. He had gone to a lot of trouble to steal French's supertoxin. Why? He expelled a hoarse laugh at the absurdity that he had simply handed it to him. Only he and DeMarco knew what French had created, the enormous ramifications of what Sterling had taken. No—there was Julie Martinelli. How much did she really know?

The colonel pulled off his gloves and reached deep inside his suit to retrieve the appointment book and pen from his shirt pocket. With consciousness fading and in absolute darkness, he began writing.

Chapter Eight

Iraq
Friday, 1600 hours

Special Forces Maj. Joseph Marshall sat down at the base of the steep dune that had brought the CH-53E Super Stallion to a halt. The temperature was falling rapidly. *This damned desert.* He had crossed Iraq's borders a dozen times on clandestine missions before and during the war. This was his first crossing in almost four years. Nothing had changed. The terrain brought back memories, harrowing memories, of some of those missions. The rescue operations had been the worst. For his last mission of the short war, he had flown a Black Hawk helicopter two hundred miles into Iraq to extract a special operations team under attack. He had had to move quickly, flying across these same dunes in daylight, a deviation from normal nighttime operations, to rescue seven of his colleagues from a waist-deep ditch just thirty-five feet from an enemy position. He had saved their lives. The poor bastards had held off a company of Iraqi soldiers plus some armed Bedouins who joined in the fracas for six hours until he arrived.

"Joe, this'll knock your socks off," hollered the major's gunnery sergeant, J. C. Williams. Marshall jumped to his feet.

The sergeant walked briskly up to the major, leading a pair of Delta commandos who were dragging a prisoner between them. One of the soldiers carried a shoulder-fired surface-to-air missile launcher. The soldier dropped both his prisoner and the launcher at the major's feet. Their prisoner, an Arab boy, directed a pair of piercing eyes at Marshall. The major looked deeply into those deep, dark eyes and didn't see a trace of youth left in them, only the hard look of a seasoned assassin.

"Where'd you find him?" Marshall asked.

"At Gorgon's camp," Williams said, "or what was left of it after Ivan's gunship got through with it."

"Any other survivors?"

"There were no casualties," the sergeant said.

Marshall looked at him uncomprehendingly. "I don't get it."

Williams shrugged. "Except for this asshole, the camp was abandoned. Has been for days."

"What?"

"'Fraid so, Joe. We've got three squads combing the area. Don't think they'll find anybody, though. Looks like we've been suckered."

"Jesus. Get this prisoner aboard the carrier. I want every bit of information we can get out of him."

Radio operator Corporal Savage rushed forward, a portable ComSat receiver thrust before him. "It's patched through to a General Medlock in Washington, sir," the corporal said. "Top priority." He added in a whisper, "He sounds pissed."

General Medlock? Marshall rubbed his hands for warmth before taking the receiver. "Marshall."

"Sounds like you're having a real bad night," a voice barked over the secured satellite channel.

"The mission's over. One of the Stallions is down. Gorgon may not be in Iraq—"

"You're damned right he's not in Iraq. You've been set up—a diversion while he made his move to South America. The bastard's getting too close. I want you on a Mach-One transport to Fort Bragg within the hour. We'll pick you up there. You're to be at Bragg no later than tomorrow at oh five hundred hours.''

Marshall glanced at his mountain watch. *No way!* "What's this all about?"

"Right now it's none of your goddamn business. I don't want to hear excuses. Just get your ass moving.''

"How many troops should I deploy? I've got two units mobilized—''

"One," Medlock said.

"One unit?"

"One man.''

The general wasn't making sense. Marshall looked quizzically at Williams and shook his head. "Sir, I've got men on the ground equipped—''

"One man," General Medlock repeated.

"Who?'' Marshall snapped, letting his irritation be known.

"Your best.''

Chapter Nine

The hills of Tampico, Mexico
Friday, 1703 hours

The Businessman made his way through the gathering dusk up an overgrown path to what once had been a cabin. The years had been unkind. Time had reduced the structure to little more than a ramshackle hut, its timber severely sagging, its moss-covered walls leaning at frightful angles. The Businessman put his shoulder to the warped cabin door and wrestled it open with a crack. He passed inside.

The cabin's single filthy room offered few furnishings, which included a small table supporting an ancient oil lamp that gave off more smoke than light. The Businessman wasn't alone. He could sense more than see the three figures watching him, mere shadows beyond the lantern's pale glow. They were killers of the worst sort, and he knew them all well. They had all made their way to Tampico alone, each using a different route.

"Sit," ordered a deep, menacing voice that cut through the gloom like a foghorn.

The Businessman sat on one of the table's chairs, which sagged and cracked under his weight. He scratched his closely

cropped silver beard, a nervous habit left over from his
Sterling masquerade, anxious to consummate a deal with these
people.

The glow of a cigarette pierced the gloom to his left like a
burning eye, followed by a stream of smoke that reeked of
heavy Russian tobacco. When the Businessman's eyes adjusted to the dimness, he could see the cigarette's owner, a
woman with short, black hair, watching him. It was Tarra,
Gorgon's first lieutenant. The Businessman's eyes shifted to
the figure seated next to her, a man with a black beard and a
squashed nose, the Arabian driver who had also helped in
Sterling's abduction.

But it was the massive man seated aloof in the corner, a
huge shadow fondling a curved Bedouin dagger, who demanded his undivided attention. Gorgon sat there, intently observing the Businessman, studying him like a leopard eyeing
its prey.

"I cannot see you," Gorgon said, his accent a hybrid of
Middle Eastern dialects.

The Businessman leaned forward, allowing the lamp's scant
illumination to bathe his face.

Gorgon laughed when he saw the Businessman's altered
features. "Well done. Your new face improves you."

Gorgon's grin vanished and the stark creases of his forehead
deepened when he looked into the Businessman's eyes that
stared back with frank candor. Gone was the serious academic
gaze that was the Businessman's signature, replaced by the
furtive glances of a conspirator, a man with a plot. Those eyes
were a warning to Gorgon. A scheme simmering in the Businessman's head was dangerous. There was no room in the
plan for a self-indulgent plot hatched by one of his confed-
erates. Operation Harness demanded absolute loyalty from his
troops. The arrangement must be carried out exactly as ordered; otherwise his plan was finished. And Gorgon needed
what only the Businessman could provide.

"Do you have it, Herr Wynett?"

The Businessman nodded.

"Show it to me."

"Impossible. It must remain frozen."

Gorgon seemed to accept that. "You had no difficulty?"

"None. Detrick's security is pathetically lax. In two weeks you will command a formidable plague."

Gorgon leaned forward, his head bobbing vulturelike. "Very good. Then let us hasten to Mazatlán—"

The Businessman raised his hand in a halting gesture. "Not so quickly, Mr. Gorgon. First we will discuss my payment."

There came stifled laughter from the other two, followed by another waft of heavy cigarette smoke. Gorgon eased back in his chair, and when he spoke there was benign superiority in his voice. "No advance compensation. I do not trust you. Most men would simply abscond with my generous down payment and live comfortably for the remainder of their years. You would do the same, I am certain."

The Businessman's eyes grew dark and angry. "I gave you my word I will deliver—"

"You brought me no proof. I will pay you after I have the tanks . . . nothing before. I have decided."

The Businessman's head flew back and out came forced laughter. "Then go to Mazatlán alone, Mr. Gorgon."

The giant slammed his fist against the wall, splitting the planks. "You will do as I order."

"No, Mr. Gorgon. This is my business arrangement. I will synthesize the organism without your muddling interference. When I have incubated the virus in the quantity you require, I will allow you to purchase it. Your cost will be ten million American dollars—two million for each tank."

Gorgon rose quickly to his feet. "You are mad to come here and demand new terms."

"A service fee, my friend. My price has doubled. What I have is worth far more than I am asking."

The others, stunned by the Businessman's brazen demands, glanced mutely at Gorgon for instruction. The giant said slowly, "You will not leave this room alive, Herr Wynett."

The Businessman, fueling his confidence, dismissed the

threat with a smirk and played his last card. "Then you will have nothing. Your ridiculous plan will be finished. If this is about money, Mr. Gorgon, then you place a very low value on His Excellency's regime. The price of a thermonuclear device, even if a reliable one could be assembed and purchased, would be one hundred times what I am asking. I am offering you a weapon far more effective and far easier to deploy. If you cannot acquire the sum, then tell His Excellency he must go back to plotting his revenge on a small scale with amateurs."

Gorgon stepped into the light, revealing cold, dark features chiseled from coal. He scrutinized the Businessman with piercing eyes that discharged hatred through thin slits. Gorgon knew enough about men to understand the Businessman would deliver what he promised—for his price. He could trust him. Gorgon drove his dagger's curved blade into the table's splintered top between the Businessman's left index finger and thumb. His guest didn't flinch.

Gorgon, grinning an odd blend of amusement and contempt, said, "I have been chosen to change the face of the world. I do not care what it costs. I will defeat the evil enemy and crush their arrogance. I have but one weakness—you, my Achilles' heel. I will not tolerate treachery. I will show you."

Gorgon plucked the dagger from the table and, with startling swiftness, spun dancelike on his heels and hurled it across the room with remarkable strength and accuracy. There came a dull thud as the blade struck bone, followed by the gasp of a man expelling his final breath. The Arabian driver died instantly, his head pinned to the wall, his brutish face contorted in an incredulous look of horror. Only the hilt of Gorgon's dagger still protruded from what had once been his left eye. Tarra gave a throaty chuckle, amused by the noisy evacuation of the corpse's bowels and bladder.

"Remove his brain," Gorgon said to her, "and send it as a warning to those who paid him to betray me."

Tarra gave the Arab driver a lingering kiss on his still trembling lips before wrenching the dagger from his eye and driving the blade into his skull with a sickening crack. Wynett winced.

Gorgon said to the Businessman in a voice that sent a cold warning, "For money he told my enemies the location of my camp. *For money!* I should have killed him slowly, but I am in haste. Now I must keep moving. What proof will you offer that you will not betray me?"

The Businessman had negotiated shrewdly, leveraging his advantages and sealing the deal under his own terms. "You have my word. And that, my friend, is all I will give you until my work is finished."

Frederick, Maryland
Saturday, January 16
1203 Hours

There came a severe knock on Julie's door, and a deep, resonant voice full of authority snapped, "Miss Martinelli?"

Julie swung away from her Macintosh computer and drew in her breath sharply when she saw two men—a black man in a suit and an army security officer—standing on the threshold of her apartment. She had expected official-looking men with unnerving stares to show up on her doorstep. Still, the specter of authority scared the hell out of her, her intuition shouting warnings.

"You are Miss Martinelli?" the black man asked again, stepping into her apartment. He was tall, with huge shoulders and sharp, intelligent eyes that scanned the room with its clutter of computer peripherals and books.

"Who are you?" Julie asked. "How did you get in here?"

"The door was open . . . ajar, actually," he said. "You should be more careful. Your ID please."

"I asked who are you? I want to see *your* ID."

"Miss Martinelli, there isn't time. We're twenty-two minutes late."

"Your ID—now."

He stepped assertively forward, maneuvering around the pillars of books stacked across the floor. He reached inside his coat pocket, produced a shiny black wallet and opened it: STONY ROBINSON, CIA.

Oh shit. Julie leaned back into her cheap wicker chair, unable to think clearly. So she was being taken into custody—by the CIA! The adrenaline surged to her head, producing strange light patterns in front of her eyes. High treason and violating countless international treaties, for starters—who knew what other charges would be filed against her. No Ph.D. No residency. No future. Her career was over, her life in ruins. *Don't panic; think this through logically.*

Had she made the right decision sending Senator Baker that self-righteous letter, which she now realized was full of vague suspicions and naive righteousness? And no proof. She was certain Dr. French had created a dreadful new organism—a creature she undeniably had dreamed up—but there was no way to prove she wasn't intimately involved in his project. Could she trust Dr. Sterling? Perhaps he had implicated her. With no tangible defense she would go to prison as an accessory. Maybe there would even be a manslaughter charge thrown in there somewhere.

"Your ID, please," Robinson said.

Julie held up the Detrick identification tag still clipped to her camel V-neck sweater. He put his nose to within inches of the tag and scrutinized it with intense, narrowly focused eyes that saw and recorded every detail.

"Your Stanford ID," he said.

Julie found her purse, fished out the plastic university ID card and offered it to him. He looked hard at it before giving a slight nod to the security officer, who spoke into a handheld radio. "Command, three-eight. We have her. ETA in three minutes."

The radio crackled an acknowledgment.

"Miss Martinelli," Robinson said, "please collect your things and come with me."

"Let me finish sending a note to my adviser," she said, her fingers hovering over the keyboard.

"There isn't time."

"Then a phone call. I want to call my father."

"No time."

"He's a lieutenant colonel in the army."

"I know, Miss Martinelli. We have a vehicle waiting."

"I'll need to power down the equipment."

Robinson's impatient sneer warned Julie that she'd made one request too many. "It will be taken care of."

What was the point dragging out the inevitable? she decided. Julie nodded and picked up her blue leather jacket and purse, then felt the security officer's fingers encircle her arm above the elbow and lead her—not too gently, she thought—into the hallway. *We have her.* On her way out she shot a sideways glance at her cat, Tad, sitting rigid on the chair by the door, his acute hazel eyes watching her leave, his ears pinned back in disapproval. Tad was her one true friend, the only creature on Earth that seemed to care what happened to her. *See ya later, Tad—maybe.*

A third security officer stood just outside her door. Several neighbors were huddled in a small group, talking in hushed tones that stopped abruptly when Julie emerged from her apartment. The door across the hallway opened and a young couple—he wearing a terry-cloth robe that barely covered the tops of his thighs, she wearing only a T-shirt—watched her with surprised looks. He pushed her gently back behind him, protecting her. The two were very much in love, or so Julie thought, and she couldn't help wonder what it would feel like to have a kind man always be there for her.

As the security officer led her into the hallway, she decided there would never be a good man in her life. She was intelligent, independent—and selfish. That was why no man with the generous qualities she desired would ever be interested in her. Sure, men always looked approvingly at her body, and there was never a shortage of suitors as long as she left her brains and independence back in the lab. She always intimidated her dates, or so many of them had told her. She had an obsessive need to control, mandatory if she was to succeed in

74

the male-dominated field of biochemistry. And when her emotions and mind were at war within herself, it was always her mind that successfully conquered all.

As a scientist, Julie Martinelli knew she would always remain an observer. Those qualities were too deeply etched since childhood to believe she might one day change—to become someone willing to give and accept people who were less intelligent than she. So, until then, she was content to experience life through textbooks, computer programs, on-line databases and electron microscopes, studying life at the molecular level, never living it.

Julie pulled out her keys.

"Leave it open, please," Robinson said. "Sergeant Ryan will power down your equipment. Whatever else you may need will be provided."

I won't need much in jail. "I've got a cat."

"We'll take care of it, Miss Martinelli."

"There's coffee on a hot plate—"

"We'll turn it off."

Agent Robinson avoided the main entrance and led her out through the building's side entrance, where a Ford Econoline passenger van sat idling, waiting for them. Julie realized she was shaking. *Hang in there; maintain control.* She had always found it easy to numb out her feelings.

"Let me take your coat," Robinson said, sliding open the side door. He helped her inside, then slid in next to her, while the security officer climbed in front with the driver. The van left immediately.

Julie's mind raced through the logic of the situation, trying to formulate a defense, but all she could imagine was the ugly interrogation that was sure to come. Not until the van pulled onto the Washington National Pike leading to D.C. did Julie dare ask, "Are you taking me to the State Department?"

Without looking at her, Robinson said, "State Department? No, ma'am—Dulles International."

"The airport?" She tried unsuccessfully to keep the emotion out of her voice, which came out as anger. "Why? Where are you people taking me?"

Robinson directed his uninterested gaze out the window. "Dulles, ma'am. That's where they usually keep airplanes. Your father has a C-20 waiting for us."

"My father? He doesn't know anything. Don't drag him into this."

Stony Robinson snapped his head around and looked at her—really looked at her—for the first time. "He has communicated with you, hasn't he?"

She shook her head, more confused than ever. "Not since this whole thing started."

"He was supposed to communicate with her." Robinson looked sharply at the security officer in front, who just shrugged. "He told me this morning he would call her."

Julie suddenly realized that the computer in her apartment had been linked to Stanford's mainframe via a modem since six-thirty that morning, tying up her phone line. No one could get through. "Communicate what? Where are you taking me? Someone please tell me what's going on!"

Robinson's staunch demure melted; he looked genuinely embarrassed. "I've spent one *fucked* morning in Pentagon briefings—I'm in no mood for this." He shed his military manner and said to her apologetically, "Your father was supposed to brief you, Miss Martinelli. There's been another incident at Detrick. As a personal favor, he asked me to pick you up on my way to meet him at Kirtland Air Force Base. He's taking you with us to Brazil."

Chapter Ten

Mato Grosso, Brazil
The Amazon Basin
Saturday, 1647 hours

The Businessman called his plantation Stonecutters Garden, a name he had chosen to remember his days in London. He arrived at dusk, alone, emerging from the rain-spawned mist that hung like great cobwebs from the jungle's thick foliage. He had made quick work of the two-mile hike from the road, a path with a pair of tire tracks rutted into clinging moss. There he had abandoned his truck and continued on foot, a rucksack draped carefully over his shoulder, his hand always upon it.

Finally the overgrown path with its immense canopy of trees gave way to high stalks of sugarcane. The crop belonged to him. Though the soil of this region yielded poor results, the Businessman smiled knowingly every time he inspected his harvest. Only an utter fool would break his back tending this patch of cleared acreage that fought a never-ending battle against the invading ocean of jungle. He knew of more lucrative ways to earn a living off this wilderness. And indeed he had.

The Businessman stepped from the last row of stalks and

saw a man on horseback, partially silhouetted against the estate's high pole lamps, ride straight at him. The rider wore a huge straw hat, boots, a garment that looked like a leather dress instead of pants and a white shirt opened wide to show off a broad and woolly chest. He carried an automatic rifle, and an enormous holstered revolver hung loosely from his hip.

"The beard distinguishes you, *chefe*," the rider called down to him in Portuguese. The dark cavalier dismounted, and the two men patted each other spiritedly on the shoulders, the usual welcome of the region.

"Come inside, Doctor," the rider said to his employer, gesturing toward the farmhouse, a grand English manor worth far more than the land on which it sat would ever earn. "I will round up the others and we will drink to your return."

"Later, Tucco," the Businessman said in the rider's native Portuguese. "First I must inspect the barn."

"The barn?" Tucco teased. "Your bed is too soft?"

The Businessman was not in a whimsical mood after a hard eighteen-hour trip. "First we will work. Then we will drink together."

Tucco spat and led the way through a twelve-foot chain-link fence topped with barbed wire, which surrounded the estate on all sides. Each stout support pole, buried deep inside slabs of granite, had been built to withstand a tank assault. Inside, they crossed landscaped grounds accented with marigolds and edged by several acres of closely cropped sod maintained by an elaborate underground sprinkling system. The two made their way to an impressive stone barn, which housed feed, trucks and farm equipment. They passed inside.

The Businessman rarely visited the barn; on its best day the storehouse reeked of an offensive mixture of manure and oil, which he refused to inhale, however briefly. But he knew few places would serve him as well. "The cellar, Tucco," he said.

The rider removed his straw hat and wiped his already perspiring brow. "So late, Doctor? First we sleep—"

"Now," the Businessman demanded.

A resigned Tucco lit an oil lamp and led the way to the

back of the barn. He raised the light over a slab of stone, half hidden by the straw, and passed the lantern to the old man. Tucco found a pick and, hissing and grunting, pried up the slab and tilted it over with a bang. A waft of damp and fetid air drifting up from below drove Tucco back with a scowl on his face; no one had gone beneath the barn in more than a year. The Businessman extended the lantern over the black opening and peered into it. A wooden staircase, half rotted from unchecked moisture, descended into the gloom.

The Businessman said to Tucco, "There is equipment on my truck. Take eleven men with you and bring it down here. Be certain they are careful with it. Then you will clean and paint the cellar and make it habitable."

Tucco cocked his head at the strange request. "I will do whatever you ask, *chefe*."

"There is one more item you must initiate immediately." The Businessman's eyes grew dark and firm. "We will need more men who can use guns. Many more. I have a formidable client, Tucco. And we must be strong when he comes here for his merchandise."

Tucco's grin vanished. "Already I do not like this customer of yours."

"He is a strong man, Tucco. An extraordinary man. In forty-eight hours I want at least ten more men with guns on my payroll. Now please hurry."

Tucco vanished to wake his roustabouts. The Businessman stepped into the hole and, with one hand on the wall for support, carefully tested each twisted plank before applying his full weight. His first visit to the barn's basement would be a short one; a year of fungus and mildew had rendered the air beneath the barn unbreathable. A handkerchief over his mouth, the Businessman lifted the lamp high to let its light touch every corner. The cellar reminded him of a catacomb, a place of death and decay. Squat wooden arches supported the low ceiling, and niter and moss had all but covered the cinder-block walls. Soon it would become a nursery, a place where new life would grow.

Satisfied, the Businessman nodded and hugged his rucksack maternally under his left arm. He had brought his adopted children home. Now he would nurture them and make them multiply.

Tarra had chosen an ideal hiding place, a patch of tall grass beyond the field's leveled crop of sugarcane, directly across from Wynett's main gate. She lay spread-eagle in the mud, concealed by the tall blades, watching the Businessman's estate through a pair of low-light binoculars.

Her arrival at dusk that afternoon—three hours before the Businessman—afforded ample time to study the movements of the farm's thirty soldiers, workers and their families. She took meticulous notes. She recorded Wynett's interest in the stone barn behind the house and watched a contingent of roustabouts march single file into the jungle, most likely to retrieve equipment. He intends to keep it in the barn, she concluded.

Tarra stared patiently through the binoculars and watched.
And waited.

PART TWO
Containment

"Mankind already carries in its own hands too many of the seeds of its own destruction."
   —President Richard M. Nixon, abolishing the United States' biological weapons program November 25, 1969

Chapter Eleven

Marshall and Williams heard it before they saw it, four massive turbofan engines powering up, the telltale sound of a military transport about to taxi. The Jeep's driver, a young corporal named Boyd, keenly aware of General Medlock's tight schedule, accelerated toward the huge hangar at the end of the airstrip. The major and his gunnery sergeant both reached for a handhold, bracing for the sudden turn that threatened to throw them headlong onto the tarmac.

Thanks to a stiff Atlantic headwind, their aircraft arrived at Fort Bragg—Delta Force's home base—twenty minutes behind schedule. Medlock's strict orders didn't allow Marshall and Williams time to shower at Bragg's "stockade" quarters. Nor, to their objections, were they permitted to secure additional gear. Each would have to make do with a single duffel bag, which contained a shaving kit and a change of clothes, and another, longer case, limiting them to one weapon each.

"A lot of folks are up late," Williams said to the major. "An op's under way."

Marshall acknowledged him with raised eyebrows.

Joseph Massucci

The Jeep rounded the hangar and jerked to a halt beside an aircraft that had just finished refueling, a red tank truck unhooking from its wing. The aerial beast, easily the size of a city block, was a Lockheed C-141 Starlifter, a cargo transport capable of moving entire battalions, including tanks and choppers.

"Word around here says the Starlifter's from Kirtland Air Force Base," Corporal Boyd said, "but there's no record of the aircraft scheduled to land here."

"Nor is there likely to be," Marshall said, then added unkindly, "Where I come from, corporals don't pump the officers for information."

"Yes, sir."

A soldier wearing combat fatigues and a serious frown, cradling an M-16, beckoned Marshall and Williams out of the Jeep.

Corporal Boyd screwed his neck around and said to the two as they jumped onto the runway, "Hey, good luck, you guys." The tone of his voice said he was genuinely concerned for their safety.

Marshall returned a halfhearted salute; the corporal seemed to know a lot more about what was going on tonight than he did. He and Williams started to brush past the no-nonsense guard, who stopped them with a quick snap to attention.

"Your IDs," the soldier ordered. He was a young man with a narrow face, wearing a tight expression that suggested a six-inch railroad spike had been driven up his ass. The C-141's engines surged to taxi power, making it difficult to hear. "Quickly!"

The two fished through their fatigues, then flashed him their cards. The guard scrutinized the IDs under the light of a hammer-sized flashlight, then directed its beam into a pair of annoyed faces. Satisfied, he presented the two with a rigid parade-ground salute.

Marshall bolted up the staircase that had been rolled to the transport. Someone called down to them, "Move your butt, Joe!"

The voice belonged to a man in camouflage fatigues standing backlit in the forward doorway of the Starlifter, just behind the flight deck. Marshall recognized that voice. He stopped midstride. "Tony?"

The man stepped onto the landing with a hoot and offered his hand. "You bet your nuts. Your butt's mine now, Joe." He belted a laugh that rang out over the engine's roar.

Marshall accepted the sincere handshake. Col. Anthony Martinelli, salt-and-pepper-haired and about to find out what it was like to turn fifty, offered Marshall—twelve years his junior—a congenial smile and enthusiastic eyes. Age hadn't sapped the colonel's energy level; in fact he looked younger than Marshall remembered, solidly built and ready for action of any kind, the tougher the better. Colonel Martinelli had pulled the right strings to get Marshall into the Special Forces. He had been his mentor, a military father figure. But they had lost touch over the past year; a special assignment had swallowed him whole.

Colonel Martinelli acknowledged Williams with a casual salute. "Glad you're still taking care of my young man. How's your aim these days?"

"Never better, sir." Williams grinned.

"Good. We may need your unique talent." Then he looked at Marshall, his eyes turning serious. "I heard you had a rough night in the desert."

Marshall waved away any discussion of the past twenty-four hours. "We'll talk later. I never thought I'd see you again at Bragg. Why aren't you spending the army's retirement money in the Canadian Rockies?"

"Who has time?" the colonel said, leading the way back into the transport. "I'm up to my eyebrows in the most interesting assignment of my career. I want you to know something, Joe; I insisted you be part of the team I'm putting together. I wanted you to be in on this."

Marshall stopped him cold. "Tony, I left a lot of good men in Iraq, some of them hurt bad."

"Is Gorgon important enough to haul your butt over here on short notice?"

Marshall's hardened expression affirmed that it was.

"We're going to nail the bastard this time," Martinelli said. "I'll have you back at Bragg within the week."

Marshall gave his mentor a curt nod. They had no sooner set foot inside the Starlifter than the ground crew pushed the steps quickly away. The transport began to roll along the taxiway.

"Get cozy," Martinelli shouted over the throttling engines, pulling the door shut behind them. "There'll be a briefing as soon as we're up. When this is over we'll all retire on our bonuses." He gave the two a reassuring thumbs-up before disappearing into the flight deck.

Marshall took one look around the inside of the Starlifter and nearly dropped his duffel bag, his jaw open noticeably. This was no cargo aircraft. The Starlifter had become a flying command center, complete with sophisticated surveillance electronics and overhead displays. And people—Marshall estimated at least fifteen, plus crew—scrambling like traders in the soybeans pit at the Chicago Board of Trade. What was going on here?

"You're late," a steel-chisel voice barked at the two. The voice belonged to an older man dressed in common khakis and a short-sleeved shirt minus any indication of rank. He wore a holstered military-issue .45 under his left armpit. He reminded Marshall of a peregrine falcon, lean and tough, his movements quick and constant. General Medlock?

Before Marshall could introduce himself, the falcon pointed to a pair of fold-down seats along the fuselage. "Strap in." Then he shouted into the flight deck, "Let's get this circus in the air."

Marshall and Williams stowed their gear under the seats, buckled in and settled back for takeoff. Men in uniforms squirreled away maps and charts, technicians in white overalls strapped themselves in before banks of electronic equipment racked in high metal cabinets, and a couple of civilians buckled themselves into cushioned seats around a conference table.

At the far end of the crowded cabin, a dozen treacherous-looking soldiers, most black or Hispanic, raced through a sliding hatchway into the Starlifter's rear compartment. Marshall caught a glimpse of a squat, black, disassembled armored helicopter before the last soldier pulled shut a bulkhead door behind him.

Impressive.

The turbofan engines roared to full power and the eighty thousand–plus pounds of combined thrust pushed Marshall and Williams sideways in their seats. The aircraft began swaying and bumping along the runway, gathering speed. With a final bump the aircraft was airborne, banking right, steadily gaining speed and altitude.

When the transport reached twenty thousand feet, Marshall decided he had waited long enough to find the head. He unbuckled and headed aft.

"No one gave you permission to move around in here," spat the peregrine falcon with the .45. Marshall noted that the man wore the frayed look of a leader in the midst of a battle he knew he couldn't win.

"We haven't met," Marshall said, softening his features with a winning smile. "I'm Major—"

"I'm General Medlock," he snapped, his eyes narrow and intense. "This is my operation."

Bing . . . bing . . .

The C-141 leveled off at twenty-five thousand feet with a signal from the pilot that it was safe to move around the cabin. There followed a rush of activity as the passengers resumed their preparations—for what, though, Marshall hadn't a clue. Several men descended on the general, demanding his immediate attention. Marshall was quickly forgotten. The Starlifter's cargo area quickly became a conference of solemn, cheerless looks, furtive conversations and civil nods.

The tough-looking soldiers returned to the main cabin. Huddled together, they exchanged rowdy banter while checking an arsenal of automatic weapons and strapping intimidating knives to interesting hiding places on their bodies. Commandos, Marshall concluded, and well equipped.

"Stay clear of the general," Williams advised. "Whatever this is all about, it's his show. And he doesn't seem too happy about it."

"It would behoove you to take your friend's advice," came a feminine voice behind them.

Marshall whirled and peered into the most striking pair of brown eyes he had ever seen. Julie squinted back at him as though she were uncomfortable around soldiers who looked like they had just stepped off a battlefield. She wore her long, black hair pulled back in a ponytail, her perfect body stuffed into a pair of tight overalls. She wore no makeup that Marshall could detect. He noted her face was perfectly angled, with high cheekbones and an elegant nose, but it was those hypnotizing dark eyes that held his undivided attention. Why hadn't he noticed her before?

"This is the worst possible time to get in the way," Julie warned. "I suggest you either make yourself useful or find a corner and stay put."

Her voice had just the right intonation to put a professional edge on a thoroughly feminine quality. The academic type, Marshall figured. *Nice.* He smiled at her, a cynical grin softening the hard lines around his equally piercing brown eyes. "And how do you suggest I make myself useful around here?"

She scrutinized his solid, eternally serious face, then let her eyes run down his sooted six-foot-three frame. "Depends. You're the Delta major, right?"

"At your service."

"You could always covertly kill somebody."

And feisty, too; he liked that. "I have a softer side you might like to get to know. I studied philosophy in college—existentialism."

Her eyes brightened. "Ooo . . . perfect. Then strap your macho ass into a seat and contemplate Kierkegaard and your army boots.''

Marshall, smiling, bowed slightly. ''Yes, ma'am.''

''I've got a better idea,'' she said, brushing briskly past him, her perfectly angled nose wrinkled. ''Find a shower stall and knock yourself out.'' She whispered to Williams, ''Tell your commander he stinks.''

Williams's stone features melted into a broad grin. ''Right away, ma'am.''

Marshall, basking in a sudden wave of self-consciousness, began buttoning his well-traveled shirt. ''I don't even know your name,'' he called after her.

''Martinelli,'' she said, taking a seat beside the white-frocked technician. The two quickly became engrossed in some technical discussion.

Tony's daughter. Marshall hadn't recognized her. He had met Julie once, and then only briefly, perhaps ten years ago when she was barely out of high school. What was she doing here?

''You look like you just swallowed a turd you thought was a Reese's cup.'' Colonel Martinelli laughed, slapping Marshall hard on his shoulder. He gestured to his daughter. ''Don't look so surprised. She's quite capable.''

Marshall didn't doubt it for a moment. ''Since when did the brass start allowing relatives in the same combat unit?''

''I got approval from the joint chiefs to put this team together any way I want. It's that damned important.''

''Did she enlist?''

''Nope. Julie's interning at Detrick to finish her Ph.D. She's already one of the best biochemists in her field. We need her here.'' He was quite the proud papa, Marshall noted.

''What field, Tony?''

''Genetic engineering.''

''Ten minutes to briefing, people,'' General Medlock announced to the group, then beckoned the colonel to follow him aft.

Marshall grabbed his mentor's arm before he could rush away. "Where can I wash up?"

Colonel Martinelli gestured forward. "The head's behind the flight deck, Joe. And while you're in there, flush that shirt of yours out of this aircraft."

Chapter Twelve

The Starlifter

Marshall emerged from the C-141's wash stall clean shaven and scrubbed as thoroughly as the telephone booth–size head would allow. His hair was toweled and slicked back, and his fresh, untucked shirt agreed with the group's lax dress code. A voracious appetite had returned, threatening to upset his plans to cop a nap. He wondered if anybody had thought to bring along a couple of sandwiches.

"Let's get started," General Medlock shouted, igniting the cabin's already eager atmosphere.

Marshall ignored his protesting stomach and joined Williams on the fold-down seats away from the conference table around which the rest of the group was gathering. The sandwich would have to wait.

"The name of this highly classified operation is *Containment*," the general began, raising his scratchy, nail-hard voice. "Some of you got to know each other over the past two days. For the benefit of the newcomers we'll introduce ourselves. I'm General John Medlock, a member of the Biochem Advisory Council, chairman of BERT and commander of this task force. I'll be monitoring this operation from Washington.

The man to my right is Colonel Anthony Martinelli, deputy commander of the Alpha Special Forces Unit. He'll be in command once this transport touches down.''

Marshall shot a sideways glance at Williams. *What the hell was Alpha?*

"Colonel Martinelli brings with him a wealth of experience from several Special Forces units, including Delta, the Green Berets and a stint with the British SAS,'' Medlock continued. "He's stationed at Fort Detrick and is the army's premier troubleshooter when it comes to bioterrorism. Alpha is his baby. And you people are the Alpha unit.''

Some of those in the room—notably the military types—didn't blink at the news, while the civilians exchanged puzzled looks.

"Alpha is the code name for BERT—Biological Emergency Response Team,'' Medlock continued. "Uncle BERT is a small, fast-reaction team of scientists, military officers and specially selected antiterrorism commandos. Martinelli, please introduce your team.''

"Yes, sir.'' The colonel stood before his captive audience. His eager grin was infectious. "The gentleman to my right is Stony Robinson, the best damn deputy squad leader ever to wear an army uniform.''

A black man in civilian khakis seated next to the colonel stood and bowed smartly before the group. Stony was sturdily built, tall, with keen eyes that exuded confidence and a sly grin that boasted he was fully capable of taking care of himself and a whole lot of others when the need arose.

"The CIA recruited Stony from engineering at Fort Sherman,'' Martinelli said. "We borrowed him from the CIA. His training system is the best the army has ever produced—hell, it's the best anywhere in the world. And he's used that system to train the most able commandos I've ever had the pleasure to inspect. We are indeed lucky to have his services.''

Colonel Martinelli acknowledged Stony's men—eight soldiers—standing along the aft fuselage. Far from the spit-polished professionals typical of Special Forces units, they looked more like ex-cons than the army's elite, Marshall noted. Some wore beards and mustaches, none was clean shaven, and their hair varied from ponytails to bald. Very unmilitary. He assumed they, too, were CIA.

"These commandos are Alpha's muscles," Stony said in a resonant voice that reminded Marshall of Lou Rawls. "We recruited these men from the military's covert strike force for drug trafficking, and I've taken them through nine months of special commando training. They can speak Spanish, Portuguese and English without an accent. We handpicked each of them on his ability to infiltrate and operate covertly in what we consider to be hot spots on continental North and South America."

So far Marshall wasn't impressed. He was prepared to pit his troops hand-to-hand against these pukes anytime, any place.

"Next is Telecommunications Lieutenant Dennis 'DOS' Spangler, who is one of the best satellite reconnaissance analysts in the business," Martinelli said, indicating a balding, thin-faced man in his midthirties, wearing a white technician's smock and owllike, metal-rimmed glasses. "Spangler will use a newly developed ComSat transceiver to make sure every finger knows what the hand is doing. He'll also be monitoring every broadcast frequency within eight hundred miles of our staging area. Spangler's job will be to keep surprises to a minimum."

During the colonel's introduction, Lieutenant Spangler kept his studious eyes fixed on a stack of three-and-a-half-inch diskettes he was shuffling in his hands like playing cards. Marshall pegged him as the nerdy computer sort, long on brains, handy with electronics, short on everything else.

"Next is our special-op pilot Captain David Youngblood from Task Force One-Sixty, night reconnaissance flying in Desert Storm."

A blond-haired jock dressed in jeans and a Georgia Bulldogs sweatshirt, seated comfortably with his right snakeskin cowboy boot resting on the conference table, acknowledged the colonel with a raised fist. He was the macho ladies-man type, Marshall noted, the antithesis of Lieutenant Spangler. Youngblood riveted his women-charming blue eyes on Julie and settled into a smug grin. She couldn't help but return his flirtatious smile.

"Youngblood will be flying a prototype of the Boeing/Sikorsky RAH-66 Comanche NOTAR light helicopter, which is stowed in back. For those of you unfamiliar with aircraft, NOTAR stands for 'no tail rotor.' It's quieter, safer and twice as fast as conventional choppers in sideways and rearward maneuvering."

Marshall gave Williams a raised-eyebrow nod of approval.

"The team's molecular biochemist is Julie Martinelli," the colonel said with a special note of pride. "I don't have to tell anybody by now that she's my daughter. Her field is theoretical biochemistry, specializing in molecular bioengineering. One day we're going to read about how she engineered a vaccine for the common cold."

The colonel's introduction drew polite laughter, prompting Julie to give her father a scolding pout that quickly melted into a charming smile. She had the cutest upper-lip pucker when she smiled, Marshall noted, though he preferred the beauty of her more serious look. Youngblood seemed taken by her too. The chopper pilot's dreamy gaze suggested he was fantasizing about what she looked like out of those overalls, and he appeared quite pleased with the result.

"And, finally, meet Major Joseph Marshall and Gunnery Master Sergeant J. C. Williams on loan from Delta," the colonel added. "The major and his sergeant were part of an elite command in operations Desert Shield and Desert Storm. They handled many of the riskiest, most covert jobs in the war: deception operations along the Kuwait coast, reconnaissance missions inside Iraq and rescue operations. They'll be riding shotgun for us. We'll rely on their broad experience of staying alive in hostile territory to defend our staging area. We're singularly fortunate to have them on our team."

Marshall fidgeted uncomfortably in his fold-down seat,

unsure of what to make of his role as a peripheral observer—
a goddamn baby-sitter.

"Lady and gentlemen," Colonel Martinelli concluded,
"welcome to Alpha unit. I needn't point out that some members of this team are not connected with the military. If it
wasn't so damned important, we wouldn't be asking civilians
to participate. There simply wasn't time to go through regular
channels. We needed the best and got clearances to recruit
each of you for this operation."

Marshall resisted the urge to fidget some more. He hadn't
left his men in Iraq and flown ten thousand miles at Mach 2
to listen to pep talks. He was pumped for action.

"One more thing, people," Colonel Martinelli added.
"While aboard this transport, the general and I need to know
what you all think. We don't have the time to coddle behind
military politics. So there will be no rank distinctions until we
land. We expect candor—frequent and relevant."

That's all Marshall needed to hear. "Tony," he called to
the front, "where is this aircraft going?"

General Medlock spat, "Antarctica."

There were puzzled looks around the cabin.

Medlock looked directly at Marshall and said, "This is a
medical transport. It's on its way to provide routine hospital
services to a NATO meteorological research team on Britain's
South Shetland Islands on the Antarctica Peninsula, something
this transport has done each month without fail for the past
three years. This month, however, a mechanical problem will
force it to make a brief unscheduled landing at an abandoned
airstrip thirty miles outside of Sinope, in Brazil's Amazon basin. Texaco built the airstrip to shuttle in seismic trucks and
drilling rigs. It's huge. Hasn't been used in two years, though.
The runway is serviceable; our people have made repairs.
That's where most of you will get off. That airstrip will be
Alpha's staging area, and you'll direct surveillance from the
field's single hangar. The structure has a sagging roof and no
utilities, but otherwise it's intact. Colonel?"

Colonel Martinelli withdrew a page from a folder and laid

it upon the conference table before him. "What I'm about to tell you is highly classified. This priority-one State Department cable was issued two days ago. It says the U.S. government has information that Saddam Hussein has ordered terrorist attacks against the United States mainland. And I quote, 'We believe these attacks will be deliberately designed to cause U.S. fatalities and/or destruction to U.S. facilities. We consider the Southeast as the most likely target, although no region can be completely precluded.' End quote. This warning has been sent to all U.S. military bases, international airlines, U.S. energy companies and other multinational businesses. Our State Department analysts issued the warning because of growing tensions over violations documented by the U.N. weapons inspection team in Iraq. But that's not the real reason. This is."

Martinelli picked up a palm-sized remote-control unit. Someone dimmed the cabin's lights, and an overhead projection TV snapped on. All eyes turned upward. An image of a corpse-lined street filled the large screen. An infant wearing a nightgown and bonnet, its face eerily placid as though it were a doll, lay in the foreground.

"This is the Iraqi settlement of Kumar, about two hundred miles west of Al Kufra," Martinelli said.

The next picture made even Marshall wince. It was a close-up of a young man's face, an expression of convulsive terror. His beard and coat were smeared with dried vomit, his barren eyes sunken into his skull.

"On Tuesday," the colonel said, "a deadly nerve gas swept through Kumar and killed one hundred and three men, women and children. Unofficially, Iraq accused the United States of deliberately murdering the people of Kumar as a warning to show the effects of a highly lethal nerve gas, which Hussein has stockpiled and hidden since the war. There is no substance to this charge, of course. Israeli intelligence suspects that the incident was the result of a spill from an Iraqi tank car en route from a manufacturing plant in Rabta. However, we may never be able to prove that. In any event, neither side has taken the issue public."

"They screw up and blame us," Marshall said. "That's nothing new."

"What's new, Joe, is Hussein may use the incident to divert attention from the international outcry against his biological and chemical weapons arsenal," Martinelli said. "He's looking for a way to rebuild a coalition—an excuse to retaliate using the same weapon—and this incident gives it to him. Hell, I wouldn't be surprised if he didn't deliberately wipe out this settlement as a means of setting his plan in motion."

"Why are we fencing with that asshole?" It was chopper pilot David Youngblood, speaking in his Georgia drawl. "Why don't we just blow off his balls with another full-scale air assault?"

"Because of this man," the colonel said.

The next slightly out-of-focus video image was a long shot of a huge, sinister-looking man with narrow eyes and short Afro hair, dressed in a combat trench outfit. No one would deny that even from a distance he was frightening to look at. Marshall leaned intently forward. This wasn't the first time he had seen this rare photograph.

"Abdul Banna," the colonel said, "better known to the terrorist underground these days as Gorgon."

Marshall, for one, needed no introduction. This was no mythical snake-haired bitch whose glance could turn beholders into stone. The man on the screen was a murderer of the worst sort, who enjoyed killing and never hesitated to take a life to protect his anonymity. Gorgon was the reason his Delta squad had been on nearly continuous alert for the past two years. A half dozen of his men were dead because of him. Now he could add last night's incident to that dismal list.

Colonel Martinelli noted Marshall's keen attention. "I thought you'd be interested, Joe. This isn't your ordinary terrorist, people. Gorgon is a freelance mercenary. Very good. Very lethal. He isn't driven by religious fanaticism—only money. Believing him to be operating out of either Iraq or Libya, the Italian government has sentenced him to death in absentia for the hijacking of the cruise ship *Ameno* and the murder of her crew. He is being sought by antiterrorist officials on three continents for hijacking, assassination and political violence. Israeli intelligence now estimates he has more than three hundred mercenary soldiers at covert bases throughout the Middle East. However, we believe his network is much broader and includes an infrastructure in the United States. For the past eighteen months the CIA has been working to develop sources, identify Banna's associates and day-to-day movements and devise a plan to intercept him.

"On January thirteenth, the U.S Embassy in Cairo received a warning from a reliable Arab informant," Martinelli said. "The caller—a well-paid Lebanese national who has worked for Banna for the past seven years—said that Hussein hired Gorgon to carry out a terror assault on the U.S. mainland. Israel has confirmed this information. We have reason to believe Gorgon will use a highly lethal organism in that attack."

Unsettled murmurs swept through the cabin.

"What organism?" Marshall probed.

"Indulge me for one moment, please, Joe. There is one more man I want all of you to meet." Colonel Martinelli raised the remote control and another face filled the screen. This one was a passport photo of an older man with a weight problem. "Meet Dr. Carl Wynett, a former biochemical engineer with Friedrich Chemical Company of Gronau, West Germany. In the underground he is known as 'the Businessman,' and for a good reason. Wynett has made his fortune selling arms to Iraq. During the past four years he has sold at least seventy tons of arms to Hussein."

The screen dissolved into another face—a distinguished-looking gentleman, sixtyish, a pair of spectacles perched on his nose above a neat, silver beard. The quality of the image was not as good as that of the first, but it was clear enough for Julie to recognize the man who had duped her at Fort Detrick.

"A surveillance camera at Detrick took this picture," the colonel said. "This also is Dr. Carl Wynett. Only the name

100

on his Detrick ID tag last Monday said Dr. Reinhard Sterling.''

The next screen showed two faces, on the right the distinguished image of Wynett, and beside it a head-and-shoulder portrait of a man who bore an uncanny resemblance to Wynett's altered image. The new face was studious, decisive, utterly self-assured.

"The man on the right is the real Dr. Sterling, one of the world's leading experts in bioengineering.'' For a moment there was only the steady rumble of the Starlifter's engines. "Sterling was scheduled to take part in a debate at Detrick sponsored by the American Society of Microbiologists. Wynett showed up instead. His masquerade was clever enough to con Senator Michael Baker, chairman of a special Senate investigation subcommittee, and gain him access to a specially retrofitted BL-4 lab at Detrick.''

"Has there been any word from Dr. Sterling?'' Julie asked.

"His wife confirms dropping him off at the Frankfort Airport,'' the colonel said. "We're not sure when Wynett took his place. But there's been no word from Sterling after he boarded his flight. A police search is still under way in both countries.''

"What in God's name was Wynett after?'' Lieutenant Spangler asked.

"Something to sell to Gorgon. Something very rare and very potent.'' Colonel Martinelli passed the remote control to his daughter. "I'll defer the specifics of that question to my expert.''

Julie passed a five-inch compact disc to telecommunications officer Spangler, who inserted it into a CD-ROM player attached to the overhead monitor. She stood before the group, her eyes fixed on the remote control in her palm. This was not the confident, self-assertive woman Marshall had met earlier, he noted; she appeared deeply troubled about something. When she spoke there was controlled anger in her voice.

"Wynett stole a vial containing a genetically engineered T_4 supertoxin,'' she began. "It was a hybrid. A Detrick researcher found a way to splice tetrodotoxin into a Group A streptococcal pathogen. He created an airborne virus at least four hundred times as lethal as conventional neurotoxins. Wynett now has it."

Marshall's empty stomach suddenly felt queasy. He glanced at Williams, who shook his head in disgust.

Julie punched a number on the remote control, and a black-and-white image of a laboratory filled the screen. "This is Detrick's BL-4 lab following Wynett's visit."

The next image showed what used to be a man, half clad in a damaged environment suit, contorted like driftwood on the lab's floor, his features no longer recognizable.

"This is what's left of Colonel James Westbrook, commander of the United States Army Medical Research Institute of Infectious Disease," Julie said. "Wynett sealed Westbrook and a technician inside the lab after opening dozens of vials containing the world's most lethal viruses and bacteria. He then turned off all life-support systems."

She zoomed in on a pocket-size notebook opened beside the corpse, greatly enlarging barely legible scribbling. It was a list of sorts, each line more erratically written than the previous one.

"Before he died," Julie said, "Westbrook wrote the name 'Saint Vitus' seven times in his calendar notebook. This was no prayer. Saint Vitus is the code name for the synthesized supertoxin—"

"Please note," General Medlock cut in, "that the name itself is highly classified."

"Of course," Julie allowed. "Although it may be months before anyone can enter the lab to be certain, we're assuming Westbrook was trying to tell us what Wynett had taken."

"Miss Martinelli," Lieutenant Spangler asked, "just how dangerous is this pathogen?"

"When tetrodotoxin protein was successfully introduced into the virus, a highly lethal new organism was born," she said. "Tetrodotoxin is found naturally in the skin, ovaries, liver and intestines of the blowfish or puffer fish. It's one of the most poisonous substances known. Laboratory analysis has demonstrated that it is more than one hundred and fifty thousand times more potent than cocaine. I would conservatively rate it five hundred times stronger than cyanide. A single lethal dose of the pure toxin could rest on the head of a pin.

"The army was interested in the new organism because of the speed with which it attacks its host's central nervous system. It's extraordinarily communicable, requiring only several hundred particles to produce an infection, compared to influenza, which requires several million. And unlike nerve gas, which can dissipate rapidly in poor weather conditions, an organism can breed and spread. An outbreak of Saint Vitus could produce a localized plague for which there is no antidote. However, the organism can survive only in an environment of pure oxygen. Once contaminated by carbon dioxide, succeeding generations mutate rapidly into less volatile strains, which is useful to the military from a tactical standpoint—after a few hours soldiers can occupy the contaminated area. Specific data are not available. The only remaining sample is now in Wynett's possession."

"And you think Wynett intends to sell this . . . this bug to Gorgon?" Youngblood drawled, more a conclusion than a question.

"Absolutely," interjected the colonel, standing. "In fact, we're certain Gorgon hired Wynett for the theft. Our informant was working with Wynett at the time of the Detrick theft. Apparently Gorgon got wise to him. Our spy turned up dead in an abandoned shack in Tampico, Mexico. His brain had been removed and turned up at the State Department via pouch mail as a warning. Gorgon was fucking with us. However, it did tell us he had left Iraq, which bought us some time."

"But only one vial?" Lieutenant Spangler said. "How much of a threat can one vial pose?"

"It's an unprecedented threat, DOS," Julie said. "Either Wynett or Gorgon can incubate as much of the organism as he wants. They have no lab data about the specimen; Wynett knows it's terribly lethal, but little else. He has no way of knowing that if a gallon of Saint Vitus was aerated over New York City, the organism would seek and kill ninety-six percent of the population in less than one hour. Assuming Wynett knows advanced molecular biochemistry, in two weeks he could produce enough virus to infect the airspace from New York to San Diego.''

The men around the table sat rigid, their expressions suggesting they were visualizing corpse-strewn streets in their own neighborhoods far more gruesome than the image of the Iraqi settlement of Kumar.

Colonel Martinelli broke the uneasy quiet. ''Perhaps you now can appreciate what Hussein is up to,'' he said. ''What better way to counter worldwide objections to his use of nuclear, chemical and biologic weapons than to reveal in such a dramatic fashion what the U.S. Army is brewing in its own labs? He wants to hoist us with our own petard. A malicious act of revenge, pure and simple.''

Marshall's mind was reeling, trying to digest the flood of information and grasp all its ramifications. ''Total candor?''

Colonel Martinelli nodded.

''Why was Detrick messing with this stuff in the first place?'' he asked. ''I thought we were out of the offensive biological weapons business.''

''Detrick is a defensive research facility,'' Medlock interjected, his firm voice doing its best to convince. ''This situation is the unfortunate side effect of that research.''

''I agree with the major,'' Lieutenant Spangler said, standing. ''This is going to feed a new-age biological weapons race whose end could become the most efficient way to exterminate man from this planet.''

''The man who dreamed up this poison should be up here risking his neck with us,'' Youngblood shouted, fueling the objections. ''I want to know the fucker's name!''

''I did it,'' Julie shouted. The cabin fell abruptly quiet, and all eyes shifted to her. ''Saint Vitus was my *fucking* idea.''

Julie dropped into her seat and locked eyes with Youngblood. He was too surprised to do anything but stare back at her. Marshall looked away from her. For a few awkward moments no one spoke—no one knew how to react to the news. The revelation that the colonel's own daughter was responsible, however indirectly, hung over the team like a thundercloud.

"What my daughter means," began Colonel Martinelli, his tone apologetic, "is that she originally proposed a theory for the new organism as part of her doctoral thesis. But it was just an idea; she declined to pursue it. The notion was purely theoretical—she had no technological means to pull it off. Unfortunately Detrick's experimental gene-splicing technique is much more advanced than anything the universities have. Dr. David French, an army biochemist, created the new strain without approval or authorization. And he paid for it with his life."

"No one is happy about this, least of all me," General Medlock said. "Nevertheless, the people of the United States have a very big problem. We can't allow Gorgon to get his hands on this toxin—goddammit, we can't let him set foot in the United States. Now that you've all asked your questions, it's time we do something about this fiasco and make sure it doesn't lead to further loss of life."

Medlock glared into the somber faces around the cabin, looking for dissension. He found none. Despite their objections he knew he could count on them all to do their jobs.

"Good," he said. "Martinelli?"

The colonel surveyed his team, his infectious grin gone, his fatherly eyes now a pair of dark spheres. "Hell, the world's not coming to an end, people. We're going to get back our bug and with it Gorgon. Wynett owns a plantation in Mato Grosso in Brazil's Amazon basin about sixty miles east of the airstrip where we'll be staging. He calls the place Stonecutters Garden. It's a front for his gun-running business in South America and a damn good hideout. Our recon satellites are monitoring increased activity on the plantation, and word's out he's recruiting men who can handle guns to strengthen his already formidable security force. We believe Wynett's on his way to the farm with Saint Vitus. If he shows up there, officially the U.S. can't touch him. That's where we come in.''

"So we enter a sovereign state illegally and assault the plantation," Marshall said. "How does that get us Gorgon?''

"By letting Wynett brew his poison," the colonel said.

Unsettled murmurs throughout the cabin confirmed that no one liked the idea.

"Keep in mind, people, that Gorgon no doubt has been paid a great deal," the colonel said. "If he doesn't get his hands on this supertoxin, he'll find another way to carry out Hussein's revenge. That's why we're going to let Saint Vitus bring Gorgon out in the open where we can deal with him permanently. The next time Gorgon and Wynett meet, we'll take down both of them. Very quietly, very efficiently. We are not, I repeat, *not* interested in making arrests. Our first task will be to get as many of Stony's men as possible onto the plantation as hired guns. Those of Stony's men who aren't recruited to beef up Wynett's security force will work in the fields as roustabouts, picking sugar. Once inside they'll be our reconnaissance and will make damn certain the vial Wynett stole doesn't leave that plantation. And when I give the order, they'll be our firepower.''

"Too dangerous, too risky," Marshall said. "The price of failure is too high.''

Colonel Martinelli, his eyes coming alive again, said, "There's no risk of Gorgon getting his hands on Saint Vitus. Wynett's incubated pathogen will be worthless.''

More quizzical looks. "I don't get it, sir," Lieutenant Spangler said. "If the vial he stole from Detrick is the real thing, what's stopping him from producing more?''

"As a chemical engineer," Colonel Martinelli said, "Wynett lacks the expertise to incubate a synthetic neurotoxin. He's going to need help from a molecular biochemist. We know he's used such a specialist at least twice before, a professor on the staff of the biochemistry department at the University of São Paulo. The man's got a lot of problems, drinking being only one of them, but he knows his science and Wynett trusts him. He's under our surveillance right now. If Wynett contacts him to assist, one of our people will attempt to take his place. If successful, our man will make sure the culture medium Wynett uses in the incubation process is toxic to the organism. Wynett will deliver to Gorgon a harmless stew.''

''Suppose Wynett doesn't go for it?'' Youngblood asked. ''What if you can't get a man next to him?''

''That's a very real possibility,'' the colonel said. ''In that event Stony's men will simply eliminate Wynett and return what he stole to Fort Detrick. Under no circumstances can we allow Wynett to incubate a lethal strain of Saint Vitus in any quantity.''

The notion hit Marshall like a bag of wet cement: *He intends to send Julie to Wynett's plantation.* Sure, she knew more about this virus than anybody else, but using her was far too risky, Marshall decided. She wasn't trained for covert sting operations. What if she panicked? He shook his head, appalled by the idea.

''Sir,'' Marshall said. ''No disrespect intended, but Julie won't last ten minutes inside Wynett's camp. He'll cut her throat before she can open a notebook.''

The colonel looked astonished. ''Are you suggesting I send in my own daughter to work with Wynett?''

Marshall scanned the faces in the cabin and saw no other likely candidate. ''Who else do you have in mind?''

Colonel Martinelli leveled a shrewd gaze at Marshall. ''Me.''

Chapter Thirteen

São Paulo, Brazil
Sunday, January 17
0804 hours

Dr. Jorge da Silva welcomed his drunken stupor. The alcohol's heavy sedation numbed the deep cut above his right eye and his four broken teeth. He didn't look much like a member of the University of São Paulo's biochemistry department. He had been foolish to resist the two goons, each easily twice his weight, when they pushed their way into his apartment more than two hours ago. The three of them had been waiting since dawn for a telephone call. Dr. da Silva had been sitting rigid for two hours, staring through fogged vision at the two men, American FBI agents or some other U.S. government agency that specialized in torment. And waiting. To his distorted eyes they looked more like gorillas than men.

When the telephone finally rang, the anemic doctor let out his breath in a sharp gasp, then winced at the pain in his chest from a collapsed lung. What he needed was another drink to further numb his pain and fear. But nothing was offered. By the third ring, one of the goons had squeezed a listening device into his ear and nodded for the doctor to answer. Dr. da Silva was no hero; he did exactly as he was told.

"Dr. da Silva," he said into the mouthpiece, trying not to slur his words.

"I need you again," Wynett said from his jungle estate's study. The plantation's satellite link sounded remarkably clear. "I can give you one week's work. Please be ready by eight tonight at our usual rendezvous."

Dr. da Silva looked at the two goons glaring back at him with dark expressions.

"Sorry, Carl," da Silva said, paraphrasing the speech the special agents had rehearsed with him. "I have a collapsed lung, of all my dumb luck. A spontaneous thing. I was just leaving for St. Luke's Hospital." Dr. da Silva coughed for effect and was rewarded with a peculiar ache in his chest. His captors had made sure his excuse rang true.

A lengthy pause followed, and for an eternal moment da Silva feared Wynett would hang up on him. If that happened he feared the goons would mash him into the floorboards like a bug. *Steady.*

Finally Wynett said, "I am sorry to hear about your health. Nevertheless, it leaves me in a bind, since I am in haste. I am prepared to pay you double."

He is up to something big—and that means cash, da Silva thought. *Too bad I won't be part of it.* "I would never live to spend it, Carl," da Silva said with a nervous laugh, watching his guards, then added slowly, "Why not use Armstrong this time?"

"Who?"

"Dr. Henry Armstrong, the department's new American instructor I told you about," he lied. He'd never uttered the name before. "We have become good friends. He teaches biology, but his field is molecular biochemistry in medical research. He is very good."

"I do not recall your mentioning his name." Another pause, then, "Can I trust him?"

"We are pals." Dr. da Silva shot a sideways glance at the goons and ad-libbed, "He does have one fault, though; an outstanding felony child molestation charge in the States. He needs cash. He will jump at a chance for freelance work.''

Another long pause. ''Describe him to me.''

One of the gorillas held a 5 × 7-inch photo of Col. Anthony Martinelli not a breath away from the doctor's face, too close for da Silva's bloodshot eyes to focus properly.

''He is older than I by 10 years, and stockier. He wears his hair short, and it has much gray in it. He is clean shaven and has a medium build.'' He leaned back to focus on the photo. ''Nothing spectacular.''

One of da Silva's guards signaled him to end the conversation; the longer da Silva talked to Wynett, the greater the chance of him blowing this. ''Carl, I have to go to St. Luke's.''

''No,'' Wynett snapped. ''I must speak with your Dr. Armstrong immediately.''

One of the goons nodded.

''You can contact him through my secretary at the university. He should be there now.''

''Thank you, Dr. da Silva. I will miss our chess games. Does Armstrong play?''

Dr. da Silva looked questioningly at his captors, whose expressions remained blank; they were unprepared for the question.

''Yes, sir,'' da Silva volunteered, a mischievous grin melting his pained features. He would like to repay the men who had beaten him. ''We play regularly. The man is a pro.''

''Very good. Again, I am sorry about your health.''

One of the goons disconnected the line, and Dr. da Silva replaced the receiver with a trembling hand, expelling a long, relieved sigh, which prompted another bout of chest pain. He looked expectantly at his captors, but neither man's dark face offered any feedback on his performance.

One of the gorillas produced a bottle of Canadian Club and passed it to da Silva. The doctor eagerly accepted the reward and downed a quarter of its contents in two impressive swallows. His captors traded amused glances—in five minutes the spiked liquor would put da Silva into a comalike sleep. When he woke in forty-eight hours with a demonic hangover, the doctor would be unable to explain how he ended up in a hospital in Salina, Kansas.

São Paulo, Brazil
0815 hours

No one in the biology department of the University of São Paulo heard Dr. da Silva's office phone ring. Not surprising, considering it had been replaced with a device that looked like a telephone but, in fact, had far different functions—ringing not being one of them. The simple switching device automatically transferred all incoming calls from Dr. da Silva's office via satellite to a small office in the World Trade Center in New York City, a room leased by the United States Central Intelligence Agency.

Two people worked the office. One of them was Mrs. Hilda Gonzales, a heavy middle-aged woman with six children, who had worked AT&T's international switchboard for more than two decades. Each time her console buzzed with an incoming call from the device, before answering she switched on a cassette tape of a typewriter banging in the background. She had taken a stack of messages for Dr. da Silva. Her routine this time was no different.

"Chemistry department," she said in Portuguese.

"I need a reference regarding a Dr. Henry Armstrong," Wynett said.

"One moment please. I will transfer you to his office."

"Madam, first I would like to speak to his superior."

"The dean will not be in today," she said, "but I can let you talk to his assistant."

"Very good."

Mrs. Gonzales put the caller on hold, switched off the cassette tape and looked at her boss for a cue. The dark man wearing a darker suit, the phone's receiver already pressed to his ear, gave her a nod. She connected the call.

111

"This is Dr. Ribera," the agent said, also in Portuguese. "How may I help you?"

"My name is Ernst Stenger from the Bianco Nacional Bank of São Paulo," Wynett said. "I need a loan reference for a Henry Armstrong. Is he employed by the University?"

"Yes, Mr. Stenger. He teaches biology."

"May I ask how long he has been employed there?"

"About four months."

"Would you be kind enough to give me a personal reference regarding his loan application?"

The CIA agent sighed for effect. "Mr. Stenger, I can vouch for Dr. Armstrong's integrity as a teacher—he is very good at what he does. But I will have to decline comment about his personal affairs."

"I understand. Thank you, Dr. Ribera; you have been very helpful."

"May I transfer you to his office?" The special agent held his breath. *Go for it, bastard.*

"I would appreciate that very much, Dr. Ribera. Thank you."

The special agent nodded to Mrs. Gonzales, who redirected the call through the satellite system to Sinope, Brazil. He replaced the receiver and, sighing deeply, gave her a sincere nod of gratitude.

Sinope, Brazil

Ten minutes after the Starlifter had touched down on the abandoned airstrip in the jungles of Sinope, the flight crew already had unloaded half its equipment and supplies, stacking them neatly along the runway. The transport's engines idled at twenty-five percent; it would be airborne in another ten minutes.

"We got company," Stony huffed, rushing across the tarmac to the colonel. He carried an M-16 rifle cocked and cradled. "A couple people are barricaded in the hangar. Four, we think, and armed. They know we're here—one took a shot at

112

us. Another bolted into the jungle. Four of my men surrounded the structure. The others are searching the brush.''

"Goddammit," General Medlock spat. "This place was supposed to be secure. Word's going to get out."

"Who are they?" Julie asked, huddling next to them.

"Most likely guerrillas and cocaine traffickers," Colonel Martinelli said. He wiped his sweat-soaked brow with the back of his camouflage cap and replaced it over his equally soaked hair. "These valleys are a source of most of the world's coco leaf. The jungle is full of illegal airstrips and drug labs. When our people repaired this runway, a drug lord probably secured this airstrip for his own use."

"How charming," Julie said.

Marshall pushed in beside the colonel. "So what are we going to do about it?"

"Colonel, don't fuck around," Medlock said. "Secure that hangar, and fast." He looked at his watch. "I'm out of here in seven minutes."

"Get your men inside that hangar, Captain," the colonel ordered Stony. "Take prisoners, if you can. But I want that hangar cleared in five minutes. And be discreet."

Stony nodded and disappeared into the jungle.

Colonel Martinelli looked severely at Lieutenant Spangler and said, "I want your ear glued to that radio. If you get the call from New York, give it to me. I don't care what I'm doing, you come get me. You understand?"

A pallid Lieutenant Spangler looked as though he could have done without this unscheduled skirmish. "Yes, sir."

The hangar was little more than a ramshackle barracks, overgrown with jungle. When his men were in position, Stony entered first. He jammed his boot solidly against the door and expected it to burst inward. Instead, the planks shattered in a blizzard of mildew and rot. He flattened his back against the planks beside the door and chanced a quick glance inside. It was dim inside the hangar, too dark to make out specifics, but he could hear hurried scuffles and could see figures rushing into the shadows, taking up positions.

"Do it!" Stony shouted.

His commandos burst inside, their silenced weapons popping single rounds into the figures skulking in the shadows. Stony could hear men screaming and kicking out the hangar's planks in their desperate bid to flee the attack. A lone shotgun blast from the inhabitants blew a hole in the hangar's roof. The shouting quickly dwindled to a few short anguished cries, interspersed with sporadic suppressed pops as the commandos rushed into each corner, pumping rounds into anything that moved. An eerie quiet followed. In a few short seconds Stony's men had secured the hangar. Its inhabitants lay dead, their bodies riddled with wounds. None of Stony's men had even broken a sweat.

Outside, Williams pushed a curious Julie back from the hangar's doorway and kept his Galil pointed at the underbrush along the runway, scanning for movement.

Marshall followed Colonel Martinelli into the hanger, and both men took a quick inventory of the dead. Four men lay scattered across the floor, their dusty faces soaked in red.

"I want light in here," the colonel demanded.

Shutters were drawn back while the colonel surveyed the carnage. Marshall shouldered his Franchi and also inspected the dead. He stood over one of the casualties, a man lying across the transom. The major's jaw tightened. The luckless man was at least sixty, with thin white hair and worn-out clothing, his hands callused from hard work. At his side lay an antique shotgun, which Marshall doubted would do much damage even if it could fire. The corpse stared vacantly out the ravaged door as if he had some particular destination in mind. Neither he nor his companions were going anywhere.

"Looks like you saved us from some formidable villains," Marshall mocked.

Stony whirled from one of the dead and glared at Marshall. "Sorry to mess up your day, Major. We're not about to blow this operation over a couple of vagrants."

"Knock it off," the colonel ordered. "We have work to do. Get these bodies out of here."

In the confusion, Lieutenant Spangler almost missed the flashing yellow light on his portable satellite transceiver. "Jesus!" He dashed across the runway and bolted straight into the hangar, unmindful of any danger.

"It's New York, sir," he yelled, slipping on headphones to monitor the call.

"I want it quiet in here!" Colonel Martinelli's voice boomed into every corner of the hangar. Julie pushed past Williams and stood watching from the doorway.

The colonel lifted the receiver from its cradle on Spangler's transceiver and put it to his ear. "Armstrong here."

"Dr. Armstrong?" asked a voice on the other end, an older gentleman with a German accent.

The colonel allowed himself an inaudible sigh. "That's what I said."

"I was told you could help me."

The colonel gave Marshall a serious nod. "Depends. Who is this?"

"My name is Dr. Carl Wynett. I am a research scientist. Dr. da Silva assured me that I can trust you. I will pay you ten thousand American dollars cash for one week of lab work as my assistant. Are you interested?"

Martinelli paused several heartbeats for effect. Marshall yanked the headphones off Lieutenant Spangler's head and placed them over his own ears to monitor the call.

"What kind of lab work?" the colonel asked slowly.

"Routine. How soon can you be ready?"

Martinelli glanced at Captain Youngblood leaning in the doorway. He knew it would take at least three hours to assemble and prep the RAH-66 Comanche light helicopter. "First thing in the morning—if I'm interested."

"Sir, if you want the job, you will tell me so immediately, then meet me outside the currency exchange office on Iguatemi Street at eight tonight."

Jesus Christ! One thousand miles to São Paulo in less than twelve hours in a chopper that's still in pieces. That's cutting it too fucking close, pal. "Ten thousand cash?"

"Yes."

"How will I know you?"

"I will find you—assuming you are on Iguatemi Street at eight tonight."

Martinelli allowed another pregnant pause. "Sure, why not?"

"Very good. By the way, your friend also assured me I can count on you for a good game of chess."

Martinelli paused again, this time uncertain how to respond; he hadn't uttered the word *'checkmate'* since college, and even then he'd never been much good at the game. The quickest way to blow your cover is to make claims about yourself you can't fulfill, he reminded himself.

"I can hold my own," he allowed.

"Good. Tonight at eight, then."

The line went dead. Martinelli replaced the receiver and looked into the questioning faces of his team. "It's a go," he said, his expression oddly barren of confidence.

Julie, agreeably surprised that the hastily prepared plan was working, touched her father's arm and quizzed, "I want you to tell me what can happen when phosphate contaminates a nutrient medium."

"We'll go over the lessons one more time later." Colonel Martinelli looked at his watch and scowled. "I've got less than twelve hours to get to São Paulo." He yelled at Youngblood, "I want that chopper assembled *now*. Joe, I want you and your sergeant to help him. Goddammit, I want this place looking like an op staging area, not a drug-infested latrine." The pilot and the gunnery sergeant vanished from the doorway, but Marshall stayed stubbornly behind.

The colonel ordered Stony, "Get your men into town—*now*." *Town* was a farming community of drifters who hung around drinking and waiting for work as Wynett's farmhands or mercenaries. Mostly they drank. With luck, some of Stony's troops would be in Wynett's employ within twenty-four hours, completing the second phase of the colonel's plan.

"Yes, sir." The ungroomed commandos followed Stony

116

single file into the jungle, while a tight-lipped Marshall watched them leave. If it weren't for their weapons, they could pass for a chain gang, he thought.

The colonel said to Marshall, "Your job is to take care of my people while I'm gone." He took Julie's hand into his. "Take care of my daughter."

"I can take care of myself, thank you very much," Julie reminded him. "I don't need one of your grunts standing guard over me."

Marshall grimaced at the word *grunt*.

"You'll do exactly as Joe says," the colonel said, curt.

"What bothers me, Tony," Marshall said, "are too many 'ifs' in this plan of yours. How are you going to pull off this masquerade?"

Colonel Martinelli scowled; this wasn't the time for self-doubts. "I've been eating, drinking and living this material for the last two years at Detrick."

"He knows biochemistry very well," Julie offered.

"Relax, Joe. We're going to nail these bastards." The colonel towered over Lieutenant Spangler still sitting on the floor next to his transceiver, cradling the headphones. "You look like you can play a mean game of chess."

Lieutenant Spangler gawked at him through his owllike spectacles and nodded. "Yes, sir. I can beat my computer one out of three games."

"Good. You have one hour to teach me."

La Strata Air Base
Cuzco, Peru

Peruvian Air Force Capt. Laszlo Valachi found himself in the middle of an uncommonly busy day. His morning had been busy honoring a Peruvian Defense Council request to monitor and record all transmissions originating from a remote Brazilian rain forest. The order at first seemed routine—another snooping session on the local drug traffickers. But this morning's events had proved most interesting. For the past four hours the air base's surveillance equipment had recorded scrambled satellite relay signals transmitting on a frequency usually reserved for high-speed data links. Captain Valachi wasn't a telecommunications expert, but he knew this was no drug trafficker with a shortwave set. So much for early-morning activities.

The second incident occurred just before noon. Valachi had monitored a distress call to the Brazilian Air Force Command Center in Cuiaba from a NATO transport plane requesting permission for an emergency landing at an abandoned airstrip outside of Sinope. The airstrip was less than sixty miles from the source of the satellite transmission. Thirty minutes later, the pilot reported a critical oil leak had been repaired and that the transport had resumed its flight plan to Antarctica.

Coincidence? Probably. Nevertheless, the captain reported the activity to the Defense Council and took the initiative to order his tiny but powerful air-force squadron—two Russian-made MiG-23s and a Hind MiL gunship—onto yellow alert.

Chapter Fourteen

Colonel Martinelli waited outside the neon-lit currency exchange office on Iguatemi Street and scanned the corrupt visages of each unsavory passerby. This wasn't a good part of town. He rubbed his two-day-old beard, then glanced at his watch again. *Damn—seven minutes late.*

After flying at full throttle for more than six hours at treetop level, Captain Youngblood had delivered him to the outskirts of São Paulo an uncomfortably close thirty minutes earlier. Still, he wasn't at his appointed rendezvous. He had to jog nearly two miles down dark, narrow side streets before finding a driver willing to take him to the worst part of the city after dark. Not an easy task, he quickly learned. His only comfort was his ever-present custom-made Beretta, hidden in a back holster under his sweat-soaked shirt.

He carried at his side a duffel bag stuffed with toiletries and spare magazine clips sewn into the lining. While he waited, his mind swirled with facts and tables from the crash course in microbiology his daughter had given him, tutoring sessions he compared with trying to take sips from a fire hose.

119

He glanced again at his watch. Where was Wynett? Maybe he suspected something and backed off. Maybe Operation Containment was already over, only he just didn't know it.

"Good evening, Dr. Armstrong," a voice with a thick Portuguese accent said from behind him.

Martinelli whirled. A man, his face half obscured by a large straw hat, regarded the colonel closely while drawing heavily on a fat cigar. Its glow cast a pale light on a grizzled face that looked direly neglected.

"You *are* Dr. Armstrong?" Tucco asked in choppy English. Martinelli nodded.

"You are late," Tucco said. He noted the colonel's perspiring features. "You have been running?"

"I couldn't get a cab," Martinelli said.

Tucco nodded, understanding. "Turn around, *faz favor.*" He made a circling gesture, instructing the colonel to face the other way. Martinelli reluctantly complied. Tucco frisked the colonel and quickly found his holstered Beretta. Tucco withdrew the handgun and admired its precision craftsmanship.

"An odd possession for a schoolteacher," Tucco said.

"As long as I'm in this country, it goes where I go," Martinelli said.

Tucco removed the clip and returned the weapon to the colonel. "You cannot come armed. There are too many new faces arriving at his place, and I have no time to check all of them properly."

A quick inspection of Martinelli's duffel bag yielded nothing of interest. Then he scrutinized the colonel's appearance.

"You must shave before we arrive. He does not care about the farmers. But those who work close to him must groom."

Martinelli just grunted. *An eccentric bastard, this Wynett.*

Tucco directed the colonel inside a waiting car with a jerk of his thumb. The colonel slid into the front seat next to the driver, a Brazilian not much more than a boy. Tucco squeezed the colonel to the middle. The driver pulled the tiny late-model Ford—rare for this city—into the light São Paulo traffic, heading south toward the airport. Sandwiched tightly between the two, Martinelli winced at the powerful odor of sweat emanating from the three of them and the brim of Tucco's straw hat tickling his temples.

"Care to tell me where we're going?" Martinelli said. "I thought this was a local job."

"You thought wrong, *amigo*," Tucco said, then drew deeply on his cigar, filling the car with thick, acrid smoke. "I hope you enjoy helicopter rides."

Sinope, Brazil
Monday, January 18
0530 hours

Julie doubled over her cot, writhing in agony from the severe pain spreading to every muscle of her body. She knew what it felt like to be terribly ill; she had once had an acute case of salmonella that put her in a hospital for two days. But this pain was far worse than any food poisoning. She touched her right arm and contorted in agony. The bloated appendage had become a black, throbbing sack, which threatened to rupture in a pool of rancid blood if she dared rub it.

Saint Vitus!

She had become infected. The virus had reduced her body to an obscene mockery of its former splendor, quickly ravaging her every organ, muscle and tissue beyond any conceivable hope of repair.

She whisked off the sheet and stared in horror at two appalling bags of yellow sap that had once been an enviable pair of legs. "Ganciclovir!" she shouted, but the sound coming from her shriveled throat sounded like the hiss of a crushed snake. . . .

Julie sat bolt upright in her cot, clinging desperately to her soaked sheet, which threatened to strangle her. *Another damned nightmare.* Trembling, she slid from under the mosquito net and put down a socked foot next to a Cane toad, which she first mistook for a round, squat teapot. She and the

121

toad exchanged curious blinks before the warty teapot hopped under the frame of her cot. *Marvelous.* Better vermin that hopped, she reassured herself, than ones that slithered.

Neither the climate nor the early hour agreed with Julie. She had slept fitfully, thanks to a nonstop string of bad dreams and the night's heavy rain, which sounded like firecrackers striking the hangar's corrugated iron roof. Her nightmares alternated between seeing the virus as an incarnation of Satan and seeing her father's decomposing remains. By morning Julie felt like the old hangar looked—worn and undesirable. The heat, even for dawn, was oppressive. Pulling a sweat-drenched T-shirt down past her waist, she trudged across the rotted and warped planks toward the bathroom before she remembered there wasn't one. Nor was there any running water.

"You sure can pick them, Dad," she muttered to no one.

The other members of Alpha were faring far better this morning. Youngblood was the late riser, still stretched out on his cot, sleeping off the effects of nightlong, low-level flying. Lt. Dennis Spangler sat behind his computer terminal, having already listened to the night's radio static on every long- and shortwave frequency.

Marshall was the only genuinely cheerful one this morning. He enjoyed the old hangar; on more than a few occasions he had paid to sleep in rooms far worse than this. He just hated the waiting.

He stifled a belch that tasted of his sardine breakfast and began his predawn regimen of push-ups, stomach crunches and deep-knee squats. With his body active, he let his thoughts drift to Tony and what he was getting himself into. He didn't envy him, didn't envy his role in this whole ugly affair. He did admire the colonel's courage. Tony was taking one hell of a personal risk; one mistake would cost him his life—and maybe a lot of others. There was a brilliant daring in the colonel's plan, though, and the circumstances were just peculiar enough to see it work. Sure, the stakes were high, but the reward was even higher—Gorgon.

Then his thoughts drifted to Julie. Too bad she wasn't more

sociable; he really wanted to get to know her better. Or did he just want to get laid? He conceded that possibility. Maybe this old hangar had gotten to her. No—it was something else. Maybe she felt guilty for putting her father in danger, a situation he did not envy her. Or maybe she was just a bitch who harbored a contempt for men who were only interested in her body.

He shrugged her off, grabbed his Franchi and jogged into the jungle to relieve himself.

The old Brazilian trapper noted signs that the trespassers were awake. He saw fleeting movement through the hangar's glassless window, then heard what might have been laughter. But it was the sudden appearance of a woman in the crooked doorway that softened the cracks around his dull, tired eyes. What he saw riveted his attention as no other sight in the jungle ever had. Stretching her arms aerobiclike, thrusting her ample breasts boldly at him, Julie was the most beautiful woman he had ever seen. He just stared at her, his eyes open wider than his mouth, and allowed her image to burn into his mind, where he hoped it would linger forever.

The Brazilian half-breed jabbed a skinny hand through a mane of pure white hair, replaced his yellow baseball cap and stroked his enormous drooping mustache, giving his jungle-beaten features their first grooming in weeks. What a fine wife she would make for his son, Roberto, he thought. He damn well intended to make a good first impression on her—perhaps his future daughter-in-law. He thought of his own wife. The last time he had slept with her had been twelve years ago, two years before she had died of tuberculosis. Loneliness had made him a bold man—a foolish man.

"Move and you're a dead man," said a cold voice behind him. "Understand? Just nod if you do."

The trapper's hand instinctively touched his archaic double-barreled shotgun, only to find a polished black boot on it. He chanced a look over his shoulder and stared into the business end of an exquisitely machined shotgun. He did not doubt that the gun's owner, a tall, sturdy soldier dressed in camouflage fatigues, would use it to blow his head apart. A sharp click drew his attention quickly to his right, erasing any lingering hopes he might still harbor about his chances. A powerfully built black man, standing naked to the waist in the underbrush, was watching him through the scope of a high-powered rifle.

"I asked you a question," Marshall repeated.

The trapper nodded.

"Who is he?" Williams called.

"Damned if I know." Marshall said to the trapper in poor Portuguese, *"Que vós?"*

"This is my camp," the old man answered in equally poor English. "You make me sleep in the rain with the turtles."

Marshall raised his weapon into a more civil position, but kept his boot on the trapper's shotgun. "Says he lives here," he said to his partner. "He looks like part of the clan Stony's boys shot up yesterday. He's lucky to be alive."

Williams kept his Galil pointed. "Careful, Major. He might be looking to get even. He might have more family around here."

"He could be useful." Marshall ordered the old man to stand. "Tell me your name."

The trapper scrambled quickly to his feet. "José."

"I'll make a deal with you, José. Let us stay at your camp for a few days and I'll pay you in *bolivares* what it would take you ten years to earn off the jungle." Marshall made the deal irresistible by adding, "And I'll leave you twenty cases of sardines."

The old trapper showed the major a rotted set of teeth. "The woman," he asked timidly. "Is she your wife?"

"Julie?" Marshall laughed. "She's not my type—she's no-body's type."

The old trapper's expression registered hope. First he would eat sardines; then he would arrange for the woman to marry his son. This was a good day, a very good day.

Marshall picked up the trapper's shotgun, with its wooden stock half eaten by algae and fungus, and led the way back to the hangar. The trapper followed, grinning, flapping behind in his sandals.

Lieutenant Spangler's announcement shot through the hangar like a gun blast. "The colonel's in!"

Julie was the first at his side and peered over the telecommunications officer's shoulder at several 8×10-inch glossy black-and-white aerial photographs he was studying with a handheld magnifier. Marshall had just entered the hangar with the trapper in tow when he heard the news. He tossed the trapper's shotgun to Williams and went to the lieutenant's workbench, pushing himself between Spangler and Julie, leaving the old man standing wide-eyed and alone in the doorway.

The computer-enhanced KH-14 satellite images had arrived from Washington courtesy of General Medlock a few minutes before as encrypted digital files. Lieutenant Spangler downloaded the files into an automatic image processor that looked like a high-tech Maytag dishwasher. The unit's 64-bit microprocessor took less than four minutes to decompress and unscramble the data, reconvert the bits into 2,400-dpi images and print three high-resolution photos on glossy photographic paper. The detail of the computer-enhanced black-and-white aerial images of Wynett's Brazilian estate was extraordinary.

"The conditions were good," the lieutenant said, studying the photographs with the magnifier. "The rain ended early and there was a break in the clouds. No haze, low-morning-sun angle . . ."

Marshall took the first photo and scrutinized the black-and-white image. "When were these photographs taken?"

Lieutenant Spangler checked his console's digital clock against the photo's time mark. "The first was taken forty-eight minutes ago, sir. The others are one minute apart. Wynett's got one heck of a spread." He used his pencil's eraser to point out the photo's more interesting features. "This is the main house—looks big enough for about twenty rooms—and the structure behind it could be a stable. The estate is surrounded by a tall fence, and these look like guard towers on the east and west corners. These spheres behind the house are satellite dishes.'' The lieutenant's pencil slid to a cluster of houses behind the estate. ''These structures probably house the farm-hands. I don't see any roads leading in, though.''

''Nice going, DOS,'' Julie said, moving around Marshall and sliding next to the lieutenant's right shoulder. ''How can you know my father's in there?''

Spangler tried to ignore the distraction of her breasts nestled against his back. ''Simple—there's a helipad in the middle of this unharvested field of sugarcane,'' he said, pointing out an object in the photo's upper right corner. ''See the chopper's main rotor blades? No one could find this helipad from the ground.''

''Yeah, but there's no way to tell if the colonel was aboard.'' It was Williams, squeezing next to Julie.

''There's more detail on the second photo.'' Lieutenant Spangler put another photograph under a table magnifier, a close-up of the area between the helipad and the estate's main gate. ''Two men are walking toward the house. Another man with a rifle, probably a guard, is following about ten paces behind them.''

''So you think one of the first two men is my father?'' Julie asked.

''Does this help?'' He put the third photo under the magnifier. The close-up showed two men, one wearing a large straw hat and white shirt, the other a shorter man with salt-and-pepper hair, carrying a duffel bag. ''I'll bet a month's pay the man on the right is the colonel. He's carrying the duffel bag. See?''

Marshall conceded with a nod. Julie took the photo and examined it with Spangler's hand magnifier. ''He doesn't look like he's being coerced.''

''Just the usual precautions,'' Spangler said.

''What do we do now?'' Julie asked, giving the photo back to the lieutenant. ''How can we help him?''

Everyone looked to Marshall for an answer. The major just shrugged. ''We do just what the colonel ordered—nothing.

Code: Alpha

Tony's a resourceful man who managed to get himself right where he wants to be. Now he's about to find out just how much he knows about biochemistry.''

Stonecutters Garden

Tucco led Colonel Martinelli from the sugarcane fields into the more civil world of Wynett's estate. Martinelli took in the magnificent grounds, astounded. The lawn, a hardy green carpet unblemished by weeds, flowed neatly around cobblestone paths and walls supporting superbly pruned shrubbery and trees of every variety and color. Wynett obviously appreciated horticulture artistry and indulged that admiration with impressive results. But the real treasure was his English Tudor house, standing sentinel over the grounds like a grand mountain. Massive irregular granite blocks gave it the solidity of a fortress. *Impressive.* Martinelli couldn't help wondering how many guns Wynett had sold to transform part of the Amazon rain forest into a posh European countryside.

As they stepped inside the fence, an iron-grilled gate closed automatically behind them, and someone shouted in Portuguese to stand clear. There came a loud crack followed by the whine of an electric generator. *Cute.*

Martinelli assumed they would go into the house straightaway to get settled. He guessed wrong. Tucco led the way along an ornate cobblestone walkway, then across several acres of sod that led down to a charming stone barn. Between the two structures sat a cluster of satellite dishes and hefty petroleum storage tanks surrounded by a high barbed-wire fence. There were a dozen men with tools working in and around the barn. A few, however, carried rifles and looked as though they knew how to use them. Martinelli scanned each farmhand's face. He released his breath slowly when he spotted one of Alpha's men, a shovel slung over his shoulder, walking toward the barn. How many more of Stony's men had made it in? he wondered.

A black man in stiff overalls emerged from the barn and

walked straight toward them. Martinelli's expression tightened; it was Stony, sweating profusely, his disinterested gaze fixed well past them. He carried a shovel, evidence that the special-op captain had been unsuccessful in convincing Wynett he could be trusted with a rifle. As he passed the two, Stony's right hand came up quickly and batted an imaginary mosquito away from his ear. He walked past them, never making eye contact with either man.

The sound of kids screaming drew Martinelli's attention back to the barn. A couple of black boys, running and pushing each other, raced inside, staying just ahead of a black woman chasing and scolding them. Martinelli's brow furled with a look of displeasure. Women and children complicated their plan. How many more were in here?

Tucco noticed the colonel's expression. "You like watching the boys, yes, Doctor?"

"Say what?"

Tucco, grinning, waved away the remark. "*Chefe* has told me about your problem in America."

"Yeah? You'll have to fill me in on it sometime."

The two entered the barn. Its darkened interior was a welcome respite from the region's early-morning sun. Inside, two workers stopped grooming a magnificent equine specimen long enough to shoo away the spirited boys darting underfoot. Tucco led Martinelli to the back of the barn, where another of Stony's men—a commando nicknamed Buckshot—stood sentinel over a hole in the floor, armed with a Kalashnikov automatic rifle. Martinelli grinned. *Nice going, Buckshot!*

Tucco said something to Buckshot in rapid Portuguese, and the soldier allowed the two to pass, refusing to make eye contact with the colonel. Tucco stepped into the hole and descended a flight of twisted steps reinforced with solid hardwood planks leading beneath the barn. Martinelli followed. The air-conditioned basement was much brighter than the barn above, thanks to a dozen rows of fluorescent fixtures suspended from the ceiling's twisted rafters. Two heavy-duty ventilation units attached to makeshift aluminum ductwork were doing their best to pump out the cellar's disgusting odor of mildew, with moderate success. The walls had been recently scrubbed and whitewashed, the paint fumes masking some odor. A lovely concerto by Vivaldi from an unseen sound system provided exceptional background music.

Martinelli didn't like what he saw down here. Wynett had transformed the cellar into an advanced molecular biology laboratory, complete with lab benches, test tubes, beakers and diagnostic equipment. To the colonel, the cellar's most interesting pieces of equipment were two stainless-steel fermentation units, which resembled old-fashioned diving bells, their bases enclosed in steel pedestals. A myriad of pipes protruded from the units, and a lone porthole on each curved top provided the only glimpse of its interior.

Martinelli was intimately familiar with these apparatuses. At Fort Detrick he had worked with similar units engineered to grow cultures for biochemical products that normally ended up in pharmacies and hospitals. The microorganisms from these modified units, however, could end up in warheads. They hadn't counted on Wynett getting his hands on such sophisticated equipment, let alone two fermentation units. Wynett would be able to work much faster than they had estimated.

At the far corner of the cellar, half hidden in an overstuffed chair positioned before a Sun computing workstation, sat Dr. Carl Wynett. Wynett's appearance surprised Martinelli. The old man looked more like Dr. Sterling than did the photographs of Sterling. He also looked tired and worn, the deep lines on his aged face evidence of an ambitious work schedule, a man pushed to the max. Wynett pulled himself wearily from the stuffed chair and offered his hand to the colonel.

"Welcome to my little garden in the forest, Dr. Armstrong," Wynett said, adding with a grin, "Behind my back my employees call me the Businessman, a name I find amusing. You may call me Carl. I trust your trip here was not too uncomfortable?"

Martinelli accepted his host's firm grip. *Spending the last fourteen hours aboard two different helicopters, first rushing to São Paulo, then back again, isn't my idea of a comfortable weekend, pal.* "I enjoyed the ride," he lied.

Wynett regarded Martinelli curiously. He had expected someone like Dr. da Silva, a squirrely lab assistant, long on brains at the expense of his body, which he further diminished with alcohol and drugs. Instead, Dr. Armstrong was a man who obviously took his health seriously and, as a result, looked ten years younger than his fifty years. His hands were not those of a scholar, he noted; they were athletic hands with strong, thick fingers and callused palms. Curious.

Tucco stood behind the colonel, watching him.

"Let us begin our business," Wynett said, waving Martinelli into a folding chair next to his. "It is critical that I get this laboratory operational this morning. Later we will have time to chat so I can learn everything about you. I trust you are familiar with the fermentation process?"

"Fermentation?" Martinelli feigned a surprised look. "Since when do you ferment cocaine?"

It was Wynett's turn to look surprised, though his expression was genuine. "You believe I asked you here to help me refine drugs?"

"I assumed—"

"Do not assume anything while in this laboratory," Wynett said, his voice curt. "It could prove very costly to both of us."

Martinelli nodded an apology, afraid he had overplayed his naiveté act. "Of course."

Wynett's deep facial lines softened. "Excuse my impatience this morning. I have spent the night unpacking this laboratory and making it operational. I have very little tolerance left. I am not a drug dealer, I assure you, Dr. Armstrong. You must first understand that I asked you here simply to consult with me. I forbid you to touch this equipment. Any adjustments will be my responsibility alone. If you believe a parameter should be changed, you will immediately inform me and, if I agree, I will adjust the process. Is that absolutely clear?"

Jesus. "Consult about what?"

Code: Alpha

"A culture medium. Its maintenance is tedious work. I cannot allow my fatigue to introduce errors. That is why I will pay you a large sum simply to be my watchdog."

"May I ask the nature of the microorganism?"

"A synthetic T_4 neurotoxin."

Martinelli let out a low whistle, a reaction Wynett did not seem to like.

"Is there a problem, Dr. Armstrong?"

The colonel gave Wynett his best embarrassed shrug, reminding himself about the first rule of cover stories: Never make promises about yourself you can't keep. He intended to cover his ass. "I've never worked on a synthetic neurotoxin before. But, hell, I'm willing to learn."

"No one has worked with this organism before. That is why we must exercise extreme care. Because the organism's precise growth-factor requirements are unknown, I have chosen a complex synthetic medium. I am concerned that if the medium is too rich, the nutrients may become toxic. I would like your opinion on the construction of that medium."

"Of course."

Wynett punched several keys on the computer, and a table of numbers scrolled down the display. "I have analyzed the cells in the blood specimen and refactored the requirements based on the growth results I require. Study this list carefully. If I have overlooked anything, you will please bring it to my attention. My notes are in this journal. Please familiarize yourself with them."

Martinelli opened the notebook to a random section with the heading *Viral Pathology*.

Then he looked at the screen and grimaced.

Water	*1 liter*
Energy source:	
Glucose	*25 g*

Nitrogen source:
  $NH4Cl$ .... *3 g*

Minerals:
  KH_2PO_4 .... *600 mg*
  $FeSO4 \cdot 7H2O$ .... *10 mg*
  K_2HPO_4 .... *600 mg*
  $MnSO_4 \cdot 4H_2O$ .... *20 mg*
  $MgSO_4 \cdot 7H_2O$ .... *200 mg*

Organic acid:
  Sodium acetate .... *20 g*

Amino acids:
  DL-Alanine .... *200 mg*
  L-Lysine .... *250 mg*
  L-Arginine .... *242 mg*
  DL-Methion. .... *100 mg*
  L-Asparagine .... *400 mg*
  DL-Phenyl. .... *100 mg*
  L-Aspart. acid .... *100 mg*
  L-Proline .... *100 mg*
  L-Cysteine .... *50 mg*
  DL-Serine .... *50 mg*
  L-glutam. acid .... *300 mg*
  DL-Threonine .... *200 mg*
  Glycine .... *100 mg*
  DL-Tryptoph. .... *40 mg*
  L-Hist. • HCl .... *62 mg*
  L-Tyrosine .... *100 mg*
  DL-Isoleucine .... *250 mg*
  DL-Valine .... *250 mg*
  DL-Leucine .... *250 mg*

Purines and pyrimidines:
  Adn. sulf. • H_2O .... *10 mg*
  Uracil .... *10 mg*

Guan. • $2H_2O$	*10 mg*
Xanth. • *HCl*	*10 mg*

Vitamins:

Thiamine • *HCl*	*1 mg*
Riboflavin	*5 mg*
Pyridoxine • *HCl*	*1 mg*
Nicotin. acid	*1 mg*
Pyridoxamine	*3 mg*
p-Aminobenz.	*1 mg*
Pyridoxal • *HCl*	*3 mg*
Biotin.	*1 mg*
Cal. pantothenate	*5 mg*
Folic acid	*1 mg*

Jesus Christ, he's way ahead of me! "Interesting."

"Oxygen is crucial to the organism's growth. How do you suggest I accomplish that?" The old man was testing him, Martinelli knew.

"Continuously aerate the synthetic medium with pure oxygen. What about phosphate contamination?" It was the colonel's turn to test him.

"I am considering adding insoluble carbonates to the medium to prevent excessive changes in hydrogen ion concentration. The timing of that introduction may prove critical. We will need to work out a schedule."

Martinelli just grunted, still staring at the screen. *Bastard isn't going to be tricked by me or anyone else.* "And temperature?"

"Incubation will be carried out at elevated temperatures for precise periods. The culture collection will be transferred at regular intervals to ten-liter tanks, where they will be frozen in a vacuum. I have written a program that will regulate the incubation temperatures. The tank transfer also will be automatic."

The more Wynett talked, the more horrified Martinelli became at his inability to sabotage the incubation process. *He doesn't need anybody's help, and he knows it.* He realized he was helpless to prevent Wynett from producing large, potent batches of Saint Vitus. His stomach heaved involuntarily. He would need to work out a new plan to thwart the incubation—but how? "Let me look this over and make some notes. Can we take this up in a couple of hours?"

Wynett looked suddenly exhausted. "Take the remainder of the morning and be accurate. Meanwhile I must lie down. After lunching we will begin."

Chapter Fifteen

Julie stepped to the hangar's glassless window. Outside, the others were sitting against the wall. She watched, amused, while Williams showed José the trapper how to hand-load ammunition, while the major cleaned his disassembled Franchi. She forced an expression that could pass for an amiable smile, but said nothing.

"So tell me why it's so important that she becomes your daughter-in-law?" Marshall asked the trapper.

The grizzled old man held out his hands palms-up. "She is *magnífico*."

Marshall laughed at him. "What if she disappoints you and your son, José? What if she doesn't satisfy?"

The old man shook his head fiercely. "She would not. She would give me many grandsons." The trapper's arms surrounded a large, imaginary family. "I can see that it is her nature to please a man."

Julie couldn't keep from grinning.

"Well, I wouldn't know anything about that," Marshall said solemnly.

Williams let out a belt of laughter. "Joe, you sound like a man who hasn't been laid in two months and knows he ain't gonna get any down here."

"This can't be happening!" Lieutenant Spangler shouted from inside the hangar. "This can't fucking be happening!"

Julie reeled away from the window with a start.

Marshall bolted inside the hangar. "What is it, Spangler? What's happening?"

The lieutenant handed him the unscrambled telex. "It's from General Medlock, a priority-one message."

083100Z ******** JHW047
TOPSECRET ****** PRI-1
FROM: MEDLOCK-ZJHM01—BAC
TO: ALPHA-ZJCM01

RE. OP CONTAINMENT
SHORTWAVE TRANSMISSIONS ORIGINATING IN YOUR AREA HAVE BEEN DECODED * SOURCE GORGON * REPEAT * SOURCE GORGON * PROCEED WITH EXTREME CAUTION.
A CODE RED HAS BEEN ORDERED * ALERT COLONEL MARTINELLI TO TERMINATE ORGANISM IMMEDIATELY * REPEAT * TERMINATE ORGANISM IMMEDIATELY* WYNETT AND GORGON SECOND PRIORITY

NEXT COMMUNIQUE: 1600

END MESSAGE
083214Z
BREAK

Julie noted uncharacteristic anxious creases on Marshall's forehead as he read the communiqué, which triggered waves of dread that went off like an alarm in the pit of her stomach. "What's wrong? What does it say?"

"Gorgon's come early for his merchandise," Marshall said,

passing the telex to his sergeant.

"Say what?" Williams said, scanning the message.

"Gorgon's here," Spangler said. "Medlock suspects he may move now."

"That's his style," Marshall said. "He'll never follow anyone else's schedule. Doesn't say how many men he has with him, though."

Youngblood, alerted by the shouting, emerged from his work area on the opposite side of the hangar. The old trapper came too, stroking his long, white mustache and listening, trying to understand the situation.

Julie appealed to Lieutenant Spangler. "Get word to my father right now."

"Do what the lady says, DOS," Marshall ordered.

"No can do, Major," the lieutenant said. "Wynett's jamming signal is ingeniously layered. Nothing has been getting in or out of that compound unless it's on his private satellite channel. I'm having a hell of a time trying to crack it."

"Then contact Stony's men in Sinope," Marshall said. "The next one in will brief the colonel."

Spangler's perspiring brow threatened to slide the wire-rimmed glasses off his nose. "Too late. The last one went in two hours ago. Wynett's hard up for men."

"Jesus," Marshall spat.

Julie grabbed Marshall's arm. "One of us must go inside and warn him."

Marshall riveted a hard gaze at Youngblood. "Can you drop me five miles from Wynett's compound without anyone knowing about it?"

The pilot shrugged. "Probably, but—"

"José," Marshall said to the trapper, "I'm enlisting you into the Special Forces of the United States Army. You're going to lead me through the jungle right up to Wynett's compound."

The old trapper drew himself up a full two inches taller than his normal five-foot frame, though still more than a foot shorter than Marshall. He stood at attention and shouldered his ancient shotgun. "I get you there."

"Lose that weapon first," Williams said to him. "I'll issue you an Uzi."

Lieutenant Spangler stood quickly. "Sir, the colonel's orders state that you're to guard this staging area. Hell, General Medlock's orders—"

"Screw Medlock's orders," Julie said. "There's not going to be an Alpha unit left if we don't warn my father."

"Use your goddamn heads, people," Youngblood said. "Barging in there now will blow their cover and get a lot of people killed. Stony's men can take care of themselves. Stay put, Major. This is an upscale party and you're not invited."

Marshall dismissed him. He couldn't stomach the thought of waiting until the fighting was over. "Get your chopper ready. Or do I have to fly it there myself?"

Stonecutters Garden
Sunday, 1840 hours

"We got problems," Stony said, falling into stride beside Colonel Martinelli. Stony had waited until after dark before risking contact with the colonel in an increasingly suspicious attitude among Wynett's men toward the newcomers.

"Guns?" Martinelli whispered.

"Yeah, guns."

"How many have you secured?"

Stony shifted the shovel to his left shoulder to conceal his face from every angle except straight ahead. "Only two of my men are part of Wynett's armed security force. The rest are picking goddamn sugarcane. Getting our hands on weapons isn't going to be easy. They're too heavily guarded."

"Do it," Martinelli snapped. "I don't care how, just do it. We're taking out Wynett tonight."

"What about Gorgon?"

"Fuck him. We're putting Wynett out of business now."

Stony scowled. "That's not good enough."

"It has to be good enough," Martinelli said, raising his voice.

Stony stopped midstride. "Sweet momma . . . it's the bug, isn't it?"

Martinelli nodded. "Wynett didn't take our bait. I couldn't convince him to change the culture medium. He's creating incredibly potent strains of the virus and securing them in tanks that are practically indestructible. And he's way ahead of schedule—only seven hours for each batch. The bug is amazingly prolific when it amplifies. He already has five tanks—he wants seven. Tomorrow I get paid and he ships me out."

"Jesus. You're scaring the shit out of me, Colonel. You've got to slow him down."

Martinelli shook his head. "Can't do it. He won't let me near the equipment, and he's got his best men defending the lab. Even if I could smuggle a charge down there, an explosion would rupture the incubators and release the organism. We're moving tonight."

"I'm looking for strong men with dry throats," said a husky female voice from the cobblestone path ahead.

Martinelli looked up suddenly at Wynett's housekeeper, Reneé, an attractive middle-aged black woman educated in the States. Reneé had done a splendid job turning Wynett's jungle retreat into a civilized country home. From their first meeting, the colonel had genuinely liked the good woman for her amiable but firm manner.

"Well, are you men thirsty or not?" she said, her generous smile broadening.

"You're a godsend, Reneé," Martinelli said, returning her cordial grin.

Reneé gave Stony a handsome smile that suggested more than a drink offer. If she thought it strange that these two were sharing company, however casual, she kept her suspicions to herself.

"Evening, ma'am." Stony rubbed his scaly, fly-bitten neck,

basking in a wave of self-consciousness at the smell of manure venting off his filthy overalls.

"The boss man's in a very good mood tonight," she said. "He put a keg of beer on the patio and everyone's welcome to share it. It's from Germany. And I'll be putting salmon on the grill directly."

"Delightful, Reneé," Martinelli said. "Tell the doctor I'll be there after I log the latest readings."

But Reneé was looking at Stony. "What about you, handsome?"

The special-op commander bowed politely. "Yes, ma'am."

Another handsome smile. "Good. That's very good. I'll see you both on the patio."

Reneé continued her rush toward the house, and both men resumed their leisurely stroll toward the barn, wary of other foot traffic on the cobblestone path ahead and behind them.

Martinelli's expression turned cold. "How do we protect them, Stony? I don't even know how many families are in this compound."

"Six—about twenty-three men, women and children who aren't part of this. I'll be damned if Wynett isn't trying to make a go of this farm. He's playing fucking Lawrence of Arabia way out here where he thinks no one can touch him. He's only succeeded in building a prison for himself and his people trapped inside."

"What about that fence?"

"Twenty-five hundred volts from an isolated generator behind the barn. Wynett's banking on it to keep out trouble. I don't like it. He's putting too many eggs in one basket. If that defense is breached, he's shit out of luck."

"What else?"

"Our radios are useless, thanks to Wynett's jamming station. It's one hell of a setup. He's a paranoid son of a bitch."

"So we're effectively out of touch with the others."

"Exactly."

"That's bloody wonderful. Get your men near some guns, and fast. I don't care how you arrange it."

"What about you?"

"I've got my Beretta and two magazines. I'll take down Wynett."

When they reached the barn, Martinelli realized he'd been talking much too loudly. Angry with himself, he abruptly broke from Stony and proceeded to the back of the barn, where he bid a good evening to Buckshot, still guarding the cellar steps, the Kalashnikov slung over his shoulder. Martinelli descended the wooden steps into the laboratory. Stony took a seat before a wiry old black man holding a hammer and a horse's leg between his knees, tapping on a new set of equine shoes.

"Join me for beer on the patio?" Stony asked.

The old man just grinned and shook his head.

Outside, Tucco emerged from the deep shadow of a spruce tree and stuck a fat cigar in his mouth. He lit it without a word, then drew in the heavy smoke, pondering the snippets of conversation he had just overheard. He exhaled the smoke slowly, trying to make sense of the odd acquaintance between a newly hired farmhand and Wynett's lab assistant.

La Strata Air Base
Peru
Sunday, 2000 hours

Air Force Captain Laszlo Valachi met the MiL-24A troop chopper as it touched down on the Peruvian air base's helipad. Three men in Russian Army uniforms, toting hefty gear bags, climbed from the chopper's troop compartment and marched straight toward him. After a curt salute, the lead soldier said to Valachi, "I am Colonel Golovko. You are aware of my orders?"

The Peruvian captain nodded. This morning's Defense Council communiqué instructed him to give full support to three *spetsnaz* special forces officers en route from Iraq—a high-priority mission involving terrorists. The soldiers had made good time; he hadn't expected them until morning.

141

Colonel Golovko presented the captain with a brown envelope. "This is your new directive. Your gunship and its pilot are now under my command."

Valachi frowned. "What is so important that I should give them to you?"

"I need to make a brief trip across the border. I intend to kill a terrorist who enjoys shooting down Russian jets with children aboard."

Chapter Sixteen

Stonecutters Garden
Sunday, 2118 hours

From the gloom of the jungle came a shadow. A shade blacker than the enveloping darkness, the figure moved with stealth and purpose among the tall stalks of sugarcane. The shadow stayed well away from the harvested field, where a great bonfire blazed. A half dozen farm workers had formed a semicircle around it, feeding the flames with armfuls of dried stalks.

Tarra didn't look at the fire, careful not to destroy her night vision, and moved quickly through the tall rows of unharvested cane. She stopped beneath Wynett's electric fence, where she could feel its powerful electromagnetic field ripple over her flesh. Crouching, she opened the rucksack and removed its contents, arranging the items on the ground with meticulous precision. She anchored a spool of uninsulated twelve-gauge Beldon wire to the ground and hooked its free end to a projectile seated in a large cocked crossbow that appeared too heavy for her slender frame. She raised the formidable weapon against her shoulder, angled it and pulled the trigger. There came a muffled snap as the steel projectile shot up into the night, boosted by gas from a CO_2 canister. There followed a stinging metallic hiss as the spool rapidly gave up countless meters of wire. One second . . . two . . . three . . . four . . . The arrow landed tip-first inside the compound, digging deep into the sod with a solid thump. Its long tail of wire dropped onto the electrified coils of barbed wire atop the fence.

Crack!

The compound's lights sputtered out, plunging Wynett's Amazon estate into a blanket of darkness.

The sudden loss of power to the barn prompted a startled outburst of protests from the roustabouts working inside. Most of the men were genuinely afraid of the sudden blackness and bolted outside. Buckshot, however, didn't move from his post by the cellar's entrance. Stony's right-hand man flung his Kalashnikov off his shoulder and pointed its muzzle at the barn's huge door, the only way in and out. The open cellar door at his feet provided modest illumination from the lab's emergency lights. No one would get near the fermentation tanks unless he allowed it.

Only one other worker remained inside the barn with Buckshot—the wiry old stable hand, his fists filled with horseshoes. Unfazed by the darkness, the old man set down his tools, lit a lantern and hung it high on a stall beam. Buckshot gave him a cautious nod of thanks.

The barn door creaked open. Buckshot fixed the barrel of his weapon on the roustabout leading a horse inside. With his attention focused on the barn door, Buckshot didn't see the old stable hand pick up a Browning automatic, a silencer fastened to its barrel. The old man pointed it with military accuracy and squeezed the trigger. A 9mm slug caught Buckshot hard in the chest just under his rib cage and slammed the special-op commando back against the barn wall.

Tucco was the first to arrive at the generators, two hefty diesel-powered machines enclosed in a huge steel cage. The air was heavy with the smell of burned wire but, luckily, there was no fire. The compound's only illumination came from Wynett's manor. Lit up in grand style, the house was immune to the electrical outage that had blackened the rest of the compound, thanks to the house's isolated generator.

A group of men, some carrying flashlights, others with guns, gathered around the generator cage. Even the armed men looked spooked. Tucco scoffed at their petty fears of the dark. He needed muscle and support, not a legion of infants.

"Darkness comes and everyone believes we have ghosts," Tucco spat, chomping down on his cigar. "I command a crew of idiots."

Tucco unlocked the generator cage and found his way to the breaker panel by the uneven beam of his flashlight. The generator hummed evenly. Tucco located the main breaker, grabbed the handle and pushed it back into place. There came another loud snap of protest, followed by a frightening flurry of sparks. A second try netted the same result; the circuit wouldn't close. He would need to find the source of the electrical short and correct it before he could restore power to the compound. The trouble most likely originated with the fence, he reasoned, the damned, power-hungry fence.

Tucco spat orders to his men, directing them to search for the source of the shorted circuit. Yelling and whooping, the workers charged off into the darkness.

Tucco moved to the entrance of the generator cage, cursing himself for hiring infants instead of men. Puffing his cigar, his eyes scanned the vague movements rushing through the bushes. He froze. At that moment even Tucco considered the possibility of ghosts.

A deep chill swept through his soul and he withdrew his huge revolver. Before he could cock it, something with the force of a sledgehammer struck him solidly in the center of his chest, slamming him back against the bank of circuit breakers. Tucco didn't feel the metal arrow that had transfixed his lungs and protruded from his back. The 2,500 volts surging from the opened circuits through his body masked all other sensations.

*   *   *

Stony's head jerked up, his eyes fixed on the darkened estate. The only lights came from Wynett's house, which looked like a bright castle against the black jungle. He glanced at the bonfire across the field and saw several workers lying around it, lifeless. Even the mule was lying on its side. His steel-set eyes scanned the fields, which were alive with moving shapes, animated shadows moving in and out of the rows of sugarcane. Who were they? In one wild instant, he realized his worst fears—*Gorgon's troops are here.*

He dropped to the ground and rolled next to a stack of cut sugarcane, trying to become one with it. He ripped off his white T-shirt and looked carefully around, his eyes constantly moving. He tried to make sense of the ghostlike figures stalking toward him, and cursed his blinded night vision. *Sweet Jesus, I love you dearly, but I'd sell my soul to the devil for a rifle.*

He glanced at the front gate. Closed. Without power he knew it couldn't be opened. He would have to cut his way into the compound. He thought of the families trapped inside and shook involuntarily. *Steady—think!* Rigid military training forced him to remain absolutely still. He knew that to reveal himself now would be tantamount to a death sentence.

Two black boys crouching over a jar of fireflies saw the figures racing across the lawn. To their little eyes, the shadow people were playing a game of hiding. The boys climbed onto the porch of Wynett's manor, sat down on the top step and talked about joining them.

''Mom,'' one of the boys called into the house in Americanized English. ''They're playing in our yard.''

Reneé, a towel in her hand, stepped onto the porch and followed the boys' gazes across the lawn. ''Who's playing, Myron?''

Her handsome smile vanished. In her two years as Wynett's housekeeper, she had never seen the grounds so dark. She had forgotten how black the jungle could be. What had happened?

As her eyes adjusted to the dimness she saw them, though not clearly—figures moving around the perimeter of the estate, taking up what could only be aggressive positions. Something was wrong, terribly wrong. Masters of stealth, these were not Wynett's people. Whoever they were, whatever their purpose, she knew they were responsible for the darkness that had overtaken the plantation. Dread ripped at Reneé's soul. *Dear God, don't let them hurt my boys!*

"Git home, both of you," she hissed, trying to mask her alarm. "It's past bedtime. Go on. Git home. *Git!*"

The boys' playful grins vanished; the tone of their mother's voice told them that all was not right with their little world.

"I said git home!" Reneé screamed.

Terrified, the boys charged off the porch, crying and scurrying into the darkness toward the little cottage they called their home.

"Do you intend to spend the rest of the evening deliberating your next move?" Wynett snapped, irritated.

Colonel Martinelli ignored the old man's prodding and remained seated statue-still before the chessboard, staring at the ornately carved chess pieces. Instead of thinking of chess moves, his mind was focused on taking down Wynett's men.

"Another marathon match," Wynett groaned, only half interested in the intellectual contest he knew he'd already won. Dr. da Silva had lied to him; Henry Armstrong was no player.

Wynett stood up from the table, stretched, and stepped to the window of his elegantly appointed second-story sitting room to watch the plantation workers secure the farm for the night. It was just an excuse to savor the moment, to enjoy the evening. He relished its welcome respite from the clammy South American heat. God, how he loved nights in the jungle.

He drew back the bedroom curtains and peered across the darkened compound.

Bloody hell—another problem with the generator. He waited for the backup generator to take over. When it didn't, he realized the problem was not with the generator, but with the system itself. He heard his men shouting at each other in the darkness, running to investigate. Something else he saw from his second-floor vantage point made him stiffen. There was other movement out there in the moonlight, intruders emerging from the jungle, breaching the fence, stalking toward his house from different directions in several slack skirmish lines.

Wynett stood rooted to the sill. His civil eyes grew cold and dark as he considered the ramifications. *The bastard intends to rob me.*

Wynett watched impotently as a roustabout led his magnificent quarterhorse across the barn's threshold, their silhouettes framed by a lantern-lit doorway. A shadow appeared from nowhere and brushed silently behind the worker. The horse bolted. The roustabout slumped to the ground without so much as a moan. Five more figures filed quickly inside the barn. The tanks. They had come to take Saint Vitus from him.

Below, his housekeeper stood on the veranda, looking suspiciously at the shadowy activity on the lawn. Wynett almost shouted down a warning to her, but thought better of it. Instead he withdrew from the lighted window and backed into the safety of the room's corner.

"Stony?" Reneé called from the porch.

There came no reply.

The figures broke into a run toward the house. *Jesus, save me!* Before she could move, a Teflon-tipped arrow pierced her larynx, smashing her through the screened door, ripping it from its hinges. She fell heavily onto the floor of the foyer, groping at the frightful flow of blood pumping from her throat. Her vocal cords were shattered, her jugular vein severed.

Choking, her back arched in agony, Reneé stared helplessly at a man in black fatigues standing in the doorway.

Stony sprinted across the lawn, keeping well within the shadows. The night's heat extracted rivers of sweat from his pores that washed over his skin in tiny streams. Wynett's manor loomed twenty yards away. He crept through a tight grove of birch trees, choosing each movement with care, knowing that his life depended on his ability to remain unseen. One thought consumed him: *Warn Colonel Martinelli and the others.*

Do it now or die.

With daring boldness Stony sprinted toward the house, expecting a bullet in his back. None came. He flattened against the side of the manor, his eyes searching for the intruders. No one was coming. Bathed by the house's queer half-light, he crabbed along the wall and looked into Wynett's first-floor study. The room stood dark and empty.

With deft agility, Stony hauled his solid frame up through the open window and set down without a sound inside the study. He moved nimbly to Wynett's desk and took a seat in front of the shortwave transceiver. He ignored the sweat pouring down his face as he powered up the set and put on the headphones. He heard it immediately, the high-pitched squeal of the jamming signal. He slid the frequency dial first right then left. The squeal continued unchanged, evidence that its power for the signal came from the same isolated generator that supplied the house. He flung off the headset. *Damn Wynett and his paranoia!*

Two strides took him to Wynett's gun rack, a splendid oak cabinet that housed a classic collection of hunting rifles. He deliberately willed himself to slow down, fighting the urge to take in great lungfuls of air. He pulled on the cabinet door and found the case locked. *Damn!* The beveled glass was reinforced with steel rods.

Stony swept around, his eyes scanning the room for a weapon. A table lamp . . . a bronze paperweight . . . a half-filled bottle of Scotch . . . a mantel clock . . . Then he saw it. Wynett's big-game Browning rifle hanging trophylike over the mantel. He was there in an instant, lifting the intimidating weapon from its mount. Cartridges? He returned to Wynett's utility cabinet and opened the bottom drawer with a creak that to him sounded like a scream. He paused, listening. Nothing.

He rummaged through several boxes of shells until he found what he needed and scooped up a handful of thirty-caliber cartridges.

The study's door squeaked open. Stony's head jerked up. The intruder acted with practiced restraint, as if listening for the intensity and duration of activity in the study. Stony slid a single cartridge into the gun's chamber and pulled back the hammer with an audible click. He lifted the huge weapon.

The door moved again, this time with bold force behind it. Stony had only the barest glimpse of a large figure dressed in black fatigues and carrying a weapon before he jerked the trigger. The blast transformed the door into a blizzard of splinters. A blood-spattered wall to the left of the doorway bore the only evidence that a man had been standing there.

The gunshot startled Martinelli from his chair, the Beretta appearing automatically in his hand.

"I'm afraid that weapon will be useless," Wynett said from his secure spot in the corner. "Sit down and move your queen out of danger."

Martinelli flattened against the wall next to the window, his Beretta pointed down in a two-handed grip. He could see nothing outside. What had happened to the lights? Who had fired a rifle inside the house?

"Dr. Armstrong, you are about to meet a client of mine," Wynett said, his voice civilly calm. "I advise you to move away from the window and do not resist. I am telling you this so that you may live."

Martinelli swore bitterly. "What weapons do you have up here?"

"Sit down," Wynett ordered, his voice curt. "Or they will cut you down like a holiday pig."

Stony stared down at Reneé's corpse, her wide, glassy eyes gazing helplessly up at him, warning him. Years of training, the resources of an elite army—all of it had failed to protect her. He turned away from her, feeling suddenly cold despite

150

the heat, dull and empty in his head, tired, old, too old. He bounded up the steps two at a time to the house's second level.

Martinelli thrust his Beretta at Wynett. "Don't you fucking move."

"Intruders are in my laboratory," Wynett said. "They are taking what we have worked so hard to produce these last few days. And neither you nor I can stop them."

"Gorgon," Martinelli spat.

Wynett's expression darkened. "How do you know that name—"

The bedroom door opened with a crash. Martinelli whipped around, his Beretta pointed. Stony stood on the threshold, his muscles glistening like oiled ebony, his eyes ferreting the interior of the bedroom. He pointed the Browning at Wynett.

The colonel lowered his handgun. "Stony, what's happening? Where are the others?"

Stony stepped into the room, keeping the huge gun pointed at Wynett. "Dead. Ambushed."

The colonel sighed in defeat. "Jesus Christ, he can't get the organism. I won't let it happen. We have to do something. We have to do something!"

"We can't get word out," Stony spat. "This fuck's got every channel jammed."

Wynett looked accusingly at Martinelli. "Who are you gentlemen?—CIA?"

They all heard it, a creak of the hallway floorboards. Martinelli signaled Stony with a curt nod. The commando captain needed no orders. Stony roared into the hallway, the gun braced on his hip. There were two of them dressed in black fatigues, messengers of death creeping down the corridor. Stony didn't know if they were black men or had merely painted their faces to become one with the night. It didn't matter.

"It's suppertime," he hummed.

The first raider jerked his weapon. Stony squeezed the trigger and let the Browning explode. The blast from the huge gun at close quarters tore the first intruder in two. His upper torso disintegrated in a brisk shower of bone and red pulp, while his disembodied legs kicked about the hallway.

A shot from the colonel's Beretta over Stony's shoulder put a slug in the center of the second intruder's forehead. The raider jerked backward and actually thought he could retreat with his wound before spilling headlong down the hallway. Martinelli whipped around and pointed his Beretta at the opposite end of the hallway. It was clear.

Stony raced down the corridor to the top of the staircase, discharging the spent cartridge as he ran and inserting another. There were two more on the steps. His Browning took the first intruder directly in the chest, hurling him into his comrade with the force of a freight train. Stony reloaded. Before the second man could rise, another blast from Stony's gun tore his head clear off.

Wynett slammed the door of the sitting room, barricading himself inside. Martinelli whirled and pumped four rounds into the door. "You son of a bitch."

The colonel saw movement from the opposite end of the hallway an instant before a metal arrow came hurtling toward his head. He sprang backward. The projectile whisked by his face and plunged into the bedroom's oak door with a solid thud. The colonel dropped and rolled into a darkened bedroom across from Wynett's, discharging two quick rounds down the hallway as he moved.

Stony could hear other men below entering the living room. Reloading, he saw the shadow of another intruder approaching the bottom of the staircase. Stony raised his rifle.

He never fired. A glint of metal appeared from the darkened bedroom behind him. With startling swiftness, a machete thrashed out and nearly sliced through his right arm above the elbow.

Stony spilled forward with a bloodcurdling howl, more from surprise than pain. The Browning clattered loudly down the steps. The shock of spontaneous amputation came an instant later.

Code: Alpha

Colonel Martinelli flattened against the bedroom wall and moved toward the door, snapping his second magazine into the handle of his Beretta. Something cold and sharp pricked the back of his neck. He froze and screwed his eyes around. A frightful woman dressed in black held a sighted crossbow cocked and ready to put an arrow through his throat. The crossbow was merely for stealth. For serious firepower, Tarra would revert to a Russian-made AK-47 automatic assault rifle hanging on her shoulder.

"He will not let me kill you yet," Tarra said. "He wants to interrogate the military commander who set this trap for him."

Down the hallway, Stony glared up at the giant looming above him. What he saw made him forget his arm wound that was rapidly draining away his life with each heartbeat. Gorgon stared down at him with cold, dead eyes. The killer carried a machete in his right hand and in his left a crossbow made of steel.

Stony tried to lift his head but found it unbearably weighty. "Just like chickenshit to hit a man from behind."

Gorgon's features did not betray the slightest emotion. He lowered his crossbow until the Teflon-tipped arrowhead was a breath above Stony's left eye.

Stony swallowed hard. "Like I said . . . chickenshit . . ."

There came a loud snap as the arrow pinned Stony's head to the hallway floorboards.

Chapter Seventeen

José the trapper rubbed the stubby barrel of his new Israeli Uzi and gave Williams a cheery wink of gratitude. Youngblood increased the throttle of the chopper, while his passengers braced themselves for liftoff. The aircraft didn't move. Youngblood sat rigid, listening to his headset, then cut the engines to idle.

"Get this thing in the air," Marshall shouted over the engine's roar.

Youngblood screwed his head around and yelled something about taking aboard another passenger. Marshall craned his neck around and glimpsed a fleeting figure dressed in camouflage fatigues carrying a gear bag around the opposite side of the aircraft. There came two thuds on the compartment door. Williams slid it open and Julie tossed her gear bag up to him.

"Out of the question," Marshall hollered.

She climbed aboard with the sergeant's help. Julie wasn't in the mood to argue about this with anyone, least of all with the major. The notion of traveling with these men through a

154

Code: Alpha

Brazilian jungle at night wasn't her idea of a fun-filled evening in the tropics. She took the seat across from Marshall and strapped herself in. "I go where the virus goes."

The whine of the Comanche's jet engines drowned out Marshall's curses of protest. The helicopter lifted into the night sky, leaned windward and proceeded due west at treetop level.

Stonecutters Garden

Colonel Martinelli looked into Tarra's green eyes, trying to read his foe, trying to understand this strange woman who was a finger-jerk away from putting an arrow through his throat. He could see nothing in her eyes, not the smallest hint of emotion behind her steely features. Any resistance, he realized, would be suicidal. He let the Beretta slip from his hands. "Can I at least know your name?"

"I will ask the questions," said a huge man in the doorway.

Tarra's features softened—became almost attractive—in the presence of an intimidating man dressed in black fatigues and armor padding. Martinelli's heart pounded savagely. Gorgon, carrying a crossbow at his side, scrutinized the colonel with eyes that were like two dark holes, absorbing every detail, every conceivable threat, all in the instant it took Martinelli to expel a breath of resignation.

Gorgon said, "I am the man you so desperately wanted to meet, Captain—or is it Colonel?"

Wynett knew exactly what he had to do and the limited time in which he had to do it. He removed a bulky pack from the closet's top shelf, opened it and unfolded a full-body environment suit, complete with air tanks and hood. On the room's mahogany table sat an innocuous-looking thermal container. With his eyes fixed on the container, he began dressing.

Colonel Martinelli's furtive eyes stole around the bedroom, rejecting one option after another. In one shattering instant he conceded the inevitable—*I am a dead man.* He had often imagined dying in battle a brave, willful soldier. He didn't feel courageous right now. He was scared shitless and needed to relieve himself.

Gorgon signaled Tarra with a jerk of his head. She grabbed the colonel's arm and dragged him cruelly back against the wall. He resisted, and she clubbed him on the side of his head with a heavy chain and cuffs, a vicious blow that left him senseless. She had little difficulty shackling him to the room's water pipe.

Gorgon picked up Martinelli's Beretta and admired the weapon. Leering down at his prisoner, he said, "You are a fool to plot an ambush for me."

The colonel strained impotently against the chain. "Go to hell."

Gorgon pointed the Beretta at Martinelli. The colonel screwed his eyes shut, anticipating the terrible blast that would end his life. There came a sharp crack, followed by Martinelli's shriek of anguish. The slug had shattered his right kneecap, almost amputating the leg at the knee.

Tarra grabbed Martinelli by the shirt and pulled him roughly upright. "We know about your base on that miserable airstrip in Sinope. We have watched you and your men infiltrate this encampment. And now we have taken the tanks with your creation while you die in this rotting jungle."

Martinelli wasn't looking at her; his unconcealed gaze of hatred was riveted on Gorgon. His mind reeled with thoughts of Julie. All he could think about was his daughter trapped in the hangar, a sitting duck for this bastard.

"I wish to know everything about your paramilitary group and how you came to know my business," Gorgon said.

Martinelli said nothing. Gorgon discharged a second round into the colonel's left knee, prompting another shriek from his prey. The giant laughed, a menacing rumble from deep within his chest. "I will put the next bullet in your groin."

Gasping, fighting the onset of shock, Martinelli pulled futilely on his wrist shackles and forced his mind to focus on Julie. *Don't black out now . . . not now. . . .*

Gorgon said to Tarra, "Bring Wynett in here. We have business to finish."

She swung the Kalashnikov off her shoulder, charged into the hallway and crouched in a firing position in front of Wynett's door. Two short blasts from her assault rifle tore the oak planks from their hinges. She caught only a fleeting glimpse of Wynett, clad in a full-body environment suit, disappearing behind the door to the bathroom. Tarra assailed the opposite wall with a second, longer, burst.

"He is wearing an environment suit," she shouted over her shoulder.

Gorgon knew immediately what Wynett planned to do. He threw the Beretta against the wall with enough force to shatter plaster. "He intends to kill us with his creation!"

Tarra emptied the Kalashnikov's thirty-round clip into the bedroom wall, producing a blizzard of plaster, wood splinters and shards of aluminum ductwork. Wynett huddled inside the porcelain bathtub as the rounds tore apart the room around him. He fastened his environmental hood securely in place and inflated the suit, making himself impervious to the outside atmosphere. He cradled the thermoslike canister in his arms.

"Gorgon," Wynett shouted, "I very much want you to meet a friend of mine."

Tarra replaced the clip of her assault rifle. "I will need a grenade."

"No! You will release the agent! We must leave here at once!" Gorgon swung his crossbow around and discharged a steel arrow into Martinelli's chest. The colonel grimaced in agony. The arrow pierced his right lung, missing his heart by two inches. Gorgon fled the room and hastened down the hallway with Tarra at his heels, his spiked boots echoing back on the hardwood floorboards.

They charged out onto the veranda, where the two soldiers stationed there snapped sharply to attention. "Burn this house and everyone in it," Gorgon ordered, before storming off the porch toward the jungle.

Upstairs Wynett waited a prudent thirty seconds after hearing Gorgon's retreat before crawling from his bathroom sanctuary and walking stiffly into the spare bedroom in which Martinelli lay dying. The Businessman ignored the colonel and watched through the window as Gorgon's soldiers fled through his fields of sugarcane, vanishing into the jungle. He opened his revered canister and carefully withdrew a glass vial.

Fighting off the anesthesia of unconsciousness, Martinelli raised his swooning head and saw Wynett's vial. "Don't do it," he said, his voice strained, his breath short. "Christ, you don't know what you stole...."

Wynett disregarded him. He shook the bottle furiously, breaking up the frozen ball inside, before opening it. Martinelli let out a sigh of despair and sank back into a pool of his blood. "It's too late ... you bloody fool, it's too late...."

Wynett hurled the bottle through the open second-story window and watched it shatter onto the veranda below at the feet of the two mercenaries. He giggled with childlike glee as one of the soldiers crushed the innocuous-looking shards of glass with his boot. The hot, humid ambient night air immediately began melting the ice crystals. Neither soldier at first felt anything unusual, despite having ingested the most powerful neurotoxin in existence.

Colonel Martinelli felt a short-lived euphoria that rapidly mounted to a feeling of dread. His mind grew numb; his senses dulled. A cacophony of strange noises filled his head, while still stranger phantasms obscured his vision. His brain screamed; his mind, full of human paradox, betrayed him. He knew the sensations had nothing to do with his wounds. This was different. He felt as though an army of ants was swarming through tunnels burrowed beneath his flesh. He drew in a deep breath and expelled a cry from the worst chest pain he had ever experienced. He tried to speak, but instead of words he expelled flecks of blood and lung tissue. His limbs began undulating, dancelike.

Wynett, rooted to the window, watched Gorgon's mercenaries below struggling on their knees in deep agony. The Businessman found the sight thoroughly amusing, his throaty laughter fogging his face shield. "You will not cheat me, Mr. Gorgon. You cannot see my army, but they will find you. Wherever you hide in this jungle, my army will find you and kill you."

A shriek, long and terrifying, drowned out Wynett's glee. The Businessman drew back from the window and stared in mute surprise at Martinelli, his throat swelled to six times its normal size.

Gorgon and Tarra whirled at the terrible shrieks of agony coming from Wynett's manor, inhuman sounds that sent shudders through all who heard them. He could see no sign of the flames that by now should have consumed the house.

Tarra slid the Kalashnikov off her shoulder. "I will finish him."

Gorgon grabbed her roughly by the arm. "No! It would mean death to go back. I have what I came for. Let us leave here and unharness the beast."

Wynett watched with detached curiosity as his lab assistant became an abomination of humanity. As the virus devoured its victim's nervous system, rapidly reproducing itself, Col. Anthony Martinelli became a beast. The thing lashed out at Wynett with a roar, trying to rip its arms from their sockets in a mad effort to tear the shackles and pipes from the wall. Wynett recoiled, awed by what he saw. He hadn't considered this, hadn't considered this at all. The colonel's bucking became so severe that Wynett feared he would break the shackles and come tearing after him in a foaming rage. Homicidal aggression as a result of brain-cell destruction, he reasoned. He had no way of knowing how wrong he was.

Wynett was so taken by the macabre sight that he failed to notice the stuffy air inside his suit. At first he attributed it to his exhilaration. When the air grew increasingly foul, he rechecked his tanks, designed to deliver two hours of air with normal exertion. The gauge read slightly less than full, yet he could barely breathe.

He fumbled with the valve, felt something odd and strained around to look at it. One of Tarra's bullets had taken a hefty bite out of the valve, rendering it inoperable. In a rush of panic, he realized he was suffocating inside a polyethylene coffin.

I must leave here!

Wynett bolted from the bedroom, consumed with the singular thought of escaping the farm before exhausting the precious pocket of air inside his suit. He knew the virus had a short life span, a matter of minutes, after which succeeding generations mutated into increasingly less volatile strains. Could the air outside his suit already be safe? He was loath to find out.

Without warning, his legs swept from under him, spilling him headlong down the second-floor hallway. He twisted around to see what had tripped him and cried out in revulsion. It was Stony, his good arm flailing in a spastic arc. The man was quite dead, the arrow through his head had seen to that, yet his corpse was moving as though eager to avenge its owner's death. Wynett didn't doubt that the thing would have pounced on him if Gorgon's arrow had not effectively pinned its head to the floorboards.

Wynett clawed on hands and knees down the staircase to the living room and beheld another nightmare. In the center of the room, struggling to rise, lay his housekeeper, Reneé, an arrow splitting her throat. She offered him a grin that was the hideous rictus of death. Her lips seemed to be struggling to form words. If the good woman could speak, Wynett believed her corpse would have acknowledged him with a caricature of her former cordiality and scolded him for this mess.

He looked away, revolted.

Wynett stumbled blindly out of the house, fleeing this nightmare. Gone were Gorgon's stricken soldiers who only moments ago had collapsed on the veranda. He looked warily around for them, fearful they would come charging out of the night and drag him to hell with them. His vision blurred, his oxygen-starved mind evaporating.

And then he saw it. A light. The lantern-lit barn. That was his destination, his salvation. He staggered toward it, arms outstretched, groping for the door that to his eyes looked both within his reach and miles away. Although the wind was quiet, the sculpted shrubbery swayed as though alive, inexplicably reaching for him. Wynett shrank past them, horrified.

He stumbled through the barn's doorway and fell heavily onto the straw-covered floor. He lifted his head. The view of the barn's floor was more shockingly gruesome than he could have imagined. Gorgon's soldiers had used the barn as a morgue for the slain farmhands. The carcasses refused to lie still. The victims of the massacre lay twisting and arching, as though straining to rise and launch a collective effort to retaliate against the forces that had murdered them.

Wynett pulled himself into a sitting position with his back against the stone wall. He could go no farther. His hollow eyes stared vacantly at the corpses, watching their grotesque movements, trying to see through this trick of his oxygen-starved mind. Why wouldn't they lie still?

The corpse of a young black man at his feet turned its barely attached head to look at him. Instead of the glassy stare of a dead man, he thought he saw real anger in those sallow eyes. The corpse's mouth split into an appalling sneer, revealing teeth that gnashed and snapped at him. Wynett screwed his eyes shut, blocking the terrible image from his mind.

Lie still!

The air inside his suit was exhausted. Blackness descended. Either he would take his chances with the virus-contaminated air or he would suffocate. He contemplated doing nothing, thus putting a definitive end to his horror; however, his survival instinct would not allow him to remain passive. His gloved hands released the seal with a hiss and swung the hood off his head. Sweet air refreshed his lungs, lifting the mist from his oxygen-starved mind.

The illness came quickly. It started as a bitter taste in his mouth; then his head began to ache, as though a dull metal drill were boring into his brain. Strange phantasms paraded before him. He could feel the organism at work within his brain, devouring his mind, hollowing out his skull.

But he did not die.

The virus indeed had mutated. Instead of death, it carried the seeds of insanity. He was helpless to prevent the corruption of the very fabric of who he was.

Wynett's eyes, sunken and hollow, darted from one corpse to the next. He didn't believe in the soul, yet as he watched the unnatural movements of the bodies, he knew they were mere shells, flowing with a powerful new life force. Saint Vitus. The organism could move what death had stilled. A grin formed on his lips when he considered how much the organism would be worth. Far more than he dared dream. A hiss erupted from his throat and rose in pitch before turning to laughter—a laughter born of madness.

Oh yes, Mr. Gorgon, you will pay!

Chapter Eighteen

Stonecutters Garden
Tuesday, January 19
0520 hours

The Russian-made MiL-24 Hind-E assault gunship descended from a purple-rimmed sky, its belly-mounted spotlight probing the strange fog below. The Peruvian pilot, a seasoned captain named Juan Batlivala, saw no activity on the barren plantation. What the hell had happened down there? It would be daylight in ten minutes, and before that happened his orders were to have the aircraft down and the troops dispersed.

He didn't like this mission, didn't like the way it had been hastily organized and executed. He hadn't been properly briefed, nor given an explanation for the order to fly without a forward weapons officer. He had no authority to enter Brazilian airspace. He knew little about the three *spetsnaz* soldiers in the gunship's troop compartment or what they hoped to find on this bizarre estate in the middle of the Brazilian jungle. Colonel Golovko had given him only an altitude and a compass bearing. Nothing else. Captain Batlivala wanted to finish this mission, fast.

He set down the gunship between the house and the barn,

creating a whirlpool of white dust that enveloped the aircraft long after he cut back the jet engines to ground-idle and disengaged the rotor. Visibility was zero. What was this strange dust?

He powered off the troop compartment's red lights, an aid to night vision once the troops were outside, and turned on the exterior spots. The main cabin door slid open and out jumped the three special forces soldiers, with AK-47 automatic assault rifles. The powerful halogen lamps turned the fog into a golden nether world, where men became wispy apparitions. The pilot watched them vanish into the strange mist. "Sweet Mary, mother of God, stay with me," he muttered.

The pilot opened the scrambled TAC channel to his Peruvian air base four hundred miles northwest of the plantation. He spoke in Spanish into his helmet's mouthpiece: "Specter One to Father. We are down."

The sharp *whip-whip-whip* of a descending military helicopter roused Wynett from a sound slumber. He sat up slowly, unsure of his surroundings and with no memory of how he got here. His head felt like mud and his ears buzzed. He wasn't even sure who he was, nor did he especially care. His dark, scarlet eyes scanned the barn's body-strewn floor, his mind yielding only the tiniest bits of the previous evening. He thought he recognized most of the corpses' bloated and twisted faces, visages seemingly carved from wood. Were they friends of his? If so, the camaraderie must have been part of another lifetime an eon ago. Perhaps someone else's life.

Then he remembered a Henry Armstrong—no, he had another name, didn't he? A general or some other military title? It didn't matter. The image of his helpless lab assistant chained to a bedroom wall struck him as terribly amusing. The phrase *You don't know what you stole* percolated up from the depths of his memory, though he couldn't recall the context in which he had heard it.

In a loud voice full of spirit, he began singing in German,

"Somebody calls you, you answer quite slowly, the girl with kaleidoscope eyes. . . ."

The three Russian soldiers approached the barn, vigilant for any signs of life. They weren't interested in the house. A thermal scan of the plantation from a reconnaissance satellite detected a single entity inside the barn that still gave off enough body heat to be classified as a living human being. There were no such heat signatures inside the house.

Special Forces Colonel Golovko stooped beside a man-shaped carcass lying before the barn door. He had almost missed the corpse, mistaking it at first for a thick, twisted tree trunk. The remains—shriveled, leathery, unrecognizable—sent a rush of nausea through him. He had seen corpses before, many in deplorable condition, but he had never seen one as unsettling as this. *What happened here?* The *spetsnaz* commander decided to forgo a probe for the cause of death, which he knew would have been futile. Then he heard singing, a deep baritone voice, coming from inside the barn.

"The barn door is bolted from the inside," his first lieutenant reported.

The colonel spotted an open window along the side of the barn. His rifle held ready, he led the others to it in silence. The singing stopped.

The barn's interior was dark, too dark to make out specifics. Colonel Golovko could see vague shapes spread over the floor, possibly men, but he couldn't be sure without a closer inspection. Holding his rifle loosely at his side, he grabbed the window frame with his free hand and lifted a leg inside. The barn reeked of death. The smell of manure laced with decay caused his stomach to heave involuntarily. He paused, straddling the windowsill, listening, straining to make sense of this gruesome warehouse of shapes and shadows.

Golovko heard movement, a shuffling among the straw. *Rats?* With stunning swiftness, a man dressed in a strange white suit sprang up before him, pointing something at him. The light was practically nil, and several moments of stunned silence passed before the Russian officer identified that "something" as an American-made automatic assault rifle.

There came a sharp report that resounded off the barn's high-beamed ceiling. The point-blank burst into Golovko's chest hurled him backward out the window, giving Wynett a clear shot at his two comrades squatting behind in the fog. The next two bursts from Wynett's weapon produced a line of plum-shaped holes across each soldier's chest. They spilled backward, their rifles spraying indiscriminate rounds into the side of the barn.

Wynett discarded his empty rifle and retrieved Golovko's AK-47. He checked the clip, pulled back the bolt with a precision click and braced the stock solidly against his shoulder. He loved the feel of a Kalashnikov.

The Hind pilot heard muffled shots above his idling engines. He strained to see what had become of the Russian colonel and his *spetsnaz* soldiers, but he could see nothing beyond the swirling dust cloud created by the rotor's downdraft. A shadow of a man appeared through the lamplit fog just beyond the cockpit door. *Thank God they're finished—*

But it wasn't Colonel Golovko. Nor was it one of his men. A white-bearded man wearing the remains of a peculiar oversuit walked up to the gunship's cockpit door. The pilot felt an odd rush of emotions as he stared into the business end of a Kalashnikov.

The bearded man sang to him, "The girl with kaleidoscope eyes."

Captain Batlivala reached for the TAC controls. Wynett squeezed the trigger. A burst from the assault rifle shattered the Plexiglas door and raked across the cockpit, tearing the pilot through his shoulder harness.

Chapter Nineteen

The jungle
Tuesday, 0515 hours

Gloom.

An endless forest of dense, dark foliage grabbed and scratched at Marshall's group, holding them willfully at bay. Youngblood had inserted them into the jungle seven hours ago, and since that time the group had hiked five miles through the jungle, excellent time, considering the thick terrain. The air was damp and rotten, the heat steamy even before sunup, the ground an unbroken carpet of dense, clinging, wicked-smelling humus. Marshall acknowledged an overpowering claustrophobia as they hacked their way beneath the dark, cathedrallike canopy of branches that blocked out every trace of moonlight. The sun would rise in another fifteen minutes, but it would take hours before they noticed its light. Even at noon, only a dim half-light ever touched the jungle floor.

José ceased chopping the undergrowth with his machete and called back to Marshall, "Animals and birds are gone. Insects too. We are alone. Very strange."

Marshall, suddenly aware of the jungle's unnatural stillness, brought the others to a halt with a raised hand. "This is far enough."

Williams swung the Galil rifle off his shoulder and unfolded its metal stock. "Something here ain't right, Joe."

"I can feel it too." Marshall marched past José and directed his high-powered lamp toward the overgrown wall of vegetation ahead. What he saw unsettled him. Instead of pervasive green, a vulgar tropical blight had destroyed the foliage, leaving in its wake withered and white husks. *Jesus wept!* He didn't need a botanist's degree to know that this flora damage was no natural infestation. The devastation reminded him of a swath of jungle scorched by Agent Orange or a similar defoliant, only this was notably different and far more potent.

Marshall waved the sergeant forward and swept his light along the ruined foliage. "Ever see anything like this? Christ, all that's left is the shell of the plant with its heart burned out." He directed the light at his map. "We're less than an eighth of a mile from Wynett's plantation. What's the connection?"

Williams let out his breath in one long, low sigh. "I think we just found our goddamned bug."

"Martinelli," Marshall called back to Julie. "I need you up here."

Julie stumbled to catch up with the others and dropped a briefcase-size package at her feet with a groan, relieving herself of the eighteen-pound box that none of the men had offered to carry. Her legs had the consistency of rubber and her sweat-soaked clothes made her feel as though she had just been dragged from the river.

Marshall directed his lamp at the foliage. "What do you make of this?"

"What the—" Julie approached what had once been a low-growing plant. Crouching, she touched the damaged flora and rubbed it into a fine white ash in her hand. "Holy Mother Teresa." She opened her instrument package and quickly brought the unit to life. The gridded amber screen displayed a waveform pattern spiked with jagged peaks, identifying the presence of airborne organisms. A sample of air, automatically fed into the unit's processor, classified each organism, its strength and the approximate area contaminated.

"A class T_4 pathogen—artificially engineered," she said, her drawn face bathed with the display's queer amber light. "One part per one hundred thousand cubic meters of air."

Marshall watched her, a finger on his lips. "Is it yours?"

"Yes."

"We have to be certain."

Julie shot him a superior glance. "This system gathers metabolic fingerprints with a microplate of ninety-six miniature wells, each filled with dye, nutrients and a different chemical. When exposed to a microbe, the wells turn various shades of violet. The computer identifies the microbe based on the color pattern."

"In English, please."

"This system is very accurate," she said. "I designed it to look for Saint Vitus. And we just found it. The virus is alive and well and living in this South American rain forest."

"Son of a bitch!" Williams spat. "And we stepped right fucking into it."

"We're on the fringe of the infestation," Julie said, reading new information from the screen. "The organism's genetic fingerprint has changed. Saint Vitus has mutated."

"Mutated into what?" Marshall asked.

"Into something harmless, or at least let's pray that it has. The organism is genetically programmed to lose its toxicity after several generations of mutation. Otherwise we would have been dead about a hundred yards back."

The *whip-whip-whip* of an approaching helicopter disturbed the jungle's unnatural quiet. A slight breeze stirred the ash into a fog. Marshall glanced at the azure predawn sky through the cracks of leafless branches. "I'll be damned . . . it's a gunship." He shot a look at Williams. "Gorgon?"

"Whoever it is, they're in for one hell of a surprise if the area is still hot."

Marshall knelt down beside Julie. "I need to know if we

have a lethal environment here or not.''

Julie, her shirt clinging to her back like a filthy wet dishrag, felt the pressure to produce an interpretation of the data beyond her—or anybody else's—abilities. ''Statistically, there's a high probability we're safe. I just don't know enough about the organism. Major, I'll need a radio linkup with Detrick to interpret this data.''

''Relay everything you get to Lieutenant Spangler as a Code Red.'' He said to Williams, ''Have you raised the hangar yet?''

The sergeant shook his head. ''I can open a channel, but Spangler still won't answer. Youngblood should be there shortly.''

Marshall swore loudly.

Julie opened her backpack and unfolded a bright orange nonporous suit with a battery-powered air supply.

''What do you think you're doing?'' Marshall asked her.

''If you men will excuse me, I'm going to find my father.''

Peruvian Air Force Capt. Laszlo Valachi bit down savagely on his Cuban cigar. Something had gone wrong. The Hind pilot had missed two radio check-ins. Eighteen years of active duty on this base told him that the Russian colonel had botched the mission and lost his gunship. *What terrorist is so damned important that Golovko would take such a risk?*

Valachi lifted the telephone receiver and secured an instant connection with his airfield's hangar. ''Full alert,'' he shouted at the officer on the other end.

Three minutes later, two Russian-made MIG-23s under his command were rolling onto the runway.

Julie's heart skipped a beat as she emerged from the jungle into an incredible white world. The estate was an abomination of decay. She sucked in her breath sharply as she scanned Wynett's estate through her suit's face shield. The effects of the organism were far more devastating than she had dared imagine. Despite the clammy South American heat, the farm

170

stood cold and dead beneath a layer of white ash that had turned the regal grounds into a shimmering snowfield. Wynett's huge stone manor rose from the decay like something out of a perverted Lewis Carroll story.

"A horse appeared," she whispered, "deathly pale, and its rider was called Plague, and Hades followed at his heels."

Julie's thoughts turned to her father. *What have I done, Dad?* Determined to find out, she crawled through a hole deliberately cut in the chain-link fence, careful not to rip her suit on the naillike ends. She proceeded toward the house, her eyes scanning every direction. The morning sun had broken through the treetops, giving an eerie warmth to the devastated grounds. She saw no one. The white, crisp grass turned to a fine powder under her boots, and she was hot, almost to the point of swooning. Julie hated her army-issued Racal full-body environment suit for not allowing the evaporation of perspiration. Its manufacturer assured comfort for prolonged wearing, unless temperatures rose above seventy-five degrees. The morning jungle already exceeded that by ten degrees, turning the inside of the positive-pressure suit into a sauna.

"Marshall," she said into the hands-free mike threaded inside her suit's hood. "The vegetation on the northern end of the plantation is devoid of pigment. I suspect that as the organism mutates, its nutritional requirements change. Maybe at one stage it feeds on chlorophyll. A breeze apparently carried the organism to the north. The epicenter of the dead zone appears to be the house."

Marshall, huddling with the others in a healthy part of the jungle well behind the estate, touched the SEND button on his belt-mounted transceiver and said into the minimike clipped to his collar, "What about the chopper? Do you see troop activity?"

"No. I'm going to investigate."

"Negative. I want you to stay put."

"Sorry, Major. I'm quite capable of taking care of myself."

Marshall turned off the mike and said to his gunnery sergeant, "I don't want her in there alone."

Williams released the safety of his Galil. "It's your call."
Marshall said to the old trapper, "You don't have to go."
José nodded firmly and pulled back the bolt on his Uzi.

"Welcome to your first biological battlefield." The major swept around and bolted through the jungle toward Wynett's estate.

Julie rechecked her bio unit. The air samples registered in the normal range, yet the display indicated trace genetic patterns she couldn't identify. She longed for her workstation at Fort Detrick and an afternoon brainstorming session with her adviser, Dr. Nancy Shaw. She snapped on her transceiver. "Marshall, are you listening?"

Marshall reached the edge of the plantation, and there he stopped, taken by the sight. He could see Julie at a distance approaching Wynett's grand manor, which rose from the fog like a medieval castle.

"Marshall?"

"I'm right here," he said. "Christ, what happened here?"

"What's the status of that radio relay?"

"Still no word from the hangar. Youngblood's almost there."

"Keep trying. I need to upload my data to Detrick for collation—" She suddenly cried out over the radio.

"What is it, Julie? What's wrong?"

No answer.

Marshall and Williams stooped through the hole in the fence and broke into a run across the field, their boots stirring up angry puffs of white ash as they ran. José trailed at a comfortable trot.

They reached Julie, who was standing statue-still, staring down dazedly at a corpse at her feet. Marshall shot glances at the other carcasses strewn over the lawn, dozens at least, effectively covered and camouflaged by the powderlike ash.

Julie looked up quickly. "You're crazy," she screamed. "You could get yourselves killed coming in here without suits!"

Code: Alpha

Marshall ignored her as he turned over the badly decomposed body with his boot. It was a boy with negroid features, clutching a handful of smooth sticks that appeared to be part of a game. A graphite arrow had struck the boy in his lower back and protruded from his chest. The arrow, fired from a high-powered compound bow, was designed to bring down large game. Quick and silent, it heightened the pleasure of killing, a sport Gorgon excelled in.

"Fucking bastards," Williams spat.

Julie crouched beside the corpse. Her heart pounded. She'd never seen a dead body outside a funeral parlor, let alone a child that looked this bad, and murdered with an arrow. She felt queerly fascinated.

Williams squatted next to her. "Looks like he's been dead for weeks."

"No more than a few hours," she speculated.

Williams looked at the biochemist, puzzled.

"Radical hemorrhaging and dehydration is one of Saint Vitus' symptoms." Julie withdrew from her instrument pack a folding plastic case with five culture containers on one side and a scalpel kit on the other. She removed a scalpel handle, inserted a blade, careful not to puncture her airtight suit, then went to work on the boy's wrist.

"Is that necessary?" Marshall said, looking away.

"Very. I'll need to analyze tissue samples." Julie parted the boy's skin, excised a piece of the radial artery and sealed it in a culture container. She filled a second container with a sample of the ubiquitous white ash.

Marshall walked among the dead, gazing numbly at the decomposed faces that still harbored traces of shock and confusion. Gorgon's raiders had ruthlessly murdered Wynett's soldiers, workers and their families. He wondered if any had managed to escape into the bush. He turned away from the unspeakable carnage and spotted the giant dust cloud rising beyond the house. He hollered to his sergeant, "Let's find that chopper." He pointed at José. "Stay with her."

The old trapper readily agreed.

Marshall and Williams followed the outline of what once had been a charming cobblestone walkway around to the opposite side of the house. A grand sight greeted them—a MiL-24 Hind-E, an advanced Russian gunship with Peruvian military markings, its twin turbo jet engines idling. Marshall couldn't tear his eyes away from it. It bothered him that they'd found no one else alive, including the chopper crew.

"Not even Gorgon could get his hands on this kind of hardware," Williams said. "Must be part of a paramilitary unit."

Marshall grunted, keenly aware of the importance of their find. Examining a Hind-E intact would be a coup for U.S. Army intelligence. There was one small problem: Peru's militia wasn't in the habit of leaving one of its premier military aircraft unattended without good reason. Its owners couldn't be far away. Julie and José caught up with them and stared mutely at the armored helicopter. The gunship, cloaked in the ash's fog, reminded Julie of a prehistoric mastodon, its scaly wings poised for flight.

"Dead men," José said, pointing toward the barn.

The old trapper was right; several corpses in dark uniforms, relatively clean of ash, lay strewn in front of the barn. The Hind crew? Marshall wondered. He said to Julie, "I want you to stay here."

"I'm searching the house." She turned and began trudging toward Wynett's manor.

"José, you stay with her," Marshall ordered.

The old trapper nodded and followed her, while Marshall and Williams broke into a run across the lawn. The major motioned Williams to take the barn, while he explored the gunship.

Marshall's pulse quickened when he reached the aircraft, an adrenaline rush from his excitement. He was certified to fly an AH-64a Apache gunship, a flying battle cruiser. The Hind was its Russian counterpart. The gunship touted four fixed 23mm cannons, 160 27mm unguided rockets, and a dozen laser-guided antitank missiles. This single aircraft could inflict more damage on a Contra stronghold than a regiment of troops with armor and artillery support.

Marshall stooped beneath the gunship's rotor blades and opened the shattered cockpit door. Inside, slumped against the controls, sat the slain Hind pilot, a Peruvian officer. A dozen wounds had produced an appalling stream of blood that soaked the armored seat and gathered on the floor in a puddle. Several rounds had shattered the windscreen, but the flight control deck didn't appear damaged. The major saw no telltale signs that the pilot had succumbed to a neurovirus, man-made or otherwise. Bullets had killed the pilot, not a virus. Bullets from whom, though? he wondered.

Marshall climbed into the cockpit, removed the corpse and took its place in the pilot's seat. He activated the electrics and hydraulics, then throttled the jet engines and idled them at twenty-five percent. The ship could be airborne in seconds. The fuel gauge registered fifty percent. He gripped the control column firmly and felt the powerful aircraft growl under his gloved hand, becoming part of him. Marshall had flown an older Hind-C captured in Afghanistan. This aircraft was similar, though quite improved. He switched on the ship's main tactical screen and summoned up the moving map of the upper continent. Everything was there for his inspection—radar installation coordinates, airfields, villages, farms, mountains and roads.

Julie stepped up onto the veranda of Wynett's Tudor manor and moved slowly, hesitantly, toward the massive double oak doors. José followed two paces behind her, his tired eyes darting from one ash-covered shape to another. Julie felt an eerie foreboding about the way the house's front doors stood open for her, swaying in the slight morning breeze, beckoning her inside. Absent were the familiar jungle sounds, which should have filled her ears even inside the suit. Her breathing accelerated, threatening hyperventilation. She tried to relax, but her pulse continued at a dead run. Against her better judgment she stepped inside.

The living room's bright panels of stained glass framed a

clear central window. Her heart pumped violently as she surveyed the scene of horror that greeted her there. What remained of a woman was sitting upright on the floor, a metal arrow jutting from her throat, staring at Julie with twin sockets for eyes. Radical dehydration had aged the corpse a decade in a few hours. *Is she laughing at me?* Julie wondered. *Jesus, it looks like she is.* She turned quickly away, letting her rapid breathing fog the face shield to block her view.

José stood rooted in the foyer. Blessing himself with the sign of the Lord's cross, the old trapper said to her, "I must wait outside."

"José, I need you with me—" But he was gone. *Damn it.* She didn't want to be alone in this house of horrors. But something deep inside compelled her to continue, with or without José's support.

She found evidence of a battle throughout the house's lower level. A numbness seized her when she stooped to examine the remains of a soldier in black fatigues heaped outside the study, its leather visage reminding her of a museum mummy. A bead of sweat rolled into her right eye, stinging it. She tried to knock it away, but couldn't reach beyond the face shield. Wrinkling her nose in discomfort, she forced herself to continue, aware of her own labored breathing.

Julie entered the study, where she imagined Wynett sitting pensively with his books and newspapers specially delivered to him from around the world; then into his dining room, an elegantly appointed chamber with dishes still set out. Wynett was a neat and orderly man, or at least employed someone to keep him that way. He had a taste for the expensive, affirmed by the original paintings and elegantly carved ivory figurines, which filled every wall and shelf space. Now the white ash covered everything like centuries-old dust.

In the kitchen Julie opened a door to a flight of stone steps leading to a black cellar. She did not descend. Her childhood imagination shifted into high gear as she visualized a pit full of ghouls waiting for her down there. She shut the door and opted to search upstairs.

Despite her best efforts to suppress such thoughts, she could think only of her father. She refused to accept the possibility that she would find him here among this collection of monstrosities, refused to accept the possibility that her bug had killed him. With the suit as her shield, as if it would protect her from every danger seen and unseen, Julie climbed the gore-covered steps to the house's second level. She reached the landing and paused, her eager eyes taking in the hallway's sinister-looking shapes created by the early-morning shadows. There were bodies everywhere. She saw several open doorways, each eclipsed in darkness. For a moment her fear was so great that she felt a firm grip on her heart trying to kill her. Pushing against it, rebellious, infuriated, she continued.

She gazed down at the twisted and shrunken face of a man who looked somehow familiar to her. An arrow, the same type of Teflon-tipped projectile that had slain the woman and boy, was buried midshaft above its eye. She gasped . . . *Stony.* She stumbled backward. How? *Stony, what in God's good name happened here?*

Fighting off a wave of nausea, Julie raised a hand to her face shield and realized she was trembling, an uncontrollable shivering that threatened to cripple her with spasms. She dreaded the thought of what else she might find up here. She drew in a deep breath and proceeded down the hallway, her suit growing distressingly warmer.

She found nothing amiss in the first two bedrooms. The third, however, was a shattered wreck of bullet holes and wood splinters—a true battlefield. Pieces of an elegant marble chessboard lay scattered among the fragmented plaster. Then she saw it—the Beretta lying in the hallway like a welcome mat. His handgun. She walked to it and picked it up. Slowly, reluctantly, she lifted her eyes to the bedroom's drapery, rolling in the breeze, beckoning her attention.

Then she saw it.

The sight forced a muffled gasp from inside her hood and she thought her heart had stopped. Only a few feet from her, chained to a water pipe beneath the window, lay a twisted ragdoll corpse of a man with distinctive peppery hair and dressed in familiar beige khakis. Its dark eye sockets were staring at her with a look of stern disapproval. *What have you done to me?* his expression seemed to ask her.

She didn't need to look long or closely to know that this awful thing used to be her father.

Chapter Twenty

The sound of automatic gunfire startled Marshall from his investigation of the Russian gunship. Through the shattered windscreen he saw Williams roll clear of a burst of erratic fire coming from the barn's window. The gunnery sergeant took up a defensive position against the side of the stone barn and returned several rapid shots with his Galil.

Julie bolted out onto the veranda, where José stood waiting for her. She stopped suddenly, her vacant eyes behind the face shield betraying the shock of seeing what had happened to her father. José just stood there, as pale as she, nervously stroking his white grizzled mustache. His gaze fell on the Beretta in her gloved hand. She gripped it awkwardly, seemingly unaware that she was even holding it.

Without a word she raced off the veranda and across the lawn, struggling in her bulky suit to get far away from the house.

Marshall jumped from the gunship, cocked his Franchi shotgun with a commanding *clack* as he ran and flattened against the barn's stone wall beside Williams. Whoever had fired on Williams from the barn was gone. He surveyed the three slain soldiers in Russian *spetsnaz* commando outfits lying beneath the barn's window, each riddled with enough rounds to assure a kill. The pieces began to fit. The Russians had followed Alpha here. Like Iraq, they had come to claim Gorgon for themselves.

"Did you see who fired?" Marshall asked.

"Yeah, an old man with a neat white beard," Williams said.

"Wynett?"

"Fuck if I—"

They heard laughter and singing coming from inside the barn—a disturbing noise of someone possessed. Williams jerked his rifle toward the window, but no one appeared. The laughter tapered off, as though the source were retreating down a long hallway.

Marshall stripped off every piece of excess gear except his cartridge belt. "Watch my back."

He took a running leap through the barn's window and rolled into a deep shadow, bringing his Franchi up all in one fluid motion. Williams covered him from the window. Marshall methodically directed his shotgun at each indistinguishable shape, every manlike silhouette. He saw no movement. Bodies, a dozen of them, lay in untidy rows across the straw-covered floor, corpses too badly decomposed for him to determine if Stony's commandos were among them. The cavernous barn reminded him of a crypt, the humid air thick with death. Williams eased through the window behind him.

Marshall moved carefully through the shadow and felt something spongy under his right foot. He glanced down. His boot rested on the neck of a corpse whose head barely remained attached by a thin strand of sinew. Disgusted, he kept moving.

They both heard the sound of stone scraping stone. The hair on the back of Williams's neck bristled. Marshall, his expression grim, moved to the back of the barn, pointing his Franchi into every darkened crevice. He found an AK-47 assault rifle, its magazine clip missing, lying next to a crack of light between a slab of stone—a trapdoor.

He motioned Williams forward. "Help me move this."

The two men lifted the boulder-size stone with an agonizing screech, unearthing a crimson emergency light source and a cool draft of mildewed air laced with the medicinal smell of formaldehyde. They set the slab roughly aside. A wooden staircase descended into a cellar.

Without a word Marshall stepped into the opening and descended. Williams followed. The air beneath the barn reeked of chemicals, and both men had to strain to see under the emergency lighting. They saw no one. The cellar reminded Marshall of Frankenstein's laboratory, with its squat arches supporting a moss-dripping ceiling over a roomful of modern lab equipment. In the center of the room sat twin high-capacity fermentation units. Here, in the middle of the primal Amazon jungle, they had found one of the better-equipped biological laboratories Marshall had seen outside a research center.

Williams let out a low whistle. "How did Wynett manage—"

They heard it again. Laughter, a deep hysterical fit, coming from behind the lab's only other door.

"I want him alive," Marshall said.

Nodding, Williams withdrew a single, special round from his SAS belt and slipped it into the Galil's chamber. The cartridge contained a nonlethal serum that could paralyze a bear for ten minutes or a medium-size man for several hours. Marshall changed the mode of his Franchi to semiautomatic, then lay spread-eagle in front of the door, belly down. Williams stood behind him and directed his rifle at the center of the door.

Marshall fired four quick shotgun blasts at the door in a cross formation, shredding the planks. The tiny room beyond was a storage closet, filled with glassware. Through the smoke and flying debris, Marshall saw a stocky, white-haired man huddled in the corner, holding a canister.

"He's got a grenade," Williams yelled.

"Move against me and I will kill us all," the man said to them. It was Wynett, wheezing heavily, his eyes crimson, the corners of his mouth twisted into a demented smile. "Tell me if you are American."

Both soldiers remained motionless. Wynett stood and stepped from the closet, his canister-filled hand raised. "I must know—"

"Major," José called from the top of the steps. "Julie is gone. She run away."

Wynett glanced up.

Williams fired. The cartridge struck Wynett square in the chest. He grunted and doubled over. Marshall bolted forward and squeezed Wynett's palm in a viselike grip, holding the canister immobile. Wynett struggled momentarily until he lost consciousness.

"Appreciate it, José," Marshall said over his shoulder. The old trapper, descending the cellar steps, looked curiously at the roomful of lab equipment.

Marshall pried the aluminum canister from Wynett's grip. "It's not a grenade."

The canister weighed only a few ounces and measured three-quarters of an inch in diameter and six inches long, evidently from Wynett's extensive collection of arms paraphernalia. Its tiny metal safety pin was still in place. Marshall had seen similar devices used in covert operations that could fire compressed gas from an ampule inside.

"What do you think's in it?" Williams asked.

"My bet is it's what we came here for," Marshall said.

Julie ran toward the farming cottages behind Wynett's manor which, miraculously, had been spared contamination. None of the surrounding foliage had been damaged by the organism, thanks to a nightlong breeze that had pushed the lethal cloud to the opposite end of the plantation. She tried to wipe the stinging mixture of tears and sweat from her eyes, but the face shield denied her gloved fingers access. Nauseous and afraid of shock, she increased the ratio of oxygen pumping into her suit. She didn't feel any better.

Julie found modest comfort in the purely mechanical act of

running across the plantation. She couldn't face Marshall and the others right now. She kept telling herself her father was dead, though not believing it. She had almost convinced herself that the thing she had seen in the house was someone else. Inwardly, however, the truth was tearing her apart. He was gone, and part of her was dying with him. Still, she believed she would find him waiting for her inside one of these charming servant houses, ready to scoop her up into his arms in a bear hug, something he had always done when she was a girl. *You know I wouldn't leave you out here alone,* she could hear him say.

Julie climbed the steps of the first house. She entered the solidly built ranch and surveyed the living room with its neatly appointed furniture. To her utter disappointment, no one was here—*he* wasn't here. She stood absolutely still, listening to the oppressive silence inside her suit, feeling the rush of another wave of grief.

She heard crying. Somewhere nearby a child was suppressing the urge to break into uncontrollable sobbing.

Julie returned to the porch and listened. The crying came again, louder—beneath her. She hurried down the steps and, crouching, peered beneath the porch. In the meager half-light, she saw a black boy, no older than ten, huddled in the corner, defending himself with a pair of sharpened sticks. He looked like a curled-up puppy, terrified of a world where everything appeared large and menacing. He just stared at her, shaking. A metal arrow protruded from his abdomen, and he seemed afraid to touch it. How could he survive that wound? she wondered.

"Jesus," she said. "Jesus . . . Jesus . . ." *I must look like a monster to him in this suit. An alien.*

She unfastened the snaps, removed her hood and shook the long, flowing hair from her face. The air filling her lungs felt rejuvenating. She hastily wiped some moisture from her face before crawling to the child and offering her hand. The boy would not give up his sharp sticks.

"Mommy promised," he said in Americanized English.

"She promised nothing would happen to us here."

Julie fought back the swell of emotion in her throat. Reaching forward, she took the sticks from him, then gripped his tiny hand. She held his hand tightly until he stopped crying and there was no life left behind those innocent, vacant eyes.

Chapter Twenty-one

Sinope, Brazil
0545 Hours

Youngblood banked his NOTAR RAH-66 Comanche in a wide arc over the hangar before setting it down on the airstrip's runway. He cut back the throttles to ground-idle and disengaged the rotor, letting the engines diminish to a growl. He saw no lights in or around the hangar, no activity of any kind. It was sunrise, but the overcast sky and the thick, enveloping trees surrounding the airstrip kept him in darkness.

Youngblood grabbed a flashlight and stepped down from the cockpit. He stood motionless before the sagging hangar, ignoring the steady rain that had begun falling. He waited and watched. The old hangar appeared deserted, and some foreboding would not allow him to relax his guard. He didn't believe in ghosts, but standing before the lifeless structure he could feel malicious spirits watching him.

Youngblood approached the bent doorway slowly, his eyes roving. His right hand unbuttoned the leather strap of his .45's side holster. Stepping inside, he slipped quickly into the deep gloom beside the doorway and listened. He could hear nothing but rain popping onto the corrugated iron roof and the distant rumble of his chopper's engine. He couldn't see anything. His right hand slid the .45 out of its holster and held it ready at his side.

He switched on the flashlight and played its beam around. Alpha's equipment sat dark and useless. Their staging base had been powered down; most likely the generator was out. The stacks of crated supplies likewise sat untouched. No one, not even jungle marauders, had intruded here. He swept the light beam across Spangler's communication console and illuminated a figure in a white technician's frock slumped face-down over the equipment.

"Spangler!"

Youngblood bolted to him, grabbed Spangler by his shoulder and turned him over. Only it wasn't Spangler. A dark man with short, black hair and a closely cropped beard, grinning at him, brandished a wicked knife. Youngblood recoiled with a shout, his flashlight clattering to the floor, and lashed out blindly with his .45. The heavy handgun connected with the intruder's jaw, a blow that sent him sprawling with broken teeth. In the confused darkness, Youngblood heard a shuffling and banging of crates as the man scrambled away, spewing a string of Arabic curses. Youngblood discharged several rapid rounds at the vague figure retreating in the dimness. There came a muted grunt as the intruder flew against the wall, ripping through the rotted planks.

Youngblood scrambled to find the flashlight and directed its beam across the floor, searching for others who might be hiding there. The light fell upon a body lying on its back, half concealed behind a stack of crates. He stepped closer, thrusting his handgun before him. This time it was Spangler. A gash the size of his palm had opened his throat, and half his blood volume had poured into an awful pool around him.

Youngblood looked away, his jaw tightening in frustration. The major's orders were to protect the staging area and everyone in it. They all had fucked up, including him.

"Sorry, DOS. I'm so sorry."

* * *

186

Marshall kicked open the double barn doors, and he and Williams half carried, half dragged an unconscious Wynett into the yard. José followed, covering them with his Uzi.

"Where's Julie?" Marshall hollered.

"She run away," José said. "Something scare her."

"Damn it! Go find her—"

"Major!" she called.

The men turned in unison. Julie raced across the lawn without her environment suit, leaving behind an ash cloud as she ran. When she reached them, he noted her eyes and cheeks were flushed from crying. His heart almost stopped when he saw the colonel's prized Beretta in her hand. "God, no . . ."

Her eyes drifted downward, spilling tears. "It was a massacre. . . . Major . . . they . . ." The words choked in her throat.

Marshall let out a long, weary sigh of regret. The loss crushed him. Williams looked away. Marshall's grief quickly turned to an outrage even Gorgon's blood couldn't abate. *Tony, why didn't your men kick his ass to hell?* He made a silent oath to his friend to finish this ugly business; he owed Tony that much.

"Dad just bought a super house in the Canadian Rockies," Julie said, forcing a smile to mask her grief. "When this was over, he planned to . . . we were going to . . ." She couldn't continue; her heart sank under the weight of a torrent of painful emotions.

Marshall touched her shoulder in a gesture of support. "Julie, I'm—"

She jerked away from him. "I don't want to hear you say it." She glared at him as though he were responsible for what had happened to her father and was surprised to see a single tear spill from the corner of his eye.

"I promise I'll get Gorgon for this," Marshall said.

Julie's eyes melted away from his. She didn't care about Gorgon; that was her father's obsession, not hers, and it had killed him. She just wanted him back in her life. Her eyes flared with anger when she saw Wynett slumped against Marshall's arm. She exploded with rage.

187

"Bastard!" She lunged at Wynett, clawing and scratching him savagely about the face and neck, screaming obscenities at him. "You did this. You did this!"

Wynett stirred groggily.

Marshall struggled to contain her with his free arm. "Julie, we need him right now . . . we need answers. . . ."

Julie didn't hear him. She continued her thrashing, obsessed with killing the old man. Nor could Williams, supporting Wynett's other arm, keep her away from his prisoner—she was that determined. José hurried to prop up Wynett so Williams would be free to subdue her. Before they could finish the hand-off, the old trapper let out a grunt and collapsed onto both knees, a Teflon arrow protruding from his side. Julie reeled back and stared horrified at José, who returned her stare with sad eyes full of longing. His eyes rolled up into his head and he dropped facedown onto the ash-covered lawn.

Marshall dropped Wynett and whipped off his Franchi. "Where did that come from?"

Williams slid the Galil off his shoulder, his eyes scanning the brush beyond the harvested fields. On the southern edge of the field, concealed by the healthy foliage, stood a man in black fatigues cocking a military-style crossbow. Williams's uncanny squirrel eyes spotted two similarly camouflaged men squatting in the brush beside him.

"Do you see him?" Marshall demanded.

The gunnery sergeant nodded and leveled his Galil sniper's rifle at the brush—a simple thirty-yard shot. The soldier in the center of Williams's scope raised his crossbow. Williams fired three rounds in quick succession. He could hit a target at a thousand yards. At thirty yards he could drive a nail into a board. Before Williams's rifle report faded, three of Gorgon's mercenaries were dead, a perfectly centered shot through each's chest.

Marshall looked bitterly at the lifeless trapper. A halo of blood flowing from under the corpse had turned the ash around him a sloppy red. The arrow could have taken out any one of them, he realized; the poor man just got in the way.

Julie whispered, barely forming the words, "José, I'm so sorry." She closed her eyes, brought her hand up wearily to her face and began to pray. "God, I can't undo this terrible thing I've done. This abomination of mine, this creature, kills whoever it touches. It killed my father. God help me, I don't know what to do."

Williams hadn't seen a fourth mercenary, a young man with long hair, sitting with his back against a tree, while his comrades fell dead around him. One of his men had been stupid, careless, he reasoned. Their orders were simply to observe, not open fire. Now three were dead. Who were these people and what sort of threat were they? He intended to find out.

The mercenary lifted a handheld transceiver and said in Arabic, "Take one of them alive."

Williams saw movement in the brush on the southern edge of the field, then more movement farther east. "Here they come, Joe."

Julie's grief turned to dread, and she thrust her father's Beretta before her, ready to use it. "What are we going to do?"

"Get inside the chopper," Marshall ordered.

Williams helped wrestle Wynett's deadweight inside the gunship's troop compartment, then climbed aboard. Julie climbed in after them.

Marshall handed her Wynett's canister. "Don't let this out of your sight."

She tucked the Beretta into one of her jumpsuit's deep pockets and accepted the strange-looking cylinder. "What is it?"

"Pandora's box—a little gift from Wynett."

Julie's stomach tightened. "I don't want it."

"Buckle in," Marshall said, then jumped out the troop compartment. Williams closed the door behind him.

"Can he fly this thing?" Julie asked the sergeant.

"We'll find out together."

Marshall climbed into the Hind's cockpit and grabbed the shoulder harness, which he realized was too damaged to do him any good. He jammed his Franchi beside the pilot's seat and advanced the throttles to flight idle. He waited what seemed an eternity for the aircraft's turbo engines to power up to seventy-five percent before engaging the rotor clutch. Overhead, the ship's five massive rotor blades began to slice the air.

Through the shattered windscreen Marshall saw at least a dozen men dressed in black fatigues charging toward the gunship in a tight skirmish line. He inched the throttles forward. As the rotor's velocity increased, he felt rather than heard brief power losses, no more than a fraction of a second each, yet persistent enough to give a seasoned pilot serious thoughts to finding another mode of transportation. He watched the tachometer dip slightly with each power interruption, aware that at high speeds a serious vibration would tear apart the aircraft.

Then he saw it beside the altimeter. A bullet hole—deep, wide, dark. It looked like an open mouth, frozen in a silent moan of defeat. *How did you miss this one?* He wondered if the aircraft's electronics had enough redundant circuits to keep the bird airborne. If not, this would be a very short ride.

"Armed men approaching from the south and east," Williams said from the narrow passageway between the troop compartment and the cockpit.

"I see them."

The aircraft's threat alarm sounded twice. Marshall switched on the gunship's radar display and saw two dots representing approaching aircraft forty miles to the east. "Fighters approaching."

"Christ, what else?" Williams said.

Marshall switched off the ship's radar, an acoustic beacon the fighter pilots could hone in on. The twin Lotarev D-136 turboshaft jet engines whipped the gunship's main rotor blades into a dishlike blur. As the engine's rpms increased, the troublesome mechanical flutter became less noticeable. Marshall knew, though, the problem hadn't gone away. It was lurking somewhere in the background like a coiled snake waiting to strike. He glanced out the windscreen; the men in black fatigues were storming toward the aircraft firing their weapons. The rounds ricocheted off the gunship's armored plating.

Williams inched open the troop compartment door, raised his Galil and squeezed off a full clip in several seconds. The gunnery sergeant's accurate report dropped four soldiers as they scattered in disorder. "Get us out of here, Joe."

Marshall drew in a deep breath, released the brakes and pulled up on the collective control lever. The gunship shuttered, refusing to move.

"Lift, you son of a bitch," he hissed through clenched teeth.

He increased the throttle. The twin engines roared. *C'mon.* Slowly, almost imperceptibly, the altimeter needle began to quiver.

Chapter Twenty-two

Stonecutters Garden

Peruvian Air Squadron Comdr. Alfonso de los Heros surveyed the green blur sweeping by below him. He dropped his MiG's nose, extended its flaps and eased the fighter to the dangerous edge of a stall. A mere four hundred feet above the treetops, a mistake now could cost Peru one of its few high-performance aircraft, not to mention one hell of a good pilot.

At two hundred knots, Commander de los Heros and his wing man had only two seconds to complete a visual inspection of the plantation. And then green, a vast ocean of monotonous green. But two seconds were enough to give them an eyeful. If he didn't know better, de los Heros would swear he had just overflown a snowfield in the middle of a tropical jungle. How was that possible? He shoved the stick forward and brought his aircraft up in a wide arc, preparing for a second run.

"Dove One to Nest," he said in Spanish into his helmet mike. "The plantation is deserted. It is . . ." He paused, groping for the right word. ". . . devastated."

Inside the Peruvian air base hangar four hundred miles to the west, Captain Valachi spat out a cigar bit and said into the open channel to the MiG pilots, "The gunship. Do you see my gunship?"

"Negative," the pilot responded.

Valachi smashed the cigar into his desk, unaware that he'd never lit it. *Scavengers!* he surmised. Scavengers working for the drug czars had killed the crew and stolen his gunship. *The fucks would use my formidable aircraft against me!* He loathed giving the order that would likely end his less-than-brilliant military career. What other choice did he have? Allow the aircraft to escape and he would be letting it butcher untold numbers of soldiers and civilians. Destroy the gunship now and he could blame its loss on Colonel Golovko, who had confiscated it on orders from the Russian Defense Council. But first they had to find it.

"Locate the gunship," he said slowly and deliberately so there could be no misunderstanding. "And destroy it."

Marshall engaged the Hind's turbo booster and felt the G-force acceleration press him back into the armored seat. He kept the engines screaming at full throttle and skimmed the treetops thirty feet below, avoiding the MiGs' radar by hiding inside the ground clutter. One hundred seventy knots . . . one hundred eighty . . . one hundred ninety . . .

His thick swirls of black hair were soaked with sweat and his shoulders ached from the tension. He could feel the tension crawling down his back. He couldn't shake the awful image of two fighters riding his ass with enough air-to-air missiles to down a dozen choppers. He kept one eye on the outside mirrors, watching for them, while the other scanned the forest below. A bleak ache gnawed at the pit of his stomach. There was nowhere to run, nowhere to hide.

"You've got this thing moving!" Williams hooted, squatting behind the pilot's high-backed seat.

"She handles like a tank," Marshall spat, his knuckles white from his overprotective grip on the pitch-control column.

"How's the fuel?" Williams asked.

"Half. Maybe enough to get us to Bolivia by way of the Rio Madeira River."

"A lot of bad neighborhoods between here and there. Are you sure about this?"

"Hell no."

Suddenly Marshall's headset crackled. "Alpha eight-seven two, this is Odessa seven-four. What's your status? Over."

"Son of a bitch, it's Youngblood!" Marshall keyed in the hangar's frequency on the communications display and spoke deliberately into his helmet mike. "We're airborne. Can't tell you our position. Code nine-two. We've missed you. What's the story at the hangar? Over."

"Spangler's dead—our terrorist friends."

Marshall sighed. "Jesus . . ."

"I wouldn't advise returning there," Youngblood said. "I'm airborne, proceeding east. Let me give you a rendezvous point—"

A warning tone in his headphones overrode Youngblood's transmission. The Hind's threat display tracked a pair of red blips above and behind them, seven miles from their tail and closing rapidly; two fighters approaching at twice the gunship's speed had them targeted and locked. The fighters had honed in on the radio transmission. Marshall activated the auto weapons console, then hesitated. Fighter pilots in high-tech confrontations were notoriously trigger-happy. And there was no way he could outduel them. *Steady.* Marshall slid a gloved finger over the countermeasure console, a much better option for the moment.

The fighters grew in his outside mirror until he could see their distinctive Peruvian markings. At the last possible moment, the fighters broke attack formation and roared past in a blur, shaking the gunship. *A scouting sweep,* Marshall reasoned. *They want their $30 million gunship back.*

"MiGs," Marshall spat.

His headset crackled again. The MiG commander's voice filling his ears spoke to him in rapid Spanish, and he didn't sound happy.

194

Code: Alpha

* * *

Julie watched Wynett sleeping fitfully on the floor of the noisy troop compartment. She gave serious thought to opening the compartment's door and shoving him out into the jungle before anybody could stop her. Or, better yet, wrapping one of the aircraft's repelling cables abound his neck and hanging the son of a bitch outside. If that meant a murder charge, she didn't give a damn.

Wynett began to stir. Julie grew rigid. His hands twitched spasmodically, and he uttered a few incoherent words, as though wrestling with a bad dream.

"Williams," she called to the front. "Get back here—*now.*"

Wynett's eyes suddenly fluttered open. He gazed up at the compartment's roof, dazed, then twisted his head around and looked at her with cold, dark eyes that terrified her.

"Sergeant!"

Wynett's voice when he spoke was deeper than she remembered at Detrick. "We have met before, have we not?"

Julie withdrew the Beretta from the pocket of her khakis, pulled back the hammer and, with two trembling hands, pointed it at his head. "This gun belonged to my father. I'm sure he wouldn't mind if I used it to blow off your fucking head."

Peruvian Air Force Commander de los Heros opened the TAC channel to the gunship and said to Marshall in Spanish, "I have you targeted and locked. You will not be permitted to continue. You will climb to ten thousand feet and proceed on a heading of two-two-four. Over."

Marshall understood something about being destroyed, but little else. He keyed the mike and said to the MiG commander, "I have a critical oil leak. I'm losing my drive train. Give me your base coordinates. Over."

"Ah, the Yankees have joined the Latin American drug trade," the pilot squawked in broken English over Marshall's headset. "Climb to ten thousand feet and proceed on two-two-four. Deviate from this flight path—even for a moment—and I will destroy you.''

Marshall grinned. ''Whatever you say, comrade.''

The MiGs roared past, regrouped on the heading back to their base and quickly lost visual on him. Marshall pushed the control column right and eased up on the throttle, turning the gunship around gracefully until it matched the MiGs' heading. He knew they would be monitoring his compliance by radar and he intended to show them what they wanted to see.

Marshall keyed the troop-compartment intercom. ''Buckle in back there. This could get bumpy.''

''What's he doing?'' Julie asked.

''Just do as the major says,'' Williams said. His tone was anything but reassuring.

Marshall brought the aircraft to a hover eight hundred feet above the treetops. He activated the ship's autofire controls, keyed the mike and said to the Peruvian pilot with as much panic as he could feign, ''Mayday. Mayday. Losing power. Fires in both engines! I can't keep her in the air—''

He dipped the gunship's nose sharply and fired four wing-mounted air-to-ground unguided missiles, then punched the countermeasure console to release several bundles of chaff. The jungle below erupted in a fireball. The radar signature would show the detonation, followed by scattered echoes of countless chaff foils, which he hoped the MiG pilots would interpret as fuselage debris.

Marshall dropped the collective and yanked the control column hard to the right, rolling the gunship around ninety degrees down hard and fast, faster than he intended. He gnashed his teeth from the G-forces and squeezed the control column while the aircraft shot away from the explosion at a right angle, low, diving for the jungle's ground cover. He pulled out of the dive and felt the treetops whipping the aircraft's undercarriage.

In the troop compartment, Julie felt as though she were riding a runaway elevator that had just plunged thirty floors. She grabbed Williams's solid frame. ''Marshall . . . !''

Code: Alpha

*   *   *

Doubling back, Commander de los Heros saw a huge, black column of smoke billowing from the jungle. He could not find the Hind—not on radar, infrared, visual. Nowhere. The MiGs roared past the fireball, making a visual sweep of the area. Had the Hind pilot been telling the truth about the engines? he wondered. Something bothered him. He throttled and climbed, and ordered his wingman to begin a methodical search of the area.

Marshall activated the moving map display. Rivers, hills, jungle, villages—there wasn't much to choose from. They were approaching the foothills of the Serra dos Parecis Mountains. His mind raced, calculating coordinates and airspeed. His plan was uncomfortably thin: follow the Parecis mountains into Bolivia and rendezvous with Youngblood at the first clearing along the Rio Madeira River. Ten minutes. Marshall needed a precious ten minutes to hide the aircraft in the protective folds of the Maderia river valley. The MiGs' radar would be useless in that terrain, forcing the pilots to mount a visual search for them. That tipped the odds slightly in his favor.

Marshall listened to the pilots' Spanish babble over the radio, probably reporting their position and describing the scorched jungle. *Take the bait, you sons of bitches, and swallow it whole.* The fighters would be burning fuel rapidly while sweeping the search area. He assumed their mission range didn't extend much beyond the plantation. Any moment they would need to head back to their base.

Marshall glanced at his watch, at the display once more, then out at the terrain. He shifted uncomfortably in his seat and felt his shirt stick to his back; he was keenly aware that the party would be over if the MiGs found them again.

The blip that pinpointed their position on the display entered the moving map's Parecis highlands a little more than forty miles from the Bolivian border. Rolling valleys were rising around them, offering cover and protection. Isolated by the

Serra dos Parecis Mountains, the Madeira River valley was a haven for drug-trafficking camps. A valley of thugs. He searched the tactical display for steep cliffs and deep canyons, any closed topography inaccessible to high-performance fighters, while offering a chopper hiding places. Real cat-and-mouse terrain. But the Parecis had none of that, only gently sloping river valleys and highlands.

"Terrific," he muttered.

As the hills rose higher around him, he felt turbulence. An updraft gave them some free lift, while a head wind blowing strongly across the ridges on each side of the valley buffeted the aircraft. He eased off the power, dropping the Hind's speed in half, and hugged the side of the valley about halfway up, the best defensive position he could negotiate.

They came without warning.

The MiGs roared past, flying over the valley in a search formation. Their sudden appearance startled Marshall, and he nearly lost control of the column. *Did they see us?* He knew a fighter pilot's vision would funnel to the bottom of the valley, perhaps missing a chopper flying halfway up. But two pilots? His headset had become unsettlingly quiet while the MiGs' engines thundered down the valley. He watched the sleek aircraft disappear, his mind cold with uncertainty. *Did they see us?* He brought the gunship over the crest of a hill and into the next valley, a wider canyon, and sank quickly to the bottom.

Halfway down the hill, the forest suddenly gave way to a clearing, an encampment. He brought the aircraft to a hover over the makeshift barracks and tents, and watched about a dozen men scatter from beneath his rotors' downdraft. Did he dare set down here? Rounds from small arms and rifle fire ricocheted off the gunship's armored undercarriage. He could see more men joining the fray, some carrying what looked like ground-to-air and antitank rockets.

His jaw tightened. This was no mining camp, he realized. He shouted back to Williams, "We're over a fucking drug factory."

198

"Jesus, Joe."

In the outside mirror Marshall saw the MiGs arcing back, regrouping in attack formation. *Shit.* He clenched the control column, lifted the collective pitch lever and increased the throttle. The gunship shot away from the encampment, making a dead run down the valley. The major's stone-set eyes watched the moving map display, searching for a smaller side valley with deep terrain he could wrap snugly around them. But there was nothing. *Nothing!*

He no longer had a plan. There was only the present moment and survival. The cat was on the mouse's tail, and he had to outrun it or be eaten.

"Joe, what are you doing?" Williams called from behind him.

Marshall ignored him. The MiGs were rapidly approaching from the rear in attack formation. *Careful.*

Marshall saw spurts of flame as the MiGs launched four AA-8 infrared homing missiles. *Four of them!* They weren't taking any chances. They were determined to end the hunt right here. He had played his bluff hand and lost; the game was finished. The missiles shrieked over the encampment and headed straight for them.

Don't look at them, for chrissake. Move your ass!

He pushed the throttle full forward, broke hard to the right and pitched up while pulling on the collective. The turboshaft engines screamed their protest. The gunship turned ninety degrees and began racing for its life at treetop level up the valley wall. He had gained a precious second. He could sense rather than see the AA's sweep around after him in a wide arc like a couple of burning arrows, homing in on his engines' exhaust.

Marshall's fingers pressed all eight countermeasure buttons. His console blared as radar-jamming circuits activated and load after load of flares and chaff decoys dropped behind the gunship like stardust. Would it gain him another precious second, he wondered? *Give it to me!*

Whomp.

One of the missiles detonated in the chaff. What about the other three?

The valley crest loomed above him, a sanctuary of solid rock. His full-throttled engines screamed—one hundred ninety knots, two-ten. *A few more seconds.* His knuckles strained from his brutal grip on the control column; his eyes locked on the crest of the valley, which seemed as far-off as the top of Everest. Marshall's gut felt like he had just been kicked by a steel-tipped boot. The threat warning tones screeching in his ears sounded like desperate cries for help, declaring the missiles' inevitable impact and the pronouncement of his own death. There was no room left to maneuver. His life and the lives of the others depended on the gunship's ability to outrace three A-88 missiles to the top of a mountain. *Damn* . . . it would be close.

"Major—" Williams shouted.

Suddenly the hill gave way to bright blue sky, and the rocky peak swept by in a blur beneath them. Marshall shoved the pitch control forward, bringing the nose of the chopper down into a steep dive. Another ocean of green stretched down and away from them into a splendid river valley like a great sweeping curtain. There wasn't time to savor the view. His every muscle strained to get the gunship out of the missiles' way. He felt no fear, only numb movement.

The ridge behind them exploded with the force of an angry volcano. The concussion from the simultaneous detonation of three A-88s pounded his eardrums and threw him viciously against the flight console as his knuckles fought to keep their grip on the pitch column. He cursed not having a shoulder harness. The Hind's speed dropped alarmingly.

The Hind's rudder pedals suddenly felt stiff and unresponsive; the hydraulics were going. Damage-control lights above the cockpit windshield warned of a half dozen system malfunctions. The chase was over. Marshall used the sudden decrease in power to maneuver the tail rotor and spin the ship around while skidding sideways down over the treetops. He wrestled with the pitch-control column, but as hard as he tried he couldn't keep the aircraft horizontal. The gunship angrily slapped the treetops, a living jungle that meant to devour them.

"Judas pri—"

Chapter Twenty-three

Marshall maneuvered the gunship into a precarious hover over the treetops. He moved his hands and feet briskly, dancelike, working the column and pedals to steady the angle of the aircraft. The engines were burning—wires, hydraulics, turbines, everything. The gunship's pendulumlike swinging became a quick recipe for airsickness, aggravated by hot, acid-tasting smoke pouring into the troop compartment.

Williams jerked open the troop compartment door to vent the fumes. He saw the MiGs disappear well beyond the next ridge, soaring around in a huge arc. He had no doubt that they would be back in attack formation, launching more missiles at them. Williams surveyed the thick treetops blanketing the valley below, then hollered to the cockpit, "No way you're gonna put her down here, Joe."

"The main rotor's going," Marshall said into the intercom. "I can't keep it horizontal. Get out of here fast."

Williams grabbed one of the gunship's two repelling cables driven by a winch powerful enough to hoist trucks. He looked at Julie, then at Wynett, who was sitting Buddha-like with his dark eyes locked on him. "God help us," he muttered, then pointed to Julie. "You first."

"Sergeant, I can't—"

Code: Alpha

"Move!"

Julie slung the instrument case over her shoulder and let Williams fasten the winch harness under her arms.

"I'm lowering Wynett next," Williams said, leading her to the edge of the compartment. "If he gives you any trouble, use the Beretta on him."

Julie didn't hear him; her eyes were locked on the swaying treetops below. "Tell me you're not serious."

Williams chuckled good-naturedly, but it came out without a trace of humor. "You don't have to do anything; I'll feed the line from here."

Fighting back a panic blitz, Julie screwed her eyes shut as Williams spun her around and eased her out of the compartment. A yelp tore from her throat when she thought she was free-falling. But the winch cable controlled her descent, though it was still much too fast, she thought. She kept her eyes closed as she sank into the branches that slapped and mauled her like claws. A half-darkness enveloped her.

Eighty feet beneath the treetops, she hit the ground with a solid thud. *Down!* Julie couldn't see the chopper through the great liana-festooned trees towering over her, but she could hear it, a sputtering reminder of those still trapped above. She scrambled out of the harness, gave the cable two hard jerks and watched her lifeline vanish up through the thick, leafy canopy. A dreadful thought occurred to her: *Suppose Wynett makes it down, but Marshall and Williams don't.* The notion scared the hell out of her. *I wouldn't just be stranded in the middle of the jungle,* she realized; *I'd be stranded in the middle of the jungle with Wynett!* If it came down to that, she decided, she would kill him with her father's Beretta.

"You're taking too much goddamn time!" Marshall yelled into the intercom.

Williams finished fastening the winch's harness under Wynett's arms. "If you even say 'boo' to the lady down there," Williams spat, "I'll kill you. Do you understand me, motherfucker?"

Wynett, smirking, said, "I suggest we remain up here, sir. A much safer option—"

Williams gave his prisoner a powerful shove out of the gunship, activated the winch and watched Wynett plunge into the forest below. The aircraft had become increasingly unstable. Williams slung his rifle and munitions pack over his shoulders and hollered to the front, "I'm outta here."

Williams grabbed the second repelling cable, swung out of the compartment and pushed himself away from the aircraft. The gunship bucked angrily away from him as he slid downward, the cable burning through his gloved hands. Swinging and sideslipping, the aircraft weaved an unpredictable path across the sky, viciously dragging the sergeant through the treetops. Williams twisted and turned, kicking a path through the branches, protecting his face with his arm.

The gunship dipped sharply, plunging him thirty feet before the cord became hopelessly enmeshed in the branches, suspending him ten feet off the ground. Williams let himself drop. He landed heavily in the mulch and dissipated the impact in a controlled roll through the high, twisted stalks. He rose shakily onto his knees.

"Sergeant!" a voice called through the din. It was Julie, half concealed in the brush. Williams sprinted to her. She had Wynett sitting beside her, the Beretta pointed at his head. He didn't appear even to know where he was. Her frenzied eyes scanned the treetops, searching for Marshall. She couldn't see him; she could only hear the gunship fighting its losing battle to stay in the air. "Where is he? Why isn't he climbing down?"

"He's coming down the hard way."

"What's that supposed to mean?"

"That chopper's too unstable. Once he lets go of those controls, the ship goes down. He has to land that thing in the trees."

Marshall could feel the mounting vibration in the pitch-control column as the rotor blades fought a valiant battle to hold on to the sky. His face, streaked with rivulets of perspiration, exhibited a blend of determination and desperation as he worked to keep the gunship airborne. He could see the MiGs finish their arch and resume an attack formation. For the moment that was unimportant. More critical was the main rotor torque gauge sinking dangerously downward as the ship lost power.

The radar-lock warning siren screeched through the cockpit. The display showed four points of light moving rapidly forward of the MiGs. They had fired four more missiles. He drew in a deep breath—possibly his last, he realized—and eased the Hind downward until he heard the treetops slapping the undercarriage.

Now!

Marshall eased down on the collective. The gunship dropped into trees, slamming him into the instrument panel like a hundred-and-seventy-pound sack of flour. He fumbled to extinguish the two Lotarev engines. The rotor blades struck the branches and shattered, hurling ribbons of steel through the jungle at 1200 mph.

He made a desperate grab at the back of his seat for support, his legs functioning like steel springs, pushing him away from the windscreen. With its nose angled downward, the gunship rolled dangerously to port, dumping him sideways against the cockpit door with a force that paralyzed his lungs and left his head feeling like a heavy lump of mashed potatoes. He was falling, but he was too stunned to do anything but ride eighteen tons of metal down through the branches. He screwed his eyes shut. The image of his mashed and broken body, indistinguishable from the scattered metal when he hit the jungle floor, was unbearable.

But there was no impact.

The aircraft slid to a stop. Marshall's eyes blinked open with a start. Dazed, unable to comprehend why he still was alive, he stared at the jungle floor twenty feet beneath him.

"Major!" The sound of Williams's voice startled his mind back. "Move your ass!"

The branches split and groaned under the weight of the gunship. The aircraft was sinking downward, twisting and cracking through the branches that struggled to hold it in their embrace.

Marshall seized his Franchi and kicked open the cockpit door. He grabbed blindly at the branches and half climbed, half slid to the ground and rolled hard onto his right shoulder. The fall left him stunned.

He became aware of another sound, a roar bearing down on them. Two hands reached under his arms, pulled him effortlessly to his feet and pushed him forward. Marshall limped blindly through the jungle on two bruised legs that, mercifully, weren't broken.

"Keep moving!" Williams roared.

Two pairs of AT-6 Spiral laser-homing missiles tore into the treetops and detonated. The twisted wreckage that had once been a Russian gunship turned onto its back like a dying dragonfly and tumbled onto the jungle floor. Hurricanelike winds shrieked through the trees and sucked the heated air from their lungs. The twin Lotarev engines exploded with an impossible concussion, turning the wreck into an angry fireball that rolled into a thick, black pillar of smoke. The MiGs roared overhead. Marshall and Williams saw none of this while racing out of the fireball's reach. Burning fuel chased after them like a fast-flowing stream of superheated lava.

Chapter Twenty-four

Williams led the way through the living curtain of jungle to a slight clearing overgrown with creepers, parasitic orchids, vines and moss. The climate of the upper river valley was damp and fetid, the heat oppressive and debilitating, the ground damp and clinging. They found Julie, Beretta in hand, standing sentinel over Wynett.

Seeing the major, she let her breath out quickly as though she had been holding it since landing. "I was beginning to think you weren't coming."

Marshall brushed coldly past her. "Put that gun away."

"Yes, sir." She added under her breath, "And it's nice to see you too."

Wynett had discarded what was left of his environmental suit and sat watching Marshall with intense dark eyes. "Have you any notion of the danger you have placed us in, sir? Our situation is hopeless without a radio."

Julie looked suddenly at Marshall. "No radio? How will you contact Youngblood?"

"We won't," Wynett said evenly. "Without a radio, we are effectively sequestered from the rest of the world. Any notion of simply marching out of this valley is absurd."

Marshall looked severely at him. "Cork it."

"Friggin' great." Julie wiggled the equipment pack off her shoulders with a groan and eased into a sitting position at the base of a liana tree. She felt the slightest nervous tickling on the back of her neck and, reaching back, touched a bug the size of a locust with long, thin legs and an ugly bloodsucking snout. She sat up suddenly. The tree was crawling with the strange-looking insects.

"Reduviidae," Wynett said. "The assassin bug. Don't let them sting you, my dear Julie. They carry Chagas' disease."

Julie sprang to her feet, brushing her shirt, while Wynett chuckled silently, his shoulders jiggling as if on springs.

A birdlike whistle startled everyone into silence. *Whoooooo! Whoooooo!* came the answering call.

Williams swung the Galil off his shoulder and directed it at the path of trampled grass leading into their floral cove.

"The natives call them the fierce people," Wynett said, his voice low. "They are soldiers of the drug cartel. They own these valleys."

Everyone looked at him.

"The Indians are terrified of them," he continued. "The value they put on their privacy is priceless. They are not after our wreckage. No doubt they believe we are a part of the militia that is at constant war with them. They will hunt us down until they find us—even if it means combing the wreckage for our charred bodies. And when they find us here alive, within the week the authorities will fish our mutilated bodies out of the Rio Madeira River, just as they have done with eighty other bodies this year alone. The corpses typically have their throats slit, their faces disfigured and their fingerprints removed with acid to make them difficult to identify—"

"Shut up," Julie said. "Make him shut up."

Marshall slapped his hand over her mouth and pushed her down behind a crude barricade of moss-covered tree stumps. "Not a word." He said to the others in a raspy whisper, "Everyone stay absolutely quiet until I tell you otherwise."

Williams saw them too, well-camouflaged figures with rifles, skulking through the jungle's gloom. He could hear the squawks of handheld radios. The sergeant rolled next to the major and scanned the movement through the scope of his Galil. There were at least a dozen out there. The forest was spawning them like a womb.

Julie saw them too, though not clearly. When Marshall removed his hand from her mouth, she looked at him, terrified. "Oh, Jesus!"

A long, undulating, sustained chorus of screams shot through the forest like a train whistle. *Whoo-hooo-hooo!*

Marshall and Williams raised their weapons.

"Fire a single round, Major," Wynett said, "and you will be killing all of us. I suggest you set your guns aside and put your hands on the back of your heads. That is our only chance."

Marshall and Williams ignored him. Suddenly they heard bullets hissing over their heads, men screaming, foliage rustling furiously, everything blurring in a drone of confusion. *We're going to buy it,* Marshall realized. *We're going to buy it in the middle of this goddamn jungle!* Faces and gun barrels pushed through the claustrophobic sea of vegetation around them, some of them firing rounds. Wynett put two fingers in his mouth and let out a deafening whistle, one long and one short. The whooping and shouting ceased for an awkward moment; then laughter broke out. The soldiers were laughing at them! The major stared bitterly into the deadly end of a firing squad of gun barrels closing in around his group, the dark faces behind the weapons eager to use them. He reached for his SAS knife.

"Don't do it," said a voice in English with a thick Portuguese accent. Marshall screwed his neck around. The voice belonged to a dark, oily-faced officer, pushing through the tight circle of soldiers that had enveloped them. The officer scrutinized each of them with a look of contempt. His lips formed a grin when he saw Wynett sitting among them.

"Ah," he said. "It's the good doctor. And he has brought friends with him."

"Good day, Colonel Perez," Wynett said. "It is always a pleasure."

Williams slid a furtive hand down the length of his Galil.

The colonel's ferreting eyes leaped to the sergeant. "Touch the trigger, colored man, and my men will cut out your heart."

Chapter Twenty-five

A small but well-armed contingent of soldiers marched their prisoners through the gates of a hidden jungle encampment that accommodated a single barracks in need of a good paint job. A driving rain had returned in sheets, washing the mud off them. Activity inside and outside the wretched compound consisted solely of natives in loincloths hoisting bales of coco leaves on their shoulders and binding them to mules. It occurred to Marshall that the drug lords were using the forest's indigenous people for the menial harvesting chores the same way Southern plantation owners used slaves to pick cotton. The civilized world had introduced commerce to the jungle, and the industry was thriving.

Marshall held no illusions about his fate. As the senior American military officer commanding an illegal operation in a sovereign state, he knew he was finished. If they had been apprehended by the *Borlo*, Brazil's secret military police, at least he could have looked forward to spending the rest of his life alone in a dark concrete cell, slowly losing his eyesight. But they weren't in police custody. By morning he would be dead, his features erased with a knife.

As for the others, they would die too, he realized. There would be no prisoner exchange or daring rescue attempt—

even if General Medlock knew their whereabouts. The U.S. State Department would deny Alpha's existence. Inside the United States military establishment, Marshall and his group did not exist; Dr. Carl Wynett, Col. Anthony Martinelli and his commandos did not exist. And certainly Saint Vitus did not exist. They were on their own.

Marshall surveyed the barracks and allowed his eyes to wander the length of a radio tower rising from its corrugated iron roof like a high-tech steeple. He stole a sideways glance at Williams, who acknowledged him with raised eyebrows. Julie and Wynett, sloshing through the mud with hands clasped behind their heads, didn't appear to notice the hardware that provided the only thin portal to the civilized world. He knew Julie only cared about the canister still hidden in a pocket of her khakis.

The barracks' interior was as dismal and rude as its exterior. The place reeked of rot, sweat and urine. Fungus seeped between cracks in the floorboards like sloppy mortar. An abomination of torn plaster, bare light fixtures and decomposing furnishings, the barracks housed men who were more repugnant than the jungle vermin it was built to keep out. Inside, Marshall counted five men, all unwashed and unshaven, each toting an automatic rifle. They were thugs of the worst sort, beasts wallowing in their native wasteland.

One of the guards, all hair and muscle, reminded Marshall of Blackbeard the pirate, complete with eye patch. The brute stood whirling a large-gauge chain as if it were a pocket watch while considering each of them with his single good eye as they entered. His woolly beard shifted and his eye glistened when he saw Julie. He lumbered to her. She shot a frightened glance back at Marshall when the brute began thoroughly frisking her, her eyes urging the major to do something, anything, to help her.

Blackbeard quickly found Wynett's strange aluminum canister hidden in a buttoned pocket of her khakis and tossed it to the oily-faced colonel who had apprehended them.

"You mustn't touch that," Julie shouted. "Please."

The colonel considered the canister in his palm. Marshall stiffened, a reaction the colonel was quick to notice. "Tell me what this is?"

"Joe," Julie shouted, "for God's sake don't let him open it!"

Marshall stifled a rush of frustration, struggling to keep his feet planted and his arms firmly at his sides. He couldn't do a damn thing.

"The container is mine," Wynett said, stepping forward. "I will tell you its secrets, but for a price."

The colonel laughed and nodded. "My friend. Always the deal maker, yes, Herr Wynett? We must talk."

The colonel cocked his head. A guard pushed Julie curtly down the hallway, while two others led Williams at gunpoint down a flight of narrow stone steps leading beneath the barracks.

Marshall tried to conceal the defeat his eyes must have shown as they led Julie away, the corrupt laughter of her captors echoing back. He couldn't listen anymore. He dug his heels into the slippery floorboards and lunged at the guard closest to him, a man not much older than twenty. He saw a blur of movement behind him and felt a cruel blow to his kidney as his hands clawed for the guard's rifle. He fell to his knees, the haze of unconsciousness rapidly descending. Blackbeard's heavy chain wrapped around his neck and yanked him roughly backward. He grabbed ineffectively at it before another hammerlike blow to his kidney knocked him insensible.

"I wish to know your name," said the colonel, stepping into Marshall's view. "I wish to know the names of the men I kill."

The chain around Marshall's neck slackened so he could breathe. "Fife," he gasped. "Bernard Fife. My friends call me Barney."

"American CIA?"

"Deputy sheriff of Mayberry."

The colonel nodded to Blackbeard, and the chain again tightened its death grip. All Marshall could manage was a lame sucking noise deep in his throat. He saw the officer's lips move but could hear nothing. Mercifully, the bottomless void enveloped him and he was out cold.

Julie waited alone in a small, dim room that served as the soldiers' sleeping quarters, with filthy mattresses strewn across the floor in no particular order. There were no windows, and the only exit was through the door by which she had just entered. She wasn't there long before a soldier joined her. It was Blackbeard. He closed and bolted the door behind him and let his good eye follow her body's shapely contours.

"Listen to me very carefully," Julie implored him. "You must convince your colonel not to open that canister. He doesn't know what he has. You must get him to return it to me so I can destroy it. The contents of that container will kill us all."

Blackbeard laughed—a deep, ugly rumble that made her wince—and leveled a lustful gaze at her. Julie doubted he understood a word of English. He was breathing heavily, his hot, foul breath pouring over her. He unfastened his pants and let them drop to his ankles, revealing a scrotum that looked like a hanging wasps' nest.

Julie covered herself with crossed arms. "Marshall!"

Marshall thought he was dreaming. How else could he explain the subterranean nightmare of shadow and gloom that reminded him of a B horror movie? But this was no dream. The stench that assaulted his nostrils, a horrendous blend of rot and excretion, was more effective than smelling salts. He woke with a start, his senses clearing, and assessed his predicament. He sat naked to the waist, strapped in a sinister-looking chair in the barracks' sub-basement. The leather straps—one around each arm and leg, another around his forehead, another around his chest—held him completely immobile. He caught only the barest glimpse of Williams from his peripheral vision strapped similarly to a chair beside him. *What in God's glory is happening?*

214

Code: Alpha

The cellar's only light came from a harsh incandescent bulb dangling above them. There were large puddles everywhere and a constant echo of dripping water. He could make out a shadowy collection of cauldrons and ovens lurking beyond the cobwebbed archways, and beyond them stacks of petroleum drums. Between an archway, a fiendish-looking hulk of a man with a long drooping mustache sat sharpening a wicked knife on a foot-driven whetstone. A dungeon, Marshall thought, a dungeon right out of the Dark Ages.

"Where's Julie?" Marshall asked.

"It's about time you woke up," Williams said. "Welcome to the party."

"Where's Julie?"

"They're not gonna waste her down here," Williams said, then let out a huff of nervous laughter. "They're not gonna waste her on a death of a thousand cuts."

"I don't know what you mean."

"An Oriental contribution to the art of execution. A guard happily told me all about it. See the drain under your chair?"

Marshall tried to look down, but the strap held his head upright. "No."

"Take my word for it. Genghis Khan over there intends to cut fine, razor incisions from our temples to our ankles. He's making the blade so sharp the incisions will hardly bleed. He'll cut us until we slowly bleed to death. The guard guaranteed we'll be aware of the pain until the very end."

Marshall sat watching the executioner, who was silhouetted by the flurry of sparks from the whetstone. "Charming."

Wynett stood staring at the room's paint peeling down the walls in long sheets, while Colonel Perez examined each piece of Alpha's gear laid out on the room's only table. He was particularly interested in Julie's instrumentation pack. Finally he faced Wynett, riveted his old friend with a cold gaze, studying him.

Wynett offered the colonel a smirk.

"You are a puzzle to me," the colonel said. "You are a

well-respected farmer and a man of considerable property, yet you steal a gunship belonging to Peru's military with your American friends. As an officer of Brazil's elite militia, I have access to all military intelligence coming in and out of this country. I am not aware of an operation involving foreigners in our valleys. Why is that so?''

Wynett gestured to the room's only other soldier, a guard, standing behind him. ''It isn't prudent to speak in front of him.''

''He will stay.''

''As you wish. The gentlemen and the woman are part of a commando special force that illegally infiltrated your borders to kidnap me. I assume the gunship offered a way out of the jungle. I cannot be certain because I was insensible when they abducted me and commandeered the aircraft. I can assure you, sir, that neither I nor they have any interest in your drug camps.''

The colonel remained still, giving no indication that he believed or disbelieved the old man's story.

''Now I must ask you for a favor, Colonel,'' Wynett continued. ''It is imperative that you deliver me to U.S. authorities. They will reward you quite generously, I promise you.''

The colonel blew out the smoke of his cigar. The aroma suggested his fondness for Cuba. ''Why are you so important? Why would the U.S. military go to these lengths to retrieve you from this country?''

Wynett looked puzzled, as if the thought hadn't occurred to him before. ''Why not?'' he finally exclaimed. ''It's bloody good fun.'' He couldn't contain his laughter, and began giggling.

The colonel shook his head, truly disappointed. His old friend was mad, the colonel could see it in those dark eyes of his, and grossly unreliable. What had happened to him? The colonel returned his attention to Julie's waterproof instrumentation pack and, brushing cigar ash from the controls, pressed several buttons until the unit came to life. Its gridded amber screen displayed a waveform pattern he could not comprehend.

"It is a transceiver? But much too sophisticated for voice communications. This device records and unscrambles our transmissions. Yes?"

Wynett shrugged. "I believe the system identifies metabolic fingerprints from air samples. You must ask the woman for specifics."

The colonel returned the case to the table, then retrieved Wynett's six-inch aluminum canister. "Such a curious container. You will tell me what this is."

"I will tell you everything in exchange for transportation to the States. I must be in Virginia no later than thirty-six hours from now."

"I can arrange transit for you to São Paulo. That is all."

Wynett shook his head firmly. "That is most unacceptable, Colonel."

Frowning, Colonel Perez removed the canister's safety pin and, holding the trigger arm secure, thrust the cylinder beneath Wynett's nose. "Tell me what is inside or I will open it."

Wynett drew in a deep breath and put his hands on his head as though expecting the ceiling to fall on him. "Sir, I should warn you that it is dangerous to hold that container in so careless a manner. If you release the handle, you will fill this room with gas."

Wynett swung his arms down from his head with surprising swiftness. The vicious impact struck the colonel's canister-filled hand, and the cylinder clattered to the floor, hissing and sputtering. The colonel looked at his prisoner, astonished. Wynett screwed his eyes shut.

There was no visible gas cloud, but an acute odor accosted the colonel, a stench unlike anything he had ever experienced. The guard reached for Wynett but never laid a hand on him. He doubled over, unconscious before he hit the floor. Colonel Perez drew his sidearm, a Walther PPK fitted with a twelve-bore silencer. His eyes burned terribly. He exploded in a coughing fit, fell to his knees and began hacking up pieces of his lungs.

*　　*　　*

Blackbeard knocked Julie senseless with a wild brush of his hand, then grabbed her shirt and tore it off her back with one quick motion. She screamed. He ran his huge, callused hands down her back.

She whirled around, enraged, and slapped his face. "God damn you!"

Blackbeard's features darkened as he withdrew a handgun from his shoulder holster. He cocked the hammer.

He didn't see Julie lock her hands in a double fist. She struck the side of his head as though she were taking a home run–size swing at a hardball. "Asshole."

The brute stumbled backward with a grunt. His feet became entangled in his loose pants, and he scrambled to keep his balance. Julie lunged, throwing her weight on him. Desperately she grappled with him to get the handgun. The weapon fired, and a bullet tore into his leg. The brute howled as he lost his balance and, together, they fell backward against the wall with an awful crash, shattering the rotting planks and landing heavily in a heap together. Blackbeard looked in stunned disbelief at the splintered edge of a board jutting through the right side of his chest just beneath his rib cage. Julie rammed his hand against the wall, forcing him to drop the gun, then rolled off him.

Blackbeard struggled to rise but the board kept him impaled. He returned Julie's astonished stare with an eye that radiated dark waves of loathing. She crawled to the handgun. He snarled at her and spewed blood between his broken teeth when she picked it up. Flailing his arms, he grabbed for her, but she reeled out of his reach. She examined the weapon, a well-traveled .45. She didn't know enough about guns to determine if its safety was on or off.

Blackbeard slammed his palms against the wall. He let out a wail and, with animallike determination, began rocking back and forth, struggling to split the board from the wall and free himself.

Julie moved into the corner, as far away from him as the room would allow. "Marshall!"

Code: Alpha

* * *

The executioner lifted his considerable bulk from the stool and moved to his prisoners, directing a lecherous gaze first at Marshall, then at Williams. He appeared to derive erotic pleasure from running his hideously scarred thumb down the length of the knife's blade. He was ready to begin.

The executioner touched his knife's razor tip to Williams's right temple. The sergeant inhaled sharply.

Marshall glared at the brute. "You fucking swine."

The executioner ran the tip of the blade lightly down the side of Williams's face and neck, stopping at the edge of his shoulder. Tense and resentful, Williams felt the veins on his temples and arms stand out like branches as he strained helplessly against the straps, sweat cascading down his ebony features. The brute stepped back to admire his handiwork with a perverse look of pleasure.

"Stings a little," Williams huffed, almost giddy. "Bastard didn't hurt me!"

The executioner grinned, an amused look that told both men there was much more fun to come. He turned his attention to Marshall, touching the ominous blade to the back of the major's right ear as if considering how best to cut it off in one clean slice.

Marshall remained absolutely still and stared into the brute's dead eyes. The executioner jerked his hand, and Marshall felt a warm, slow trickle down his neck. "The bastard cut me!"

The brute grinned again, opened his palm and showed Marshall his right ear.

"Jeesssuuuus Christ—"

The cage door at the top of the steps creaked open, followed by descending footsteps. The executioner's face darkened and he swept his massive torso around to see who had breached his sanctuary. He abhorred intrusions once he began. A figure, backlit by the corridor above, stole down the steps. It wasn't a barracks soldier.

The executioner tossed the major's ear into a puddle, grabbed his knife by the blade and prepared to throw it. The shadow on the steps assumed a half-crouch and raised a hand-gun with both hands. There came three hollow cracks from a silenced weapon. Three rounds struck the brute square in the chest, pushing him backward with a grunt. He didn't go down. Three rivulets of blood streamed down the front of his butcher's overalls as he staggered forward, the knife still raised. Three more muffled cracks augmented the wounds on his chest. The executioner's massive head bowed in defeat and his bulk toppled forward, landing with a heavy splash on the mud floor.

The figure descended the remaining steps and moved into the ring of light beneath the chairs.

"I am in need of your assistance, Major," Wynett said. "It is imperative that you escort me to the States and deliver me to your superiors."

Chapter Twenty-six

"Wynett!" Marshall shouted. "For chrissake get these straps off us."

"I am prepared to make a trade with your government," Wynett said deliberately. "My safe return for a major American city."

Marshall's hardened gaze locked with Wynett's. "What are you talking about? What city?"

"I must be on United States soil no later than thirty-six hours from now or there will be no deal. I want your word as a soldier of honor that you will do everything in your power to deliver me to your superiors in that time frame. Otherwise I will leave you here and take my chances with the Brazilian guerrilla militia."

"What city?"

"Jesus, Joe," Williams said. "Tell the man what he wants to hear!"

"You got yourself a deal," Marshall spat. "I'll carry you home on my back, if I have to."

Wynett retrieved the executioner's formidable knife and hardly flexed as the keen blade slit the straps binding Marshall to the chair. He similarly released Williams from his binds. The sergeant jumped up and drove his boot into the chair, shattering it with a single, solid kick. He said to Marshall, "Jesus, Joe. Your ear . . ."

Marshall retrieved his shirt and used it to mop the flow of blood running down his neck. "Fucking bastard."

"There are three soldiers upstairs," Wynett said.

"Where are the others?" Marshall asked, pressing the bloody shirt over his missing ear. "Where's the colonel?"

"He was foolish enough to open my container."

"He what?"

"The colonel and his guard became victims of *pois gratter*," Wynett said, rolling the term around his tongue like a shot of fine whiskey, "a species of Mucuna plant. I synthesized a colorless crystalline compound that rapidly assaults the respiratory and central nervous system. On the skin it feels like slivers of glass. Inhaled, it causes excessive secretion to rapidly fill the lungs. A victim will quickly drown on his own mucus."

"So what makes you immune to *pois* whatever?" Williams asked, delicately touching the fine, deep cut on his face that now stung like bloody hell.

"*Pois gratter* is fatal only if inhaled, Sergeant. To the skin and eyes it is merely an irritant. I simply held my breath while in the room"—he held up the Walther—"and borrowed this from the good colonel after he succumbed."

Marshall reached for the Walther. "I'll need that to get you out of here."

Wynett relinquished the handgun but made no secret that he intended to keep the executioner's wicked-looking knife. Williams found a sturdy hatchet under the executioner's grindstone table and noted its razor-sharp blade. Marshall checked the Walther's magazine, snapped it back and charged the breech; there were only two rounds left.

"Let's go."

The major led the way up the stone steps to the barracks' main corridor. It stood empty. They passed the interrogation room, where Colonel Perez and his guard lay stretched grotesquely across the floor. Marshall could see the two had not

Code: Alpha

gone quietly to eternity. Williams spotted his Galil among their gear on the table and made a move to retrieve it.

"Leave it for now, Sergeant," Wynett warned. "*Pois gratter* is a heavy compound and does not dissipate rapidly."

Williams grunted his protest. Electronically distorted voices reverberated from the end of the hallway.

"The radio," Wynett said to the major. "I suggest you contact your people and arrange a rendezvous."

"Where's Julie?"

"Under close guard, I suspect."

Marshall moved swiftly down the hallway and slid next to the only open door. Two soldiers sat with their backs to the door in front of the outpost's radio, one listening through headphones, the other thumbing through pages of a lewd magazine.

Marshall eased open the door with a crack. The magazine reader glanced back at him. Marshall smiled amiably. However, there was nothing amiable about the silenced Walther he held steady in his hand. The soldier stood up suddenly. A dull crack from the handgun sent him looping backward. The second soldier, still wearing the headphones, whirled in his chair. Marshall didn't give him a chance to stand. The Walther's final round turned his face into a spray of blood and shattered bone as his body flailed backward, ripping the headphone jack from the console.

"My compliments, Major," Wynett offered in professional admiration.

The three slipped quickly into the radio room. Williams searched the slain soldiers for weapons and cursed aloud when he found none.

A shot roared from the room next to them, followed by shouting that was unmistakably Julie. Marshall and Williams burst into the hallway. The sergeant, his knuckles pale from an overly tight grip on the hatchet, half ran, half leaped at the door, his right leg thrust before him like a battering ram. The heel of his boot connected solidly and the door burst inward. He spotted Julie crouching in the corner, still pointing a hand-

223

gun at Blackbeard, who lay at her feet, a shattered board jutting from his back. A large-caliber exit wound had taken off the back of his head, revealing a half-empty cranial cavity.

Marshall went to her and eased the gun from her grip. She looked up at him, her distant eyes unfocused. At first she didn't appear to recognize him. Then she saw his wound. "Oh, my God! Joe, your ear . . ."

Marshall covered the side of his head with the shirt that he still carried.

Wynett thrust his head through the doorway. "Call your people, Major."

Marshall returned to the communications room and took a seat in front of the radio, a multicalibrated transceiver with satellite relay capabilities. He reset the frequency. Suddenly a voice, loud and with minimal distortion, began cracking orders in Portuguese through the speaker.

"Radio traffic between two helicopter pilots," Wynett said. "They work for the drug czar who owns this compound and many like it. They cannot be far."

As the exchange continued, Marshall watched the VU meters' needles bounce from vehicle to vehicle. "They're approaching from the northwest." He glanced at the digital readout. "Amplitude twenty decibels—sixty miles. They'll be here in twenty minutes." Marshall thrust a finger at the large wall map. "I need our coordinates."

Williams quickly pinpointed the outpost's position and read off the longitude and latitude coordinates of the camp, while Marshall reset the transceiver to the hangar's frequency. When the digital readout indicated an open channel, he spoke slowly into the microphone: "Alpha eight-seven-two to Odessa seven-four. Factor nine-two. Code one-seven-zero-one. Post error. Position one-seven-zero, four-two-seven. Repeat. One-seven-zero, four-two-seven. January Alpha one-nine-seven-zero. January two-seven-zero-four. Repeat—"

A shrill howl blared from the speaker, pegging the VU meters. Marshall grimaced.

"What's wrong?" Julie demanded.

"Jamming," Wynett said. "Our drug lord friends are on to us. Did you get through to your pilot?"

Marshall's expression registered anything but certainty. "I don't even know if he's still out there to hear me."

"Even if you did reach Youngblood," Julie said, "he'll never find us here in the jungle at night."

Marshall looked hard at Julie. "He'll see us—I'm burning this dump to the ground."

Chapter Twenty-seven

In the dungeon beneath the barracks, Williams dumped three barrels of stored aviation fuel across the mud floor. The fumes nearly overpowered him. He watched the liquid wash around the executioner's corpse with a particular note of satisfaction.

"Get up here, Sergeant," Marshall hollered down to him. "Now."

Williams bounded up the stone steps two at a time and met Marshall up top, kerosene lantern in hand. The major hurled the lantern down the steps. The glass shattered, igniting the fuel with an audible *whump*. Within seconds the basement was consumed by flames. Both men scrambled outside, where they joined Wynett and Julie huddled in the bush. They watched the barracks in silence. The flames already were stretching their fingers up through the corrugated roof, feeling for a grip that would tear the structure down. The basement's remaining barrels of aviation fuel ignited and exploded, turning the structure into a fireball that roared high into the night. Those who sifted through the smoldering rubble in the morning would find nothing in the foundation crater but charred grit and twisted metal.

"I've never seen you so jittery, Joe," Williams said.

Marshall looked curiously at his sergeant. "Jittery? I'm not jittery. Eager, maybe, but not jittery.''

Williams pointed to the major's hand. "Then what's with the shaking?"

Marshall was surprised to see his right hand shaking spasmodically, as though he were scared shitless. He ignored it, touched the bandanna Julie had fashioned to cover his ear and watched the blaze in silence. He saw the flames as Saint Vitus, a deadly and uncontainable force that consumed flesh the way the fire was consuming the barracks. He loathed to think that Gorgon now possessed it. Why didn't Tony's men kill him in this godforsaken jungle and be forever rid of him? The virus had become Marshall's real adversary now. He, Gorgon and Saint Vitus were inseparable, their fates inextricably intertwined. Like it or not, he was a soldier on a high-tech battlefield, the organism a part of the arsenal of a powerful enemy he swore to bring down.

Marshall heard the murmurs of a chopper approaching from the south—low, just above the tree line. Although he could see nothing in the night, he recognized the telltale wisps of the NOTAR RAH-66 Comanche, its rotors in whisper mode.

Julie heard it too and clutched Marshall's arm, panic swelling up inside her. He put a strong arm around her shoulder and pulled her close to him. He lifted her chin and searched those deep brown eyes of hers for the self-assured woman he had grown fond of. He hardly recognized her. "I'm taking you home."

Julie responded with a forced smile.

Williams stepped out of the bush and began waving his arms. A half a minute later, Youngblood's sleek, black helicopter descended from the night sky and set down in a clearing a prudent distance from the conflagration.

"You really piss me off," said Youngblood, climbing down from the cockpit. "I've been chasing you all goddamn day. Now hustle your asses. I picked up two choppers on radar approaching from the north about fifteen miles out."

"The major will need medical attention," Wynett said to the pilot.

Youngblood's boyish grin vanished when he recognized Wynett from the briefing photo. Then he noted the solemn look on each of their faces and Marshall's hastily bandaged ear. "Sweet Mother . . ."

Wynett attempted to help Julie into the chopper's passenger compartment, but she pushed him rudely away. "Don't you ever touch me." She slung her instrument package over her shoulder and stepped up into the chopper. Williams and Wynett followed.

Marshall climbed into the cockpit next to Youngblood and strapped himself in.

"Jesus, Major," Youngblood said, "what happened back there? Where's Colonel Martinelli, Stony and his men?"

"Just get us out of here, cowboy. Get us out of this damn jungle."

PART THREE
Lucy

"While the United States debates the development of a massive defensive effort against nuclear attack . . . the fact remains that this nation is almost entirely defenseless against chemical, biological and toxic weapons of mass destruction. Some of these weapons may already be secreted within our borders; others could be synthesized by our enemies within a matter of hours, or days at the most."

—Defense Consultants
Joseph D. Douglass, Jr.
and Neil C. Livingstone

Chapter Twenty-eight

Tuesday, 1445 hours
The Caribbean Sea
Twelve miles off the coast of St. Martin

The coastline of the Virgin Islands sank beneath the wing of the twin-engine seaplane as it banked into a clear Caribbean sky. Neither of the two cabin passengers paid notice to the view. Tarra withdrew a fully loaded Uzi from her leather rucksack and gripped the weapon firmly, drawing strength from its sleek power. She checked the clip, drove it home with a precision snap, then screwed on a fourteen-bore silencer.

Gorgon knew she loathed flying. He smiled at her preoccupation with the weapon, which seemed to have a calming effect on her. Her nervousness amused him. He couldn't resist taunting her anxious look during the plane's occasional sudden loss of altitude during the ascent. My poor Tarra, his spirited eyes mocked her. He touched her chin with playful fingers. "I know one experience that can always thrill you. Yes?"

She slapped away his hand, scornful.

"Put your thoughts elsewhere," he told her. "Think of pleasant things. Think of the tanker."

Seven hours.

That was how long it took the seaplane to cover twelve hundred miles of open sea before reaching the intercoastal waterway of South Carolina. The cabin's transponder signaled that they were in range of their target.

"We are landing?" Tarra asked, eager to be out of the plane, even if it meant trading it for a raft on the open sea.

Gorgon said nothing as he moved to the cabin's electronics rack and activated a modified Doppler radar unit. The size of the tanker ten thousand feet below them made it impossible to miss, even if the seaplane had inadvertently strayed miles from the shipping lanes. He fine-tuned the scan and relayed the ship's coordinates to his pilot. The aircraft banked awkwardly to intercept it, dipping too steeply to port and spilling Tarra hard against the bulkhead. She cushioned the impact with her Uzi.

Gorgon frowned at her. "Put it away."

He picked up the microphone, flipped the low-powered radio to TRANSMIT and adjusted the directional antenna on the aircraft's underbelly. When he spoke his voice was cold and serious, his English flawless. "Charleston, Charleston, this is Cessna four-seven-nine-two. Emergency. Repeat, emergency. We are four-six miles east-southeast of you, thirty-one degrees north latitude and eighty-two degrees west longitude. Two on board. Engine fire. Oil pressure zero. Losing altitude. I will attempt a water landing. Repeat. I will attempt a water landing. Stand by. . . ."

The radio had only enough power to broadcast the Coast Guard distress call thirty miles in a single direction. That was far enough. Tonight he wanted only one ship to hear his call.

Central Virginia
Twenty-five thousand feet

Reluctantly, and with great effort, Marshall dragged himself from beneath the mist-fogged depths of an exhausted sleep, recalling with more than passing irony that they were returning home aboard the same C-141 Starlifter that had taken them to

Sinope. Only tonight the huge aircraft bore little resemblance to a flying command center. There was no team left to command, no operation to monitor. After Youngblood had delivered them to a neutral air base in Kingston, Jamaica, a crew of American army medical volunteers had ushered them into a retrofitted vacation trailer, a cozy compartment with padded high-backed chairs. A medic had stitched and patched what was left of Marshall's right ear and gave him something to ease the throbbing.

Once aloft, Marshall and the others spent the afternoon debriefing on a four-hour conference call patched directly to General Medlock at the Pentagon. Now the team was indulging in long-overdue sleep. Marshall and Williams had conditioned themselves to function capably for days without adequate sleep, as long as they could doze for at least twenty minutes twice a day. Marshall agreed with Charles Lindbergh that any sleep at all adds to wakened strength, whether it was minutes or even seconds. Julie wasn't as fortunate. She was out of touch with her body's needs and hadn't felt the least bit sleepy or hungry since leaving Brazil. She felt restless and agitated, and couldn't wait to be on United States soil.

"We'll be landing in about twenty-seven minutes, people," the pilot's serious-sounding voice informed them over the aircraft's intercom. "There are garments for each of you in the lockers. Please put them on at this time."

Julie, grateful for something to do during the tedious ride home, opened one of the lockers and sorted through the suits. Her expression registered confusion. These weren't civilian clothing, nor were they standard army gear; the locker was full of coveralls and masks or, as Julie instantly realized, biological isolation suits. There were sizes for everybody. Someone wanted to make damn sure they didn't bring any strange pathogens ashore.

"The army's not taking any chances," Julie said to Marshall. "They're treating us as though we have the plague."

Marshall kept his eyes shut, ready to drift back to sleep if she would let him. "Come again?"

She held up a face mask. "They want us to wear these environment suits. A precaution, I'm sure, just like the first astronauts coming back from the moon. Routine isolation."

Williams's eyes fluttered open. "Gimme a break. I feel fine."

Slowly, reluctantly, Marshall opened his eyes and found it difficult to focus them. "We are okay, aren't we?"

Julie didn't answer. She was mulling over the situation in her mind, processing the data. They had all been exposed to a mutated strain of Saint Vitus. Did the Pentagon know something she didn't?

"Our bodies are fouled," Wynett offered from his seat in the corner of the trailer. "The abomination has made a home inside our bodies."

Youngblood, reclining next to him, stirred irritably and re-adjusted the cowboy hat over his eyes.

Williams snapped his seat upright. "You're full of shit, Wynett. I feel fucking fine."

Wynett smiled darkly, his face bathed in the trailer's eerie half-light. "No symptoms yet, Sergeant. Give it time. The virus is exploring our bodies, adapting as it propagates. Your people are aware of this and certainly will monitor us very closely. We are offering them a rare opportunity to study the effects of the organism on humans. They will learn much from our autopsies. Relax, sir; you will know what Saint Vitus has planned for you—but in its own time and in its own way."

Marshall dragged himself out of the pillowy chair and said to Julie, "Give Wynett another sedative so I don't have to hear his voice."

"He's already ingested the max. His mental state is extremely unstable. He'll go in and out of delusions. One moment he'll seem normal, the next . . ." She shrugged.

Marshall tried the door handle at the rear of the trailer. It wouldn't move. He grabbed the intercom mike and said to the cockpit, "What's with the locked door, Jack?"

"Relax, Joe," the pilot's metallic voice blared over the trailer's intercom. "We'll be on the ground in a few minutes.

Code: Alpha

Then you can ask the brass all the questions you want."

Marshall didn't like what he was hearing; the pilot was stalling until he could hand them over. But to whom and for what purpose?

"I want you to tell Medlock we're not putting on environment suits," Marshall said into the mike. "Jack, we're not infected. This bug works fast. You should have seen what it did to the plantation. We would be dead by now if it were still dangerous." He appealed to Julie. "Tell him!"

"No one's said you're infected, Joe," said the pilot's disembodied voice. "Washington just wants to be careful."

"Jack, you're bullshitting me."

The pilot's voice turned cold. "Joe, you can make this easy or you can make this difficult. Either way, once we're on the ground all of you will be wearing those suits."

The U.S. Eastern Seaboard
Twenty-two miles off the coast of Charleston, S.C.
2213 hours

A man aboard a small craft might have mistaken the 80,000-deadweight-ton crude-oil tanker *Lucy* for a moving mountain in the night. The length of two football fields, the tanker was traveling from Venezuela with a cargo for Universal Oil Company's refinery in Yorktown when Capt. Sergio Carlucci, master of the *Lucy*, received a radio message from a distressed plane. The call alerted him that a single-engine aircraft with two persons on board was going down somewhere in these waters. A routine call to the Coast Guard only added to the puzzle. The ship's radio officer had been unable to send or receive any other transmissions, nor could he locate the source of the problem. Captain Carlucci, a quiet, religious man with a strong sense of duty to aid his fellow man whenever possible, immediately ordered his engines cut to a crawl and posted his nineteen-man crew as lookouts.

A pair of high-power binoculars to his eyes, Carlucci surveyed the shallow swells. He saw nothing but blackness. And it was calm, perhaps too much so. His usually confident manner tonight was restless and apprehensive, his hopes of finding anybody alive out there diminishing with each minute. He stood by the rail, legs apart, and hid from the rest of his crew the deep lines of doubt etched around his fifty-four-year-old eyes. Darkness had settled in like a black shroud on their chances of spotting survivors. At least the weather was in their favor. Skies were clear with only light trade winds and calm seas. Unfortunately, the moonless night reduced the already small chances of finding wreckage or a lifeboat. A pity. Life was so precious. A few minutes more, Carlucci decided, and he would have no choice but to order the engines back to eighteen knots. . . .

"I can hear it!" shouted a port-side lookout, *Lucy*'s first officer Francesco Amorosi. The young officer stood stiffly at the rail, listening.

Captain Carlucci moved quickly to his side. Both men stood staring into the darkness, breathless, neither uttering a sound. Then Carlucci heard it too, a distant whistle piercing the night like a frantic bird cry. A minute later Carlucci was on the bridge turning the rudder hard over to port, initiating an emergency maneuver called the Williamson Turn, named after its developer, Comdr. John A. Williamson of the U.S. Naval Reserve. When the ship swung sixty degrees from its initial heading, Carlucci shifted to full rudder in the opposite direction until the tanker returned to its reverse heading. Because of *Lucy*'s size and speed, the ship would have passed whoever was out there by some distance. The Williamson Turn allowed the vessel to reverse direction and head back along its original path, a critical procedure to locate a person who had fallen overboard. Carlucci handled the controls himself, refusing to let anyone take responsibility for the precision turn. The former Italian naval officer completed the maneuver flawlessly, then ordered the engines cut to dead slow ahead–stop speed.

Carlucci, his gray-flecked hair glistening with sweat, raised the handheld radio to his lips but, as with ship-to-shore radio, he could neither receive nor send messages. Cursing, the captain retrieved a bullhorn from storage, stormed out onto the wheelhouse "wing"—an outdoor deck off the bridge that offered him a view of the ship's fore and aft upper decks—and called down to first officer Amorosi in Italian: "I want all deck- and searchlights directed into the water. Divide the men and position them on each side of the ship. And pray to God while you hurry; we will not get a second chance."

The crew on *Lucy's* port side spotted something on the fringe of the searchlights—a small rubber dinghy with two men on board wearing florescent orange life jackets, waving their arms. Carlucci piloted the vessel with its 600,000 barrels of crude oil to approach them. It took the crew less than twenty minutes to pass a line with a safety strap to the dinghy and bring both men aboard. The rescue went smoothly, by the book. Once completed, the fully laden oil tanker swung slowly around in the Atlantic and resumed its original course and speed north toward the Chesapeake Bay.

Carlucci watched the rescue from the wheelhouse wing deck. He nodded agreeably when he saw that both men could walk without assistance. Good. Very good. "Bring them up to the bridge," he called down to Amorosi through the bullhorn. "Tell them I will have my steward standing by with hot coffee while the medic examines them."

Captain Carlucci was pleasantly surprised when the door to the wheelhouse opened and he discovered that one of the lives he had helped save tonight was a woman's. His four other officers gathered to greet the survivors, and there were handshakes all around. The two guests remained mostly cold and detached—understandable, considering what they had just been through, Carlucci thought. He could not deduce their nationality. He watched the woman while the ship's medic tried to examine her for injuries. She remained uncooperative and reacted with irritation to his probing. Her dark, closely cropped hair and penetrating green eyes on an otherwise attractive face betrayed her rebellious soul, a youthful style Carlucci found offensive.

Her companion, a massive, intimidating man with dark features, appeared interested only in the bridge's instrumentation, which he surveyed meticulously with his probing eyes. While the steward served coffee to the guests and the officers on the bridge, Carlucci stood detached, regarding the two curiously. Both were wearing oilskin jackets beneath their life vests and carrying shoulder bags as though they had expected a water landing. Neither appeared particularly fazed by the crash, an experience that would have stricken most men with nervous shock.

"I apologize for inconveniencing you, Captain," Gorgon said in perfect, though accented, English, a language all foreign officers on American petroleum company ships were required to speak.

"Nonsense," Carlucci said. "It is my duty." He said to his communications officer, "Are you able to use the radio?"

The officer shook his head. "Still no luck, sir."

"Then use the MariSat transceiver to contact the Coast Guard though the Houston office. Inform them of the rescue."

"Your radios do not work," Gorgon said. "A seaplane circling your ship at four miles is equipped with very powerful radio jamming gear. It is the same aircraft that brought us to you." Gorgon withdrew a Ruger Mark 1 with suppressor from inside his jacket and pointed it at the captain's head. He drew back the hammer. "I am taking command of this vessel."

The radio officer reacted first. As he reached for the telephone receiver on the main console to alert the crew, a burst from Tarra's silenced Uzi tore his heart in two before he could depress the call button.

The chief steward made a dash for the door, sidestepping Gorgon. The terrorist lashed out and grabbed the steward's head, breaking his neck with a swift, hard pull backward.

The two remaining officers on the bridge watched in horror as Tarra swung her weapon around and executed each of them with a brief, silenced burst. Not a single round damaged any of the bridge's instruments. She watched with alluring eyes until the last of her victims had stopped kicking. Gorgon discharged a single round into the back of each's head to be certain. Tarra had effectively cleared *Lucy*'s bridge but spared Carlucci, whose kind, fatherly eyes were glazed in shock. He could only stare helplessly at Gorgon, silently asking why.

He soon had his answer. Tarra peered into the hood of the ship's JRC radar display, set the range for forty miles and adjusted the antenna beam for a narrow eastern scan. She moved the cursor over one of the phosphorescent signatures in the southwest quadrant and touched the identification button. The smaller vessel's transponder affirmed its identity.

"I have them," she announced. "Bearing one-eight-seven. Range, twenty-six kilometers. They are on a crossing course on my starboard."

Gorgon noted the ship's compass heading and instructed Carlucci, "You will alter your course seven degrees to starboard."

When the captain did not move, Tarra said, "I will do it."

"No!" Gorgon's deep voice resonated off the bridge's stark walls like a gun blast. He riveted his steel eyes on Carlucci. "You will do it."

Carlucci could hardly form the words. "Put away your weapons. This ship carries a highly volatile cargo. A catastrophe out here will benefit no one."

"I am well aware of what you carry, Captain," Gorgon said. "Cooperate, and I will need no weapons. Cross me, and I will destroy your hundred-million-dollar ship and its cargo."

"For God's sake, why? Who are you? What do you want?"

"You need only know," Gorgon said, "that I am the man who has taken your ship. I will have your cooperation as well."

Chapter Twenty-nine

Fort Detrick
2243 hours

The quarantine trailer crept back into the loading dock of one of Fort Detrick's bunkerlike buildings dedicated to biological research. The faceless structure looked disturbingly like a prison. Inside the trailer Julie, stuffed into a pair of bulky environmental overalls, slid next to Marshall on the trailer's wraparound sofa and waited, for what, she wasn't quite sure. She had given him one of her black bandannas to cover the bandages over his right ear, and he wore it like a headband. She liked the way he felt so close to her—strong and full of confidence—even if she had to feel him through a thick layer of nonporous material.

Marshall didn't notice her; his eyes were fixed on his left hand. After they had boarded the Starlifter, his hand had become prone to spastic fits of trembling, as though the limb had a mind of its own. The fingertips of his right hand were numb most of the time and his mouth was always dry. He tried to put it out of his mind by focusing instead on where they were going. He thought it strange that no one was talking to the survivors of Alpha about their eventual destination.

Their handling had been quick and methodical, like a shipment of machine parts. Their only view of the night was through a narrow windscreen at the rear of the trailer.

Marshall moved to the window and didn't like what he saw. An armed contingent of soldiers was overseeing their arrival under a forest of intense carbon-vapor lamps mounted on high stands. Dronelike technicians in white down coats were draping a polyurethane fabric shield over the trailer. *A gigantic prophylactic,* Marshall thought; *they don't even want us breathing the air.* He appealed to Julie. "What is this place?"

Julie joined him at the window. "The Slammer."

"Come again?"

"They're putting us in the army's biological receiving lab, eighty-three thousand square feet of lab space devoted to studying bacterial pathology. Casualties of a biological war are supposed to be brought here for observation and quarantine."

"You know a great deal about this facility, young lady," Wynett said, his alert eyes watching her closely.

Julie ignored him and explained to the others: "I spent two days of my internship here participating in a crisis exercise. I was role-playing a patient."

"Welcome to the real world." Youngblood snorted, squeezing next to Julie for a glimpse out the narrow window. He wasn't interested in the building. He wanted a closer look at the Bell-Ranger helicopter sitting under the spotlights of Detrick's helipad. It had the military markings of a VIP aircraft, the sort usually equipped with advanced telecommunications equipment intended for a mobile command vehicle.

"Helloooooo," he said, studying the chopper until it disappeared from his view. His gaze shifted back to the loading dock. Scowling, he took his seat and said, "Quarantine, my ass. I feel like a fucking prisoner."

"And so you are, Captain," Wynett said, adjusting the strap of his face shield before putting it on. He looked like a fat scuba diver in his environment suit. "When you surrendered your weapons and stepped into this compartment, you ceased to be a soldier. Your war is over. Now you are lab specimens.''

Williams appealed to the major. ''Say the word and I'll have us out of here in thirty seconds. I'll kick a hole right through that glass.''

''Spare us the heroics, Sergeant,'' Wynett said, trying without luck to make the mask fit comfortably over his face. ''Violate the integrity of this trailer and you will risk spreading a plague that could very well ravage your country.''

''Don't bullshit me,'' Williams barked. ''I feel fine. And since when did you care about spreading—''

''That's enough,'' Marshall snapped. But he could well understand the others' frustration; he too loathed confinement of any kind, especially hospitals.

The trailer gave a sudden jerk as it came in contact with the receiving dock, and there followed the sound of a heavy crash door grinding shut behind them, sealing them inside the fortresslike quarantine building. The intense light from the carbon lamps vanished as the doors closed, replaced by the warmer glow of the garage's incandescent bulbs.

''Please exit the vehicle and proceed into the building,'' a feminine metallic voice blared through a bullhorn with enough volume to penetrate the trailer's aluminum skin. ''Do not remove any personal possessions from the trailer. Do not attempt to breach the quarantine area.''

Julie draped the instrumentation package over her shoulder. ''This goes where I go.'' She slid on her face mask.

Marshall likewise snapped the mask over his solid features before pulling back the exit handle. The door opened easily, and he felt a distinct draft of air flow past him.

''Negative pressure,'' Julie noted, her voice muffled by the face shield.

''Say what?'' Williams asked, wincing from the too-tight mask over his bulging jowls.

''Air pressure inside the building is lower than the air outside,'' Julie explained. ''If there's a leak, the negative pressure

244

will draw outside air in, preventing stray organisms from escaping.''

"I'll sleep better tonight." Marshall waved them forward.

The group proceeded single file out onto the receiving dock. Their respirators concealed from them the smell of the dock's heavy oils, which sat in smeared puddles over the cracked concrete. They exited through a lone door into a small room outfitted with a tiny refrigerator, offering token hospitality to the center's new guests. The receiving room reminded Julie of the tiny kitchen in her campus apartment.

The door closed automatically. They could hear a high-pressure shower flooding the garage area, rinsing the trailer and their footprints with industrial-strength disinfectant and bleach. A second door opened into the complex.

"You are now in quarantine," the metallic voice informed them through the ubiquitous intercom system. "Please leave your suits in this room and proceed inside."

Williams yanked off his mask with a protesting snap. "Thank you."

The others peeled off their environment suits and tossed them unceremoniously in a pile in front of the refrigerator. Wynett chose to keep his suit and mask on. Julie led the way into the complex's L-shaped corridor, a sterile place with white walls and fluorescent lighting. Somewhere far-off a telephone was ringing. She proceeded down the longer of the two hallways, with the others following.

The facility resembled a clinic with its stark walls, a pervasive smell of antiseptics and closed doors with clipboard holders outside. Marshall thought he smelled alcohol, without realizing that the air itself was sanitized, the environment controlled down to the last drop of moisture and air pressure. He already disliked the place for its resemblance to a hospital. He hated hospitals.

Julie opened a door, passed inside and snapped on the switch, filling the darkened surgery with harsh fluorescent light. She set her instrumentation case on the examining table, then opened one of the room's many cabinets and surveyed the well-stocked supplies.

When she returned to the hallway, Williams was emerging from the room next door. "There's a dentist's chair in here," the sergeant said.

"I think this is a goddamn CAT-scanning unit," Youngblood said, closing a door to another.

"It's a magnetic resonator," Julie corrected him, then gestured to the doorways down the hallway. The other rooms are biochemical labs, and there's also an X-ray area."

"Where's the staff of doctors and nurses?" Marshall asked.

"There aren't any," she said. "This center is completely isolated from the biosphere. There's no need for anybody to risk coming down here with us, even wearing an environment suit. All examinations can be done remotely. There are fifteen private quarters in here, a kitchen, lounge, dining room, laundry, a gym—"

Farther down the corridor, a telephone began ringing again. Marshall cocked his head at Williams. "Check that out."

Williams nodded and moved briskly down the hallway.

The others continued their tour. "So how long do we have to stay in here?" Marshall asked Julie.

"At least twenty-four days," she said.

"Say what?"

"We could be here longer. Twenty-four days is the incubation period for most viruses. Unfortunately, St. Vitus is a complete mystery. Some tests can take months."

"You mean the rest of our lives," he spat.

"Joe, remember what we're dealing with."

"You're starting to sound like the rest of the brass. Maybe you want to make sure this creature of yours stays locked up, even if it means burying us in here with it."

Julie's face flushed with anger. "That's unfair!"

"While you people bicker amongst yourselves," Wynett said, removing his mask and running a hand through his tousled mane of white hair, "someone please direct me to a shower. I wish to turn in."

"Joe, the phone's for you," Williams shouted down the hallway. "It's General Medlock. And he doesn't sound happy."

"Terrific." Marshall thrust a finger at Wynett. "Consider yourself my prisoner. You and I are going to get to know each other very well. You don't eat, you don't sleep, you don't take a crap without asking my permission first. You got that?"

Wynett responded with a throaty chuckle.

Marshall said to Julie, "See if you can get some of this equipment up and running. I want blood tests started tonight."

"Joe," Williams hollered, "answer the goddamn phone."

Marshall rushed down the hallway to find the telephone.

While the others ventured off to find their quarters, Julie slipped into the corridor's last room—her favorite lab. The room was filled with refrigerator-size equipment covered with plastic dust covers. She found the light switch, and when the overhead fluorescent lights blinked on, her grin mirrored her satisfaction.

She pulled the plastic cover off a Sun minicomputer, powered it up and rolled a chair in front of the workstation. Despite the center's seventy-four-degree ambient temperature, she felt chilly. She longed for her favorite mug filled with flavored coffee and cream. Maybe she could persuade Marshall to brew some for her in exchange for a communications hookup with her Stanford adviser. She put the machine in a terminal emulation mode and logged on to Stanford's VMC mainframe. Just like home.

Out of habit she sent a quick message to her adviser, Dr. Nancy Shaw: U THERE?

Julie was surprised when a message beeped back almost immediately: I HEARD YOU WERE BACK IN TOWN. WHAT'S UP?

Julie looked at her watch and frowned. She typed: YOU'RE AT THE OFFICE LATE.

I DON'T SLEEP MUCH THESE DAYS. GENERAL MEDLOCK SAID YOU WERE COMING IN, AND I KNEW YOU WOULD LOG ON AND CHECK YOUR MAIL. NEED ANYTHING?

I MIGHT AFTER I GET SETTLED. ANYTHING GOING ON?

I LEFT A FEW NOTES IN YOUR E-MAIL IN-BASKET. NOTHING URGENT.''

THANKS. I'LL LOOK AT THEM TOMORROW.

I'LL BE HERE FOR A WHILE, IF YOU WANT TO CHAT.

THANKS. THERE'S A GREAT DEAL I'D LIKE TO TALK ABOUT. BUT NOT RIGHT NOW. TOMORROW. SEE YA. . . .

Julie logged off the VMC mainframe system and requested Detrick's mainframe environment.

PASSWORD?

She typed APRIL to log on to the army's mainframe and requested access to the lab's programs.

*****RESTRICTED ACCESS DENIED*****
*****RESTRICTED ACCESS DENIED*****
*****RESTRICTED ACCESS DENIED*****

"Oh, you bastards.'' Someone anticipated she would want to look at those files and wasn't about to oblige her curiosity.

Her fingers performed a well-choreographed dance over the keyboard as she disassembled the Master User ID file into its program code. The army's security measures were competent, but not nearly clever enough to keep her from simply rewriting the code so the program would authorize her password. She had yet to find a computer she couldn't ''crack route''—penetrating to the deepest level of the computer's operating system. Detrick's network was no exception, and once she cracked into the system's server, she would have the omniscience of the center's highest-ranking officer.

She reassembled the machine language and repeated her request.

RESTRICTED ACCESS. ENTER USED ID

She typed in ZJCM01.

PASSWORD?

She again entered APRIL.

The computer hardly blinked as it checked her authorization, found nothing wrong with it, then obediently displayed a list of options. She highlighted the first item on the menu:

Code: Alpha

The computer complied, showing her the Slammer's layout from its electronic security system all the way down to the ast penny nail.

Lucy
U.S. Eastern Seaboard off Charleston, S.C.

Lucy's first officer Francesco Amorosi didn't like the way Carlucci had summoned him to the bridge. The captain's intercom message, brief and unbecomingly curt, smacked of trouble. Had he fucked up? Hardly. The rescue had gone superbly well under his direction, and he already had visions of a company commendation and his picture in the employee magazine. And maybe a bonus too. Nothing less for a hero. Still, something about the captain's summons bothered him. It wasn't like Carlucci to get a bug up his ass and bark orders at his men like a boot-camp sergeant, especially after saving lives. He should be sharing the crew's jubilation. What the fuck was his problem?

Amorosi entered the wheelhouse and found the main lights switched off, forcing him to grope about in the glow of the ship's multicolored instrumentation. As he reached for the main light switch, something cold and hard touched the back of his neck, something made of steel. Startled, he feigned a calm response and raised his arms in an gesture of capitulation. The twenty-seven-year-old seaman didn't need much imagination to visualize someone with a gun standing behind him a finger-jerk away from blowing off his head. What was going on? Robberies, though common while anchored in African waters, were rare at sea. He knew better than to resist. He had no intention of giving his life to protect someone else's cargo.

"Are you First Officer Francesco Amorosi?" asked a deep, sonorous voice behind him.

Amorosi kept his gazed fixed forward. As his eyes adjusted to the dimness he saw another figure standing between two of the ship's radar consoles. It was Captain Carlucci; the poor man didn't look at all well. Now Amorosi understood the captain's curt radio message. It had been a warning made under duress. His eyes begged the captain for an explanation, a reassuring signal that all would be well. But Carlucci's eyes remained downcast, helpless, deeply ashamed of what was happening to him. Amorosi's hands began shaking.

"Are you Amorosi?" the deep voice hissed, its owner's lips close to the young mate's ear. "I will not ask you again."

The young officer drew in his breath sharply and screwed shut his eyes, expecting the worst. He nodded.

"Good," Gorgon said.

Amorosi winced when the cold metal jabbed the back of his neck and prodded him forward. He walked several paces between the consoles, his legs moving automatically, the gun barrel boring into his neck. Spent shells on the floor felt like rocks under his feet. Gorgon ordered both men out onto the bridge's port wing deck.

The open air had grown cold and windy and the night black. They were entering a storm system. Amorosi, in the lead, saw several figures huddled against the chest-high metal wall. He could smell a peculiar stench in the chilly night air, a smell that reminded him of sawdust. Some primordial instinct told him that this was the smell of death. He heard a woman's voice, a throaty moan combined with long, heavy breaths, as though she were enjoying some deep satisfaction. His mind couldn't comprehend the contradiction of sight and sound and smell.

A figure rose from the shadows, stepped into the glow from the wheelhouse and riveted a pair of haunting green eyes on Amorosi. Despite the dimness he recognized the woman from the sea rescue, standing naked to the waist, rubbing blood-soaked fingertips over her ample bosom.

"He is yours," Gorgon said to her.

Tarra smiled alluringly and took Amorosi's trembling hand into hers. Her touch felt wet, warm, soft, reassuring. His breathing eased; he didn't want her to feel the convulsive fear that had tied his chest into knots.

Code: Alpha

She led him into the shadows at the end of the deck, and Captain Carlucci heard a sucking sound that suggested deep, lustful kissing. It didn't last long. Amorosi let out a shriek, a hideous sound Carlucci would never forget. He cursed in his native Italian and forced himself to move to help the boy, but Gorgon launched a huge hand, blocking his way.

"Why do this to my men?" the captain implored.

Gorgon put a finger to his lips, and they both listened to the young mate's anguished whimpering. Amorosi's tortured cries grew muffled as though he were being roughly gagged. And then came a silence, an emptiness far more unsettling than any shriek.

Carlucci shivered as Gorgon put a bearlike paw on his shoulder and led him forward. The captain looked past the silent figures sitting with their backs against the wall. In the corner sat Tarra, rubbing her hands seductively over Amorosi's naked chest. Gorgon ordered her away, then pressed a flashlight into Carlucci's hands.

"See what she has done," Gorgon said, gesturing to the line of motionless figures.

Carlucci shivered. He held no illusions that he too would sit here among these corpses if he didn't do exactly as the beast ordered. Cursing his lack of courage, he knelt before the figures and switched on the flashlight with trembling fingers. He probed each face with the light and recognized his chief steward, radio officer, ship's medic and chief engineer. All of them were dead, of course. Carlucci crawled on hands and knees for a closer look at the fifth man. At first he did not recognize him. Amorosi's blood-soaked cheeks were bloated as though he had been forced to eat something he had violently resisted. A strange appendage still protruded from his mouth.

"My God . . ."

Amorosi's eyes ceased blinking and turned lifeless, staring vacantly back at the captain in solemn resignation, warning him that any resistance simply wasn't worth risking a similar fate. Carlucci bowed his head, deeply ashamed. *Forgive me, my son, for letting you die at the hands of these barbarians.*

Would he vomit or pass out? He probably would do both, and in no particular order.

"You will follow my instructions," Gorgon said. "Disobey me, and you will sit here among them."

Carlucci rose unsteadily to his feet and, fighting the urge to retch, turned away from his hideous group of comrades, his face a white plaster. "Why . . . murder him . . . *and* torture him . . . ?"

Tarra cocked her head questioningly. "Torture? He shared with me an experience any man would give his life to enjoy."

Carlucci directed his rage-filled eyes at the woman and said in a voice still phlegmy with fear, "For the love of God, you fed him his own testicles."

She ran her tongue over her lips. "He would tell you how much he enjoyed it . . . if he could still talk." She giggled wickedly.

Carlucci threw up all over himself. Half-digested beans dripped down the front of his shirt and smelled of vomit. He collapsed onto both knees until the contents of his stomach had emptied onto the rubber mat between his legs. He noticed another odor; he had urinated in his pants.

A large hand rested solidly on his shoulder. "Tarra has a peculiar need for men," Gorgon said, his voice queerly apologetic. "At the age of eight years, four men raped her and left her for dead in the desert. The incident only aroused her hunger for coitus—she obsesses on it as few women do—and she satisfies her contempt for men in this perverse way. Never again will she be used by a man. Do not let her see your love for this ship or it will anger her; she is very jealous. Meanwhile, you still are *Lucy*'s captain. I will not take that from you. I need a man sufficiently skilled to handle this vessel. Only her true master will know how this ship will behave under all circumstances. You will keep normal radio contact with the owner of this vessel and proceed without incident to your destination in Yorktown. Do exactly as I say and you will live and prosper from our acquaintance. Disobey me, and

252

I will let her kill you—her own way. Do we have an agreement?"

A wave of total helplessness washed over Carlucci; his fear of these monsters was more crippling than anything he had ever experienced in his life. "But you killed my officers . . . my first mate. . . ."

"Tarra will be your first mate, and I will provide you with a new crew. In exactly twenty minutes I want you to stop all engines and stand by. Will you carry out those simple instructions for me, Captain?"

Carlucci, shivering spasmodically, nodded.

"Good. Captain Sergio Carlucci, you will now take charge of the bridge."

An hour after Gorgon and Tarra had come aboard, only Captain Carlucci knew that *Lucy* had been hijacked. If the remaining crew of sixteen suspected anything, no one came forward with their suspicions; no one called the captain to ask questions.

On Gorgon's command, Carlucci stopped all engines and ran out the cargo boom.

Carlucci quickly dismissed the barrage of inevitable questions from the ship's officer of the deck that followed. And then they waited. A fifty-foot tramp steamer slipped alongside in the moonless night and offloaded three truck-size pallets. Seventeen minutes later, *Lucy* resumed her original heading and speed, with fifteen of Gorgon's soldiers who brought with them a special cargo.

Chapter Thirty

Quarantine

Marshall slipped inside a closet-size room off the quarantine center's recreation area and sat down at a tiny desk with a reading lamp and a push-button telephone. The door closed with a solid click, causing a pressure change in his ears. The room was a soundproof anechoic chamber. Marshall picked up the phone's receiver and said abruptly, "Tell me what the hell is going on."

He heard only the low static of a poor connection, as though Medlock had hung up. Finally the general's voice, chillingly terse, said, "Know just one thing, mister: you don't talk to me like I'm one of your goddamn grunts."

Marshall pictured Medlock's vulture face and clenched beak on the other end ready to chomp off his head in a single bite. The major breathed a sigh of apology. "Sir, it's been a bad week. And it isn't helping matters that we're locked up with a raving psychotic. You can make it up by sending me and Williams back to Fort Bragg."

"I can't do that, Major," Medlock said, his tone tempering. "You'll stay in quarantine for at least three weeks. And sorry about the arrangements; under the circumstances it's just not possible to stow Wynett anyplace else. Besides, we'll need to interrogate him." The apology was in his statement, not his voice.

"Sir, what about Gorgon? As I explained to you this afternoon, we have to assume he's planning an assault on the U.S. mainland with at least five tanks of the organism—"

"Slow down, Joe. It's being handled."

"Handled? What's being handled? Who's handling what?"

"We're assembling a group of commandos from all Special Forces units and flying them to our staging area at Oceana."

"Sir, let me mobilize Delta."

"I must be speaking Arabic." Medlock grunted. "Didn't I make myself clear about your quarantine?"

"I want you to put Major Warren in charge of Squad Six. He knows the drill. I can feed him intelligence—"

"Negative. The situation is being handled."

Marshall could barely contain his anger. "Sir, don't write us off yet. Hell, nobody's even examined us yet. I owe Colonel Martinelli—"

"You'll do exactly as I tell you, mister. Be thankful you're alive, for chrissake. Meanwhile, you're still part of Alpha. You can help me a great deal by getting Wynett to talk. I need every goddamn piece of information you can get from him."

"General . . ."

He heard a click; then another voice came on the line. "Major, this is Commander Frank Haake of the State Department. I need to ask you some very specific questions about Operation Containment. Just give me five seconds to make sure this machine is recording everything."

Marshall sank back wearily in his cheap fabric chair. The silence inside the soundproof room was unsettling. He couldn't remember ever feeling this impotent.

Lucy

Gorgon's fifteen soldiers, their faces blackened, swept through *Lucy* with meticulous precision and speed, leaving in their wake a trail of corpses. Four mercenary soldiers split off from the main assault group and descended deep into the bowels of the tanker. With sawed-off shotguns braced in front of them, they marched methodically through the engine room, control room, boiler room and lower pump room. They checked behind every pipe and conduit large enough to conceal a man. Their weapons and cartridges were carefully chosen to protect the machinery, pipes and bulkheads from damage.

Lucy's crew never had a chance to offer even token resistance. Seaman Dinelli, the ship's chief engineer, reacted instinctively to the sight of the death squad storming into the boiler area. The Italian officer's fist closed around the only weapon he could find—an eleven-pound steel wrench. An ear-splitting blast from a shotgun tore off his wrench-toting arm at the elbow, while a second blast blew the pale look of shock from his face . . . and every other feature.

One of Dinelli's maintenance men, a young Filipino, grabbed the intercom mike, opened a channel to the bridge and shouted in poor English, "Captain, there are guns . . . men in the boiler—" A blast, and then he too was dead.

The three remaining crewmen in the engine room, their hands raised in an unmistakable gesture of surrender, stared helplessly at the row of stubby shotgun barrels pointed at them. Their startled faces, white and strained, pleaded for mercy. A series of rapid blasts from the shotguns transformed them into a heap of slaughtered corpses.

Their business of killing finished, Gorgon's mercenaries filed out of the engine room, leaving behind rivers of blood streaming like rain through the grated catwalks.

The assault had been easy, far easier than the elaborate scheme had called for, evidence of Gorgon's commitment to painstaking planning and careful execution. None of *Lucy's* unarmed crewmen had offered any serious resistance. The tanker was a product transport vessel, not a warship, and there were no weapons aboard to oppose the assault.

Minutes after the mercenaries boarded, all but one of Carlucci's crew lay dead. The lone survivor—a young crewman named Palombini—was led hands on head outside to the ship's upper deck, where he sat under close guard in the chilled night air. Gorgon walked out to him. Tarra strolled at his side, as did a slumped Captain Carlucci, his eyes downcast.

Gorgon towered over the young crewman who had lost four fingers on his right hand in the brief struggle to take the ship. He was cradling his bloodied hand in his lap, his face wet from weeping. Gorgon's intense dark eyes memorized every fear-induced line in the young Italian's face as he sat huddled on deck, trembling.

Gorgon said to him in English, "Your injuries are unfortunate for a man so young. Tell me how much you loathe me for what I have done to you."

Palombini didn't understand him, his stricken eyes staring questioningly at the captain.

"He is a good man with a family," Carlucci said. "He operates the ship's cargo pumps, a job very useful to us."

Gorgon shook his head viciously. "That is not why I had him spared until now. I wanted you to see this."

Gorgon signaled Tarra with a quick jerk of his head. She drove her Uzi into the young crewman's disbelieving face and squeezed off a single round. Palombini let out an animallike yelp and spilled backward, spouting blood from both his mutilated hand and his head wound. Tarra knelt down and gently kissed his forehead.

"I wanted you to see the death of your last crewman."

Carlucci, his face pale, collapsed onto his knees and wept openly, his fists clenched in frustration and despair. Crushed was his spirit to challenge these unspeakable atrocities. He kept asking his God, *What should I have done? What should I have done?*

Chapter Thirty-one

Quarantine
2255 hours

Julie didn't hear him slip into the room behind her. She had no idea how long he'd been standing there watching her stare at the computer screen before he gently placed his strong hands on her shoulders and began massaging the muscles at the base of her neck with deep, sensual movements of his thumbs. His probing fingertips felt very good, but his closeness made her uncomfortable. Feeling her tense up, he spun the chair around and squatted in front of her.

"You don't like that?" Youngblood drawled, taking her hands into his. "Let me try something else."

Julie's eyes grew wide when he leaned forward and planted a perfect kiss on her lips. She rolled backward, ramming her chair into the computer workstation's table.

"I'm sorry," Youngblood said. "That really wasn't planned. Ever since I met you I've wanted to do that. No woman has ever interested me as much as you. God, you're beautiful . . . and smart, very smart."

Julie was speechless. Not that she didn't find Youngblood attractive; she did, just as she imagined every other woman did who laid eyes on him. She just couldn't picture them together. No, that wasn't it, was it? She couldn't picture herself with any man, especially a good-looking one she had to work with. Relationships always got in the way of her work; besides, this wasn't the time or place for romance. *There you go rationalizing again.* The truth was she didn't know how to respond to Youngblood's affections, or anyone else's for that matter. She hadn't been programmed for affection, hadn't done any research on intimacy. Romance 101 wasn't a required course in her Ph.D curriculum. Nor had she ever seen how it was done at home, she realized, having been raised by a stoical father who kept his feelings hidden from her.

"Julie," Youngblood said gently, "what I'm trying to say is that when we get out of here I'd like to take you out to dinner, or to a show, or . . . hell, anywhere you like. Just name it. But if you're involved with someone else . . . or just don't want to . . ." His voice trailed off and he gave her a sad, though thoroughly charming smile.

"Is there a problem?" Marshall's curt voice boomed from the doorway. "A problem that takes two of you to solve?"

Julie and Youngblood whipped around with a start. Something was wrong—Julie could see the tension lines on Marshall's face. For a hopeful instant she thought it might be jealousy.

"I'm calling a meeting in the lounge," Marshall said. When neither of them moved, he added, "Right now."

Youngblood rose stiffly from his squat in front of Julie. "Jesus, Joe, can't it wait till morning? It's been a long day and we're all spent. Maybe after a good night's sleep—"

"Save it, mister," Marshall said, his voice as empty and frigid as Arctic rock.

"Yes, sir," Youngblood snapped.

Julie grinned. Yes, perhaps he was jealous. Interesting.

"And as for you," Marshall said, riveting his hardest military stare at her, "I want you to draw blood samples from everybody and find a way to test it. Send the samples to your friends upstairs, if you have to. Do whatever you need to do, but I want to know by morning if we're sick."

"Oh, so I'm your nurse now."

But Marshall was gone, the sound of his boots echoing heavily down the corridor, sending a not-to-subtle warning for everybody to hustle their ass.

Marshall directed everyone to a seat in the center's lounge, a congenial study area that offered several overstuffed sofas and deep chairs, a wet bar and two circular tables ideally suited for card games. The room could have passed for a lounge in a university student union. Julie commandeered one of the tables and laid out a medical pouch containing a syringe kit and blood specimen vials.

"Oh, Jesus," Youngblood said when he saw the needles. "I hope you've done this before."

"Only once." She grinned, attaching an eighteen-gauge needle to the first syringe. "On a hamster. And I'm sorry to say it died in the process."

"I need to build up iron in my blood with a midnight snack." Youngblood stooped before a knee-high refrigerator behind the wet bar and opened it. "Helloooo. Can I interest anybody in a cold beer? I also have blush and white wine . . . and diet Cokes."

"A blush sounds perfect," Julie said.

"You got it," Youngblood said, grabbing a chilled zinfandel.

Wynett sank comfortably into an overstuffed chair that meant to swallow him and said to the chopper pilot, "What is the chance of securing a Scotch and water?"

Youngblood opened the lower cabinet of the wet bar and inspected two rows of hard liquor. "Someone thought of everything."

"Negative on the liquor," Marshall said. "Alcohol is off-limits in here."

Youngblood frowned; he had had his heart set on one of those beers. Williams, grinning, sensed a barroom brawl brewing.

260

"Major," Wynett said, "surely you are not pretending to still be on duty? There is a time to make war and a time to recharge. I believe it is now time to indulge our vices."

Williams chuckled good-naturedly; he knew Marshall's prohibition of alcohol when on duty. That meant they would be drinking lots of Cokes.

"The Army's gone to a lot of trouble to make this prison comfortable for us . . . too comfortable," Marshall said. "Forget the booze. We're not sacrificing our edge for a couple of beers."

"What edge?" Youngblood snorted.

"Stow it," Marshall said.

Julie held up the syringe. "People, let's just get this over with so I can turn in. Who's first?"

When no one volunteered, she beckoned Youngblood with a mischievous crook of her finger. In bold macho fashion, he took a seat at her table and rolled up his sleeve. "Hurt me, baby."

"Make a fist," Julie instructed. He created an impressive muscle for her. She wrapped a rubber tourniquet around his arm above the elbow and searched for a suitable vein to tap. She found one and hastened the dreaded anticipation by getting quickly to the point. Two minutes later she had three vials full of his blood, which she labeled and secured in the carrying case.

"Who's next?"

Again nobody volunteered, so Marshall volunteered Williams. When the gunnery sergeant made no effort to move from his chair, Julie brought her syringe and tourniquet to him.

Youngblood, flexing and unflexing his needle-pricked arm, said, "So what did Medlock have to say?"

Marshall settled his weight against a table and folded his arms over his chest. "General Medlock isn't going to let us out of here until he's certain we're not sick. And that could take weeks. Meanwhile he's going after Gorgon, though he won't say how or when. But Gorgon's ass is mine. We've got to convince Medlock there's nothing wrong with us. The sooner we get a clean bill of health, the sooner we get out of here.''

Williams and Youngblood bobbed their heads in agreement.

"Spare us your military bravado, Major," Wynett scoffed. "Your war is over. Now please, I wish to return to my quarters, preferably with a bottle of Seagram's and a cache of ice. I would very much like to fall into a deep sleep with both those items under my arms.''

Marshall dragged a chair from beneath the table, spun it around in front of the old man and sat astride it. "You're our ticket out of here. I need to know what Gorgon plans to do with those tanks you brewed up. And you're going to tell me everything.''

"Major, I don't see the point belaboring—"

Marshall lunged forward, spilling his chair, and grabbed the front of Wynett's shirt into his fists, popping two buttons. Stunned, everyone looked mutely at him.

"Listen to me, you shithead," Marshall hissed, his rage held fragilely in check. "I've had a very bad week, thanks entirely to you. Don't fuck with me.''

Wynett, sitting arrogantly composed, said, "You still don't understand, do you, Major?''

"Understand what?''

"That Gorgon owes me ten million American dollars.''

Marshall's grip on him tightened and his teeth clenched. "For chrissake, what's that got to do with anything?''

"Gorgon stole from me. I fully intend to secure payment from him or reclaim my merchandise. I don't want your muddled interference.''

Marshall released Wynett and looked hard at him. For the first time he saw him as he truly was: a madman. "Is that all this means to you? Money?''

"I am a realist, Major," Wynett said, "not a fool driven by misplaced notions of honor, God or patriotic duty. I have no intentions of writing Mr. Gorgon from my books. I cannot stay in business if I give away what I labor to produce.''

"You're not going to see a dime from this.''

"I disagree, Major. Your superiors will provide whatever I request. They will even take me to Gorgon under military escort, if I decide that will serve my best interest. I still am deliberating my options."

"Screw your options. You're gonna hang."

"There will be no charges filed against me. Not now. Not ever. Considering what I know and the short time before Gorgon reaches your shores, your superiors will need to act very quickly. I will give them a statement for a price: twenty million American dollars and no charges against me. The deal is nonnegotiable."

Julie knelt next to Wynett's chair with her syringe kit. "Roll up your sleeve."

Wynett ignored her, keeping his eyes locked on the major's. The two just stared at each other, deadlocked, each knowing full well what was at stake. Julie helped herself to Wynett's arm and wrapped the rubber tourniquet above his elbow. He didn't react when she inserted the needle into his vein; in fact, he didn't appear to feel anything. Three minutes later Julie put away her syringes, retreated to the table with his blood specimen and watched Wynett carefully. Almost immediately he began to perspire as though the climate-controlled room had become too warm for him.

"I believe you are next, Major," Wynett said. "Though I doubt Miss Julie will draw anything but idiocy from those veins of yours. . . ."

Wynett looked suddenly pale. A wave of nausea swept over him, and his arm where Julie had pricked him began to burn. He directed his suspecting eyes at her, his fingers touching a tender welt on his forearm. When he spoke his words were slightly slurred. "What have you done to me, Miss Julie?"

Marshall glanced questioningly at her.

"A sedative," she said. "If you want specifics, it's an alkaloid—$C_{17}H_{21}NO_4$."

Wynett let out a huff of laughter, his eyes assuming an inward look. "Scopolamine. My dear Julie, I am disappointed. I would have preferred *datura stramonium,* a far more effective sedative and much more interesting to the patient, though I have seen it used only by a remote tribe in Brazil. Believe me, it is worth the trouble to obtain it.''

''Sorry, but scopolamine was all I could find. It's a proven method of loosening tongues.''

''You'll have to . . . do . . . better. . . .''

Wynett's eyes rolled back into his head and his jaw dropped. He appeared deathly ill, and for a moment Marshall feared he would go into cardiac arrest. The major looked at Julie, who signaled reassuringly that the old man's reaction was normal.

''He's yours to question,'' she said, ''until he passes out.''

''How long?''

''I may have given him too much. He can go under at any moment. He'll fight you. And you'll have no way of knowing if his information is accurate.''

''Terrific.'' Marshall, willing to try anything, expecting nothing, knelt before Wynett's chair. ''Okay. Tell me all about it.''

Wynett rolled his head around in euphoric rhythm. ''You may have stumbled onto something, Miss Julie, though it is not as pleasant as Scotch.'' Then he frowned. ''Bastard stole my merchandise. . . .''

Williams moved next to Marshall and whispered, ''He's hung up on this deal with Gorgon. Go with it.''

Marshall looked hard at the old man. ''What will he do with your merchandise?''

''Bastard . . . stole my merchandise. . . .''

''Yes, yes. Is your merchandise worth the price?''

Wynett's eyes suddenly opened, and he appeared alert. ''Oh, yes. I gave him quality merchandise.''

''How much does he have?''

Wynett grinned. ''Five.''

''Five? Five tanks?''

''Yes. Twenty-five liters.''

''Twenty-five liters of Saint Vitus?''

''Yes.''

"How will he deploy it?"

Wynett's eyes drifted shut and he appeared troubled. "Several ways ... missiles ..."

"Missiles? He has Scud missiles?"

Wynett shook his head. "No, sir. Even the improved Scud-B's surface-to-surface launcher could not adequately deploy a viral warhead. ..."

"What then?"

"Procyon computer-guided, independently targeted warheads ..."

"Jesus. How did he get his hands on those?"

Wynett smiled. "He purchased them from me."

Julie looked questioningly at Marshall and mouthed, "What's a Procyon?"

"He will harness the creature," Wynett said. "Operation ... Harness ..."

"Tell me about Operation Harness."

"Distribution ... law of supply and demand ... addiction ... you are addicted to it and he knows it."

"Addicted?" Marshall looked at Julie for an answer. She had none. "Are you saying the virus is addictive?"

Julie shook her head. Marshall realized how stupid the question sounded as soon as he'd asked it.

Wynett slurred, "You will welcome him inside your borders because you are addicted. ..."

"You're not making sense."

"Trojan House ... you will welcome him and the creature inside ... and then he will be free to strike ... the missiles are merely his backup." Wynett's head began rolling from side to side and his speech became notably more slurred. "Sweet crude ... sweet crude ... sweet crude ..."

"Sweet crude? Do you mean oil?"

"No one will stop him ... you will welcome him inside ... you are addicted to it ... you need it. ..."

"Wynett—"

"No one will stop him ... you are addicted ... you need what he carries. ..."

"I don't understand."

"So secret . . . floating city . . . floating bomb . . . no one can touch him . . . too dangerous. . . ."

Marshall's icy stare was riveted on his interrogatee. "I need to know where Gorgon is taking the virus."

Wynett let out a huff of laughter. "Pay me first. . . ."

"Negative."

". . . grand lady . . . follow her down to a bridge by a fountain . . . she sits in the sky . . . with diamonds . . ." Wynett laughed deliciously.

Marshall appealed to Julie. "What's he babbling about?"

"He's fighting you."

"I can see that."

". . . marshmallow pieeessssss . . ." Wynett's head rolled forward onto his chest, where it remained, unmoving. He was out cold.

Marshall rose stiffly to his feet. He felt suddenly tired. "Marshmallow pies? Was he just babbling?"

No one had an answer. With Wynett out Marshall knew there was nothing more he could do tonight; besides, he needed time to sort out the old man's rambling. "What about the blood analysis?" he asked Julie. "How long before you know something?"

"I'll put the specimens in the pathology lab's PCR unit and let it run through the night. We should know something by morning."

Marshall nodded agreeably.

"There is one unfinished piece of business before I can get started," she said.

"Name it and you got it."

She stuck an eighteen-gauge needle on a syringe. "I need some of your blood."

General Medlock pushed himself away from the small conference table and considered everything he and his staff had just heard over the table's 360-degree speaker. The general's solid military demeanor allowed a smile. In fact, he felt giddy.

Code: Alpha

The session had gone surprisingly well, better, in fact, than he had dared to hope. The fidelity from the quarantine center's strategically placed microphones surprised even him, giving him the bizarre feeling that he had been part of the group's meeting two floors below. Leaving Wynett in quarantine with Marshall had been a masterstroke. The general stood up, stretched the cramps from his legs and moved to a rack of audio gear at the opposite end of the conference room. He squeezed the technician's shoulder, quietly thanking him for the audio hookup.

"I want you to send a copy of that tape over to my office for analysis," Medlock said.

"Yes, sir."

General Medlock turned to Dr. Nancy Shaw sitting rigidly at her computer terminal, a solemn frown pasted on her face. He placed his hands on her shoulders. She shrugged them away.

"I just want you to know how much I appreciate what you're doing for me," Medlock said.

"Don't make this any worse by bullshitting me, General," she said, her eyes glaring. Her blunt features were taut and intense and stone serious, chiseled from seventeen years of fighting higher-academia politics. "I'm not one of your grunts, nor did I volunteer to be here. I fully intend to file a complaint with the State Department at my first opportunity."

Medlock waved away her threat. "Exercise whatever rights you think you need to, ma'am. But I know you'll feel differently after shaking hands with the president and hearing him thank you personally for your help during this crisis."

"I don't like spying on people, especially one of my students. Why don't you level with them? Why manipulate them like this?"

"Because I'm out of time. Small cohesive groups will draw on extraordinary powers of problem-solving when they're backed against a wall. Marshall's a very resourceful man. I'm counting on him to find out what an interrogation team may not. Bonding is a powerful motivator, and I will exploit it to the fullest.''

''That's bullshit, General.''

''Considering the lives at risk here, I'll use every resource available in whatever ways I see fit. And that includes your services. Are you clear on that point or do I have to get an executive order?''

''Yes, sir, General. Very clear.''

Medlock's birdlike features broke into a self-satisfied smile. ''Good. I want you to use your database to unravel Wynett's babbling. Draw correlations. See if it means anything. Get me whatever you can.''

Medlock didn't wait for her acknowledgment. He returned to the conference table, where the members of his task force were brainstorming each part of Wynett's interview, developing hypotheses. ''Okay, people. What's it all mean? Higgins?''

Maj. Samuel Higgins, BERT's logistics officer, cleared his throat as he stood. He worked best on his feet, pacing. ''We agree that Wynett's reference to sweet crude means a lighter grade of crude oil, which has little or no sulfur.''

''No shit,'' Medlock spat. ''So how's he going to use it?''

Major Higgins smiled broadly. ''Wynett told us. 'Floating city, floating bomb.' Gorgon may be smuggling the virus aboard an oil tanker.'' Heads around the table bobbed in eager agreement.

''What about those goddamn Procyons? Jesus, that sucks. Can he launch them from a tanker?''

Dr. Theodore Gruber, BERT's science consultant, nodded. ''No problem. Even the smallest tanker would have a deck wide enough to accommodate the launch platform and electronics van.''

Lieutenant Hernandez couldn't contain his eagerness. ''The name of the ship. Find out the name of the goddamn ship and we've got him!''

''Lucy!'' Dr. Shaw shouted from her workstation. ''Gorgon's tanker is named *Lucy*.''

Code: Alpha

All eyes turned to her. "Where in hell did you come up with that?" Medlock said, standing.

"The song," she said, barely containing the excitement of her find. "That's what Wynett was raving about. He was teasing us, reciting the lyrics to the Beatles' song 'Lucy in the Sky With Diamonds.' He was telling them, yet hiding it from them."

Medlock looked to the others for validation. He counted two nods, the rest shrugs. "Never listened to them," the general said, making his way around the table to her workstation. "I prefer Nat King Cole."

He glanced over her shoulder at the hypercard program on her Macintosh screen. His eyes quickly followed the stacks of opened cards, reviewing her search path. She had simply entered key words from Wynett's rambling into the program and let the computer find correlations from the hypercard's optical storage database. One of the last windows showed the crimson back cover of the Beatles' *Sgt. Pepper* album, complete with lyrics. Some of the highlighted words on one of the songs matched bits of Wynett's ravings. The final card displayed an oil tanker registry; the seventeenth name on the list, flying a Liberian flag, was *Lucy*.

"Doc, you're a genius," Medlock said, putting a hand on her shoulder. "A goddamn genius. Send Miss Martinelli an electronic message. Get her to talk about the interview with Wynett. See if she's filed any notes on her computer. Will you do that for me?"

She shrugged off his hand. "Do I have a choice?"

Medlock patted her shoulder affectionately, then returned to the conference table. "In one hour I want every piece of information you can secure on that tanker," he said to the group, "engineering blueprints, schematics, everything."

"What about Wynett's offer?" Lieutenant Hernandez said. "Are you willing to pay his price?"

"Negative," Medlock said. "Every offer can be negotiated. I want to meet this son of a bitch face-to-face."

Dr. Shaw stared at her computer monitor, her arms folded

defiantly across her chest. Spying on Julie was too easy. She simply could share her computer session and open any file on Julie's personal storage disk for General Medlock's inspection. That was worse than spying; that was prying into Julie's personal mail.

"Sorry, honey," she said to the screen.

Chapter Thirty-two

The U.S. Eastern Seaboard
Wednesday, 0603 hours

Capt. Sergio Carlucci moved carefully among the mélange of crates and steel containers Gorgon's soldiers had stacked in the ship's lower pumping room. The inventory of armaments was as unconventional as it was extensive. He ran his fingers over an unopened crate's military symbols and serial numbers, speculating what new weapon lay hidden inside. How powerful? And for what purpose?

He stole frequent glances at two mercenaries assembling a curious piece of military hardware that reminded him of a Gatling gun, only much larger. They worked quickly and with seasoned mastery, transforming unassuming pieces of metal into a formidable weapon. When finished, they would install it on the ship's upper deck, Carlucci figured, as they had done with other exotic killing machines they had brought with them. The soldiers allowed him to watch. Gorgon wanted Carlucci to see the extent of his considerable firepower, a strong persuasion against resisting.

Besides, Carlucci still was *Lucy*'s master. His orders were to operate the ship normally; see that everything about *Lucy*'s journey remained absolutely routine—or as routine as seventeen highly trained killers would allow. To do that he needed limited freedom, including access to the lower decks. The captain took full advantage of this privilege to investigate the extent of Gorgon's hold on his vessel, probing for weaknesses. So far he had found none.

Carlucci slipped into the pump room's maintenance shop, one of the few areas that had been specified off-limits to him. No one was inside. He spotted the cylinders immediately. At first he mistook them for beer kegs; they were the same relative size and shape. But vats of beer would have been grossly out of place among Gorgon's crates of armaments. Five in all and arranged neatly against the far wall, these were no ordinary containers. He knelt before the first and ran his hand down its gunmetal gray surface. It was unlike anything he had ever seen before, each tank capped with a very sophisticated, very strong valve mechanism. He was afraid to touch it again. Were they bombs? If so, they resembled nothing like he had ever seen during his sixteen years as a naval officer.

He stood and surveyed the rest of the workshop. On a bench sat six disassembled conical projectiles, each a meter high. They reminded him of missiles, except smaller. He moved to them, sticking his nose to within inches of one, scrutinizing the integrated circuit boards inside. They were warheads, he realized, warheads for missiles.

Next to the workbench sat an open crate containing tubelike cylinders, each the same relative shape and size of a wine bottle. There were dozens of them in this single crate, and there were many crates. He tapped one of the cylinders with his pencil. Hollow. Empty tubes and warheads. How would they figure in Gorgon's plan? He looked again at the larger keglike tanks, deliberating. Somehow they were the key, he knew.

Carlucci checked the bulkhead door to see who was watching him. No one was coming; no one knew he was in here. His confidence rising, he returned to the larger tanks and probed the valve on the first, determined to learn Gorgon's secrets. The valve was made of a material more durable than steel. He tried to move what he thought must be the valve's lever. Frozen. Only someone intimately familiar with this mechanism—an engineer—could open these tanks, he concluded.

He would have to find another way to open them. The notion hit him with a rush of excitement. If these tanks were crucial to Gorgon's plan as he believed they were, opening them might render him impotent. Tampering also could get him killed, he realized. Was his life too high a price to pay to thwart Gorgon? He thought not. The last twelve hours had been worse than any nightmare. His men, good men under his care, were dead. He had allowed them to die. This moment offered him perhaps his only chance to stop the madness that had overtaken his ship and avenge the deaths of his crew. *Take it!*

He pulled a pair of pliers from his coat pocket. Too small, too ineffective. A wrench lay on top of an oil drum. He seized it and considered the fourteen-pound steel tool. Too large for the tanks' valve, it nonetheless might prove useful. Did he have the courage to go through with it? Did he have the courage to die?

Captain Carlucci swept around, wrench in hand, and hovered over the first tank. Gazing downward, he saw the container as his own coffin. There was only his own heartbeat and the deep rumble of the ship's engine. His father had once told him that conquerors and cowards feel exactly the same fear. Conquerors just respond to fear differently.

He raised the wrench high over his head and brought it down onto the tank's valve. The blow produced a crash that echoed through the ship's lower hold, yet it hardly dented the metal. He would have to work harder—much harder. He raised the wrench and began hammering the valve again and again, some blows finding their mark, others bouncing harmlessly off the tank's side. *Open, you son of a bitch!* But the tank remained stubbornly intact, refusing to succumb to his attack.

When Carlucci raised the wrench for perhaps the tenth time,

something firm and strong caught his hand in midair and held it tightly. Wheezing, out of breath, he glanced helplessly upward. Another hand, easily the size and strength of a bear's and possessing the strength to crush his bones with a single flex, held him immobile.

The solid, mechanized clicks of cocking shotguns drew his attention to the hatchway. Two soldiers stood inside the maintenance room, ready to fire.

Gorgon twisted the wrench from Carlucci's hand. The captain winced in agony.

"You made a grave mistake," Gorgon said, tossing the wrench aside. He stooped to inspect the tank's damaged valve and frowned. "One more day. I need you alive only one more day."

Carlucci didn't comprehend any of it. "Why? To what end will all this serve?"

Gorgon allowed a smile, an expression of sympathy for those insignificants who would never understand his destiny. "You will never understand why. You only need know that your kind will pay with blood for the sins of your leaders. As for *how*, it is time you learned who I am and what role you are playing in the new world I will fashion. Come with me. I will show you something."

Gorgon and Carlucci rode the tiny service elevator up to the superstructure's master deck, one level below the bridge. They entered the captain's quarters. Behind a glass partition four of Gorgon's men hovered over a conference table layered with charts, maps and diagrams.

Gorgon led Carlucci to the head of the table so he could see everything. The captain gazed down at a marine chart scribed with a detailed route into the Chesapeake Bay and ending in the York River at West Point. Another sheet was a comprehensive schematic of a refinery. A third was a diagram of the refinery's off-loading dock. Still another drawing, the most puzzling to the captain, detailed a product pipeline network starting at Yorktown and leading to major population centers throughout the east-southeastern United States. Circled in red were New York, Philadelphia, Baltimore/Washington, Richmond, Atlanta and Jacksonville. He understood little of what he saw.

On the table sat one of the tube-shaped cylinders Carlucci had found in the crate in the maintenance shop. This one was open, its top unscrewed and sitting to one side. Inside was a thermal vessel, capped with a small valve. The cylinder's interior reminded Carlucci of a miniature version of the larger tank he had tried to open. He couldn't take his eyes off it. Next to the cylinder sat a curious-looking orange object made of polyurethane, a foot in diameter, with ribbed sides.

"The tanks you treated so irreverently," Gorgon said, "hold a genetically altered virus developed by the United States military. If you had succeeded in opening the tank, we all would be dead. I have enough and more of the organism to kill every man, woman and child in North America and in every ally nation in the U.N."

Carlucci shook his head. "Even if this . . . this . . . weapon is what you say, you cannot use it. The movement of this tanker is severely restricted. And she is slow."

Gorgon laughed wickedly. "The voyage of this tanker is only the means, Captain, not the end. Tonight you will dock and off-load your cargo as scheduled." He drew the pipeline schematic to him. "Look at this diagram. Yorktown represents the beginning of a major distribution network for transporting refined crude throughout the north and southeast United States. No doubt you are aware how such a pipeline system works, Captain?"

Carlucci remained silent, offering nothing that might help him.

"Refined crude oil," Gorgon explained, "is sent to distribution terminals throughout the country through a pipeline network such as this one. To isolate one product from the next— a higher octane gasoline from a lower octane product—a cylindrical separator known as a 'pig' is put into the pipe ahead of each product." He picked up the orange, ribbed object. "This is a pig designed for a petroleum pipeline. It rides ahead of the product, pushed by the pressure of the liquid behind. When it arrives at a distribution terminal, an operator diverts the incoming product to the appropriate storage tank. The pig is recovered in a simple relief valve."

Gorgon picked up the cylinder from the table and handled it reverently, as though it were a precious artifact. "One of these cylinders will be placed inside each of my pigs. Each cylinder will carry one quart of my organism. Tonight I will put seventy-four of these containers into the pipeline system at Yorktown. These containers will open automatically and release their contents the moment they are removed from the relief valve. No other intervention is required. The contents of each container will contaminate at least seven hundred square miles. Within twenty-four hours, my people will be avenged."

Carlucci said nothing, his mind spinning with the enormity of Gorgon's plan. He couldn't speak, only listen. Gorgon's voice rumbled with a volcanic fervor that spoke of his madness. That he was entirely mad in his brilliance, Carlucci did not doubt.

Carlucci's eyes shifted to the charts, but he was unable to focus them. At that moment he knew what he had to do, knew his destiny. He had spent his career as a seaman protecting the ships and crews under his command. Today he must develop a plan to destroy this ship and sink her. A scheme began to form in his head, and he began to tremble. The ship's closed-loop inert-gas system pumped carbon monoxide from the exhaust of the huge diesel engine into the cargo tanks, replacing the oxygen. The system minimized the chance of accidental combustion. That was the key. Turn it off, and the cargo could ignite with a single spark. Gorgon would be dead, and with him this horror he carried.

Would he be allowed near the pump-room controls? And, if so, how would he introduce that spark?

For a long moment there was silence. Suddenly Gorgon shattered the silence with laughter that sent tremors of dread to the core of Carlucci's soul.

"As you can see, Captain," Gorgon said, "my new order has already begun."

Chapter Thirty-three

"Jesus, I don't believe this."

The results from the pathology lab's Polymerase Chain Reaction unit weren't what Julie had expected to see. The columns of numbers scrolling down her monitor showed in great analytical detail the DNA sequence of thousands of mutant genes in the blood cells of each sample she had drawn the night before. Had a biological change taken place in their systems? Without a doubt. Would they survive? Well . . .

"Looks like you're having a bad morning," a deep voice said from the doorway. "I can come back."

Julie whirled. It was Williams. "Sergeant . . . you startled me. Come in . . . please."

Williams, dressed in a T-shirt, shorts and running shoes soaked from a hard three-hour workout in the center's weight room, closed the pathology lab's door behind him and approached her workstation. His eyes were fixed on the monitor, searching for some encouraging news among the numbers and symbols. But nothing he saw made any sense to him. "Thought I'd drop by in case you needed something."

277

"You mean in case I could tell you something."

Williams dumped his huge frame into the cheap molded chair next to her. "Now that you mention it."

For the briefest moment she considered lying to him, telling him what he wanted to hear, that she could find nothing unusual in his blood. He'd never know; *only you can interpret the data,* she thought. But lying to her friends would only make a bad situation worse. *Stop being a caretaker and deal with this appropriately,* she scolded herself. Besides, he would know soon enough. She wanted to share her findings with someone, share her feelings. Why not with Williams? She felt safest around him. Why? *Because he doesn't pose a romantic threat to you, that's why.*

"I might know something this afternoon," she said slowly, "after I run more tests."

"You're stalling." His congenial grin vanished, and he looked suddenly weary and beaten. "How bad is it?"

She sighed and shook her head. *Here goes.* "You and Joe can forget about Gorgon; the army will never let any of us out of here. We can all look forward to a hefty medical disability."

"How long do we have?"

"I can't tell you that." She pressed a finger to the screen. "Do you see these numbers?"

Williams leaned forward and stared glassy-eyed at the screen. "Don't know what any of it means."

"I'm still running tests to find correlations from the tissue and plant samples I took from the plantation. It'll take weeks to sift through the data. Even then I may never get a straight answer. What's fascinating about Saint Vitus is the fiendishly clever way it adapts to its environment. The organism catalyzes its own replication in simple chemical systems without the help of enzymes. That's why it spreads so fast. It brings together two molecular building blocks to create its own template molecule and accelerates their coupling to form a second template. The new molecule catalyzes its own reproduction. It makes copies of itself by promoting this reaction between its two building blocks while they're bound to the template. It's really quite remarkable.''

Williams wore the confused look of a third-grader mistakenly stuck in a calculus class. "Haven't a clue what you're talking about."

She smiled apologetically. "Sorry. What I'm getting at is each generation of Saint Vitus is less toxic than the one before. Man built artificial toxicity into the organism, while nature gives it up in exchange for adaptability."

"Is that supposed to be good news?"

"Yes. That's why we're still alive." Julie rolled her chair away from him and parked it in front of the lab's electron-scanning microscope. She clicked on the postcard-size display. Williams followed and peered over her shoulder at the display's luminous circles of life.

"I can show you slides of each of our blood cells," she said. "There are abnormalities with the same genetic fingerprint in mine, yours and Joe's cell cytoplasm. Youngblood's sample shows no deformation because he didn't come in direct contact with the organism on the plantation. He's the only healthy one among us. That suggests Saint Vitus isn't airborne contagious once it infests the host. Wynett's the worst. His blood shows evidence of gross malignancy, which isn't surprising, considering the length of time he was exposed to the virus. I'd like to see a magnetic resonator image of him. He most likely has tumors in advanced stages in his brain."

Williams let out a long, weary sigh. "After putting my ass on the line so many times, I'm gonna buy it from a goddamn germ."

"It's too early to start planning your funeral, Sergeant. The toxicity could take years to break down our immune systems."

Williams's brow furrowed. "Did you see the major's hand this morning? The trembling's gotten worse."

Julie looked hard at him. "No, I haven't. Sergeant, I don't know what this synthetic aberration in a mutated state will do to us or how long it will take before we see symptoms—it's a total black box. And there's something else I can't figure. I found a gene I can't identify imbedded in the infected cells. I suspect it has something to do with a mutated version of Saint Vitus, but I won't be sure without further testing. If I can talk the army into giving me time on one of its Crays, I might be able to identify the enzymes and see what Saint Vitus is up to."

Williams sank back into his chair. "I'd like to keep this between us for now. If the brass gets wind of what you've found, they'll bury us in here."

"They already have. I'm going to need the medical opinion of a highly specialized team, something on the order of the NIH's Recombinant DNA Advisory Committee. And that means turning over this data to someone on the outside. I'll consult with my adviser, Dr. Shaw. She'll know how to get discreet answers."

"Just make sure she can keep her mouth shut for now. When are you gonna tell Joe?"

Julie turned away from him. "None of this will matter to him. He doesn't have any feelings."

"He feels, Julie. He feels a great deal more than you're likely to ever know. Except he's *programmed* not to show it." He emphasized the word *programmed* as though it would mean something special to her. "After fifteen years in the service, he's forgotten how to show his feelings. It'd do him a world of good if you could bring him out of his suit of armor—before he dies stuck in there. All he knows is you'd rather talk to this computer instead of him. He needs to know you trust him."

She looked at him, hurt. "This is very difficult work. I need to find the precise shape of the virus. To do that I need to crystallize the protein, then take a long series of X-ray pictures. Processing these photos through a computer will give me a three-dimensional image."

Williams rolled his eyes. "There you go, making excuses just like those workaholic assholes in Washington who only know how to organize committees. When you sit in front of that screen you're a queen in your own world. Safe and sound.

The computer doesn't talk back to you or make you feel vulnerable; it does just what you tell it to do. You control it. It's safe, as close to a kingdom as you're likely to find . . . except there's no people in there."

"What's your point, Sergeant?"

"Don't have a point, except the way I see it you're using your work to avoid Joe—same as Joe's using Gorgon to bury his feelings for you. Maybe a man like Joe is something you've never experienced before. And you're not comfortable with the way he makes you feel."

"Sergeant—"

"So go back to your keyboard; it won't reject you. At this rate you'll both become just like your machines—you a computer, him a tank."

Julie sat speechless. He couldn't possibly know how she felt about her work or about Marshall. Deep down, though, she knew he was flirting with the truth. *You're afraid Joe will reject you, abandon you. And that scares the hell out of you.*

Williams was on his feet, heading for the door. "You've got work to do and I need a shower." He opened the lab's door, turned and added, "Maybe you'll live long enough to find out what you're missing—about Joe, that is."

USAMRIID
Fort Detrick

General Medlock's hand remained frozen around a polystyrene cup half filled with cold, black coffee. It had been a long night. He needed sleep, and his drawn expression showed it. He had removed himself from the discussion around the conference room table to mentally devour several pages of statistics on crude oil tankers registered to U.S. oil companies. On one of the pages an analyst had highlighted the name *Lucy,* an eighty-thousand-deadweight-ton oil tanker registered to Universal Oil Marine Transport Company in Houston. An eighty-thousand-deadweight-ton oil tanker—that translated to six hundred thousand barrels of crude oil.

Maj. Samuel Higgins, BERT's logistics officer, was on his feet, listing the technical issues of the crisis on an electronic "chalkboard" that could print out hard copies of anything written on it with a washable marker. "*Lucy* loads medium-gravity crude from Universal's oil fields in Venezuela. She has a cruising radius of seventeen-thousand nautical miles. Her route takes her across the Caribbean, up the United States' Eastern Seaboard to the Chesapeake Bay, where she'll dock at her company's refinery in Yorktown."

"It fits." Medlock grunted.

"*Lucy*'s perfect, sir," said Lieutenant Hernandez, a young officer with serious lines of maturity blemishing his baby-smooth features. "She's small by tanker standards, which means she won't need special port handling. Fully laden and retrofitted with armaments, she'd pose one hell of a threat if he intends to use her to gain entry to this country. At the very least he can threaten a first-class oil spill if we try to intercept her—that's if Gorgon doesn't release the bug first. That bastard's got himself a floating fortress."

Medlock stared over his coffee cup at Lieutenant Hernandez with eyes cast in steel. "You sound like you wish you were on that goddamn ship with him."

The young lieutenant's enthusiastic grin evaporated like a desert mirage. "Sir, I was only pointing out—"

"Where the hell is *Lucy*'s schedule?" Major Higgins interrupted. "We need to find out where she picks up a river pilot." He thrust his marker at Lieutenant Hernandez. "Get on the horn to Universal's headquarters in Houston and find out where *Lucy* is now and which pilot station she uses. Find out if anybody's noticed any change in her routine radio messages. I want to know if she's done anything out of the ordinary."

Lieutenant Hernandez punched a preprogrammed button on his phone and relayed the major's instructions to his staff.

"Let's ask Universal to take a look," Major Higgins suggested. "One of their choppers can drop in for a surprise inspection."

"Negative," Medlock said. "When we find out where she

picks up a pilot, we'll put in our own man. Though I'd bet Gorgon won't allow a pilot anywhere near the vessel.''

"He won't have a choice."

The phone in front of Lieutenant Hernandez rang. Thirty seconds later the lieutenant relayed to the group: "Houston says *Lucy*'s last routine message came three hours ago over the MariSat channel. She's at thirty-seven degrees north latitude and seventy-six degrees west longitude, approaching the Chesapeake Bay. She'll arrive at the pilot station offshore of Cape Henry this afternoon. She's scheduled to dock at the company's Yorktown refinery at 1830 hours tonight. And so far there's been nothing unusual about her voyage. Let me take this to a Code Yellow, sir.''

Medlock shut his report with a snap. "Negative. Let's go slow and easy until we get more facts. Make a call to the joint chiefs and brief them. Meanwhile let's try to get a man aboard on a recon. Find an enlisted seaman who can pilot that tanker upriver and get him wired. If they won't let him aboard, that'll at least tell us what we need to know. If I have to I'll call the Chief of Naval Operations and have him order a blockade.''

Dr. Theodore Gruber, BERT's science consultant, cleared his throat apologetically while running his fingers through his surviving wisps of white hair that always drifted up and outward. Slouched in a bland blue blazer and gray slacks that looked like he'd just awakened wearing them—and he had— Gruber was an MIT engineering professor, who last year headed Raytheon's technology development program. "Excuse me, gentlemen," he said. "I believe this Gorgon fellow has made a serious error.''

All eyes shifted to Gruber. Medlock said, "Let's have it, Ted.''

"A Procyon missile," Gruber said, making copious notes on the yellow legal pad in front of him, "is designed to deliver an explosive warhead with a maximum range of nine hundred and fifty nautical miles. Let's assume he is using a conventional warhead canister that jettisons on reentry and spins to the ground while dispersing its contents—the only way a bacterial and chemical agent can disperse from a warhead.''

"What are you getting at?" Medlock spat, impatient.

Gruber slid back his chair, walked slightly stooped to th[e] head of the table and took the black marker from Major Hig[-] gins. He wiped off several of Higgins's notes on the board t[o] make room for his crude sketch of the slope of a missile pat[h] from the tanker. "As designed, the missiles' trajectory is fa[r] too steep for the warhead, and upon reentry it would be trav[-] eling much too fast.''

Medlock leaned back thoughtfully in his chair, touching hi[s] fingertips together. "Ted, are you saying his warheads won'[t] work?"

"Not unless he's reengineered the boosters to reduce th[e] trajectory and speed—and that would take a team of engineer[s] and technicians. It's a gamble, to be sure. And to complicat[e] matters for him, a storm front is moving across the northeas[t] seaboard from the west, and he's riding straight into it. Dis[-] persing an airborne toxin in thirty-knot winds would be inef[-] fectual. No, he must have something else planned. Perhaps he[ ] is taking the neurotoxin inland for a larger attack.''

"That's why we're not going to let him reach that refinery,'['] Medlock said. "The only question is how.''

"I say our best option is a covert commando assault of the[ ] vessel," Major Higgins said. "Once on board, a commando[ ] team can neutralize the missiles by simply taking out the elec[-] tronics truck. Then Gorgon's vulnerable to a full-scale as[-] sault.''

Medlock nodded. The speed of organizing a small, cover[t] assault force intrigued him. At the very least it was the genesi[s] of a plan—a solid plan. "Too many unanswered questions[,] too many risks," the general said. "If we're to have any[ ] chance at all, we must do a recon of the tanker first. I wan[t] to know how many men Gorgon has on board, where he keep[s] the tanks and even what they look like. That's going to take[ ] a lot more time than we have.''

"Perhaps not," Gruber said, wiping his writing hand on a[ ] blue tie emblazoned with golden statistical symbols. He looked directly at Dr. Shaw seated in the far corner of the room. "Would you kindly download and print out Julie Martinelli's collated data on the organism? I need to know if they are still airborne contagious." Then he appealed to Medlock, his exhausted, academic features enlivened. "I think it's time you cut a deal with this Carl Wynett."

The White House
Oval Office
1154 hours

The president and Senator Baker were absorbed in a lively discussion about the limits of Hussein's nuclear capability when Michael Brennan was shown into the Oval Office. Director of the Central Intelligence Agency, Brennan didn't need an appointment to meet with his boss. He had access to the president twenty-four hours a day. Unassuming and sporting horn-rimmed glasses and a crew cut, Brennan looked more like a staff accountant than head of the world's most powerful intelligence organization.

The president and his guest turned in unison as Brennan entered the office, their discussion ending abruptly.

"Excuse me, Mr. President, Senator Baker," Brennan began, sporting uncharacteristically serious lines on his usually benign features.

The president gestured the CIA director to a blue highbacked chair beside him, inviting him into their circle of discussion. "What is it, Mike? I don't like it when you get that look on your face."

Senator Baker touched the president's arm. "Perhaps I should go."

The president looked at Brennan for affirmation. "What about it, Mike? Want him to leave?"

Brennan sat down stiffly on the proffered blue suede chair in front of the office's ornate fireplace. "That's not necessary, sir. This also concerns the senator. In fact, in a way he started this whole business."

Senator Baker hid his curiosity beneath an expression that remained noncommitally passive.

"Whatever you say," the president conceded.

Deliberately, and with what seemed to the others glacially slowly, Brennan removed his glasses and used a handkerchief to wipe the oil from beneath each eye. Then he tucked the handkerchief inside his coat and cleared his throat.

"Mr. President . . . a situation has developed that I think you should know about."

Chapter Thirty-four

Quarantine
1300 hours

Marshall knocked twice on the door and didn't wait for permission before slipping into her room. He found Julie sitting at the small circular table, her father's Beretta lying before her like a funeral wreath. She had been grieving, which her dark glistening eyes affirmed. Startled by his unexpected appearance, she quickly wiped away her tears with the back of her hand and brushed back her hair with her fingers.

"You're not welcome in here right now," she said, fumbling through her sweater pockets for a tissue. "Please respect my space."

"I knocked first."

She looked at him coldly, then blew her nose into a tissue. "I want to be alone."

"You're always alone." He closed the door quietly behind him and walked around her bed, slowly, his eyes drifting down to her father's Beretta. He took the weapon slowly into his hand and felt his mentor's strength in its heavy, elegant metal. He sat down on her bed and contemplated the weapon, paying his respects to its owner. The gun was so much like the colonel. It was as though he were here with them, his soul residing in this finely crafted handgun.

"It reminds me of him," she said at last, tucking the spent tissue into her sweater pocket.

Marshall looked thoughtfully at her. He didn't tell her that those were his thoughts too.

"He once told me," she said, "that a gun gives a man a perverse power only God should have. Still, I love it. It reminds me of who he was, what he was. I never touched his guns, but I can't let go of this one . . . I can't let go of him."

Marshall saw the Beretta for what it really was: a handsome handgun without a magazine clip, an impotent piece of metal unable to protect its owner. Useless. The Beretta was just like him: a custom-made, finely tuned weapon, unable to do its job.

Marshall replaced the Beretta reverently on the table in front of her. "I'll never forget him."

Despite her best effort to control herself, tears rolled freely down her cheeks. She was vulnerable now, he could see. She wasn't accustomed to showing her feelings, especially intense new ones.

"Joe," she said, her voice unsteady, "I . . . made some terrible mistakes. I . . ." She reached as though to touch him, kept her hand there, but dared go no further. He took her hand and completed the bond she seemed reluctant to make. His touch gave her strength and lifted a great burden from her. She felt safe. "I miss him so much. I'm nothing without him."

"You're everything without him," Marshall said firmly. "You're the strongest woman I know."

Julie forced a smile. "I've been thinking about how everything has changed since he died. How I've changed. Without him I have no compass, no one to guide me. How am I going to make it on my own, Joe?"

"You don't need anyone to guide you." He tugged on her arm ever so slightly. She slid off the chair easily, as though waiting for his cue, and almost landed in his lap on the bed.

He slid his arms around her. "What if I told you that I'm the one who needs *you*."

Julie wrapped her arms around his neck and hugged him more tightly than she intended, pressing her face into his strong, muscular neck. She wept freely, no longer ashamed to hide her tears from him. The man in her arms wasn't her father, yet she felt as though she could share her most intimate feelings with him. He was a more potent reservoir of strength than she had ever dreamed. His effect on her was liberating.

"Oh, Joe. I've treated you terribly."

"Forget it. We're exactly the same, you and I, shaped from the same mold. We can help each other." He pushed her gently away from him so he could look deep into her moist brown eyes. She returned his gaze, unable to speak. A rush of compassion filled him, and he saw her for the great woman she was. He felt an overwhelming desire for her, coupled with a profound respect for her frail vulnerabilities and insecurities. He leaned forward and kissed her lips ever so lightly. They felt wonderful. When he drew away, she looked at him, and they both knew it was right—no, perfect—to be together.

This time she kissed him, a long, deep, lingering kiss that set new boundaries. A great exhilaration seized her, obliterating every fear and regret within her soul. She kissed him again, and this time there was a painful urgency in her kiss, as though this were the last time she would be with a man. She was hungry for him.

It was Julie who undressed Marshall, pushing him down on the bed with gentle insistence, then taking her time exploring his strong, handsome contours as she removed each item of his clothing. She smiled as she ran her hands admiringly over his muscular chest, then brushed a finger playfully over his face, feeling his sandpaper-rough week-old beard. She loved the musky way he smelled. He watched her, happily, feeling his excitement build as she handled him. Her touch was electric, and she could readily see the effect it was having on him. She wanted to keep him prone and continue touching him, but he didn't let her—not yet. Instead, smiling, he sat up and pushed her back onto the bed and undressed her completely. And he too was pleased by what he saw. Her body was absolutely perfect.

He pulled her into his arms, though awkwardly, new lovers that they were. Pressed against him, she felt indescribably warm and wonderful. The clumsiness passed, and quickly, naturally, they became one.

"You feel so good," she breathed into his ear.

He ran his hands down the supple curves of her back. "So do you," he whispered, than locked her in another deep kiss. They explored each other's mouths, letting go completely, giving themselves freely to each other.

USAMRIID
1330 hours

General Medlock pushed his way into the interrogation room and looked questioningly at Lieutenant Hernandez standing by the door, waiting for him.

"He'll talk only to you," the lieutenant said.

"Then get your men out of here," Medlock snapped.

The lieutenant led his staff quickly from the room, and Medlock secured the door behind him. The general dragged a folding chair across the concrete floor with a screech and sat down in front of Wynett. "So start talking."

"I regret that this meeting must be a short one," Wynett said. "Simply stated, I sold Abdul Banna the armaments to defend the ship and I know how he will use them. You are in a very dangerous situation, General. I do not envy you. An explosion on any of the tanker's decks will effect the release of the organism you wish to contain. Your mistake now could cost millions of lives. If you are to have any chance at all, you must take immediate action. Unfortunately, that puts you at a negotiating disadvantage."

"What's that supposed to mean?"

"It means, General, that in exchange for my information in

any quantity and quality I choose to give, you will give me exactly what I want."

"And that is?"

"I need a supercutter to escort me to the oil tanker *Lucy* while she still is on the Chesapeake Bay. Once under way, I will supply you with information that will allow your men to board the vessel and disable the Procyon missiles. That is all I can offer you. The rest will be up to you."

Medlock scowled. "That's insane. Why the hell would you want to meet Gorgon now?"

"I have unfinished business with him."

"Maybe you want to team up with him again. Maybe he needs you with him before he can carry out his attack."

"That is the first risk you must take. General, time is short and I need to ask you one question."

"No one's stopping you."

"I am dying, am I not?"

Medlock shrugged. "Ask a doctor."

"Sir, you must be candid with me if we are to continue our business relationship. I am certain that you know the results of Miss Martinelli's blood tests. I simply am asking you to share them with me."

General Medlock let his breath out in a long sigh. "Yeah, you're dying." He waited for him to react. When he didn't, he added, "A brain tumor."

Wynett nodded, and his eyes grew distant and reflective. "I suspected as much from the headaches. Then let us begin. What a fine tomb *Lucy* will make."

The White House Situation Room
1415 hours

General Medlock walked briskly to the foot of the elongated table and stood almost at attention across from the president of the United States, who faced him with his hands locked behind his back. Medlock quickly scanned the room. Around the table sat the director of the CIA, the chairman of the joint chiefs and the national security adviser—the men who embodied the president's mantle of power, whose faces he knew. In the corner lurked an ashen-faced Senator Baker, conspicuously avoiding the general's gaze. There were no aides present. A pessimistic mood hung over the room like a noxious cloud of smoke.

The president quickly drew the general into their circle of discussion. "I'm not at all pleased," he began, "with the way this situation has been handled. I understand you've been managing this disaster ever since the organism was stolen from Detrick. What I can't understand is how you allowed matters to come to this. I'm appalled that Saddam's terror group has penetrated U.S. territory under our noses, carrying with them this . . . this . . . scourge of yours." The president almost spat in disgust.

General Medlock frowned; Saint Vitus wasn't *his*. "Sir—"

"I want this stopped," the president said, glaring at the general as though Gorgon were coming after him personally, "and I want it done immediately. If you can't do it, damn it, I want somebody who can. That organism must not be released, not by a missile, not by any means. My God, this can precipitate a plague the likes of which . . ." He grew rigid, a hand on his forehead, barely containing his rage. When his passion quelled, he continued, though strained. "Under no circumstances can this incident become public. He's trying to castrate me with my own knife. I won't become the brunt of an international scandal over this abomination, regardless of how this situation turns out. Most of all, I don't want an Iraqi victory hanging over my head, not now, not ever." The president hurled the words at him, hammered them at him.

"Sir—"

The president raised a hand, his face drawn and bitter. He damn well intended to get his way. "I don't want an explanation, General. I want you to carry out a single directive."

"Yes, sir."

"After considering every option, we have only one choice"—the room was silent, all eyes on the president—"a tactical thermonuclear warhead.''

There it was. The phrase floated in the air like the very plague the solution was meant to stop. No one dared move, no one dared breathe it in for fear of contamination. Medlock was the first to react, his lips parting in a bleak, wintery smile.

The president looked at him, astonished. "Did I say something funny, General?"

"Sir, a nuclear detonation over the ship is a drastic step that will hardly keep this incident quiet—"

"For the past three-quarters of an hour," the president said, "these gentlemen and I have been debating every option to resolve this crisis, from effecting an assassination of Hussein to doing absolutely nothing. The joint chiefs are already at Code Yellow and are standing by to address Congress. This is an act of war. Saddam believes Allah has given him another chance. We've considered every available option and each poses a risk that his terrorists will launch those missiles— every option, that is, except one. We agree that a nuclear detonation in U.S. waters, however abhorrent, is preferable to the release of the organism. A point-one-megaton nuclear warhead is just large enough to vaporize the ship, while evaporating most of the crude oil and scattering the remains over a four-mile area. If we detonate before the tanker reaches the Chesapeake Bay, the impact on civilian areas will be minimal. Drastic? Yes. Effective? One hundred percent.''

"The fallout—"

"We'll evacuate. The radiation will dissipate out to sea, unlike your monster that breeds and spreads.''

"Sir, what you're suggesting poses unacceptable risks, not to mention the scandal of nuking our own waters.''

The president's glance circled the room; he seemed to be debating whether to share with the general an ugly secret. "The U.N. weapons inspection team in Iraq," the president said slowly, "has already made public Hussein's attempts to test a primitive nuclear device. Iraqi scientists have openly declared to United Nations inspectors that they are rebuilding Iraq's nuclear weapons program. We will fabricate evidence that this maniac smuggled a small-yield nuclear device into U.S. waters aboard the tanker and detonated it. No scientific investigation team will be able to discern the difference. Sure, a lot of people will want my ass when this is over. But I'm sure the American people will stand behind me when I initiate a plan to finally overthrow that tyrant.''

General Medlock placed his hands palm-down on the table's mirrorlike mahogany surface and leaned forward. ''With all due respect, sir, let me offer you another option. We don't believe Gorgon plans to launch the Procyons. We believe the missiles are merely a backup threat to camouflage a larger operation, the scale of which we can only speculate. A Special Forces team is standing by in Oceana to carry out a covert assault on the tanker. We can deal with this quietly and effectively; no one need know this organism or Saddam's terrorist plot ever existed.''

Warily, the president listened to the general, hoping to hear another way out of this crisis, but in the end he wasn't persuaded. He shook his head. ''The organism is a great threat to the American people, regardless of how he intends to use it or when. The bastard's smirking at us, for chrissake. He knows this country—any country—is entirely vulnerable to this sort of attack. We've got a fleet of warships and attack aircraft standing by at Oceana ready to sink that tanker, yet we can't use them. We can't use them. This is worse than nuclear blackmail. No, General. I wish there was another way out of this, but every minute we allow that tanker to continue, we are risking more lives. There simply isn't time for further discussion.''

''Then allow a compromise, sir, one that won't undermine your option.''

''What is it?''

''We'll stand by with your nuclear option. The moment something goes wrong with my plan—if any bugs are released or a launch becomes imminent—we nuke the ship, special op team and all. We can accept the sacrifice in the interest of saving a lot more lives. You can have it both ways.''

Code: Alpha

The president didn't like the general's proposal. He wanted guarantees, which only the nuclear option seemed to provide. Too much was at stake—perhaps even his own life. During the planning of the liberation of Kuwait, the joint chiefs had quickly ruled out a nuclear option as unnecessary. In this situation not only was it necessary, but mandatory—and in U.S. waters! Could he really have it both ways? He wished it were so.

"No deal," the president said.

"Sir, my commandos are the best. The elite from every Special Forces unit—SEALs, Delta, Green Berets . . . We're patched into the navy's LINK II combat information system and are monitoring the tanker's movements from our control center in a hangar at Andrews Airfield. We're ready to move. The name of the operation is Maximum Containment."

For a full minute the president said nothing, his back to the group. The silence was frightening. Then he turned, riveted an acute glare at Medlock and said, "General, can you guarantee me one hundred percent that the organism will not be released?"

Medlock drew in a deep breath and told the president what he wanted to hear. "Yes, sir."

"Then you have my authority to act. And God damn your soul if you're wrong."

Chapter Thirty-five

Quarantine
1700 hours

"He's gone," Julie whispered into his ear.

Marshall woke suddenly from the deepest sleep he had enjoyed in a month, with no idea where he was and no memory of how he had gotten here. Dream-soaked images of Julie swirled through his mind. Had he just heard her voice or was he still asleep? Then the events of the afternoon came flooding back, and he remembered he was in her bed. It felt good. His desire for her stirred again when he smelled her sweetness flowing over him and saw her standing above him. He wrestled her down onto the bed, rolled on top of her and drove his semitough member between her legs. She was fully clothed in an abrasive jumpsuit.

"Did you hear what I just said?" Julie said, pushing him off her. "Wynett's gone."

"Jesus." Marshall fumbled in the darkness to find his watertight chronometer on the table. The luminous dial said he had been asleep for more than three hours. He switched on the lamp. "Gone? What do you mean *gone?*"

Julie sat up and swung her legs over the edge of the bed.

"We searched the whole frigging center, and the son of a bitch isn't here. Williams and Youngblood are going through every room again."

Marshall pulled on his jockey briefs with a snap and stormed out of her room and down the hallway, his bare feet slapping the sterile linoleum. His mind was racing. Gone? How was it possible?

He found Williams sitting cross-armed at one of the lounge's tables and noted the sergeant's look of frustration. The remains of a penny-poker game and empty Coke cans littered the table, while Dan Fogelberg's "Part of the Plan" blared from the center's audio system.

"Going to church in your Sunday best, Joe?" Williams snorted as the major charged through the lounge.

Marshall, clad only in barely adequate briefs, jabbed the CD player's off button with his index finger. "So where is he?"

"Hell if I know," Williams said. "But he ain't in here."

"How thoroughly did you check the pathology lab?" Marshall asked. "He's nutty enough to lock himself inside a goddamn freezer."

"He ain't here," Williams repeated, a note of annoyance in his voice.

Youngblood strode into the lounge and dumped himself into a chair across from Williams. "You're not going to believe what I just saw." The pilot paused to survey Marshall's perspiring chest and briefs and knew he had just crawled from the sack. Julie's sack? He watched disapprovingly as she tossed Marshall a pair of khaki pants and a long-sleeved flannel shirt.

"Believe what?" Marshall demanded.

"Medlock's people pulled Wynett out of here," Youngblood said.

Marshall stepped into the khakis. "What are you saying? How do you know?"

Youngblood cocked his thumb in the general direction of the center's communications room. "I saw it on the outside monitors. A bunch of officers whisked Wynett out to the hel-

297

ipad and loaded him onto a UH1B troop transport chopper. It's on tape, if you'd like to see for yourself. My guess is a delegation of top brass will follow in the VIP command chopper; the pilot's started his preflight.''

"Don't look now, ladies," Marshall said, buttoning his flannel shirt, "but I think we've just been conned."

"What's that supposed to mean?" Julie asked.

"We're not contagious, and Medlock knows it."

Marshall stormed down the corridor, slipped inside the phone room, lifted the receiver and waited an impatient thirty seconds for someone to answer. A woman finally said, "How can I help you?"

"Talk to me. What the hell's going on up there?"

"This is Sergeant McGinnis. I'm filling in for Lieutenant Lowe, who isn't available. What can I do for you?"

"Where are they taking Wynett?"

Her youthful voice dropped a full octave. "I'm sorry, Major. I'm not authorized to give you any information. General Medlock will brief you personally in the morning. I have strict instructions. I'm sorry."

"Let me speak to someone whose nose isn't buried six inches past the brass's sphincter."

"I have strict instructions, sir. I'm sorry." Her tone had taken on the dull, mechanical quality of an answering machine.

He threw down the receiver. "This is bullshit."

"Meet me in the computer lab in two minutes," Julie hollered down the hallway. "And dress warmly."

Marshall scrambled out of the telephone room. "Say what?"

"I'm getting us out of here," Julie said, then disappeared into her computer lab.

"You heard what the lady said," Marshall said, his adrenaline pumping. "Move your asses and dress warmly."

Marshall hustled back to his quarters and grabbed his boots and a pair of wool socks from his closet before joining the others in the computer lab. They were all putting on extra layers of flannel shirts and tucking them into overalls. Williams was strapping his wicked black-blade serrated knife to his right ankle, while Julie sat in front of her computer, her favorite coffee mug, half-filled and cold, in her hand. Beside the terminal lay her father's Beretta.

Marshall slid his chair next to Julie's and stomped his boot on. "So tell me your little secret. How are you going to get us out of here?"

"While you were on the phone," she said, "I found a message waiting for me in my electronic in-basket."

"What's it say?"

Youngblood and Williams pressed behind them as Julie jabbed the keyboard's PF2 key to access her incoming electronic mail. The main menu gave way to a screenful of addresses and subject lines listed in the descending order in which they were received. At the top of the list was a message from a Dr. N. Shaw.

"Who's N. Shaw?" Marshall asked.

"Nancy's my Stanford adviser." Julie pressed the PF1 key to view the note:

JULIE—
I'M SORRY I DIDN'T TELL YOU BEFORE THAT I'M HERE AT DETRICK TWO FLOORS ABOVE YOU. I'M UNDER A STRICT GAG ORDER. THERE'S A TASK FORCE UP HERE LISTENING AND WATCHING EVERYTHING YOU SAY AND DO. WYNETT HAS INSISTED ON MEETING GORGON'S HIJACKED OIL TANKER, WHICH WILL REACH THE CHESAPEAKE BAY IN ABOUT TWO HOURS. A COVERT ASSAULT TEAM WILL BOARD AND ATTEMPT TO STOP HIM. THEY'RE CALLING THE OPERATION MAXIMUM CONTAINMENT. ALL HELL'S BREAKING LOOSE UP HERE WHILE MEDLOCK GETS READY TO FLY TO HIS COMMAND HANGAR AT ANDREWS AIRFIELD. I'M NOT SURE WHERE THE TROOPS ARE STAGING.

THE GENERAL DOESN'T WANT YOU INVOLVED. I WANTED YOU TO KNOW WHAT'S GOING ON—I'M TIRED OF ALL THE SECRETS AND ALL THE BULLSHIT. MY JOB HERE IS JUST

ABOUT FINISHED ANYWAY AND I'M GLAD. SORRY I HAD TO
BE SO SNEAKY. PLEASE HIT PF4 NOW TO DELETE THIS NOTE.

NANCY

"Bastards have been spying on us all along," Youngblood
said.

Marshall put a finger to his lips, signaling each of them to
remain quiet. He whispered into Julie's ear, "Get me out of
here."

She grabbed her legal pad, scribbled a note and showed it
to them. *Any idea where they're taking Wynett?*

Marshall snatched her pad of paper and pen and scribbled,
My bet is Oceana. That's three hours minimum. He thought a
moment, then finished, *That's IF we can drive a car out of
here.*

"I vote we follow Wynett in a chopper," Youngblood whispered.

Marshall responded with a questioning shrug.

Youngblood grabbed the pad of paper from Williams and
wrote, *There's a chopper on the helipad.*

Marshall laughed out loud when he read Youngblood's
note. "You've been hanging out with Wynett too long."

Youngblood said, "I don't think you have any other option."

"I think it's a splendid idea," Julie said. "They're treating
Wynett like a goddamn VIP. Well, I'm not letting him get
away scot-free. Besides, we're plumb out of time." She typed
a command into her computer, slid back in her chair and bit
her lower lip. They all watched the word WAIT appear briefly
in the lower left corner of the screen before the screen returned
to the system prompt.

Marshall said, "What are you up to?"

Julie raised her hand for silence. They all listened but heard
nothing. They sat there for ten seconds waiting for something
to happen . . . twenty. . . . Nothing did.

Youngblood shook his head. "All dressed up and no-where—"

"*Quiet!*" Marshall shouted.

More silence. Youngblood, smirking, stepped into the hall-way and mocked, "No one here 'cept us ghosts. . . ." He stopped, his jaw dropping. "Well, I'll be the south end of a northbound horse."

Marshall stood suddenly. "What is it?"

Julie too was on her feet, her expression hopeful.

"The crash door"—Youngblood looked at the major, his face wide-eyed and boyish—"is open."

Marshall bolted into the hallway. Youngblood was right; the electronically controlled door leading into the receiving-dock area stood ajar. Beyond it they could hear the muted sound of a larger mechanical door moving—the service-bay door to the outside.

"Yes!" Williams said, his fist raised in victory.

Marshall swept Julie into a bear hug as she dashed from the lab. "You're beautiful."

"Nothing to it." She laughed, hugging his neck. "A simple shell program I put together last night in case of an emer-gency."

Suddenly the center's emergency red lights began flashing and the alarms erupted in a deafening cacophony of sound. A metallic, emotionless voice boomed over the intercom: "Quar-antine has been breached. Do not attempt to leave quarantine. Repeat. Do not attempt to leave quarantine."

"We're screwed if that door shuts!" Julie shouted.

The four of them sprinted down the hallway.

"Quarantine has been breached. Do not attempt to leave quarantine."

Marshall burst into the receiving room and entered the cen-ter's cavernous loading dock, where a fierce January storm poured into the garage. The quarantine trailer was gone. A loud, staccato buzzer and spinning yellow light warned them to stand clear of the great steel service-bay door rolling shut.

"A fail-safe routine," Julie said. "The security program is

automatically compensating for the failure my command introduced into the system and is sealing the building.''

"Everybody out!" Marshall hollered. Williams and Youngblood bolted across the loading dock.

Marshall grabbed Julie around the waist and tackled her back into the center. "Sorry, honey," he said. "You're staying here." He planted an impeccable kiss on her lips and snatched the Beretta from her. "I'll see you tonight."

Before she could protest, he sprinted into the receiving room and slammed the steel door behind him, automatically locking it with a mechanical click.

Stunned, Julie drove her shoulder against the metal door; she might as well have rammed a brick wall. "Marshall!"

The service-bay door had less than three feet to go before Marshall too was sealed inside. Youngblood, peering beneath it from the outside, beckoned him to hurry. "Get your ass out here, Major!"

Marshall bolted across the dock, jumped down onto the concrete and raced toward the massive door as it rolled closed. He flattened onto his buttocks as though sliding for home and pushed his legs under the door. His upper torso wouldn't clear. He felt the door's crushing weight begin to press down on him. He couldn't stop it.

Two pairs of hands grabbed him by his legs and yanked him cruelly out into the cold January night. The service-bay door closed behind him with a pneumatic mechanical thud.

Chapter Thirty-six

The wind had picked up considerably as the weather deteriorated. Youngblood blew on his hands and rubbed them together for warmth. "I wish I had my bomber jacket."

"I wish I had a bomber," Marshall said, grabbing Williams's hand and pulling himself to his feet. The major led the way across to the helipad, where the VIP command helicopter sat idling. A large uniformed security officer stood rigid by the open compartment door, watching the three men approach through the driving curtain of sleet, not quite sure what to make of them. He put a hand on his holstered .45.

Marshall ducked under the rotor blades and thrust Martinelli's empty Beretta before him. "Don't take this personally."

The guard's roving eyes darted from one man to the next, then back at the chopper as he looked for a bold way out of his cornered predicament. Marshall pegged him as a reckless jock who would eat a urinal deodorant cake on a dare. While the major kept the Beretta tucked neatly under the guard's chin, Youngblood relieved him of his sidearm.

Marshall beckoned Williams forward. "Take care of him."

303

Before the soldier could protest, Williams drove the palm of his hand into the bridge of the guard's nose. He was out cold, his nose broken.

Youngblood opened the cockpit door and said to the pilot, "New orders. You're wanted inside."

The helicopter pilot, a seasoned flier with sharp features who didn't like getting jerked around, pulled off his flight helmet and roared at Youngblood, "Who the fuck are you?"

Youngblood offered him his best Georgian grin. "Don't shoot me; I'm just the messenger."

"My ass." The pilot reached for his radio.

Youngblood pointed the confiscated .45 at the pilot's head. "One way or another, in ten seconds you're gonna be out of my life."

Youngblood could see the pilot's bleached face even under the low light of the flight deck's multicolored instrumentation. The pilot scrambled out of the cockpit.

Youngblood strapped himself into the pilot's seat, engaged the rotor clutch and throttled the turboshaft engines for takeoff. The prop blades bit into the thick winter air.

Marshall and Williams climbed into the troop compartment, an airborne combat communications center loaded with racks of electronics. Williams secured the compartment door behind them. A frail-looking gentleman with glasses and thin wispy hair sat buckled into a seat, a briefcase full of papers spread out on the table before him.

Dr. Gruber recognized Marshall and Williams from their dossier photos. "Good God . . ." He slid a handful of papers into his worn shoulder bag and clutched it to his chest. "I suppose you want me to leave."

Marshall let him see his Beretta. "Depends. Who are you?"

"Fuck you."

Marshall flashed Gruber a congenial grin and took a seat across from him. "Have it your way. I don't really care who you are as long as you can bring me up to speed on this situation real fast."

The helicopter gave a shudder as it lifted off the helipad.

"Are you insane?" Gruber shouted. "This vehicle is General Medlock's communications link to the command hangar at Andrews Airfield. You're jeopardizing the entire operation. A lot of people are going to die if you continue this nonsense."

"The general doesn't know Gorgon like I do," Marshall said. He indicated the electronics behind him. "Nothing's in jeopardy. You have my permission to keep the flow of information moving, if that's your job. Meanwhile I want you to get on the LINK II and inform all parties that we're part of Maximum Containment on special assignment. You can start by telling me how many assault troops are staging at Oceana."

"Two hundred," Williams said, sifting through Gruber's paperwork. "It's all here."

General Medlock marched briskly into the bone-chilling wind in time to see his helicopter bank to the east and, gathering speed, disappear into the storm, leaving in its wake a whirlpool of snow. His chopper pilot rushed up to meet him. "A couple of assholes commandeered my aircraft at gunpoint."

Medlock, his stern features now grim, passed a weary hand over his face. "Marshall just earned himself a felony court-martial. I'll see he gets life for this stunt." Then he recalled Julie's prognosis and realized Marshall had nothing to lose and certainly nothing to fear from a general.

He leveled a frightening glare at the pilot. "Get my goddamn car."

Marshall made his way to the flight deck and said to Youngblood, "Where's Wynett's chopper now?"

"He's thirty miles ahead of us," he said, checking the radar. "ETA in Oceana should be about thirty minutes."

Marshall nodded and started to withdraw when Youngblood hollered back, "Can I ask you a question?"

"No."

"What's Julie like?" he asked anyway.

Marshall dismissed him with a scowl and headed aft.

"So don't tell me," he said to himself, then muttered, "Let me find out for myself."

Quarantine

Julie sat behind the quarantine center's communications console and watched the helicopter take off on the TV monitors. She was barely able to control her anger. "Marshall, you son of a bitch."

Marshall had blown her last chance to stop this nightmare. Now her Catholic upbringing was pouring guilt back into her heart, filling her with shame for her creation that was about to kill a lot of people. She no longer dreamed of being infected. Now she dreamed about starting a fire in a forest that spread around the world.

Ever since South America, Julie accepted the possibility that there might indeed be a God—or at least she allowed for the possibility of divine intervention in her life. She had come to accept the notion that a God, or some reasonable facsimile, had allowed her to live long enough to undo this terrible wrong she had committed. Stopping Gorgon would have been her penance. Now she was trapped in quarantine, impotent. Perhaps the Almighty intended to make her an example to the rest of the world—*See what happens, my children, when mere mortals meddle with creation. Julie Martinelli, the Creator. Come see what she's done.* Damn you, Marshall, she thought, for leaving me behind.

"Julie, are you there?" It was Marshall's voice coming over the UHF band.

Her trembling fingers set the broadcast channel to all frequencies. She slid the headset over her ears and pressed the transmit button.

"Marshall? Marshall, are you hearing me?"

Seconds later Marshall's voice boomed over her headset. "Set your frequency on one-two-nine. There's a scramble channel on the console. Find it and turn it on so we're in sync.''

Julie did as he instructed and a hideously garbled noise filled her ears. She heard three sharp sync tones; then Marshall's voice came in loud and clear.

"How's that?" he said.

"Fine. I'm furious with you right now."

"If you want to bitch at me, it'll have to wait."

"You had no right to leave me out of this."

"There's nothing you can do out here. I need you safe and sound where you can do me some good."

"There's no such thing as safe and sound. We're dying, you son of a bitch." Her words came out in a controlled sob.

There was a pause from the chopper, then, "No one gets off this planet alive. Stay on this channel." The LED readout indicated that Marshall had ceased transmitting.

"Bastard." Julie spun away from the console and nearly shouted out loud when she saw a woman standing in the doorway, holding a hefty stack of papers.

"Thought you might want some company," said Dr. Shaw.

Julie whipped around to compose herself, and even then all she could manage was, "Nancy . . ."

"I eavesdropped on your last conversation and figured out what was going on," she said.

Julie looked past her academic adviser to see if the cinderblock corridor was empty.

"Don't worry," Shaw said. "I'm the only one who bothered to listen in. Everybody else was either too busy getting ready for the showdown or making plans to get upwind of Dodge. Anyway, I knew Marshall wouldn't take you with him."

"He's a bastard. He doesn't give a damn about me."

"Cut the crap and save the self-pity for your analyst. He did you and himself a favor. You're both right where you belong. If he didn't give a damn about you he'd have brought you along and let you kill yourself."

Julie frowned at her. "Why did you come down here? I may be contagious."

"No, you're not, otherwise Medlock would never have taken Wynett out. It's all in here." Shaw lifted a stack of printouts the size of the D.C. telephone directory. "Here are the numbers you wanted run through the Cray. I did it on General Medlock's orders. Knock yourself out."

"Nancy, I'm scared shitless."

Dr. Shaw gave her a mock look of surprise. "You? Scared? I don't buy it."

Julie struggled to lift her left hand, which seemed terribly weighty, and showed the doctor trembling fingers that were bent unnaturally at right angles. Shaw bit her lower lip.

"It feels so strange," Julie said, "like it no longer belongs to me."

The general's personal white Lincoln Mark VII LSC skidded to a stop in front of him, its wipers pushing sloppy piles of sleet to each side of the windshield. General Medlock, his neck veins throbbing, climbed into the backseat and yelled at his driver, "Get me to Andrews Airfield as fast as you can drive this thing."

Marshall searched the chopper's armament cabinet, found a 9mm magazine clip and pushed it into the handle of the empty Beretta. He grabbed a leather pilot's jacket from a locker and slipped it over his heavy clothing. Williams did likewise.

Marshall sat down next to Gruber and snatched the shoulder bag he still clutched to his chest. "I need every piece of information you've dug up about Gorgon's movements in the last forty-eight hours."

"It's all right in front of you," Gruber said.

Marshall sifted through Gruber's satchel and found a map of Virginia detailing the tanker's route approaching the Chesapeake Bay. He spread it on the chart table before him and noted a dotted line plotting the tanker's projected course up the York River to a refinery just north of Yorktown. Marshall followed its route with a quivering finger, an impairment Gruber was quick to notice.

"It's getting worse, isn't it?" Gruber asked.

Marshall looked suddenly at him. "What's getting worse?"

"Your viral affliction. It's affecting your motor coordination. I think I understand what this is all about; you want to kill Gorgon before Saint Vitus kills you. A noble exchange. But you're denying the fact that you can't possibly be effective in your condition. All you'll succeed in doing is getting others killed. You're a terrible threat to the success of this operation."

Williams thrust a finger at the old man and shouted, "There's nothing wrong with us. I feel fucking fine!"

The pencil in Marshall's hand suddenly snapped, though he wasn't aware that he'd put any pressure on it. "Save it, both of you." He hid his trembling hand in his lap. "Sergeant, I want you to monitor all voice communication. Tell me what's going on."

Williams put on a pair of headphones and patched into the navy's LINK II combat information system.

"If Gorgon intended to launch," Marshall said to Gruber, "he could have done it by now—he could have struck dozens of targets hours ago without jeopardizing his escape. Why is he boxing himself in? Why does he need to dock that tanker?" Marshall paused, considering, then said, "Unless he intends to take Saint Vitus inland."

"We considered that," Gruber said. "He surely must realize he's a dead man without the threat of those missiles. There's a sixty-percent probability that something's gone wrong with his launch system. We're running the logistics though the Cray—weight ratios, payloads, trajectory, thrust, weather, everything. In any event, the assault team's first priority will be to take out those warheads. There's no margin for error."

"What if he starts pumping crude oil into the bay?" Williams offered. "You're going to piss off a lot of watermen."

"An environmental mess is the least of our problems,"

309

Gruber said. "We haven't even factored that into our equation."

"Where's the ship now?" Marshall asked.

Without much thought, Gruber said, "Thirty-two miles from the mouth of the Chesapeake Bay." He looked at his watch and twisted uncomfortably in his seat.

"What's your problem with the time?" the major asked.

"The president won't allow the tanker to reach the bay."

"Not a whole lot he can do about it," Marshall said tonelessly.

Gruber looked timidly at the major, anxiety written on his face. "Yes, there is."

Quarantine

Julie sat at her computer workstation, her legs tucked comfortably beneath her, making notes with her good hand on the stack of printouts her adviser had given her.

Dr. Shaw sat across from her, watching her pupil over a hot cup of freshly brewed coffee.

"Here's something I didn't expect to see," Julie said, circling a group of numbers on the printout. "It doesn't make much sense. There's another virus present in our blood cells along with Saint Vitus."

"A coincidence?"

Julie shook her head. "It's too prolific, too consistent. It's in every single one of our infected cells."

"Could be part of the mutation," Dr. Shaw said, stirring her coffee. "You could be looking at a new variation of St. Vitus, several generations removed."

"Not this virus," Julie said. "I've been able to track the pattern of Saint Vitus' mutations. This other virus hasn't changed a bit. And I think I can identify it."

"Is it man-made?"

"Nope." Julie looked up at her. "It's a friggin' mouse-tumor virus."

"A mouse-tumor virus? Are you certain?"

Julie flipped through her printout and confirmed, "It was gene-spliced—Saint Vitus introduced it into our systems."

Dr. Shaw, feeling suddenly warm, set down her coffee mug before her suddenly shaking hands could spill it. "Do you know what you're saying, dear?"

"I think I'm saying that Dr. French was one clever son of a bitch." Julie looked hard at Dr. Shaw. "Would you get me six cc's of the antibiotic ganciclovir?"

Chapter Thirty-seven

Andrews Air Force Base
1705 hours

General Medlock's driver negotiated a turn onto a frontage road that took the Lincoln around to the far side of Andrews' number-three runway. Every five hundred feet a soldier with an automatic rifle waved the general's vehicle quickly past. Medlock stared at the dashboard's digital clock—five-zero-five. Wynett would be on his way to the tanker, and he demanded to be part of it.

The car stopped abruptly in front of a brightly lit hangar, thick with activity. A tall, lanky officer minus a jacket, his sleeves rolled up to his elbows, opened the passenger door. "Sir, Wynett took off about seven minutes ago. We're taking him as far as Cape Henry, where the tanker is scheduled to pick up a river pilot. If he doesn't get aboard he comes right back here."

"What about Phase Two?"

"Already initiated."

Phase Two rolled out of the hangar and taxied toward the runway—two F-15 Strike Eagle bombers, followed by an EF-11 Raven for jamming support. Medlock noted the F-15's unconventional payload, two tactical nuclear glide bombs hanging from each wing. His eyes took on a distant look of resignation. "Jesus Christ, all those good men I'm sending out there. What's happening to us?"

"Sir, Marshall's chopper just landed at Oceana. Say the word and we'll have him shot on the spot."

Medlock climbed out of the car and watched the first F-15 roar off the runway and vanish into the night.

"Sir," the officer pressed, "what about Marshall?"

Medlock shook his head. "Get him on that tanker. He's the best damn chance I have."

Oceana Naval Air Station
Virginia

The skids of Medlock's command helicopter had barely touched down when Williams and Marshall were out of the troop compartment and racing across the tarmac. Special Forces Commander Alexander Stern met them halfway, holding a drawn .45 at his side.

"Jesus Christ, Joe," Stern said, "I never thought I'd be taking your ass into custody at gunpoint."

Commander Stern was a commando's commando—tough, mean and highly skilled. Large framed and eager to show off an all-muscle body, he didn't let his age of forty-seven years keep him from participating in every op under his charge. One hell of a tactical planner, he also was one hell of a soldier. "How in Christ did you manage to get yourself into this mess, Joe?"

Marshall saw the drawn .45 in Stern's hand and the dangerous squint in his eyes that said he was ready to use it on him, if necessary. "Stern, I need your help tonight."

"Damn right you do, pal. I have orders to arrest you on sight . . . or put a bullet into your fat head if you resist. I don't need this right now."

Marshall matched Stern's rock-steady eyes. "I'm asking you as a friend to let me be part of this op tonight."

Stern thrust the .45 into Marshall's face and drew back the hammer with a dangerous click. "Not a fucking chance. Jesus, Joe, don't make me use this."

"Commander," yelled a first lieutenant running across the tarmac with a handheld ComSat transceiver. "It's Medlock at Andrews. Says he has a priority-one directive for you."

Stern never took his eyes off Marshall as he grabbed the transceiver from the lieutenant and put it to his ear. "Stern here." His face remained frozen as he listened, and Marshall watched him slowly lower the .45, reseat the hammer and slip it into his side holster. "Yes, sir." He thrust the transceiver back at the lieutenant, an uncharacteristic grin breaking his features. "Medlock says you're in. Don't ask me how or why. We're out of time, Joe. Hell, maybe you and the sergeant are just what we need tonight—ha, a couple of kamikaze commandos."

Marshall, his adrenaline flowing, let out a long, silent sigh as he walked Stern back to the hangar. "How many men do we have here?"

"Two Delta squads from Bragg and every SEAL within eight hundred miles," Stern said. "We're putting thirty SEALs on the tanker in the first assault. Forty Delta troops are standing by in Sea Stallions. We have regular ground troops waiting in Yorktown in the unlikely event the bastard makes it that far upriver. General Medlock wants you and your sergeant on the tanker with the first assault."

Marshall nodded his approval. "I need a Franchi and my sergeant needs a Galil."

Commander Stern checked his clipboard. "I'm putting you on launch number nine. Lieutenant Greenberg on the dock will get you whatever you need. This weather's going to be a problem for the watercraft. Get your ass moving, Marshall. You're shoving off in five minutes."

Stern hustled back to the hangar.

"Congratulations, Major," Gruber said, appearing at Marshall's elbow. "Looks like you got your wish. If you manage to get on board the tanker alive, it's imperative that you immediately sever the power cable between the launch vehicle and the missile pallet. Do that and you'll kick the son of a bitch in the balls. He won't be able to target those missiles.''

"But he can still launch?" Marshall asked.

"Yes, the missile platform has a redundant launch system, which he can fire manually," Gruber said. "A bullet in the platform's motherboard should prevent the missiles from firing at all. Got it?"

"I got it." Marshall extended his hand to Gruber. "And thank you. I appreciate your help."

Gruber took his proffered hand. Besides a firm shake, he could feel the unmistakable tremor of a very ill man. Gruber's half-smile faded. "Good luck, Major. I know you'll do what you have to do. Just don't let that bastard kill any more people."

Cape Henry
United States Eastern Seaboard

Lt. Cmdr. Thomas Lee tightened his grip on a pair of high-powered binoculars as though that might steady his view against the even rolling of the launch's deck. Three weeks past his twentieth anniversary in the service of the United States Navy, Lee was tall, very tall, and the heavy oilskin breaker gave his substantial frame the gray, rocky appearance of Mt. Rainier.

Lee's keen hazel eyes buried beneath twin outcrops of gray brows peered through the night binoculars with a laserlike intensity that could find any object with radar precision in the roughest seas, day or night.

He spotted her immediately.

Locating something as large as an oil tanker hardly required a psychic sense; he hoped getting Wynett aboard would be just as easy.

Commander Lee lowered the binoculars, his lips curled in a half-frown. His launch looked more like a pleasure craft than an armed navy vessel, a disguise which had worked exceedingly well in drug-trafficking patrols off Miami. A good seaman's eye, though, might suspect something, and that bothered the hell out of him.

Lee, watching the tanker six miles off his starboard bow, became aware of someone at his elbow. He half-turned and saw Wynett, dressed from head to foot in an orange one-piece survival suit, staring vacantly in the direction of the tanker.

"She still isn't answering us," Lee said. "Nor has she stopped. There's a strong possibility they won't let you board. Did you consider that?"

Wynett, his distant eyes narrowing, shook his head. "I will meet with him."

Lucy

"Approaching vessel," Tarra said, her eyes buried in the ship's radar hood.

Captain Carlucci whirled at the news.

Tarra narrowed the tracking beam on the bridge's radar display to a west-northwest scan. "Range, five-point-three kilometers, bearing three-two-seven . . . on an interception course." She pressed the headset to her ear. "The river pilot is requesting permission to board."

"I can see him," Gorgon said, scanning the rising swells through a pair of night binoculars. A gray half-light was rapidly yielding to a blackness that would soon swallow the bay and give him cover. "Let him board and bring him directly to me. Impatience now will cost us everything." Gorgon lowered his binoculars and said in a low voice as though to himself, "A horse appeared, deathly pale, and its rider was called Death, and Hell followed at his heels."

"I did not hear you," Tarra said.

Gorgon shook his head. "The journey we began at the settlement of Kumar is almost at an end."

316

Code: Alpha

Marshall and Williams climbed down into the rubber Zodiac launch beside Lieutenant Greenberg, a seasoned Special Forces officer who would be their pilot and navigator.

"Commander Stern just radioed me about you gents," Greenberg said.

Marshall regarded the slightly short, slightly stocky, slightly aging Navy SEAL. Despite Greenberg's disarming, fatherly smile, Marshall didn't doubt he knew at least a half dozen ways to break a man's back. "What did Stern tell you?"

"Says you're Delta's best," Greenberg said, shaking first Marshall's, then Williams's hand. "Glad to be on your team tonight."

Clad in black rubber wet suits, hoods and taut, slipperlike boots, the three men went to work, only vaguely aware of the other teams along the dock also loading and readying their launches. There were no lights illuminated throughout the staging area, no light anywhere. Only the sounds of men working.

Marshall smeared black camouflage paint onto his face, obscuring the boundaries between wet suit and flesh, then tugged on a pair of skintight leather gloves. He clamped a miniature transceiver to his SAS belt, put the headphone over his good ear, adjusted its tiny microphone over his mouth and switched on the belt unit. Williams did likewise.

"A lot of gents in Washington will no doubt be monitoring everything we say tonight," Greenberg warned the two. He grinned. "So be careful who you hurl your curses at."

A soldier on the dock passed down munitions satchels and a pair of weapons—a Franchi military shotgun and an Israeli Galil sniper's rifle. He also gave each of them a pair of Phillips Electro-Spezial image-intensifying goggles and a tiny waterproof notebook, detailing *Lucy*'s deck plan. Marshall slipped on the goggles and focused them. The world once again

317

became visible in a strange new dawn with an eerie green-yellow glow.

"Let's go."

Lucy

A very winded and exhausted-looking Wynett met Captain Carlucci at the top of *Lucy*'s gangway. Wynett sat down heavily on a pipe, unable to breathe. He looked ghastly. His face was beaten, his skin the pallor of death, his bloodshot eyes deep-sunk in hollowed sockets, his lips bloodless. Carlucci thought the old man might pass out.

Wynett struggled to focus his eyes on the sea captain standing over him and wheezed, "Requesting permission to board, Captain."

Carlucci's suspicious eyes moved from Wynett to the disguised launch racing away from the tanker, then back to Wynett. "You are not a pilot, are you?"

Wynett, struggling to take a breath, put a spasming hand on his forehead. "No, sir. My business is with the man who commandeered your vessel."

Carlucci looked curiously at him. "Then am I to understand the American military knows about this murderous madman?"

"You are correct, sir."

Carlucci nodded. "Then God has heard my prayers tonight."

Chapter Thirty-eight

1710 hours

Cmdr. Buzz Hayes eased his F-15 Strike Eagle into a gentle bank that would scribe another forty-five-mile arc around *Lucy*. Hayes and his wingman reduced power to their twin turbine engines to conserve fuel. The night promised a long wait. The bombardier, a young lieutenant named Peter Booker, once again checked the position of each armament switch on the aircraft's newly retrofitted tactical bombing system, which functioned identically to the conventional air-to-ground bombing unit he had trained on. He noted the time in his kneeboard log; a simple tactical exercise. He glanced at the three-dimensional computer image of *Lucy* on his heads-up display, then moved the cursor over the ship's radar image and pressed a key to retarget and lock the tanker on the autotracking system. Piece of cake. The length of a football field, *Lucy* was a ridiculously easy target to track.

An alert tone blared in Lieutenant Booker's headset, and coded data flashed across the bottom of the VDI display. New orders. He mentally decoded the display information and felt every muscle in his body involuntarily tighten.

This was no exercise.

Shit—that's fucking Newport News down there! Somebody had made one hell of a mistake. Or had they? The bombardier shifted his unfocused eyes on the infinite blackness outside the canopy. "Jesus," he said into his helmet mike.

Commander Hayes chuckled, but it was a cold laugh. "You're not likely to get his help tonight." Then the pilot's voice hardened. "You got a problem, Lieutenant?"

"Negative."

The bombardier opened the scrambled UHF to the command hangar. He heard the voice scrambler beep, then said, "Hawk One to Father. Request voice confirmation."

The radio was silent for several seconds before a voice responded, "Stand by to attack target at coordinates two-six-four and one-seven-nine. Repeat. Stand by to attack target at coordinates two-six-four, one-seven-nine."

Booker didn't acknowledge. *Jesus, this is really happening!* Another tone sounded in his headset as the orange AUTOPILOT DISCONNECT light blinked on. He felt the aircraft roll left as Hayes began the bomb run. One button, the bombardier mused. That was all that stood between him and a bona fide hell. For the first time in his military career his hands were trembling . . . *trembling during a fucking mission!* One button. *Why me, Jesus? Why am I the one?* He would press one button, and two minutes later a low-yield tactical nuclear bomb would transform the tanker into a thick, stinking cloud of hydrocarbons.

The White House Situation Room

"What the hell's happening out there, General?" the president hollered into the phone's receiver.

"The deteriorating weather is slowing us down, Mr. President," Medlock said from the hangar at Andrews Airfield. "My troops will rendezvous with the ship in approximately nine minutes."

"General," the president said, "I'm taking a terrible risk with your plan. Damn it, I don't want that tanker on the bay."

"Nine minutes, Mr. President," Medlock said slowly and deliberately. "In nine minutes my men will be on board the tanker, and this business will be finished."

Quarantine

Dr. Nancy Shaw inserted the syringe into the permeable tip of the bottle and withdrew six cc's of the antibiotic ganciclovir. "Give me your arm."

Julie reached for the syringe with a trembling hand. "I'm perfectly capable of giving myself a shot."

"Give me your arm," Shaw insisted.

Julie acquiesced, allowing the injection.

"This is three times the normal dose," Shaw said, pulling the syringe out of her arm and pressing a cotton ball hard inside her elbow. "We'll give it ten minutes, then take another blood specimen."

Julie nodded and let her thoughts drift to Marshall. Where was he now? What was he doing? She didn't try to push him from her mind. Quite the contrary. She drew newfound strength from the mental image of him.

The mouth of the Chesapeake Bay
1717 hours

The Zodiac rubber water raft skimmed smartly across the bay in complete darkness. It began sleeting again as the storm gathered, rendering practical visibility to zero. Marshall and Williams peered through their night goggles at the rising storm, but could see nothing. Neither could those aboard the tanker. The foul weather was a godsend they intended to exploit to their full advantage. For the moment they didn't need to see. An Air Force AWAC plane circling 20,000 feet above them was feeding the tanker's position to the teams' GPS receivers. Lieutenant Greenberg's eyes darted continuously from the compass to the receiver, which told him the tanker was only five hundred feet to port. There were no ship lights to act as beacons.

Nine other Zodiacs with three-man crews bore down on the tanker from different headings. The plan called for the troops to rendezvous on the ship and disable the missile pallet. How they managed that feat once on board would depend entirely on their opportunities. There had been no elaborate setup, no training, little planning. There simply hadn't been time. Medlock was gambling that the tanker was too large for Gorgon's men to patrol every foot of bulwark. He figured that ten teams—thirty men—would raise the odds for success in their favor. There were a lot of crossed fingers tonight in Washington.

Marshall had too much time during the short crossing to contemplate what could go wrong. What if Gorgon saw them approaching? What if only one of the teams managed to get on board? What if the missiles fired? What if the virus was released? What if . . . what if . . . ?

They all saw it at once, a shape the size of a large island rising up before them. It was *Lucy*. She looked gigantic. Her deck and anticollision lights were out, making her virtually invisible. Marshall, sitting motionless except for the knuckle he tapped thoughtfully on his lips, watched the massive ship approach. Williams, sitting at his side, watched with a growing eagerness he found hard to contain. They felt the wind decrease as the huge wall of the tanker loomed up over them, shielding them. No one said anything.

All Marshall could think about was Julie. Thank God she was safe. He found it difficult to stop the flow of feelings between his brain and his heart. The sensations were new to him. He couldn't rid her from his mind. He closed his eyes and struggled to focus on the op. He grew rigid, rocklike, forcing himself to once again become a machine. But he couldn't. Something was different this time, he realized. It was Julie. She was with him—a part of him.

Lieutenant Greenberg let the craft bounce off the tanker's hull, which towered over them like a great cliff, then adjusted the muffled outboard motor to match the ship's speed. They worked quickly in the ship's wind shelter to secure the launch. Despite the rough water, *Lucy* rolled slowly and evenly, her fully loaded cargo tanks stabilizing the ship deep in the water. No one had seen them approach—or at least they trusted no one had seen them. The element of surprise was their most potent weapon.

Marshall could barely make out the ship's bulwark on the forward bow only fifteen feet above them. "Can you secure a line to the anchor aperture?"

Greenberg squinted upward. "Piece of cake."

"Watch that rail," Marshall ordered his sergeant. "If you see anything that looks like a head, put a bullet through it."

Williams swung his Galil assault rifle off his shoulder and scanned the bulwark above through the weapon's night scope. He saw nothing but sleet.

Lucy

Wynett followed Carlucci sluggishly across the deck, while a soldier in black fatigues and carrying a Kalashnikov fell in behind him. Wynett felt neither fear nor intimidation, only a fatigue that bore to the core of his soul. *Lucy* was everything he had expected and nothing he had imagined. Her vast size astounded him, and he could feel her solidness beneath his feet. With a road of pipes stretching the length of the vessel to the superstructure, she looked more like an industrial facility than a ship. He knew she was both fortified and inviolable.

Wynett had no memory of walking the lengthy ice-crusted deck, entering the superstructure or climbing the narrow stairwells to the bridge deck. Only after he entered the wheelhouse did his attention return to the pressing reality.

He was on *Lucy*'s bridge, which was crowded with soldiers in black fatigues. The wheelhouse reeked of death, as though an animal had died inside the walls where nobody could get rid of it.

Before Wynett could get his bearings, Gorgon peeled away

from the chart table and loomed over him, his hands arrogantly on his hips. Carlucci moved into the corner and watched. Gorgon's face turned to stone when he realized who the river pilot was. Wynett betrayed no emotion at all to again meet his partner.

Gorgon greeted his old friend with a sneer. "You." His eyes narrowed. "I would not have believed you capable of this."

Tarra swung away from the main console and let out a shriek when she saw Wynett. "If he is here, then the United States militia must know who we are and what we carry. They will not let us proceed." She grabbed Gorgon's arm. "The missiles. You must launch the missiles now and finish this."

"Give this up," Carlucci said, making his way forward. "I implore you in the name of sanity to surrender this vessel." Two of Gorgon's men pushed Carlucci cruelly back with their weapons. That didn't deter him. "It is madness to continue." He appealed to Tarra. "Tell him. Make him listen."

"I demand to know why you came here." Gorgon's voice was low, vicious.

Wynett said soberly, "To collect money."

"What?"

"Ten million American dollars. I delivered to you the most effective weapon of mass killing ever devised and you gave me nothing in return. I am here to collect my fee per our agreement."

Gorgon's head flew back and out roared a great laughter, an ugly sound that boomed off the wheelhouse's metal walls. "You are truly mad." Gorgon's face darkened, and when he spoke there was cold contempt in his voice. "In Tampico you saw how I deal with treachery. Before I kill you, you will tell me what the American military intelligence knows about Operation Harness."

Wynett's eyes fluttered, and he looked every bit the old, dying man he was. "They know we are having bloody good fun. . . ."

Gorgon gave a quick, irritated jerk of his head, and three

of his soldiers surrounded Wynett, their weapons pointed at his chest. The old man did not react with the slightest alarm.

Beep . . . beep . . . beep . . .

Tarra moved to the ship's radar console. The unit was reading sporadic signatures of several small craft approaching *Lucy* from different directions. She swung around. "Watercraft. Several of them. Range, one hundred meters."

Gorgon whirled at Wynett. "What is this trap?"

The old man said nothing.

"Alert the deck," Gorgon ordered. "Tell them to stand by for a boarding assault."

Gorgon moved to the bridge's window but could see nothing but blackness beyond the ship's forward bow. When he spoke, his tone was subdued. "No navy on earth can undo the seeds I have sown. Soon the world we once knew will change. No one can stop that. No one can stop me."

Chapter Thirty-nine

Lucy

Marshall twisted through the narrow opening between the anchor aperture and the massive chain and lay facedown on *Lucy*'s forward deck. Williams followed and slid beside him. The deck had a coating of ice, and a stunningly cold blast of wind lashed at them. Neither moved. The quiet, broken only by the churning river sweeping past the ship's sides, was eerie.

Marshall scanned the deck through his image-intensifying goggles. He could see vague shapes and protrusions across the deck. Gorgon's troops were strategically stationed, some manning the ship's armaments, some patrolling, some scanning the bay through binoculars. Through the night goggles they looked like cardboard cutouts. The terrorists appeared hypervigilant, expectant. Marshall counted seven on the forecastle, nearly invisible in their black uniforms.

Marshall screwed his neck around. His eyes widened. A soldier stood at the bulwark several feet behind him, his unmistakable silhouette a shade blacker than the night, scanning the bay forward of the ship. Williams saw him too. Marshall withdrew Martinelli's Beretta from his back holster and pointed it, but his trembling hand couldn't keep the gun still.

Williams hissed, reached for his ankle and unsheathed his black serrated knife. The sentry whirled at the slight sound. There was a blur of hand movement as Williams's knife vanished. Marshall saw nothing, not a trace of metal glinting. The soldier gave a short grunt and grabbed the base of his throat. He collapsed against the rail before sliding soundlessly to the deck.

Commander Stern steadied his balance in the small, swaying Zodiac and lifted what looked like a miniature bazooka onto his shoulder. He took an inordinately long three seconds to sight the tanker's bulwark, aimed high to compensate for the rising and falling swells, then pressed the trigger. There was a sharp puff, and the thin nylon cord unraveled quickly as it spiraled upward. The rubber four-pronged grappling hook flew over the rail and landed with a muted thud on *Lucy's* steel deck. Stern pulled, caught the hook on the bulwark and quickly secured his end to the raft. He could barely see another team aft already halfway up the ship's Jacob's ladder.

Don't think about it, he told himself. *Just act.*

"Let's do it."

Stern covered the fifteen-foot climb in just under ten seconds. His two commandos followed him, M-24 assault rifles strapped to their backs.

Stern swung his legs over the bulwark and landed in a half-crouch on the ship's darkened deck. All he could see were vague shapes rising from the tanker's open deck; there simply wasn't enough light for the goggles to amplify. His two men crouched at his side and unfolded the metal stocks of their weapons. Stern made a quick sweep of the deck through his rifle's night scope, searching for the missile platform. Where was it? There were too many unrecognizable shapes—pipes, hatches, valves. . . . *How many other teams made it on board?* The sleet made it impossible to make out anything specific. Damn it, he needed time to acquire his bearings.

Movement caught Stern's eye—man-size objects at ten yards. He shifted his rifle. Bright flashes—rapid bursts—an

327

instant sooner than his highly trained reflexes, negated his fire. A dozen rounds tore into Stern and his two men. He felt only a cold numbness as he died.

Marshall saw several of Gorgon's soldiers running aft, shouting. The unmistakable sound of gunshots ripped through the night. Marshall grimaced. Gorgon's soldiers were launching a barrage of fire at the troops storming *Lucy*'s side. *The poor bastards don't stand a chance.* The port and starboard 30mm chain cannons simultaneously began firing at the Zodiac rafts on the bay, filling the winter night with their awful pounding. It would be a massacre.

"Do it," Marshall hissed.

Williams nodded. He raised the Galil to his eye and sighted the starboard 30mm chain-cannon operator through the infrared laser-assisted scope. He positioned the laser beam on the soldier's chest halfway between his heart and throat and fired a single, silenced round. A plum-shaped wound appeared beneath the laser marker. The terrorist looped backward over the bulwark and disappeared into the bay, his huge gun falling silent. The gunnery sergeant placed his scope's beam similarly on the port cannon operator and fired. The mercenary crumpled to the deck, his cannon also abruptly silenced.

Williams kept his Galil moving, a cold, calculated sweep of the upper deck. Patiently, methodically, he fired. He took out a third terrorist running with an AK-47 braced on his hip. The soldier flew against a wall of pipes and dropped. Williams took out a fourth soldier. A fifth. A sixth. Each went down silently, the well-placed round inflicting too much damage to warrant even a cry of protest from the victim.

In the first minute of the assault, Williams had secured *Lucy*'s forward deck.

"Radio them," Tarra shouted at him. "Tell them you will release a plague if they do not call off the assault and let us pass. They will listen to you."

Gorgon remained rooted before the wheelhouse window,